THE LONG
GAZE BACK

THE LONG GAZE BACK

An Anthology of
Irish Women Writers

Edited by
Sinéad Gleeson

NEW ISLAND

THE LONG GAZE BACK

First published in 2015 by
New Island Books
16 Priory Hall Office Park
Stillorgan
County Dublin
Republic of Ireland

www.newisland.ie

'A Bus from Tivoli' by Kate O'Brien was originally published in *Threshold*, Vol 1 No 2, Summer 1957). Reprinted by the permission of David Higham as agents for the author.

'When Miss Coles Made the Tea' is from *The Cocktail Bar* by Norah Hoult, published by William Heinemann and reprinted by permission of the Random House Group Limited.

'The Demon Lover' is from *The Demon Lover and Other Stories* by Elizabeth Bowen, published by Jonathan Cape, reprinted by permission of the Random House Group Limited.

'The Eldest Child' is from *The Springs of Affection: Stories of Dublin* by Maeve Brennan, reprinted by the permission of Russell & Volkening as agents for the author. Copyright © 1997 by the Estate of Maeve Brennan.

'In the Middle of the Fields' is from *The Stories of Mary Lavin: Volume III* by Mary Lavin and is reprinted by the permission of the Estate of Mary Lavin. Copyright © 1985 by the Estate of Mary Lavin.

PRINT ISBN: 978-1-84840-420-5
EPUB ISBN: 978-1-84840-421-2
MOBI ISBN: 978-1-84840-422-9

British Library Cataloguing Data.
A CIP catalogue record for this book is available from the British Library.

Typeset by JVR Creative India
Cover design by Martin Gleeson
Printed by ScandBook AB, Sweden 2015

10 9 8 7 6 5 4 3 2 1

Contents

Editor's Introduction

In 2001, I discovered a copy of *Cutting the Night in Two: Short Stories by Irish Women Writers*. Edited by Evelyn Conlon and Hans-Christian Oeser, it is a sizeable anthology of thirty-four writers, living and dead. I hadn't encountered many all-female anthologies (of Irish writers), so I was intrigued. In my first years of discovering books, I was frequently drawn to the short story. Here was a form whose brevity belied the scale of thoughts and ideas within it. Anthologies are something of a gift for a curious reader: a chance to sit down in the company of several writers within one volume.

Until *Cutting the Night in Two*, nearly every anthology I opened – and I include books from all around the world – was heavily weighted towards male writers. Irish offerings were no different: pick up any anthology of Irish short stories published between 1950 and 1990, and there was a certain amount of predictability when it came to who was included. Scanning down the list of contributors, a reader would usually find that there were rarely more than five stories by women. Many anthologies had none, others had just two female writers, and it was always the ubiquitous names, the female stalwarts of the form like Mary Lavin, Edna O'Brien, Somerville and Ross, and Elizabeth Bowen. (Although one notable exception is *Modern Irish Stories*, edited by Caroline Walsh and published by *The Irish Times* in 1985. Of the thirty writers, sixteen are women.)

It's only in the last three decades that we've seen a small number of collections focused solely on Irish women's writing, including Janet Madden-Simpson's *A Woman's Part: An Anthology of Short Fiction By and About Irish Women 1890–1960*, *The Female Line: Northern Irish Women's Writers* edited by Ruth Hooley, *Virgins and Hyacinths* edited by Caroline Walsh, Ailbhe Smyth's *Wildish Things: An Anthology of New Irish Women's Writing* and *Territories of the Voice: Contemporary Short Stories by Irish Women Writers* edited by Louise DeSalvo, Kathleen Walsh D'Arcy and Katherine Hogan. Personal taste and bias sways the choices made by any anthology editor, but in the past, selecting a comparable number of women to feature alongside their male contemporaries often wasn't done, whatever the impetus for that was. The anthologies I mention prove that there wasn't a shortage of female writers, but collections published before 1980 simply didn't include them in large numbers. Visibility was once an issue, and in the last five years, regardless of gender, Irish writing has flourished and expanded. These writers are finding readers, winning prizes and creating a new collective: 2015 already feels like a very strong year for emerging Irish female voices, some of whom feature in this book. There is a palpable energy in Irish writing, and although many writers feel the pragmatic pull towards the novel, most are still enthusiastically committed to the shorter form.

Putting together an anthology can be construed as creating a canon, but many factors went into the selection of these stories. In choosing deceased writers, I tried to find stories that I both admired, and that hadn't already been heavily anthologised. With the exception of 'The Demon

Lover' by Elizabeth Bowen, most of these stories do not regularly, if ever, appear in anthologies. For a long time Maeve Brennan's short stories were out of print, and 'The Eldest Child' originally appeared in 1969's *In and Out of Never Never Land*. It wasn't until a new collection, *The Springs of Affection* was reissued by Counterpoint Press in the late 1990s, that the story was republished. It's even more difficult to locate the short stories of Norah Hoult – who appeared in *Cutting the Night in Two* – but London's Persephone Books have kept her novel *There Were No Windows* in print. The story that appears here, 'Miss Coles Makes the Tea', appears in Hoult's 1950 collection *Cocktail Bar*, which is out of print. Maria Edgeworth is better known for writing on social issues, and her novels, but she also wrote short stories. On the surface, 'The Purple Jar' is a cautionary tale of being careful what you wish for, or possibly the evils of capitalism, but one interpretation pitches it as a metaphor for menstruation.

I wanted this book to look back, as well as forward: to trace a line to the past when women publishing their writing was rare, and often discouraged. 'Frank's Response' comes from Charlotte Riddell's collection *Frank Sinclair's Wife: And Other Stories,* but even though Riddell was a prolific writer, she wrote under the androgynous pseudonym of F. G. Trafford until her eighth book was published. Before the start of the twentieth century, writing was often only accessible to those of a certain class. The formidable duo of Somerville and Ross wrote from a different, ascendency position, and the story here, 'Poisson d'Avril', offers both historical context of a bygone era, as well as much comedy. One of the best-known stories in this collection is Elizabeth Bowen's 'The Demon Lover'. Is it a ghost story or an account of psychological breakdown? It also references both World

Wars and the long-lasting effect each had on individuals and on the physical make-up of a city.

Much of the early work included here shows women straining against the gendered roles of the time. The young widow in Mary Lavin's 'In the Middle of the Fields' tries to run the family farm while staving off grief and unwanted male attention. In Maeve Brennan's 'The Eldest Child', Mrs Bagot, the bereaved mother of a newborn, battles grief and is instructed to be stoic and move on.

In some ways this book is a triptych: deceased classic writers sit alongside the feted names of the last two decades and the next generation of new voices. This is why the stories are published chronologically. As the title suggests, the book is rooted in the present with emerging writers, and looks all the way back to the flag bearers of Irish women's writing. And it's a long arc: there are 218 years between the oldest and youngest writer in the collection (Maria Edgeworth and Eimear Ryan, respectively).

The writers were not given a theme or any guidance as to what they could, or should, write about. As with any anthology, the diversity and range of issues raised is very broad. Certainly, there are examinations of inner lives and of things that only affect women – pregnancy, miscarriage, sisterhood – but within these stories there are universal truths. In Lucy Caldwell's 'Multitudes', a new mother watches as her baby struggles to survive, while Eimear McBride's reluctant mother in 'Through the Wall' handles maternity very differently. Siobhan Mannion's character in 'Somewhere to Be' has a jarring experience in the sea, which recalls another recent trauma. In the second of Anne Enright's 'Three Stories about Love', homesickness haunts a pregnant Irish woman living in Australia. 'You're not far away until you have a baby, and then you're really, really far away,' she says.

Leave-taking and distance is often a feature of Irish writing, from leaving behind a small town, in Lisa McInerney's 'Berghain', or an entire country, in Belinda McKeon's 'Long Distance' – although Evelyn Conlon's 'The Meaning of Missing' focuses on those who are left behind when others emigrate. There's the strange outsiderness of the woman obsessed with baths and plumbing in Anakana Schofield's 'Beneath the Taps', and along with June Caldwell's 'SOMAT', it's one of the most experimental stories in the book in terms of language and form.

Several stories deal with lost potential, missed opportunities and what happens when other people impose their expectations on us. Hélène, the young American frontier girl in Nuala Ní Chonchúir's story, wonders why she isn't encouraged to go to school. Niamh Boyce's protagonist is a grown woman, a wife, a neighbour, and yet her choices are thwarted. Many stories deal with the complexity of family relationships, including the mother and son trying to navigate a new life in 'As Seen From Space' by Susan Stairs.

There is as much overlap as there are distinct ideas among the thirty stories. Defiance and aspiration are motivators: in Norah Hoult's story, Olive is determined not to let her deafness hold her back, while the mystery behind a young girl's blindness in 'The Cat and the Mouse' by Christine Dwyer Hickey is finally revealed.

The writers are all Irish, or based here, but not all the stories take place in Ireland. Molly McCloskey draws on her US background and sets 'Frogs' in Portland for a reunion that offers promise only to turn into something else. Kate O'Brien lived away from Ireland for much of her life, and wrote many travel pieces. In 'A Bus from Tivoli', an Irishwoman abroad in Italy seeks solace and independence, only to find herself receiving unwanted attention. The heat and claustrophobia of 'The Crossing' by Lia Mills also echoes the crumbling marriage in the story.

There are mothers and daughters, pregnant women, and childless ones, young girls on the cusp of life and women at the end of it. In 'The Coast of Wales', a widow finds comfort in the routine and memory, while Eimear Ryan's character in 'Lane in Stay' reinvents herself dramatically after her husband dies.

There are ghosts in these pages, some actual, some metaphysical, and many are generated by the fact that we all have a past, receding further and further in the rear-view mirror. In 'My Little Pyromaniac' by Mary Costello, sometimes the thing you want to escape most is literally on your doorstep. An ex-boyfriend makes a current one feel uneasy in E. M. Reapy's 'Gustavo'. The woman in Anne Devlin's 'Winter Journey (The Apparitions)' has travelled all over Europe, but still is troubled by her youth. For another Northern Irish writer, Bernie McGill, a death in the present reawakens an unwanted scene from the past.

I hope that *The Long Gaze Back* finds new readers for the older writers included here, and that the new and existing voices reinforce the breadth and brilliance of Irish women's writing. The book's title is a quote from Maeve Brennan's novella, *The Visitor*, and I hope captures the sense of looking back over the long arc of Irish women's writing. Mary Lavin said there was a 'large deal of detection in the short story', and all of these stories are about figuring things out, exploration and questioning ourselves and all around us – something that fiction can encourage each of us to do.

Sinéad Gleeson,
Dublin,
Summer 2015

Acknowledgements

I'm indebted to Eoin Purcell, former commissioning editor at New Island, for agreeing to this idea after a random comment from me. Edwin Higel and Daniel Bolger have been very supportive of the project, and helped to get it over the finish line. Thanks to Mariel, Justin and all at New Island for their support of the book and for championing it. A special thank you to Hannah Shorten, who worked tirelessly to help locate stories and chase copyright clearance.

Many people offered advice on specific writers, works and anthologies, including Professor Margaret Kelleher, Evelyn Conlon, Cormac Kinsella, Rosita Boland and particularly Dr Eibhear Walsh.

Huge thanks to Martin Gleeson for all his work on the cover design and illustration.

Finally, thank you to the writers whose wonderful work makes up this collection.

Maria Edgeworth

Maria Edgeworth was born in Oxfordshire in 1768 but moved with her family to Edgeworthstown, Co. Longford when she was five. There, she wrote novels, short stories, children's literature and essays on politics and social issues. During the Famine, she worked to help the starving, and wrote *Orlandino* – a children's story – to benefit the Poor Relief Fund. She is best known for her novels, *Castle Rackrent* (1800), which garnered praise from Sir Walter Scott) as well as *Belinda* (1801) and *The Absentee* (1812). Edgeworth died in 1849 aged eighty-one.

The Purple Jar

Rosamond, a little girl of about seven years old, was walking with her mother in the streets of London. As she passed along, she looked in at the windows of several shops, and she saw a great variety of different sorts of things, of which she did not know the use, or even the names. She wished to stop to look at them; but there was a great number of people in the streets, and a great many carts and carriages and wheelbarrows, and she was afraid to let go her mother's hand.

'Oh! Mother, how happy I should be,' said she, as she passed a toyshop, 'if I had all these pretty things!'

'What, all! Do you wish for them all, Rosamond?'

'Yes, Mamma, all.'

As she spoke, they came to a milliner's shop; the windows were hung with ribbons and lace, and festoons of artificial flowers.

'Oh! Mamma, what beautiful roses! Won't you buy some of them?'

'No, my dear.'

'Why?'

'Because I don't want them, my dear.'

They went a little farther, and they came to another shop, which caught Rosamond's eye. It was a jeweler's shop; and there were a great many pretty baubles, ranged in drawers behind glass.

'Mamma, you'll buy some of these?'

'Which of them, Rosamond?'

'Which? I don't know which; but any of them, for they are all pretty.'

'Yes, they are all pretty; but of what use would they be to me?'

'Use! Oh, I'm sure you could find some use or other, if you would only buy them first.'

'But I would rather find out the use first.'

Rosamond was very sorry that her mother wanted nothing. Presently, however, they came to a shop, which appeared to her far more beautiful than the rest. It was a chemist's shop; but she did not know that.

'Oh, Mother! Oh!' cried she, pulling her mother's hand. 'Look! Look! Blue, green, red, yellow, and purple! Oh, Mamma, what beautiful things! Won't you buy some of these?'

Still her mother answered as before, 'What use would they be to me, Rosamond?'

'You might put flowers in them, Mamma, and they would look so pretty on the chimneypiece. I wish I had one of them.'

'You have a flower vase,' said her mother; 'and that is not for flowers.'

'But I could use it for a flower vase, Mamma, you know.'

'Perhaps if you were to see it nearer, if you were to examine it, you might be disappointed.'

'No, indeed; I'm sure I should not. I should like it exceedingly.'

Rosamond kept her head turned to look at the purple vase till she could see it no longer.

'Then, Mother,' said she, after a pause, 'perhaps you have no money.'

'Yes, I have.'

'Dear me! If I had money, I would buy roses, and boxes, and purple flowerpots, and everything.' Rosamond was obliged to pause in the midst of her speech.

'Oh, Mamma, would you stop a minute for me? I have got a stone in my shoe; it hurts me very much.'

'How comes there to be a stone in your shoe?'

'Because of this great hole, Mamma – it comes in there: my shoes are quite worn out; I wish you'd be so very good as to give me another pair.'

'Nay, Rosamond, but I have not money enough to buy shoes, and flowerpots, and boxes, and everything.'

Rosamond thought that was a great pity. But now her foot, which had been hurt by the stone, began to give her so much pain that she was obliged to hop every other step, and she could think of nothing else. They came to a shoemaker's shop soon afterwards.

'There! There! Mamma, there are shoes – there are little shoes that would just fit me; and you know shoes would be really of use to me.'

'Yes, so they would, Rosamond. Come in.'

She followed her mother into the shop. Mr Sole, the shoemaker, had a great many customers, and his shop was full, so they were obliged to wait.

'Well, Rosamond,' said her mother, 'you don't think this shop so pretty as the rest?'

'No, not nearly; it's black and dark, and there are nothing but shoes all round; and besides, there's a very disagreeable smell.'

'That smell is the smell of new leather.'

'Is it? Oh!' said Rosamond, looking round, 'there is a pair of little shoes; they'll just fit me, I'm sure.'

'Perhaps they might, but you cannot be sure till you have tried them on, any more than you can be quite sure that you should like the purple vase exceedingly, till you have examined it more attentively.'

'Why, I don't know about the shoes, certainly, till I've tried; but, mamma, I'm quite sure I should like the flowerpot.'

'Well, which would you rather have, that jar, or a pair of shoes? I will buy either for you.'

'Dear Mamma, thank you – but if you could buy both?'

'No, not both.'

'Then the jar, if you please.'

'But I should tell you that I shall not give you another pair of shoes this month.'

'This month! That's a very long time indeed. You can't think how these hurt me. I believe I'd better have the new shoes –but yet, that purple flowerpot – Oh, indeed, Mamma, these shoes are not so very, very bad; I think I might wear them a little longer; and the month will soon be over: I can make them last to the end of the month, can't I? Don't you think so, Mamma?'

'Nay, my dear, I want you to think for yourself: you will have time enough to consider about it whilst I speak to Mr Sole about my boots.'

Mr Sole was by this time at leisure; and whilst her mother was speaking to him, Rosamond stood in profound meditation, with one shoe on, and the other in her hand.

'Well, my dear, have you decided?'

'Mamma! – Yes – I believe. If you please – I should like the flowerpot; that is, if you won't think me very silly, Mamma.'

'Why, as to that, I can't promise you, Rosamond; but when you are to judge for yourself, you should choose what will make you the happiest; and then it would not signify who thought you silly.'

'Then, Mamma, if that's all, I'm sure the flowerpot would make me the happiest,' said she, putting on her old shoe again; 'so I choose the flowerpot.'

'Very well, you shall have it: clasp your shoe and come home.'

Rosamond clasped her shoe, and ran after her mother: it was not long before the shoe came down at the heel, and many times was she obliged to stop, to take the stones out of her shoe, and often was she obliged to hop with pain; but still the thoughts of the purple flowerpot prevailed, and she persisted in her choice.

When they came to the shop with the large window, Rosamond felt her joy redouble, upon hearing her mother desire the servant, who was with them, to buy the purple jar, and bring it home. He had other commissions, so he did not return with them. Rosamond, as soon as she got in, ran to gather all her own flowers, which she had in a corner of her mother's garden.

'I'm afraid they'll be dead before the flowerpot comes, Rosamond,' said her mother to her, when she was coming in with the flowers in her lap.

'No, indeed, Mamma, it will come home very soon, I dare say; and shan't I be very happy putting them into the purple flowerpot?'

'I hope so, my dear.'

The servant was much longer returning home than Rosamond had expected; but at length he came, and brought with him the long wished-for jar. The moment it was set down upon the table, Rosamond ran up with an exclamation of joy.

'I may have it now, Mamma?'

'Yes, my dear, it is yours.'

Rosamond poured the flowers from her lap upon the carpet, and seized the purple flowerpot. 'Oh, dear Mother!' cried she, as soon as she had taken off the top, 'but there's something dark in it – it smells very disagreeable: what is in it? I didn't want this black stuff.'

'Nor I neither, my dear.'

'But what shall I do with it, Mamma?'

'That I cannot tell.'

'But it will be of no use to me, Mamma.'

'That I can't help.'

'But I must pour it out, and fill the flowerpot with water.'

'That's as you please, my dear.'

'Will you lend me a bowl to pour it into, Mamma?'

'That was more than I promised you, my dear; but I will lend you a bowl.'

The bowl was produced, and Rosamond proceeded to empty the purple vase. But to her surprise and disappointment, when it was entirely empty, she found that it was no longer a purple vase! It was a plain white glass jar, which had appeared to have that beautiful colour merely from the liquor with which it had been filled.

Little Rosamond burst into tears.

'Why should you cry, my dear?' said her mother; 'it will be of as much use to you now as ever for a flower vase.'

'But it won't look so pretty on the chimneypiece. I am sure, if I had known that it was not really purple, I should not have wished to have it so much.'

'But didn't I tell you that you had not examined it, and that perhaps you would be disappointed?'

'And so I am disappointed indeed. I wish I had believed you beforehand. Now I had much rather have the shoes, for I shall not be able to walk all this month: even walking home that little way hurt me exceedingly. Mamma, I'll give you the flowerpot back again, and that purple stuff and all, if you'll only give me the shoes.'

'No, Rosamond, you must abide by your own choice; and now the best thing you can possibly do is to bear your disappointment with good humour.'

'I will bear it as well as I can,' said Rosamond, wiping her eyes, and she began slowly and sorrowfully to fill the vase with flowers.

But Rosamond's disappointment did not end here: many were the difficulties and distresses into which her imprudent choice brought her before the end of the month. Every day her shoes grew worse and worse, till at last she could neither run, dance, jump, nor walk in them. Whenever Rosamond was called to see anything, she was pulling up her shoes at the heels, and was sure to be too late. Whenever her mother was going out to walk, she could not take Rosamond with her, for Rosamond had no soles to her shoes; and at length, on the very last day of the month, it happened that her father proposed to take her and her brother to a glasshouse which she had long wished to see. She was very happy; but, when she was quite ready, had her hat and gloves on, and was making haste downstairs to her brother and father, who were waiting at the hall door for her, the shoe dropped off; she put it on again in a great hurry; but, as she was going across the hall, her father turned round.

'Why are you walking slipshod? No one must walk slipshod with me. Why, Rosamond,' said he, looking at her shoes with disgust, 'I thought that you were always neat. Go, I cannot take you with me.'

Rosamond coloured and retired. 'Oh, Mamma,' said she, as she took off her hat, 'how I wish that I had chosen the shoes! They would have been of so much more use to me than that jar: however, I am sure – no, not quite sure – but I hope I shall be wiser another time.'

Charlotte Riddell

Charlotte Riddell was born in Carrickfergus, Co. Antrim in 1832 and wrote numerous novels and short story collections. Her works include *The Moors and the Fens* (which appeared under the pseudonym F. G. Trafford, as did her first eight novels), *The Rich Husband, Fairy Water* and *A Struggle for Fame*. She also published short stories (including several ghost stories) and her collections include *Frank Sinclair's Wife: And Other Stories, Weird Stories, Idle Tales* and *The Collected Ghost Stories of Mrs J H Riddell*. Riddell was the first author to be paid a pension by the Society of Authors and died in 1906.

Frank's Resolve

One summer's evening, ten years after his marriage, Frank Sinclair left his office with the intention of walking home. It was pleasantly cool after the heat of the day, and as he had scarcely moved from his desk since early in the morning when he came into the City, the prospect of a walk, even through familiar thoroughfares, between endless rows of houses, seemed pleasant to him.

No person who has not been in a struggling business, can imagine the relief of mind it is to a man to feel that even for one hour the pressure is relaxed, that toward to-morrow he need not look forward with dread; and after years of anxiety, after days and nights of hard thought and painful work, Frank Sinclair was able at last to say, 'The battle is over, and I have won.'

For the battle was over, and the fight won so far as this, that in pecuniary matters he was the day forward instead of the day behind; that he had the typical five-pound note in hand without which no City man can be pronounced happy, that he was, still to speak allegorically, able to hatch his chickens before going through the process of counting them. Consequently, so far as a tranquil mind concerning business could tend to make him happy, Frank Sinclair might that summer's evening have been so called.

But he had other and nearer causes for anxiety than any mere pecuniary affair; and now that the strain of business pressure was relaxed, that the entangled skein of commercial matters had been made comparatively smooth, the man could not help thinking about home and home sorrows; about his wife who was no helpmate; about his children who were neglected; about his house which was wretched; about domestic extravagance which had added in no small degree to increase the troubles he had been daily called upon to endure, in that modern pandemonium where men pant out their lives and peril their souls, not for wealth, not even for competence, but just for the sake of a mere subsistence, the bread of which is bitter to the palate, and the waters whereof are briny to the taste.

It takes a man or woman a long time to confess that he or she has made just that one mistake which is utterly irrevocable. Old recollections, the fond memories of tender words whispered when the dusty roads of life were still untraversed, when it was all greensward underfoot, and blossoming roses overhead; the very dread, it may be, of the thought of the way still to be traversed with an uncongenial companion: all these things conspire to induce human beings to make the best of their bargain and to lay the fault of domestic unhappiness, as long as possible, on any cause save that of utter unsuitability.

Frank Sinclair had striven to do this, at any rate, and even as he walked home that evening he made excuses for the woman who was his wife, and vowed, if it lay in his power to make a better thing of the future, the future should be better than the past had proved.

Only, how was he to set about it? Between them there had grown up insensibly a barrier, strong in precise proportion as it was indescribable.

Arabella had indeed, as Patty stated, fallen amongst people whose friendship (save the mark!) and sympathy (that a good word should ever come to be so misapplied!) were effecting infinite harm.

There were persons who, never having done a day's real work in their lives, had no faith in the real work of others; who, just as every man thinks he can drive a gig through London, believed there was nothing difficult in conducting a business; who had a general contempt for men, their uselessness, their selfishness, their exacting ideas. Even the males amongst that clique had a way of saying, 'If you want a thing done well, get a woman to do it,' whilst all the time the women did nothing except complain about the shortcomings of the rival sex.

Those were the days before 'Women's Rights' was discussed either privately or publicly. 'Women's Wrongs,' a much more prolific and dangerous subject was then the popular question in certain circles. Ladies who were married, and ladies who were single, alike agreed in condemning the arrangements of Providence as regarded mankind.

People may object to the institution of women's rights, and the open discussion of their fitness for this or that trade and profession, but there can be no question that an open sore is better than one falsely healed; and that if women think themselves unfairly treated, it is better they should say so in the market-place than beside the domestic hearth; that the question should be decided by the experience of the world, rather than sulked over between husband and wife, father and daughter.

If it gives the smallest pleasure to a gentlewoman to go out and earn her own bread instead of letting some one make

competent earn it for her, there cannot, I apprehend, be any reason why she should be prevented from doing so. England is a free country, which means that we reside in a land where one human being has full liberty to annoy another to his heart's content, and why should woman be an exception to this rule? The times in which a father could exercise a certain control over his son's career have had their day, and are gone; and if modern daughters develope a taste for 'cutting their own grass,' to use an inelegant but expressive phrase, paterfamilias may be quite certain it is much more to his interest they should do so, than sit at home in that fearful state of idleness which obtains in modern English homes – thinking of the author of their being as a surly creature, who delights not in the latest costume dress, in the sweetest hat that ever came out of a milliner's shop, or in the heaviest plaits of hair that ever were bought 'cheaper than cheap,' through the kind offices of a friend in Germany.

For my own part, if women choose to go out and work with and like men, it seems to me that it is simple folly to raise any objection.

Years ago, a widower, burying his second wife, loudly expressed his intention of flinging himself into the grave after her coffin, and was indeed, only restrained from doing so by the strong arms of his friends, who with difficulty prevented the execution of his project.

The scene was a suburban burial-ground, where people were buried daily by the score; and as familiarity breeds contempt, or at least indifference, the officiating clergyman proceeded with the service, unmoved alike by the man's grief and the bystanders' expostulations.

Suddenly, however, his noisy lamentations becoming quite unendurable, the curate very mildly remarked, 'If the gentleman wishes to get into the grave, there is nothing to prevent his doing so,' which unexpected permission at once ended the scene.

The gentleman did not jump in after his wife, any more than a certain other gentleman died on the floor of the house of Commons; and it is the firm belief of the present writer that if women's rights had never met with the smallest opposition – had a wise public said, 'You shall take men's work if you desire it; you shall hedge and ditch; you shall walk four miles to your work in the winter mornings; you shall go down into the sewers; you shall drive dust carts; you shall have businesses, and leave your homes every morning at eight o'clock, so as to reach office by nine; you shall have full liberty to go out, no matter how ill you feel; you shall forget your sex, and let men forget it too, and treat you as they would men, peremptorily and roughly; you shall have households to keep, and incompetent husbands if you like, boring you when you come home for money; you shall go out in all weathers, and face all difficulties, and take all responsibilities, since such is your pleasure' – we should never have had another word of women doing men's work, or wanting to do it either.

It was the gross ignorance of women concerning the battle of life that made them ever wish to go out into it; and I hope and trust the day may come, though writer or reader may not live to see it, when, for the sake of England's honour and England's glory, her daughters, wearied of the world's clamour and the world's unkindness, may thankfully creep back home, and tell to their grandchildren and their great-grandchildren how much better and happier a thing it is to rule a household aright, and to make bright a fireside for a man's return, than to go forth through the mud and the rain, the melting heat and the suffocating dust, without a dear face and kindly smile looking forth from the open door to welcome one's return.

It is dangerous to preach an old religion when a new is abroad; and, therefore, to moderate the fury of the storm with which these remarks are certain to be assailed, I will just add in all honesty, that I believe the last state of English society to be far more healthy than that which preceded it. The sore long concealed has been exhibited at last. Instead of women saying over their tea, 'Men do no real work,' they are crying aloud in the streets, 'Give us work!' and the only matter for real regret in the whole business is that there cannot be found work enough to give them, since it would prove better for women to learn sympathy with men from actual experience than for them to refrain from sympathy altogether.

But, as has been said, on that especial summer evening when Frank Sinclair left the City in order to walk home, women's rights had not been thought of – not in England, at least, save vaguely.

The preliminary notes of war had sounded, it is true, and were carried to human ears like voices from a far distance; but what had actually come to pass was this – that wives were looking distastefully on former occupations, without having taken courage to lay hold on new; that daughters were taking part with their mothers against the stinginess which refused them unlimited credit, and insisted that a ten-pound note should last them, oh! for ever so long; that the willing service, the loving thoughtfulness of a previous generation had become a mere memory of the past, and that women had left their own especial sphere without actually aspiring to shine in that of man.

It was an uncomfortable transition state, that, in which it fared very hardly with many a man who had really very few sins of his own to answer for, and who was merely made the unhappy scapegoat, destined to bear the real or fancied transgressions of previous generations of husbands, forth into the wilderness.

The result to each male who chanced to be selected for this purpose was uncomfortable, and for a long time previously Frank had found his domestic situation unpleasant; and as he walked along, thankful at heart for the pecuniary ease time had brought, his thoughts recurred over and over again to home troubles, and he began marvelling if the fault lay at all with him, and if so, how he could remedy it.

Once more he recalled the past, carefully weighing each step, and asking himself how matters would have been had he acted in this way, or in that. Had he been too reserved? Had he been moody, irritable, apparently ungenerous? Might his wife not have mistaken his ill-concealed anxiety, for temper, his desire for economy, for meanness, his abstraction, for want of love? Putting aside the memory of that bright sunshiny time at Mulford, before they twain became one, he could not, even for the children's sake, endure that the mother of his girls and his boys should drift any further away from his affection.

He would make an effort to come to a thorough understanding with her. Sitting in the soft evening light, he would make the experiment of taking her fully into his confidence, and trying to make her understand the precise nature and extent of the difficulties which he had encountered and overcome.

Somerville and Ross

Edith Somerville (1858–1949) and Violet Florence Martin (Martin Ross, 1862–1915) were cousins who wrote collaboratively as Somerville and Ross. As a writing duo, they published fourteen stories and novels, including *The Real Charlotte, In the Vine Country, Through Connemara in a Governess Cart* and *The Experiences of an Irish R. M.* Their first book, *An Irish Cousin*, was published in 1889. When Violet died in 1915, Edith often wrote under their dual name, and published a further nine novels herself from 1919 to 1949, including *Mount Music, The Big House at Inver, An Incorruptible Irishman* and *Maria and Some Other Dogs*, published in 1949, the year that she died at the age of ninety-one.

Poisson d'Avril

The atmosphere of the waiting-room set at naught at a single glance the theory that there can be no smoke without fire. The stationmaster, when remonstrated with, stated, as an incontrovertible fact, that any chimney in the world would smoke in a south-easterly wind, and further, said there wasn't a poker, and that if you poked the fire the grate would fall out. He was, however, sympathetic, and went on his knees before the smouldering mound of slack, endeavouring to charm it to a smile by subtle proddings with the handle of the ticket-punch. Finally, he took me to his own kitchen fire and talked politics and salmon-fishing, the former with judicious attention to my presumed point of view, and careful suppression of his own, the latter with no less tactful regard for my admission that for three days I had not caught a fish, while the steam rose from my wet boots, in witness of the ten miles of rain through which an outside car had carried me.

Before the train was signalled I realised for the hundredth time the magnificent superiority of the Irish mind to the trammels of officialdom, and the inveterate supremacy in Ireland of the Personal Element.

'You might get a foot-warmer at Carrig Junction,' said a species of lay porter in a knitted jersey, ramming my suitcase upside down under the seat. 'Sometimes they're in it, and more times they're not.'

The train dragged itself rheumatically from the station, and a cold spring rain – the time was the middle of a most inclement April – smote it in flank as it came into the open. I pulled up both windows and began to smoke; there is, at least, a semblance of warmth in a thoroughly vitiated atmosphere.

It is my wife's habit to assert that I do not read her letters, and being now on my way to join her and my family in Gloucestershire, it seemed a sound thing to study again her latest letter of instructions.

'I am starting to-day, as Alice wrote to say we must be there two days before the wedding, so as to have a rehearsal for the pages. Their dresses have come, and they look too delicious in them—'

(I here omit profuse particulars not pertinent to this tale)—

'It is sickening for you to have had such bad sport. If the worst comes to the worst couldn't you buy one?—'

I smote my hand upon my knee. I had forgotten the infernal salmon! What a score for Philippa! If these contretemps would only teach her that I was not to be relied upon, they would have their uses, but experience is wasted upon her; I have no objection to being called an idiot, but, that being so, I ought to be allowed the privileges and exemptions proper to idiots. Philippa had, no doubt, written to Alice Hervey, and assured her that Sinclair would be only too delighted to bring her a salmon, and Alice Hervey, who was rich enough to find much enjoyment in saving money, would reckon upon it, to its final fin in mayonnaise.

Plunged in morose meditations, I progressed through a country parcelled out by shaky and crooked walls into a patchwood of hazel scrub and rocky fields, veiled in rain. About every six miles there was a station, wet and windswept; at one the sole occurrence was the presentation of a newspaper to the guard by the stationmaster; at the next the guard read aloud some choice excerpts from the same to the porter. The Personal Element was potent on this branch of the Munster and Connaught Railway. Routine, abhorrent to all artistic minds, was sheathed in conversation; even the engine-driver, a functionary ordinarily as aloof as the Mikado, alleviated his enforced isolation by sociable shrieks to every level crossing, while the long row of public-houses that formed, as far as I could judge, the town of Carrig, received a special and, as it seemed, humorous salutation.

The Time-Table decreed that we were to spend ten minutes at Carrig Junction; it was fifteen before the crowd of market people on the platform had been assimilated; finally, the window of a neighbouring carriage was flung open, and a wrathful English voice asked how much longer the train was going to wait. The stationmaster, who was at the moment engrossed in conversation with the guard and a man who was carrying a long parcel wrapped in newspaper, looked round, and said gravely—

'Well now, that's a mystery!'

The man with the parcel turned away, and convulsively studied a poster. The guard put his hand over his mouth.

The voice, still more wrathfully, demanded the earliest hour at which its owner could get to Belfast.

'Ye'll be asking me next when I take me breakfast,' replied the stationmaster, without haste or palpable annoyance.

The window went up again with a bang, the man with the parcel dug the guard in the ribs with his elbow, and the parcel slipped from under his arm and fell on the platform.

'Oh my! oh my! Me fish!' exclaimed the man, solicitously picking up a remarkably good-looking salmon that had slipped from its wrapping of newspaper.

Inspiration came to me, and I, in my turn, opened my window and summoned the stationmaster.

Would his friend sell me the salmon? The stationmaster entered upon the mission with ardour, but without success.

No; the gentleman was only just after running down to the town for it in the delay, but why wouldn't I run down and get one for myself? There was half-a-dozen more of them below at Coffey's, selling cheap; there would be time enough, the mail wasn't signalled yet.

I jumped from the carriage and doubled out of the station at top speed, followed by an assurance from the guard that he would not forget me.

Congratulating myself on the ascendancy of the Personal Element, I sped through the soapy limestone mud towards the public-houses. En route I met a heated man carrying yet another salmon, who, without preamble, informed me that there were three or four more good fish in it, and that he was after running down from the train himself.

'Ye have whips o' time!' he called after me. 'It's the first house that's not a public-house. Ye'll see boots in the window – she'll give them for tenpence a pound if ye're stiff with her!'

I ran past the public houses.

'Tenpence a pound!' I exclaimed inwardly, 'at this time of year! That's good enough.'

Here I perceived the house with boots in the window, and dived into its dark doorway.

A cobbler was at work behind a low counter. He mumbled something about Herself, through lengths of waxed thread that hung across his mouth, a fat woman appeared at an inner door, and at that moment I heard, appallingly near, the whistle of the incoming mail. The fat woman grasped the situation in an instant, and with what appeared but one movement, snatched a large fish from the floor of the room behind her and flung a newspaper round it.

'Eight pound weight!' she said swiftly. 'Ten shillings!'

A convulsive effort of mental arithmetic assured me that this was more than tenpence a pound, but it was not the moment for stiffness. I shoved a half-sovereign into her fishy hand, clasped my salmon in my arms, and ran.

Needless to say it was uphill, and at the steepest gradient another whistle stabbed me like a spur; above the station roof successive and advancing puffs of steam warned me that the worst had probably happened, but still I ran. When I gained the platform my train was already clear of it, but the Personal Element held good. Every soul in the station, or so it seemed to me, lifted up his voice and yelled. The stationmaster put his fingers in his mouth and sent after the departing train an unearthly whistle, with a high trajectory and a serrated edge. It took effect; the train slackened, I plunged from the platform and followed it up the rails, and every window in both trains blossomed with the heads of deeply interested spectators. The guard met me on the line, very apologetic and primed with an explanation that the gentleman going for the boat-train wouldn't let him wait any longer, while from our rear came an exultant cry from the station-master.

'Ye *told* him ye wouldn't forget him!'

'There's a few countrywomen in your carriage, sir,' said the guard, ignoring the taunt, as he shoved me and my salmon up the side of the train, 'but they'll be getting out in a couple of stations. There wasn't another seat in the train for them!'

My sensational return to my carriage was viewed with the utmost sympathy, by no less than seven shawled and cloaked countrywomen. In order to make room for me, one of them seated herself on the floor with her basket in her lap, another, on the seat opposite to me, squeezed herself under the central elbow flap that had been turned up to make room. The aromas of wet cloaks, turf smoke, and salt fish formed a potent blend. I was excessively hot, and the eyes of the seven women were fastened upon me with intense and unwearying interest.

'Move west a small piece, Mary Jack, if you please,' said a voluminous matron in the corner, 'I declare we're as throng as three in a bed this minute!'

'Why then Julia Casey, there's little throubling yourself,' grumbled the woman under the flap. 'Look at the way meself is! I wonder is it to be putting humps on themselves the gentry has them things down on top o' them! I'd sooner be carrying a basket of turnips on me back than to be scrooged this way!'

The woman on the floor at my feet rolled up at me a glance of compassionate amusement at this rustic ignorance, and tactfully changed the conversation by supposing that it was at Coffey's I got the salmon.

I said it was.

There was a silence, during which it was obvious that one question burnt in every heart.

'I'll go bail she axed him tinpence!' said the woman under the flap, as one who touches the limits of absurdity.

'It's a beautiful fish!' I said defiantly. 'Eight pounds weight. I gave her ten shillings for it.'

What is described in newspapers as 'sensation in court' greeted this confession.

'Look!' said the woman under the flap, darting her head out of the hood of her cloak, like a tortoise, 't'is what it is, ye haven't as much roguery in your heart as'd make ye a match for her!'

'Divil blow the ha'penny Eliza Coffey paid for that fish!' burst out the fat woman in the corner. 'Thim lads o' her's had a creel full o' thim snatched this morning before it was making day!'

'How would the gentleman be a match for her!' shouted the woman on the floor through a long-drawn whistle that told of a coming station. 'Sure a Turk itself wouldn't be a match for her! That one has a tongue that'd clip a hedge!'

At the station they clambered out laboriously, and with groaning. I handed down to them their monster baskets, laden, apparently, with ingots of lead; they told me in return that I was a fine *grauver* man, and it was a pity there weren't more like me; they wished, finally, that my journey might well thrive with me, and passed from my ken, bequeathing to me, after the agreeable manner of their kind, a certain comfortable mental sleekness that reason cannot immediately dispel. They also left me in possession of the fact that I was about to present the irreproachable Alice Hervey with a contraband salmon.

The afternoon passed cheerlessly into evening, and my journey did not conspicuously thrive with me. Somewhere in the dripping twilight I changed trains, and again later on, and at each change the salmon moulted some more of its damp raiment of newspaper, and I debated seriously the idea of interring it, regardless of consequences, in my portmanteau. A lamp was banged into the roof of my carriage, half an inch of orange flame, poised in a large glass globe, like a gold-fish, and of about as much use as an illuminant. Here also was handed in the dinner basket that I had wired for, and its contents, arid though they were, enabled me to achieve at least some measure of mechanical distension, followed by a dreary lethargy that was not far from drowsiness.

At the next station we paused long; nothing whatever occurred, and the rain drummed patiently upon the roof. Two nuns and some school-girls were in the carriage next door, and their voices came plaintively and in snatches through the partition; after a long period of apparent collapse, during which I closed my eyes to evade the cold gaze of the salmon through the netting, a voice in the next carriage said resourcefully:

'Oh, girls, I'll tell you what we'll do! We'll say the Rosary!'

'Oh, that will be lovely!' said another voice; 'well, who'll give it out? Theresa Condon, you'll give it out.'

Theresa Condon gave it out, in a not unmelodious monotone, interspersed with the responses, always in a lower cadence; the words were indistinguishable, but the rise and fall of the western voices was lulling as the hum of bees. I fell asleep.

I awoke in total darkness; the train was motionless, and complete and profound silence reigned. We were at a station: that much I discerned by the light of the dim lamp at the far end of a platform glistening with wet. I struck a match and ascertained that it was eleven o'clock, precisely the hour at which I was to board the mail train. I jumped out and ran down the platform; there was no one in the train; there was no one even on the engine, which was forlornly hissing to itself in the silence. There was not a human being anywhere. Every door was closed, and all was dark. The name-board of the station was faintly visible; with a lighted match I went along it letter by letter. It seemed as if the whole alphabet were in it, and by the time I had got to the end I had forgotten the beginning. One fact I had, however, mastered, that it was not the junction at which I was to catch the mail.

I was undoubtedly awake, but for a moment I was inclined to entertain the idea that there had been an accident, and that I had entered upon existence in another world. Once more I assailed the station house and the appurtenances thereof, the ticket-office, the waiting room, finally, and at some distance, the goods store, outside which the single lamp of the station commented feebly on the drizzle and the darkness. As I approached it a crack of light under the door became perceptible, and a voice was suddenly uplifted within.

'Your best now agin that! Throw down your Jack!'

I opened the door with pardonable violence, and found the guard, the stationmaster, the driver, and the stoker, seated on barrels round a packing case, on which they were playing a game of cards.

To have too egregiously the best of a situation is not, to a generous mind, a source of strength. In the perfection of their overthrow I permitted the driver and stoker to wither from their places, and to fade away into the outer darkness without any suitable send-off; with the guard and the stationmaster I dealt more faithfully, but the pleasure of throwing water on drowned rats is not a lasting one. I accepted the statements that they thought there wasn't a Christian in the train; that a few minutes here or there wouldn't signify, that they would have me at the junction in twenty minutes, and it was often the mail was late.

Fired by this hope I hurried back to my carriage, preceded at an emulous gallop by the officials. The guard thrust in with me the lantern from the card table, and fled to his van.

'Mind the goods, Tim!' shouted the stationmaster, as he slammed my door, 'she might be coming anytime now!'

The answer travelled magnificently back from the engine.

'Let her come! She'll meet her match!' A war-whoop upon the steam whistle fittingly closed the speech, and the train sprang into action.

We had about fifteen miles to go, and we banged and bucketed over it in what was, I should imagine, record time. The carriage felt as if it were galloping on four wooden legs, my teeth chattered in my head, and the salmon slowly churned its way forth from its newspaper, and moved along the netting with dreadful stealth.

All was of no avail.

'Well,' said the guard, as I stepped forth on to the deserted platform of Loughranny, 'that owld Limited Mail's th' unpunctualest thrain in Ireland! If you're a minute late she's gone from you, and may be if you were early you might be half-an-hour waiting for her!'

On the whole the guard was a gentleman. He said he would show me the best hotel in the town, though he feared I would be hard set to get a bed anywhere because of the '*Feis*' (a Feis, I should explain, is a Festival, devoted to competitions in Irish songs and dances). He shouldered my portmanteau, he even grappled successfully with the salmon, and, as we traversed the empty streets, he explained to me how easily I could catch the morning boat from Rosslare, and how it was, as a matter of fact, quite the act of Providence that my original scheme had been frustrated.

All was dark at the uninviting portals of the hotel favoured by the guard. For a full five minutes we waited at them, ringing hard: I suggested that we should try elsewhere.

'He'll come,' said the guard, with the confidence of the Pied Piper of Hamelin, retaining an implacable thumb upon the button of the electric bell. 'He'll come. Sure it rings in his room!'

The victim came, half awake, half dressed, and with an inch of dripping candle in his fingers. There was not a bed there, he said, nor in the town neither.

I said I would sit in the dining room till the time for the early train.

'Sure there's five beds in the dining room,' replied the boots, 'and there's mostly two in every bed.'

His voice was firm, but there was a wavering look in his eye.

'What about the billiard-room, Mike?' said the guard, in wooing tones.

'Ah, God bless you! We have a mattress on the table this minute!' answered the boots, wearily, 'and the fellow that got the First Prize for Reels asleep on top of it!'

'Well, and can't ye put the palliasse on the floor under it, ye omadhawn?' said the guard, dumping my luggage and the salmon in the hall, 'sure there's no snugger place in the house! I must run away home now, before Herself thinks I'm dead altogether!'

His retreating footsteps went lightly away down the empty street.

'Anything don't throuble *him*!' said the boots bitterly.

As for me, nothing save the Personal Element stood between me and destitution.

It was in the dark of the early morning that I woke again to life and its troubles. A voice, dropping, as it were, over the edge of some smothering over-world, had awakened me. It was the voice of the First Prize for Reels, descending through a pocket of the billiard-table.

'I beg your pardon, sir, are ye going on the 5 to Cork?'

I grunted a negative.

'Well, if ye were, ye'd be late,' said the voice.

I received this useful information in indignant silence, and endeavoured to wrap myself again in the vanishing skirts of a dream.

'I'm going on the 6.30 meself,' proceeded the voice, 'and it's unknown to me how I'll put on me boots. Me feet is swelled the size o' three-pound loaves with the dint of the little dancing-shoes I had on me in the competition last night. Me feet's delicate that way, and I'm a great epicure about me boots.'

I snored aggressively, but the dream was gone. So, for all practical purposes, was the night.

The First Prize for Reels arose, presenting an astonishing spectacle of grass-green breeches, a white shirt, and pearl-grey stockings, and accomplished a toilet that consisted of removing these and putting on ordinary garments, completed by the apparently excruciating act of getting into his boots. At any other hour of the day I might have been sorry for him. He then removed himself and his belongings to the hall, and there entered upon a resounding conversation with the boots, while I crawled forth from my lair to renew the strife with circumstances and to endeavour to compose a telegram to Alice Hervey of explanation and apology that should cost less than seven and sixpence. There was also the salmon to be dealt with.

Here the boots intervened, opportunely, with a cup of tea, and the intelligence that he had already done up the salmon in straw bottle-covers and brown paper, and that I could travel Europe with it if I liked. He further informed me that he would run up to the station with the luggage now, and that may be I wouldn't mind carrying the fish myself; it was on the table in the hall.

My train went at 6.15. The boots had secured for me one of many empty carriages, and lingered conversationally till the train started; he regretted politely my bad night at the hotel, and assured me that only for Jimmy Durkan having a little drink taken – Jimmy Durkan was the First Prize for Reels – he would have turned him off the billiard-table for my benefit. He finally confided to me that Mr Durkan was engaged to his sister, and was a rising baker in the town of Limerick, 'indeed,' he said, 'any girl might be glad to get him. He dances like whalebone, and he makes grand bread!'

Here the train started.

It was late that night when, stiff, dirty, with tired eyes blinking in the dazzle of electric lights, I was conducted by the Herveys' beautiful footman into the Herveys' baronial hall, and was told by the Herveys' imperial butler that dinner was over, and the gentlemen had just gone into the drawing-room. I was in the act of hastily declining to join them there, when a voice cried—

'Here he is!'

And Philippa, rustling and radiant, came forth into the hall, followed in shimmers of satin, and flutterings of lace, by Alice Hervey, by the bride elect, and by the usual festive rout of exhilarated relatives, male and female, whose mission it is to keep things lively before a wedding.

'Is this a wedding present for me, Uncle Sinclair?' cried the bride elect, through a deluge of questions and commiserations, and snatched from under my arm the brown paper parcel that had remained there from force of direful habit.

'I advise you not to open it!' I exclaimed; 'it's a salmon!'

The bride elect, with a shriek of disgust, and without an instant of hesitation, hurled it at her nearest neighbour, the head bridesmaid. The head bridesmaid, with an answering shriek, sprang to one side, and the parcel that I had cherished with a mother's care across two countries and a stormy channel, fell, with a crash, on the flagged floor.

Why did it crash?

'A salmon!' screamed Philippa, gazing at the parcel, round which a pool was already forming, 'why that's whisky! Can't you smell it?'

The footman here respectfully interposed, and kneeling down, cautiously extracted from folds of brown paper a straw bottle-cover full of broken glass and dripping with whisky.

'I'm afraid the other things are rather spoiled, sir,' he said seriously, and drew forth, successively, a very large pair of high-low shoes, two long grey worsted stockings, and a pair of grass-green breeches.

They brought the house down, in a manner doubtless familiar to them when they shared the triumphs of Mr Jimmy Durkan, but they left Alice Hervey distinctly cold.

'You know, darling,' she said to Philippa afterwards, 'I don't think it was very clever of dear Sinclair to take the wrong parcel. I *had* counted on that salmon.'

Kate O'Brien

Kate O'Brien was born in Limerick in 1897 and began her writing life as a playwright. She soon turned to fiction and her first novel, *Without My Cloak*, was published in 1931, winning the James Tait Black Memorial Prize. She is probably best known for *The Ante-Room*, *The Land of Spices* and *Mary Lavelle* (both were banned in Ireland on publication). *That Lady* was adapted for Broadway by O'Brien, and a film version was made in 1955 starring Olivia de Havilland. As well as novels, short stories and plays, O'Brien also wrote essays, film scripts, travelogues, journalism and a biography of St Teresa of Avila. Her final novel, *Music and Splendour*, was published in 1958. She died in the UK in 1974.

A Bus from Tivoli

In the hot weather Miriam liked to take, at random, one or other of the many buses that left the Piazza Termini for the villages called Castelli, in the Alban hills; or sometimes she would choose to go to Tivoli in the Sabines. Eventually she grew to like best to go to Hadrian's Villa, and to loaf about in that extraordinary estate through silent evenings. It was a place of sweet smells and lovely shades; she did not trouble overmuch to trace Hadrian's grandiose plans, under the grass; she felt sufficiently aware of the place and sufficiently aware of Rome in general to be content to walk about in peace, and to accept what the map at the gate said, and what the occasional signposts said. What she went to Hadrian's Villa for was profound silence, and the surprising richness of green and leaf. Rome, so near, was also far in summer evenings from this sad, grassed-over place of pride and sorrow.

They locked the entrance gate at seven o'clock; the man in charge got to know her, and gave her a few minutes grace as she hurried down under the acacia trees and past the little Greek Theatre. And when she was turned out she always crossed the lane to the trattoria opposite.

This was a pleasant restaurant. She sat in the garden, under vines that trailed from elm-tree to apple-tree; fireflies dashed about and late birds fussed and fluttered; strong light from indoors threw shadows about the grass, and also allowed her to read at ease. Cats, Roman and self-confident, sat at her feet, and shared her supper. By Roman standards, food was cheap in this place, and it was good. Trout, omelettes, strawberries, and peaches, and sharp wine of the Castelli. She sat in the silent dark as long as she liked. The bus descending from Tivoli for Rome passed the crossroads – a kilometer away, up the lane, every half-hour until eleven o'clock – and she was never in hurry. About half-past nine or so she would walk up the lane to catch say, the ten o'clock bus. One night she fell in, on this walk, with an elderly gardener who mistook her for Spanish – he said her Italian had a Spanish inflection. He knew Spain and had lived in a town of Northern Spain that she knew well. So they found much to talk about, and as he was old and rheumatic, by the time she parted from him at his house near the crossroads, she saw the ten o'clock bus dash past for Rome.

It was no matter; there would be another at ten-thirty. The only disadvantage was that in the evening, as at all hours, the high road from Tivoli to Rome is noisy and dusty, and there is nothing to sit on by the bus-stops.

Marian was in her fifties, and a heavy woman, one easily tired and who found life in Rome somewhat a physical ordeal. So, although she disliked the appearance of the little, brand-new café on the corner, disliked its shape, its white neon lights and its juke-box noises, she went into it, and to her surprise found a seat and a table vacant, crammed though the small interior was with lively, shouting Romans, crowded about the terrible music in the box.

44

'Could I have a glass of dry vermouth?' she said, in anxious, bad Italian.

A young man in spotless white coat beamed, bowed and went to get her a glass of dry vermouth. She looked around her, feeling sad. Always, she left Hadrian's Villa and the embowered, quiet trattoria feeling sad. But the high road, the noise, the scooters, and the public lavatory style of this as of all cheap places of refreshment set up by the Romans – saddened her unreasonably.

Unreasonable indeed, she told herself she was, and looked about and lighted a cigarette. The young man came and placed a glass of vermouth before her. Also he brought olives and potato crisps. He stood and smiled on her. She thanked him, and as he did not move she thought she should pay at once. She opened her purse. He waved the money aside.

'No, no,' he said. 'Merely I wonder where you are going?'

'I'm going to Rome. I missed the ten o'clock bus.'

'You are foreign, lady. But you are not English?'

'I am Irish.'

'Ah! Irish! And why do you go to Rome?'

'Because I'm living there.'

'I see,' he said. 'You are living there. Rome is quite near us, here.'

He was large and powerfully built young man. Very clean; scrubbed and square, and fresh-skinned; handsome in the Roman fashion, heavily muscular, with firmly, marked features. His eyes were intelligently bright – small and green-grey. He looked to be twenty-four or five.

As he stood and stared upon her, smiling kindly, Marian considered him with amusement.

'He's curiously like me,' she thought. 'He could be my son.'

For she had, as she knew with dislike, a heavy Roman look. In youth she had been normally slender, and beautiful of face; but middle age had taken the beauty away, and left her fleshy and Roman looking – Roman emperors she suggested to herself, when she contemplated her ageing head in the mirror; but Nero or Heliogabahus rather than Marcus Aurelius or Hadrian.

'And this boy is like Nero, I'd say,' she thought. 'Indeed – I'm sorry to think it – but this strong young Roman could easily be my son – in looks.'

This reflection, though amusing, did not please her, because Marian did not at all admire the Roman physical type, and very much disliked her own undeniable relation to it.

She ran her hands through her untidy hair. 'You feel too warm?'

'Yes; it's hot here. But it's always hot in Rome.'

'We have a beautiful bathroom here – with a beautiful shower.'

'Oh yes – we have all those beautiful things in my flat in Rome – your plumbing is very good—'

'Very good here. You must meet my sister. A moment, please!'

The young man bowed.

Relieved that he had left her, Marian shut her eyes and sipped vermouth.

But within a minute a hand touched her gently. A young, small, pretty girl was sitting beside her.

'My brother says that you are going to Rome. Why are you going to Rome?'

Amazed, Marian answered.

'I live in Rome.'

'But why do you live there?'

'I come often to Tivoli and to Hadrian's Villa.'

'Of course. Many people come to Hadrian's Villa. You love it?'

'I like to walk there.'

'Then why don't you stay here?'

'But – I don't want to. I live in Rome.'

'My brother wants you to stay here. Will you not?'

'Stay here? But how – what do you mean?'

'My brother – he has begged me to ask you. We have every comfort here – bath, all conveniences. We will be good to you. My brother is good. He entreats that you stay with us.'

'But – what on earth do you mean?'

'I mean what I say. My brother wants you. Could you not stay with him? He is kind.'

Marian stood up.

'Please, I beg you – let me pay now – I must go—'

The young man came forward and took her two hands.

'Will you not stay? Please, lady – my sister has told you, surely? I entreat you—'

'I am old! I'm an old woman!'

He smiled and touched her shoulder. 'I know. I see that. It doesn't matter. Stay!'

Marian put some lire on the table. He gathered them up and put them into her hand.

'Please, please – stay here a little while—'

'Oh heavens, goodnight! You're a crazy child! Why, you could both be my children!'

She ran down the steps, and in a minute the bus for Rome drew up. As it swept her away they stood and waved to her under their neon lights.

The curious, comic episode slid out of mind. Amused and puzzled by it for a day or so, she did narrate it to some friends, writers, painters, film actors – English and American – with whom she, a writer, associated in Rome.

But she told the ridiculous little story to no Italian acquaintance, because she felt that it would be impolite to do so. Also, she was sure that no Italian would believe her, and would gently dismiss her as another dreaming old lady from the queer, northern lands. Her English, Irish and American friends, however, knew her well enough to know that odd little story was true; they theorised gaily over the eccentric young Roman café-keeper; and one or two of them went so far in affection for her as to say that they saw his point – that definitely they saw his point.

Marian, however, did not see his point; and accepting that any youth who could rush such improbable fences within five minutes was in some unfixable way insane, she still wondered how he was empowered in the same five minutes of his lunatic appeal, to engage his young and sensitive-faced sister as his procuress. Nevertheless, she was a novelist and had been on earth for fifty-five years; she had encountered knottier questions than this accidental one of the café-keeper at the Tivoli bus stop. She let it slide. But she did not go to Hadrian's Villa again; and this was a deprivation.

In August, however, she had staying with her in Rome an English painter, a woman much younger than herself, to whom the Roman scene was new. She decided that she must take this friend to Tivoli and Hadrian's Villa. So they went. As they were late in leaving Tivoli after luncheon they took a taxi to Hadrian's Villa. In the trattoria they ate at leisure and fed the cats, and Marian amused Elizabeth with the story of the young café-keeper at the crossroads.

Politely, affectionately, Elizabeth said that she saw the young man's point. Marian laughed.

'Diana and Robert said that too,' she said. 'But it was a madman's point. He's only a big, fat boy. And all in five minutes! And dragging his little sister into it!'

They stayed a long time in the trattoria garden, aromatic and quiet. And when at last they reached the cross-roads they had barely missed the ten-thirty bus to Rome and had twenty-nine minutes to wait for the next, the last one. It was a fiesta night, dusty, and intolerably noisy by the roadside.

'We'll sit in the café,' said Elizabeth. 'What harm if the poor boy sees you again?'

'What harm indeed? He'll have forgotten the whole thing anyway – it's more than two months ago.'

The café had grown smarter with summer expansion, and had tin tables set now in a narrow little terrace, above the shops under the neon lights. One of these tables, in a corner, was vacant, and Marian and Elizabeth went and sat there.

Like a shot from a gun the young café-keeper was with them. His face shone with joy.

'You have come back at last! I knew you would! Dry Vermouth – I remember! Or would you not have a brandy?'

Marian asked Elizabeth what she would like to drink – Vermouth – dry Italian. He was enchanted. He must tell his sister. He would be with them in a moment. He had wished always for her to come back. She must believe him, excuse him – he would return in a moment.

And in a moment he did return – with his sister, and with bottle and glasses. Radiant, happy, sketchily asking permission, he and his sister sat down and he filled the glasses with Asti Spumante. Marian smiled. She detested the wine.

'Lady – you have come again. I have watched for you – I and my sister. Where do you live in Rome? We have searched and asked – oh, we drink now! You have returned! You will stay here now – please? Yes? You, her friend – you too? You will stay here now, as I desire – in this fine, clean house I have—?'

'It is good and clean; my brother is a good boy – and he desires this lady,' said her sister to Elizabeth.

Elizabeth had no Italian, but she understood what the girl said, and she smiled.

'I have watched, I have waited. I have not for a day forgotten you, Irish lady – is that true?' he turned to his sister.

'It is true. He loves you, signora – signorina? There is no peace. Stay with him a little, please. He is a good boy – he is kind.'

'We have all modern comforts. We will consider you and be careful. Oh, you are near Rome here; you can do as you please! Only stay with us, a little time, lady! I knew I must see you again!'

The young man's strong, clean hands were laid, hard and flat on Marian's. His bright eyes blazed on her.

'Answer him. Speak to him,' said Elizabeth.

Marian knew she must do so. Grotesque as the comedy made her feel, it also quite absurdly honoured her. And ludicrous insane as it might be, it was – take it or leave it, an actuality. This cracked young man was as he was and taken and held to this impossible and grotesque idea.

'I don't know your name, or your sister's,' she said. 'I am fifty-five years old: I take you to be about twenty-five, your sister not yet. I'd say, twenty-one. It is impossible for me to thank you or be gracious about your insane idea. I have to speak in English – I have no Italian to say what I mean – but in English I will tell you to stop talking nonsense, and that I'll be gone on the bus in a minute.'

Marian stood up. The young man rose with her, holding her two hands.

'Do not go! Oh, do not go – now you have returned! We have here every kindness, every comfort—'

'I am going! Oh please be sane!'

'I am not concerned to be sane! Where are you – in Rome? I will visit you! I will behave well, I have a beautiful summer suit, of light grey – let me come! Where are you?'

'He is good, lady. He will bring you flowers, he will bring you wine. Tell him where to find you in Rome! He is good. He loves you – he talks about you always.'

'I will come. I will visit – in my good new suit. I insist I will visit. You have returned – and you must tell me who you are – I have searched—'

'Good-bye, good-bye.'

The last bus from Tivoli came roaring down and Marian and Elizabeth fought their way on to it.

They dismounted in the Piazza Termini.

'I think you should have let him visit you,' said Elizabeth. 'His good, new suit.'

They found their bus to the Chiesa Nuova.

Norah Hoult

Born in Dublin in 1898, Norah Hoult published journalism, novels and short stories. Her first collection, *Poor Women!* was published in 1928, and Hoult wrote two further collections, *Nine Years is a Long Time* and *Cocktail Bar* (which is where 'Miss Coles Makes the Tea' first appeared). Her novels include *Time, Gentlemen, Time!, Holy Ireland, Four Women Grow Up, The Last Days of Miss Jenkinson* and *There Were No Windows*, which was reissued by Persephone Books in 2005. Hoult died in Greystones, Co. Wicklow in 1984.

When Miss Coles Made the Tea

Mr and Mrs Coles were pleased when they heard definitely that Olive had got the job as a junior assistant at the Standard Book Shop and Library. It wasn't much money, of course; only twenty-five bob a week to start, but money wasn't everything.

'It'll be nice surroundings, you see, Olive,' said Mrs Coles, who had a pale face, a lot of dark hair, and dark eyes, and a habit when she felt tired of sitting down and looking long and thoughtfully at herself in the mirror – which examination generally ended in a sigh and a shake of the head. 'Refined, that's what I mean! You should get to know a lot of *nice* people.'

And Mr Coles, who was short and stout and rubicund, and enjoyed being helpful about everything, whether it was washing dishes or contributing to a discussion at his local, put on his serious look, and said: 'With all those books around, you should pick up a real education. Because it doesn't follow that because you're fifteen and through with school, you're educated. Not by a long chalk, it don't.'

Between themselves, and not so Olive would hear, because they wouldn't have hurt her feelings for anything in the world, they agreed that with her slight deafness she was lucky to get a job.

'I mean we have to face it that there are some places, factories and such, where she wouldn't be no manner of use,' said Mr Coles. And Mrs Coles said: 'I wouldn't have let her go to a place where they might start shouting rough at her. She's like me: she's sensitive. And she hears well enough if she's only spoken to quiet and polite.'

There were certainly quite a lot of things about the Standard that Olive liked at first. For one thing, she liked being called 'Miss Coles'. It made you feel ever so grown-up and much more important. It was like being given a present of a superior personality which inspired you to walk differently, keeping your head well up, and to see that your shoes were polished and that if you had a hole in your stocking it was at least in a place where it didn't show.

It was true that the grown-up girls weren't very friendly: sometimes looking through her in a funny way as if she wasn't really there, and, especially upstairs in the Library, speaking *at* her rather than *to* her. But Olive, having sweetness in her disposition, worked it out, and saw, of course, that they were really superior.

'All the girls, 'cept me and Miss Phillips, have been to ever such high-class schools, and Miss Steadham, what does the foreign books ...'

'*Who* does the foreign books,' interrupted Mrs Coles. 'You must learn to speak nice, Olive, now.'

'*Who* does the foreign books, I mean. Well, she can speak French like we can speak English because she's been there. She was at school in Paris before the war.'

'So've I been to Paris,' said Mr Coles. 'In the last war. And I can speak French: *"Oui, oui. Voulez-vous coucher avec moi, Mamselle?"*'

'Now, Fred,' said Mrs Coles reprovingly. But unheeding, for she knew Dad liked his joke and anyone could see that being to France hadn't educated him in the same way as it had Miss Steadham, Olive raced on:

'And her clothes are posh. *Plain*, you know, Mum, but ever so *good!* And another one whose clothes must cost a lot of money is Miss Taylor. She's upstairs in the Library where they give out the books to the public. There was someone ever so important, Dad, came in to change her book: I was told who she was, but I didn't quite catch the name. I'd like to give out the books, but I shall have to be there quite a while, I expect, before I'm allowed to do that.'

Indeed Miss Coles' job was mostly fetching and carrying and putting away. Down from the shop to the basement, where the unpacking went on, and upstairs with her arms loaded with print. In the Library it was putting the books the public returned back on the shelves in their right places. It was very important to get exactly the right place; and she had to keep running over the alphabet the whole time because it wasn't just all the A's together, it was the Ab's together, and she had to remember that Shu came before Spa, and so on. It took a bit of getting *into!*

She had to admit that the other junior, Miss Phillips, was quicker than herself, Miss Phillips being pert and full of self-confidence. But Miss Coles didn't feel very inferior about this, because, after all, things have a way of evening out. She felt she was prettier than Miss Phillips, who had straight sandy hair, and a snub nose, and looked like a kid, while *her* curling dark hair fell to her shoulders in a Hollywood bob, and she knew she had long eyelashes, because it was a joke of Dad's that she could sweep the carpet with them. And she didn't look a kid because, of course, now she was at work she used lipstick.

'My mother wouldn't half give me what for if I put that red stuff on my lips,' said Miss Phillips, watching her disapprovingly one day when they were together in the cloakroom and Miss Coles was able to reply, 'My mum isn't a bit like that. She says, "You're out in the big world now, Olive, and it's right you should want to look your best!"'

But when Miss Coles got over the first glory of having a refined job she found its inconveniences increasing. Chief of the inconveniences was Mrs Dickenson. When Mr Coles said to her, 'Are you able to do a bit of reading to improve yourself, Olive?' she looked back at him with pity.

'Why, Dad, I'd hate to see Mrs Dickenson's face if she caught me reading a book!'

'Who's Mrs Dickenson when she's at home?'

'She's the boss, she's everybody,' said Miss Coles sadly. 'She's the one that tells you off.'

Mrs Dickenson wasn't in fact quite the boss, but she was the Assistant Librarian. She was the wind who blew the dust out of shelves, or caused it to be blown; she was the stick ready to beat girls who paused in their labours to giggle or gossip; she was the ear that listened to be sure you said the right thing, like: 'I don't know Madam, but I'll inquire'; she was the voice that pursued relentlessly, 'Do hurry up Miss Coles'; she was the nose that always poked itself into your business.

Mr Coles said, when the situation became clear, 'I see! She's the one that's always hauling you over the *coles*.' But Miss Coles was not amused.

Now there is in offices, and other places where toilers are gathered together, an institution known as 'having tea'. One person usually makes the tea, and the others come along to sip, and gather what rosebuds of relaxation may be allowed. At the Standard the staff were theoretically permitted ten minutes to take tea: the bosses were called first, then the intermediates, and finally the humble and the juniors. A big fat girl, named Miss Scott, who worked in the basement, usually made the tea, and her method was to pour it all out at once into the required number of tea cups. So that the last to come were most coldly served.

But when it was Miss Scott's half-day off, another girl had to understudy. In due course Miss Coles heard from one of her elders and betters, 'You're Miss Coles, aren't you? Mrs Dickenson says you're to make the tea this afternoon. I suppose you know how. Here's the key of the cupboard with the tea and the cups and biscuits. You put the kettle on the gas-ring, and do, my good child, *wait* till it's boiling if you can.'

'I know how to make tea,' said Miss Coles with dignity. 'Often and often I make it for Mum and she says …'

'How terribly interesting! Here's the money for the milk that you get from the dairy round the corner in New Street. You tell them it's for the Standard. You're up in the Library this afternoon, I believe? Ask Miss Taylor to excuse you at ten to three because you are making the tea.'

'Okey Dokey,' said Miss Coles.

It was with a slight frown that at ten to three Miss Coles set forth for the dairy. But those who are incarcerated in employment vile for most of the daylight hours know how dear the outside world can appear when viewed for but a brief glimpse, and the sight of free men and women walking up and down and looking into shop windows instantly banished the frown. Cheered and fortified, Miss Coles returned with the milk bottle, carefully she warmed the teapot just before the kettle came to the boil, cautiously with the tip of her tongue peeping through her scarlet lips she infused the beverage, and, finally, by verbal message and house telephone, it became known to the staff that tea was ready.

Each in their turn came and drank and took their biscuit, Miss Coles passing the cups to those who were to her tops in the whole wide world, since they were the élite of The Standard Bookshop. She hoped politely that they had the amount of milk that suited them; sugar, since it was rationed, they had to provide for themselves. She didn't notice that one or two raised haughty eyebrows or looked at each other in 'the sarky way' she had had occasion to observe was one of the insignia of the superior. For she was fortified by the number of times her Mum had said to callers that if there was one thing Olive could do it was make good tea. And in fact, since she was careful to pour it out fresh for each corner, she gave them a much better cup than was usually provided.

The highest drank quickly and departed, for so important were they that their absence might suspend affairs of the utmost moment; the secondary class lingered but very little longer, and, finally, Miss Coles was left with the last arrival, Miss Phillips, and a woman who though much older had only started her wartime job that week with the Standard, and was still sufficiently conscious of her lowly and confused estate to behave herself even with the juniors.

Miss Coles, feeling the change in the atmosphere, allowed herself to relax. She sat down, and for the first time filled her own cup. And the new woman having said that they were lucky to get biscuits, she dipped into warming conversation.

'My Dad often does the shopping in our house, and he's ever so good at picking up things. Every Saturday morning he sets out with Mum's string bag.'

'Isn't that sweet of him?' said the newcomer. She turned to Miss Phillips. 'So few men bother, do they?'

Miss Phillips stared blankly, but Miss Coles nodded: 'That's right! You see, what Dad says is that he's better at standing in queues than Mum, because her legs get so tired she could drop.'

The newcomer nodded appreciative understanding, and Miss Coles was encouraged to proceed. She had always known that her Dad was a special person, just as in a different way her Mum was a special person. It was nice to be able to put some of it into words.

'He's a good shopper, Mum says. She says, "Well, you mayn't look romantic, but you can certainly shop." Dad's put on weight a bit, that's what she means. Mum doesn't really mind, you see. She just likes pulling his leg, because he only laughs. You know how difficult it is to get corn-flour and jelly now, don't you?'

'I certainly do. I haven't any.'

'Well, my Dad got both last Saturday. Mum was pleased!'

'I should think she must have been.'

At this very moment when Miss Coles, at the top of her form, was about to nod, enjoying the cosy conversation, enjoying the vicarious triumph of Dad's cleverness, something happened. The door didn't open; it was flung back, and Mrs Dickenson stood dramatically in front of them. Her cheeks were flushed; behind her glasses her eyes glittered with rage; her hands were clenched. She said:

'What do you think you are doing, Miss Coles?'

It was so obvious what she was doing, that she was doing what she had been instructed to do, and serve the tea that Miss Coles nearly gaped back in wonder.

Mrs Dickenson saw the rouged lips framed in the cascade of falling hair drop apart, and these two features, which to her mind made Miss Coles look common and therefore unworthy to minister in the Standard, served as an added impetus to her rage. However, she remembered that the girl was inclined to be deaf; and with great effort made herself speak slowly and clearly:

'You are allowed ten minutes for your tea, Miss Coles: you have been here twenty minutes. *Why?*'

'I thought I was supposed to put the cups away. Miss Scott does.'

Mrs Dickenson closed her eyes as if in pain. She also closed them against the recognition that Miss Coles had scored a point in her own defence. But Miss Scott was one person; this monster of a junior who had been sitting down and chatting away – Mrs Dickenson had paused to listen at the door before rage had thrust her forward – as if she were giving a tea party, was another. Mrs Dickenson, who like many highly-strung women set in authority was not infrequently beset by black angers directed toward the stupidity and 'don't care' attitude of her subordinates, would have liked to hold her head with both hands and *scream*. She refrained from doing so, but as Miss Coles was still calmly sitting there when she opened her eyes, she did stamp her foot.

'WILL YOU RETURN TO YOUR WORK? CAN YOU HEAR ME?'

Miss Coles went. She was still too confounded to realise quite what had happened, and why Mrs Dickenson was in such a temper. When a child has broken her doll, when a woman sees her home destroyed by a bomb, when a painter finds his canvas slashed, there is a time lag, perceptible or imperceptible, before the complete realisation of loss strikes home. It was Miss Phillips who helped on the work of full enlightenment, Miss Phillips who came running in high glee down to the basement where Miss Coles had been sent.

'Oh, here you are! Cor, didn't you catch it! See her stamp her foot at you! And she didn't half go on after you'd gone.'

'I don't care. I was doing what she told me. What did she say?'

'She said to that new woman, Miss Whatshername, "To think," she said' – Miss Phillips gave a not unsuccessful imitation of Mrs Dickenson's sharp and anguished voice – '"To *think* that the Standard is reduced to employing such a type, such a nit-wit."' She stared out of the window, and she was wringing her hands. At least they were clenched, and she unclenched them. And then she said through her teeth, 'And she's *deaf*,' she said. 'Stone *deaf*.'

'I'm not,' said Miss Coles staring very hard but quite unseeingly at the pile of books she was supposed to dust before bringing them up to the Library.

'I'm only telling you what *she* said. I know you're not really very deaf. I washed my cup, and then I scrammed quick. And the other woman mumbled something and was out after me like a flash. She broke up the party all right, all right! Gosh, I never saw her in such a wax before!'

'I don't care,' said Miss Coles, and started to dust Plato's *Republic*.

She did care. She closed her eyelids, and squeezed them hard so not to let the tears come through and give Miss Phillips, who was only a kid, the satisfaction of seeing her cry. And so the sickness inside her slowly grew a shell, retaining its poison. For she knew that she couldn't, she *mustn't* tell Mum and Dad when she got home about the row, and what Mrs Dickenson had said about her. She could see their faces getting worried. Their pride in her would be spoilt. She was old enough to start protecting them now. Mum and Dad were kind; they didn't understand about unkindness.

It wasn't as if she could explain the hurt properly either, because it wasn't just an ordinary telling-off which might be fair enough, or not so fair. What she couldn't explain but only felt was her knowledge that she had wrought well, that she had made good tea, and at the end entertained successfully. She had created something; a little oasis of cosy warmth, a patch of civilised living, in the middle of the grey office routine. And then a storm had come, obliterating, so that her handiwork must never be thought of with pride, but only with pain and mortification.

After that first time she had made the tea, Miss Coles somehow never cared much for her job at the Standard. But her Mum was still pleased she was there, so when people asked her how she was getting on she said, 'All rightio,' because she didn't want to disappoint Mum. She decided to pack it in when the war was over, and go to somewhere less refined but where they paid better. Meanwhile she could always look forward to the great moment when the clock said five to six, and she could start getting ready to go out into the gay street. For, at this time, there was generally an American G.I. or two who stared ever so hard at her and said, 'Hello Beautiful!' Because that showed everybody didn't think she was so dumb.

Elizabeth Bowen

Born in Dublin in 1899 to an Anglo-Irish family, Elizabeth Bowen was a novelist, short story writer and essayist. Her ten novels include *The Last September, The Death of the Heart* and *The Heat of the Day*. Bowen published several short story collections including *Encounters, The Cat Jumps, The Demon Lover and Other Stories* and *Ivy Gripped the Steps*. Her nonfiction work focused on memoir, writing and travel. She was awarded the CBE in 1948 and made a Companion of Literature by the Royal Society of Literature in 1965. Bowen's last novel, *Eva Trout*, published in 1968, won the James Tait Black Memorial Prize. She died in 1973.

The Demon Lover

Toward the end of her day in London Mrs Drover went round to her shut-up house to look for several things she wanted to take away. Some belonged to herself, some to her family, who were by now used to their country life. It was late August; it had been a steamy, showery day: at the moment the trees down the pavement glittered in an escape of humid yellow afternoon sun. Against the next batch of clouds, already piling up ink-dark, broken chimneys and parapets stood out. In her once familiar street, as in any unused channel, an unfamiliar queerness had silted up; a cat wove itself in and out of railings, but no human eye watched Mrs Drover's return. Shifting some parcels under her arm, she slowly forced round her latchkey in an unwilling lock, then gave the door, which had warped, a push with her knee. Dead air came out to meet her as she went in.

The staircase window having been boarded up, no light came down into the hall. But one door, she could just see, stood ajar, so she went quickly through into the room and unshuttered the big window in there. Now the prosaic woman, looking about her, was more perplexed than she knew by everything that she saw, by traces of her long former habit of life – the yellow smoke stain up the white marble mantelpiece, the ring left by a vase on the top of the escritoire; the bruise in the wallpaper where, on the door being thrown open widely, the china handle had always hit the wall. The piano, having gone away to be stored, had left what looked like claw marks on its part of the parquet. Though not much dust had seeped in, each object wore a film of another kind; and, the only ventilation being the chimney, the whole drawing room smelled of the cold hearth. Mrs Drover put down her parcels on the escritoire and left the room to proceed upstairs; the things she wanted were in a bedroom chest.

She had been anxious to see how the house was – the part-time caretaker she shared with some neighbours was away this week on his holiday, known to be not yet back. At the best of times he did not look in often, and she was never sure that she trusted him. There were some cracks in the structure, left by the last bombing, on which she was anxious to keep an eye. Not that one could do anything.

A shaft of refracted daylight now lay across the hall. She stopped dead and stared at the hall table – on this lay a letter addressed to her.

She thought first – then the caretaker *must* be back. All the same, who, seeing the house shuttered, would have dropped a letter in at the box? It was not a circular, it was not a bill. And the post office redirected, to the address in the country, everything for her that came through the post. The caretaker (even if he were back) did not know she was due in London today – her call here had been planned to be a surprise – so his negligence in the manner of this letter, leaving it to wait in the dusk and the dust, annoyed her. Annoyed, she picked up the letter, which bore no stamp. But it cannot be important, or they would know ... She took the letter rapidly upstairs with her, without a stop to look at the writing till she reached what had been her bedroom, where she let in light. The room looked over the garden and other gardens: the sun had gone in; as the clouds sharpened and lowered, the trees and rank lawns seemed already to smoke with dark. Her reluctance to look again at the letter came from the fact that she felt intruded upon – and by someone contemptuous of her ways. However, in the tenseness preceding the fall of rain she read it: It was a few lines.

Dear Kathleen,
You will not have forgotten that today is our anniversary, and the day we said. The years have gone by at once slowly and fast. In view of the fact that nothing has changed, I shall rely upon you to keep your promise. I was sorry to see you leave London, but was satisfied that you would be back in time. You may expect me, therefore, at the hour arranged. Until then ...
K.

Mrs Drover looked for the date: It was today's. She dropped the letter onto the bedsprings, then picked it up to see the writing again – her lips, beneath the remains of lipstick, beginning to go white. She felt so much the change in her own face that she went to the mirror, polished a clear patch in it, and looked at once urgently and stealthily in. She was confronted by a woman of forty-four, with eyes starting out under a hat brim that had been rather carelessly pulled down. She had not put on any more powder since she left the shop where she ate her solitary tea. The pearls her husband had given her on their marriage hung loose round her now rather thinner throat, slipping in the V of the pink wool jumper her sister knitted last autumn as they sat round the fire. Mrs Drover's most normal expression was one of controlled worry, but of assent. Since the birth of the third of her little boys, attended by a quite serious illness, she had had an intermittent muscular flicker to the left of her mouth, but in spite of this she could always sustain a manner that was at once energetic and calm.

Turning from her own face as precipitately as she had gone to meet it, she went to the chest where the things were, unlocked it, threw up the lid, and knelt to search. But as rain began to come crashing down she could not keep from looking over her shoulder at the stripped bed on which the letter lay. Behind the blanket of rain the clock of the church that still stood struck six – with rapidly heightening apprehension she counted each of the slow strokes. 'The hour arranged ... My God,' she said, '*what* hour? How should I ... ? After twenty-five years ...'

The young girl talking to the soldier in the garden had not ever completely seen his face. It was dark; they were saying goodbye under a tree. Now and then – for it felt, from not seeing him at this intense moment, as though she had never seen him at all – she verified his presence for these few moments longer by putting out a hand, which he each time pressed, without very much kindness, and painfully, on to one of the breast buttons of his uniform. That cut of the button on the palm of her hand was, principally, what she was to carry away. This was so near the end of a leave from France that she could only wish him already gone. It was August 1916. Being not kissed, being drawn away from and looked at intimidated Kathleen till she imagined spectral glitters in the place of his eyes. Turning away and looking back up the lawn she saw, through branches of trees, the drawing-room window alight: She caught a breath for the moment when she could go running back there into the safe arms of her mother and sister, and cry: 'What shall I do, what shall I do? He has gone.'

Hearing her catch her breath, her fiancé said, without feeling: 'Cold?'

'You're going away such a long way.'

'Not so far as you think.'

'I don't understand?'

'You don't have to,' he said. 'You will. You know what we said.'

'But that was – suppose you – I mean, suppose.'

'I shall be with you,' he said, 'sooner or later. You won't forget that. You need do nothing but wait.'

Only a little more than a minute later she was free to run up the silent lawn. Looking in through the window at her mother and sister, who did not for the moment perceive her, she already felt that unnatural promise drive down between her and the rest of all humankind. No other way of having given herself could have made her feel so apart, lost and forsworn. She could not have plighted a more sinister troth.

Kathleen behaved well when, some months later, her fiancé was reported missing, presumed killed. Her family not only supported her but were able to praise her courage without stint because they could not regret, as a husband for her, the man they knew almost nothing about. They hoped she would, in a year or two, console herself – and had it been only a question of consolation things might have gone much straighter ahead. But her trouble, behind just a little grief, was a complete dislocation from everything. She did not reject other lovers, for these failed to appear: For years she failed to attract men – and with the approach of her thirties she became natural enough to share her family's anxiousness on this score. She began to put herself out, to wonder; and at thirty-two she was very greatly relieved to find herself being courted by William Drover. She married him, and the two of them settled down in this quiet, arboreal part of Kensington: In this house the years piled up, her children were born, and they all lived till they were driven out by the bombs of the next war. Her movements as Mrs Drover were circumscribed, and she dismissed any idea that they were still watched.

As things were – dead or living the letter writer sent her only a threat. Unable, for some minutes, to go on kneeling with her back exposed to the empty room, Mrs Drover rose from the chest to sit on an upright chair whose back was firmly against the wall. The desuetude of her former bedroom, her married London home's whole air of being a cracked cup from which memory, with its reassuring power, had either evaporated or leaked away, made a crisis – and at just this crisis the letter writer had, knowledgeably, struck. The hollowness of the house this evening cancelled years on years of voices, habits, and steps. Through the shut windows she only heard rain fall on the roofs around. To rally herself, she said she was in a mood – and for two or three seconds shutting her eyes, told herself that she had imagined the letter. But she opened them – there it lay on the bed.

On the supernatural side of the letter's entrance she was not permitting her mind to dwell. Who, in London, knew she meant to call at the house today? Evidently, however, this had been known. The caretaker, *had* he come back, had had no cause to expect her: He would have taken the letter in his pocket, to forward it, at his own time, through the post. There was no other sign that the caretaker had been in – but, if not? Letters dropped in at doors of deserted houses do not fly or walk to tables in halls. They do not sit on the dust of empty tables with the air of certainty that they will be found. There is needed some human hand – but nobody but the caretaker had a key. Under circumstances she did not care to consider, a house can be entered without a key. It was possible that she was not alone now. She might be being waited for, downstairs. Waited for – until when? Until 'the hour arranged.' At least that was not six o'clock: Six has struck.

She rose from the chair and went over and locked the door.

The thing was, to get out. To fly? No, not that: She had to catch her train. As a woman whose utter dependability was the keystone of her family life she was not willing to return to the country, to her husband, her little boys, and her sister, without the objects she had come up to fetch. Resuming work at the chest she set about making up a number of parcels in a rapid, fumbling-decisive way. These, with her shopping parcels, would be too much to carry; these meant a taxi – at the thought of the taxi her heart went up and her normal breathing resumed. I will ring up the taxi now; the taxi cannot come too soon: I shall hear the taxi out there running its engine, till I walk calmly down to it through the hall. I'll ring up – But no: the telephone is cut off ... She tugged at a knot she had tied wrong.

The idea of flight ... He was never kind to me, not really. I don't remember him kind at all. Mother said he never considered me. He was set on me, that was what it was – not love. Not love, not meaning a person well. What did he do, to make me promise like that? I can't remember – But she found that she could.

She remembered with such dreadful acuteness that the twenty-five years since then dissolved like smoke and she instinctively looked for the weal left by the button on the palm of her hand. She remembered not only all that he said and did but the complete suspension of *her* existence during that August week. I was not myself – they all told me so at the time. She remembered – but with one white burning blank as where acid has dropped on a photograph: *Under no conditions* could she remember his face.

So, wherever he may be waiting, I shall not know him. You have no time to run from a face you do not expect.

The thing was to get to the taxi before any clock struck what could be the hour. She would slip down the street and round the side of the square to where the square gave on the main road. She would return in the taxi, safe, to her own door, and bring the solid driver into the house with her to pick up the parcels from room to room. The idea of the taxi driver made her decisive, bold: She unlocked her door, went to the top of the staircase, and listened down.

She heard nothing – but while she was hearing nothing the *passé* air of the staircase was disturbed by a draft that travelled up to her face. It emanated from the basement: Down there a door or window was being opened by someone who chose this moment to leave the house.

The rain had stopped; the pavements steamily shone as Mrs Drover let herself out by inches from her own front door into the empty street. The unoccupied houses opposite continued to meet her look with their damaged stare. Making toward the thoroughfare and the taxi, she tried not to keep looking behind. Indeed, the silence was so intense – one of those creeks of London silence exaggerated this summer by the damage of war – that no tread could have gained on hers unheard. Where her street debouched on the square where people went on living, she grew conscious of, and checked, her unnatural pace. Across the open end of the square two buses impassively passed each other: Women, a perambulator, cyclists, a man wheeling a barrow signalized, once again, the ordinary flow of life. At the square's most populous corner should be – and was – the short taxi rank. This evening, only one taxi – but this, although it presented its blank rump, appeared already to be alertly waiting for her. Indeed, without looking round the driver started his engine as she panted up from behind and put her hand on the door. As she did so, the clock struck seven. The taxi faced the main road: To make the trip back to her house it would have to turn – she had settled back on the seat and the taxi *had* turned before she, surprised by its knowing movement, recollected that she had not 'said where.' She leaned forward to scratch at the glass panel that divided the driver's head from her own.

The driver braked to what was almost a stop, turned round, and slid the glass panel back: The jolt of this flung Mrs Drover forward till her face was almost into the glass. Through the aperture driver and passenger, not six inches between them, remained for an eternity eye to eye. Mrs Drover's mouth hung open for some seconds before she could issue her first scream. After that she continued to scream freely and to beat with her gloved hands on the glass all round as the taxi, accelerating without mercy, made off with her into the hinterland of deserted streets.

Mary Lavin

Mary Lavin was born in 1912 in the US, but moved as a child with her Irish parents to Athenry, and then to Dublin. Lavin only wrote two novels, *The House in Clewe Street* and *Mary O'Grady*, and is best known for her short story collections, including *Tales from Bective Bridge, The Becker Wives and Other Stories, In the Middle of the Fields* and *Happiness and Other Stories*. She won The James Tait Black Memorial Prize, two Guggenheim Fellowships, The Katherine Mansfield Prize and the Allied Irish Banks Literary Award. She was awarded an honorary doctorate from UCD in 1968, and died in 1996.

In the Middle of the Fields

Like a rock in the sea, she was islanded by fields, the heavy grass washing about the house, and the cattle wading in it as in water. Even their gentle stirrings were a loss when they moved away at evening to the shelter of the woods. A rainy day might strike a wet flash from a hay barn on the far side of the river. Not even a habitation! And yet she was less lonely for him here in Meath than elsewhere. Anxieties by day, and cares, and at night vague, nameless fears, these were the stones across the mouth of the tomb. But who understood that? They thought she hugged tight every memory she had of him. What did they know about memory? What was it but another name for dry love and barren longing? They even tried to unload upon her their own small purposeless memories. 'I imagine I see him every time I look out there,' they would say as they glanced nervously over the darkening fields when they were leaving. 'I think I ought to see him coming through the trees.' Oh, for God's sake! she'd think. She'd forgotten him for a minute.

It wasn't him she saw when she looked out at the fields. It was the ugly tufts of tow and scutch that whitened the tops of the grass and gave it the look of a sea in storm, spattered with broken foam. That grass would have to be topped. And how much would it cost?

At least Ned, the old herd, knew the man to do it for her. 'Bartley Crossen is your man, Ma'am. Your husband knew him well.'

Vera couldn't place him at first. Then she remembered. 'Oh, yes, that's his hay barn we see, isn't it? Why, of course. I know him well, by sight.' And so she did, splashing past on the road in his big muddy car, the wheels always caked with clay, and the wife in the front seat beside him.

'I'll get him to call around and have a word with you, Ma'am,' said the herd.

'Before dark,' she cautioned.

But there was no need to tell Ned. The old man knew how she always tried to be upstairs before it got dark, locking herself into her bedroom, which opened off the room where the children slept, praying devoutly that she wouldn't have to come down again for anything, above all, not to answer the door. That was what in particular she dreaded: a knock after dark.

'Ah, sure, who'd come near you, Ma'am, knowing you're a woman alone with small children that might be wakened and set crying? And, for that matter, where could you be safer than in the middle of the fields, with the innocent beasts asleep around you?' If he himself had come to the house late at night for any reason, to get hot water to stoup the foot of a beast, or to call the vet, he took care to shout out long before he got to the gable. 'It's me, Ma'am!' he'd shout.

'Coming! Coming!' she'd cry, gratefully, as quick on his words as their echo. Unlocking her door, she'd run down and throw open the hall door. No matter what the hour! No matter how black the night!

'Go back to your bed now, Ma'am,' he'd say from the darkness, where she could see the swinging yard lamp coming nearer and nearer like the light of a little boat drawing near to a jetty. 'I'll put out the lights and let myself out.' Relaxed by the thought that there was someone in the house, she would indeed scuttle back into bed, and, what was more, she'd be nearly asleep when she'd hear the door slam. It used to sound like the slam of a door a million miles away. There was no need to worry. He'd see that Crossen came early.

It was well before dark when Crossen did drive up to the door. The wife was with him, as usual, sitting up in the front seat the way people sat up in the well of little tub traps long ago, their knees pressed together, allowing no slump. Ned had come with them, but only he and Crossen got out.

'Won't your wife come inside and wait, Mr Crossen?' she asked.

'Oh, not at all, Ma'am. She likes sitting in the car. Now, where's the grass that's to be cut? Are there any stones lying about that would blunt the blade?' Going around the gable of the house, he looked out over the land.

'There's not a stone or a stump in it,' Ned said. 'You'd run your blade over the whole of it while you'd be whetting it twenty times in another place.'

'I can see that,' said Bartley Crossen, but absently, Vera thought. He had walked across the lawn to the rickety wooden gate that led into the pasture, and leaned on it. He didn't seem to be looking at the fields at all though, but at the small string of stunted thorns that grew along the riverbank, their branches leaning so heavily out over the water that their roots were almost dragged clear of the clay. When he turned around he gave a sigh. 'Ah, sure, I didn't need to look. I know it well,' he said. As she showed surprise, he gave a little laugh, like a young man. 'I courted a girl down there when I was a lad,' he said. 'That's a queer length of time ago now, I can tell you.' He turned to the old man. 'You might remember.' Then he looked back at her. 'I don't suppose you were born then Ma'am,' he said, and there was something kindly in his look and in his words. 'You'd like the mowing done soon, I suppose? How about first thing in the morning?'

Her face lit up. But there was the price to settle. 'It won't be as dear as cutting meadow, will it?'

'Ah, I won't be too hard on you, Ma'am,' he said. 'I can promise you that.'

'That's very kind of you,' she said, but a little doubtfully.

Behind Crossen's back, Ned nodded his head in approval. 'Let it go at that, Ma'am,' he whispered as they walked back towards the car. 'He's a man you can trust.'

When Crossen and the wife had driven away, Ned reassured her again. 'A decent man,' he said. Then he gave a laugh, and it was a young kind of laugh for a man of his age. 'Did you hear what he said about the girl he courted down there? Do you know who that was? It was his first wife. You know he was twice married? Ah, well, it's so long ago I wouldn't wonder if you never heard it. Look at the way he spoke about her himself, as if she was some girl he'd all but forgotten. The thorn trees brought her to his mind. That's where they used to meet, being only youngsters, when they first took up with each other.'

'Poor Bridie Logan! She was as wild as a hare. And she was mad with love, young as she was. They were company-keeping while they were still going to school. Only nobody took it seriously, him least of all, maybe, till the winter he went away to the agricultural college in Clonakilty. They started writing to each other then. I used to see her running up to the postbox at the crossroads every other evening, and sure, the whole village knew where the letter was going. His people were fit to be tied when he came home in the summer and said he wasn't going back, but was going to marry Bridie. All the same, his father set them up in a cottage on his own land. It's the cottage he uses now for stall-feds, it's back of his new house. Oh, but you can't judge it now for what it was then. Giddy and all as she was, as lightheaded as a thistle, you should have seen the way Bridie kept that cottage. She'd have had it scrubbed away if she didn't start having a baby. He wouldn't let her take the scrubbing brush into her hands after that.'

'But she wasn't delicate, was she?'

'Bridie? She was as strong as a kid goat, that one. But I told you she was mad about him, didn't I? Well, after she was married to him she was no better. Worse, I'd say: She couldn't do enough for him. It was like as if she was driven on by some kind of a fever. You'd only to look in her eyes to see it. Do you know! From that day to this, I don't believe I ever saw a woman so full of going as that one. Did you ever happen to see little birds flying about in the air like they were flying for the devilment of it and nothing else? And did you ever see the way they give a sort of a little leap in the air, like they were forcing themselves to go a bit higher still, higher than they ought? Well, it struck me that was the way Bridie was acting, as she rushed about that cottage doing this and doing that to make him prouder and prouder of her. As if he could be any prouder than he was already with her condition getting noticeable.'

'She didn't die in childbed?'

'No. Not in a manner of speaking, anyway. She had the child, nice and easy, and in their own cottage too, only costing him a few shillings for one of those women that went in for that kind of job long ago. And all went well. It was no time till she was let up on her feet again. I was there the first morning she had the place to herself. She was up and dressed when I got there, just as he was going out to milk.

'"Oh, it's great to be able to go out again," she said, taking a great breath of the morning air as she stood at the door looking after him. "Wait, why don't I come with you to milk?" She called after him. Then she threw a glance back at the baby to make sure it was asleep in its crib by the window.

'"It's too far for you, Bridie," he said. The cows were down in a little field alongside the road, at the foot of the hill below the village. And knowing she'd start coaxing him, Bartley made off as quick as he could out of the gate with the cans. "Good man!" I said to myself. But the next thing I knew, Bridie had darted across the yard.

'"I can go on the bike if it's too far to walk," she said. And up she got on her old bike, and out she pedalled through the gate.

'"Bridie, are you out of your mind?" Bartley shouted as she whizzed past him.

'"Arrah, what harm can it do me?" she shouted back.

'I went stiff with fright looking after her. And I thought it was the same with him, when he threw down the cans and started down the hill after her. But looking back on it, I think it was the same fever as always was raging in her that was raging in him, too. Mad with love, that's what they were, both of them, she only wanting to draw him on, and he only too willing.

'"Wait for me!" he shouted, but before she'd even got to the bottom she started to brake the bike, putting down her foot like you'd see a youngster do, and raising up such a cloud of dust we could hardly see her.'

'She braked too hard?'

'Not her! In the twinkle of an eye she'd stopped the bike, jumped off, turned it round, and was pedalling madly up the hill again to meet him, with her head down on the handlebars like a racing cyclist. But that was the finish of her.'

'Oh, no! What happened?'

'She stopped pedalling all of a sudden, and the bike half stopped, and then it started to slide back down the hill, as if it had skidded on the loose gravel at the side of the road. That's what we both thought happened, because we both began to run down the hill too. She didn't get time to fall before we got to her. But what use was that? It was some kind of internal bleeding that took her. We got her into the bed, and the neighbours came running, but she was gone before night.'

'Oh, what a dreadful thing to happen! And the baby?'

'Well, it was a strong child. And it grew into a fine lad. That's the fellow that drives the tractor for him now, the oldest son, Barty they called him not to confuse him with Bartley.'

'Well, I suppose his second marriage had more to it, when all was said and done.'

'That's it. And she's a good woman, the second one. Look at the way she brought up that child of Bridie's, and filled the cradle, year after year, with sons of her own. Ah sure, things always work out for the best in the end, no matter what!' the old man said, and he started to walk away.

'Wait a minute, Ned,' Vera called after him urgently. 'Do you really think he forgot about her, until today?'

'I'd swear it,' said the old man. Then he looked hard at her. 'It will be the same with you, too,' he added kindly. 'Take my word for it. Everything passes in time and is forgotten.'

As she shook her head doubtfully, he shook his emphatically. 'When the tree falls, how can the shadow stand?' he said. And he walked away.

I wonder! She thought as she walked back to the house, and she envied the practical country people who made good

the defaults of nature as readily as the broken sod knits back
into the sward.

Again that night, when she went up to her room, Vera
looked down towards the river and she thought of
Crossen. Had he really forgotten? It was hard for her to
believe, and with a sigh she picked up her hairbrush and
pulled it through her hair. Like everything else about
her lately, her hair was sluggish and hung heavily down,
but after a few minutes under the quickening strokes
of the brush, it lightened and lifted, and soon it flew
about her face like the spray over a weir. It had always
been the same, even when she was a child. She had only
to suffer the first painful drag of the bristles when her
mother would cry out, 'Look! Look! That's electricity!'
And a blue spark would shine for an instant like a star in
the grey depth of the mirror. That was all they knew of
electricity in those dim-lit days when valleys of shadow
lay deep between one piece of furniture and another. Was
it because rooms were so badly lit then that they saw it so
often, that little blue star? Suddenly she was overcome by
longing to see it again, and, standing up impetuously, she
switched off the light. It was just then that, down below,
the iron fist of the knocker was lifted and, with a strong,
confident hand, brought down to the door. It was not a
furtive knock. She recognised that even as she sat stark
with fright in the darkness. And then a voice that was
vaguely familiar called out from below.

'It's me, Ma'am. I hope I'm not disturbing you?'

'Oh, Mr Crossen!' she cried out with relief, and
unlocking her door, she ran across the landing and threw
up a window on that side of the house. 'I'll be right down!'
she called.

'There's no need to come down, Ma'am,' he shouted. 'I only want one word with you.'

'Of course I'll come down.' She went back and got her dressing-gown and was about to pin up her hair, but as she did she heard him stomping his feet on the gravel. It had been a mild day, but with night a chill had come in the air, and for all that it was late spring, there was a cutting east wind coming across the river. 'I'll run down and let you in from the cold,' she called, and, twisting up her hair, she held it against her head with her hand without waiting to pin it, and she ran down the stairs in her bare feet and opened the hall door.

'Oh? You were going to bed, Ma'am?' he said apologetically when she opened the door. And where he had been so impatient a minute beforehand, he stood stock-still in the open doorway. 'I saw the lights were out downstairs when I was coming up the drive,' he said contritely. 'But I didn't think you'd gone up for the night.'

'Not at all,' she lied, to put him at his ease. 'I was just upstairs brushing my hair. You must excuse me,' she added, because a breeze from the door was blowing her dressing-gown from her knees, and to pull it across she had to take her hand from her hair, so the hair fell down about her shoulders. 'Would you mind closing the door for me?' she said, with some embarrassment, and she began to back up the stairs. 'Please go inside to the sitting-room off the hall. Put on the light. I'll be down in a minute.'

Although he had obediently stepped inside the door, and closed it, he stood stoutly in the middle of the hall. 'I shouldn't have come in,' he said. 'You were going to bed,' he cried, this time in an accusing voice as if he dared her to deny it. He was looking at her hair. 'Excuse my saying so, Ma'am, but I never saw such a fine head of hair. God bless it!' he added quickly, as if afraid he had been too familiar. 'Doesn't a small thing make a big differ,' he said impulsively. 'You look like a young girl.'

In spite of herself, she smiled with pleasure. She wanted no more of this kind of talk, all the same. 'Well, I don't feel like one,' she said sharply.

What was meant for a quite opposite effect however, seemed to delight him and put him wonderfully at ease. 'Ah sure, you're a sensible woman, I can see that,' he said, and, coming to the foot of the stairs, he leaned comfortably across the newel post. 'Let you stay the way you are, Ma'am,' he said. 'I've only one word to say to you. Let me say here and now and be off about my business. The wife will be waiting up for me, and I don't want that.'

She hesitated. Was the reference to his wife meant to put *her* at ease? 'I think I ought to get my slippers,' she said cautiously. Her feet were cold.

'Oh, yes, you should put on your slippers,' he said, only then seeing that she was in her bare feet. 'But as to the rest, I'm long gone beyond taking any account of what a woman has on her. I'm gone beyond taking notice of women at all.'

But she had seen something to put on her feet. Under the table in the hall there was a pair of old boots belonging to Richard, with fleece lining in them. She hadn't been able to make up her mind to give them away with the rest of his clothes, and although they were big and clumsy on her, she often stuck her feet into them when she came in from the fields with mud on her shoes. 'Well, come in where it's warm, so,' she said. She came back down the few steps and stuck her feet into the boots, and then she opened the door of the sittingroom. She was glad she'd come down. He'd never have been able to put on the light. 'There's something wrong with the centre light,' she said as she groped along the skirting board to find the plug of the reading lamp. It was in an awkward place, behind the desk. She had to go down on her knees.

'What's wrong with it?' he asked, as, with a countryman's interest in practicalities, he clicked the switch up and down to no effect.

'Oh, nothing much, I'm sure,' she said absently. 'There!' She had found the plug, and the room was lit up with a bright white glow.

'Why don't you leave the plug in the socket?' he asked critically.

'I don't know,' she said. 'I think someone told me it's safer, with reading lamps, to pull the plugs out at night. There might be a short circuit, or mice might nibble at the cord, or something. I forget what I was told. I got into the habit of doing it, and now I keep on.' She felt a bit silly.

But he was concerned about it. 'I don't think any harm could be done,' he said gravely. Then he turned away from the problem. 'About tomorrow, Ma'am,' he said, somewhat offhandedly, she thought. 'I was determined I'd see you tonight, because I'm not a man to break my word, above all, to a woman.'

What was he getting at?

'Let me put it this way,' he said quickly. 'You'll understand, Ma'am, that as far as I am concerned, topping land is the same as cutting hay. The same time. The same labour. The same cost. And the same wear and tear on the blade. You understand that?'

On her guard, she nodded.

'Well now, Ma'am, I'd be the first to admit that it's not quite the same for you. For you, topping doesn't give the immediate return you'd get from hay.'

'There's no return from topping,' she exclaimed crossly.

'Oh, come now, Ma'am! Good grassland pays as well as anything. You know you won't get nice sweet pickings for your beasts from neglected land, but only dirty old tow grass knotting under their feet. It's just that it's not a quick return, and so, as you know, I told you I'd be making a special price for you.'

'I do know,' she said impatiently. 'But I thought that part of it was settled and done.'

'Oh, I'm not going back on it, if that's what you think,' he said affably. 'I'm glad to do what I can for you, Ma'am, the more so seeing you have no man to attend to these things for you, but only yourself alone.'

'Oh, I'm well able to look after myself,' she said, raising her voice.

Once again her words had an opposite effect to what she intended. He laughed good-humouredly. 'That's what all women like to think,' he said. 'Well, now,' he went on in a different tone of voice, and it annoyed her to see he seemed to think something had been settled between them, 'it would suit me, and I'm sure it's all the same to you, if we could leave your little job till later in the week, say till nearer to the time of the haymaking generally. Because by then I'd have the cutting bar in good order, sharpened and ready for use. Whereas now, while there's still a bit of ploughing to be done here and there, I'll have to be chopping and changing, between the plough and the mower, putting one on one minute and the other the next.'

'As if anyone is still ploughing this time of the year! Who are you putting before me?' she demanded.

'Now, take it easy, Ma'am. I'm not putting anyone before you, leastways, not without getting leave first from you.'

'Without telling me you're not coming, you mean.'

'Oh, now, Ma'am, don't get cross. I'm only trying to make matters easy for everyone.'

She was very angry now. 'It's always the same story. I thought you'd treat me differently. I'm to wait till after this one, and after that one, and in the end my fields will go wild.'

He looked a bit shamefaced. 'Ah now, Ma'am, that's not going to be the case at all. Although, mind you, some people don't hold with topping, you know.'

'I hold with it.'

'Oh, I suppose there's something in it,' he said reluctantly. 'But the way I look at it, cutting the weeds in July is a kind of a topping.'

'Grass cut before it goes to seed gets so thick at the roots no weeds can come up,' she cried, so angry she didn't realise how authoritative she sounded.

'Faith, I never knew you were so well up, Ma'am,' he said, looking at her admiringly, but she saw he wasn't going to be put down by her. 'All the same now, Ma'am, you can't say a few days here or there could make any difference?'

'A few days could make all the difference. This farm has a gravelly bottom to it, for all it's to lush. A few days of drought could burn it to the butt. And how could I mow it then? And what cover would there be for the 'nice sweet pickings' you were talking about a minute ago?' Angrily, she mimicked his own accent without thinking.

He threw up his hands. 'Ah well, I suppose a man may as well admit when he's bested,' he said. 'Even by a woman. And you can't say I broke my promise.'

'I can't say but you tried hard enough,' she said grudgingly, although she was mollified that she was getting her way. 'Can I offer you anything?' she said then, anxious to convey an air of finality to their discussion.

'Not at all, Ma'am. Nothing, thank you. I'll have to be getting home.'

'I hope you won't think I was trying to take advantage of you,' he said as they went towards the door. 'It's just that we must all make out as best we can for ourselves, isn't that so? Not but you are well able to look after yourself, I must say. No one ever thought you'd stay on here after your husband died. I suppose it's for the children you did it?' He looked up the well of the stairs. 'Are they asleep?'

'Oh, long ago,' she said indifferently. She opened the hall door.

The night air swept it. But this time, from far away, it brought with it the fragrance of new-mown hay. 'There's hay cut somewhere already,' she exclaimed in surprise. And she lifted her face to the sweetness of it.

For a minute, Crossen looked past her out into the darkness, then he looked back at her. 'Aren't you never lonely here at night?' he asked suddenly.

'You mean frightened?' she corrected quickly and coldly.

'Yes! Yes, that's what I meant,' he said, taken aback. 'Ah, but why would you be frightened? What safer place could you be under the sky than right here with your own fields all about you.'

What he said was so true, and he himself as he stood there, with his hat in his hand, so normal and natural it was indeed absurd to think that he would no sooner have gone out the door than she would be scurrying up the stairs like a child. 'You may not believe it,' she said, 'but I am scared to death sometimes. I nearly died when I heard your knock on the door tonight. It's because I was scared that I was upstairs,' she said, in a further burst of confidence. 'I always go up the minute it gets dark. I don't feel so frightened upstairs.

'Isn't that strange now?' he said, and she could see he found it an incomprehensibly womanly thing to do. He was sympathetic all the same. 'You shouldn't be alone. That's the truth of the matter,' he said, 'It's a shame.'

'Oh, it can't be helped,' she said. There was something she wanted to shrug off in his sympathy, while at the same time she appreciated the kindliness. 'Would you like to do something for me?' she asked impulsively. 'Would you wait and put out the lights down here and let me get back upstairs before you go? Ned often does that for me if he's working here late'. After she had spoken she felt foolish, but she saw at once that, if anything, he thought it only too little to do for her. He was genuinely troubled about her. And it wasn't only the present moment that concerned him; he seemed to be considering the whole problem of her isolation and loneliness.

'Is there nobody could stay here with you, at night even? It would have to be another woman, of course,' he added quickly, and her heart was warmed by the way, without a word from her, he rejected that solution out of hand. 'You don't want another woman about the place,' he said flatly.

'Oh, I'm all right, really. I'll get used to it,' she said.

'It's a shame, all the same,' he said. He said it helplessly, though, and he motioned her towards the stairs. 'You'll be all right for tonight, anyway. Go on up the stairs now, and I'll put out the lights.' He had already turned around to go back into the sitting-room.

Yet it wasn't quite as she intended for some reason, and it was somewhat reluctantly that she started up the stairs.

'Wait a minute! How do I put out this one?' he called out from the room before she was halfway up.

'Oh, I'd better put out that one myself,' she said, thinking of the awkward position of the plug. She ran down again, and, going past him into the little room, she knelt and pulled at the cord. Instantly the room was deluged in darkness. And instantly she felt that she had done something stupid. It was not like turning out a light by a switch at the door and being able to step back into the lighted hall. She got to her feet as quickly as she could, but as she did, she saw that Crossen was standing in the doorway. His bulk was blocked out against the hall light behind him. 'I'll leave the rest to you,' she said to break the peculiar silence that had come down on the house. But he didn't move. He stood there, the full of the doorway, and she was reluctant to brush past him.

Why didn't he move? Instead he caught her by the arm, and, putting out his other hand, he pressed his palm against the door-jamb, barring her way.

'Tell me,' he whispered, his words falling over each other, 'are you never lonely at all?'

'What did you say?' she said in a clear voice, because the thickness of his voice sickened her. She had barely heard what he said. Her one thought was to get past him.

He leaned forward. 'What about a little kiss?' he whispered, and to get a better hold on her he let go the hand he had pressed against the wall, but before he caught at her with both hands she had wrenched her all free of him, and, ignominiously ducking under his armpit, she was out next minute in the lighted hall.

Out there, because light was all the protection she needed from him, the old fool, she began to laugh. She had only to wait for him to come sheepishly out. But there was something she hadn't counted on; she hadn't counted on there being anything pathetic in his sheepishness, something really pitiful in the way he shambled into the light, not raising his eyes. And she was so surprisingly touched that before he had time to utter a word she put out her hand. 'Don't feel too bad,' she said. 'I didn't take offence.'

Still he didn't look at her. He just took her hand and pressed it gratefully, his face turned away. And to her dismay she saw that his nose was running water. Like a small boy, he wiped it with the back of his fist, streaking his face. 'I don't know what came over me,' he said slowly. 'I'm getting on to be an old man. I thought I was beyond all that.' He wiped his face again. 'Beyond letting myself go, anyway,' he amended miserably.

'Oh, it was nothing,' she said.

He shook his head. 'It wasn't as if I had cause for what I did.'

'But you did nothing,' she protested.

'It wasn't nothing to me,' he said dejectedly.

For a minute, they stood there silent. The hall door was still ajar, but she didn't dare to close it. What am I going to do with him now, she thought, I'll have him here all night if I'm not careful. What time was it, anyway? All scale and proportion seemed to have gone from the night. 'Well, I'll see you in the morning, Mr Crossen,' she said, as matter-of-factly as possible.

He nodded, but made no move to go. 'You know I meant no disrespect to you, Ma'am, don't you?' he said, looking imploringly at her. 'I always had a great regard for you. And for your husband, too. I was thinking of him this very night when I was coming up to the house. And I thought of him again when you came to the door looking like a young girl. I thought what a pity it was him to be taken from you, and you both so young. Oh, what came over me at all? And what would Mona say if she knew?'

'But surely you wouldn't tell her? I should certainly hope not,' Vera cried, appalled. What sort of a figure would she cut if he told the wife about her coming down in her bare feet with her hair down her back. 'Take care would you tell her!' she warned.

'I don't suppose I ought,' he said, but he said it uncertainly and morosely, and he leaned back against the wall. 'She's been a good woman, Mona. I wouldn't want anyone to think different. My sons could tell you. She's been a good mother to them all these years. She never made a bit of difference between them. Some say she was better to Barty than to any of them. She reared him from a week old. She was living next door to us, you see, at the time I was left with him,' he said. 'She came in that first night and took him home to her own bed, and, mind you, that wasn't a small thing for a woman who knew nothing about children, not being what you'd call a young girl, in spite of the big family she gave me afterwards. She took him home and looked after him, although it isn't every woman would care to be responsible for a newborn baby. That's a thing a man doesn't forget easy. That's many I know would say that if she hadn't taken him someone else would, but no one only her would have done it the way she did. She used to keep him all day in her own cottage, feeding him and the rest of it. But at night, when I'd be back from the fields, she'd bring him home and leave him down in his little crib by the fire alongside of me. She used to let on she had things to do in her own place, and she'd slip away and leave us alone, but that wasn't her real reason for leaving him. She knew the way I'd be sitting looking into the fire, wondering how I'd face the long years ahead, and she left the child there with me to distract me from my sorrow. And she was right. I never got long to brood. The child would give a cry, or a whinge, and I'd have to run out and fetch her to him. Or else she'd hear him herself maybe, and run in without me having to call her at all. I used often think she must have kept every window and door in her place open, for fear she'd lose a sound from either of us. And so, bit by bit, I was knit back into a living man. I often wondered what would have become of me if it wasn't for her. There are men and when the bright way closes to them there's no knowing but they'll take a dark way. And I was that class of man. I told you she used to take the little fellow away in the day and bring him back at night? Well, of course, she used to take him away again coming on to the real dark of night. She used to keep him in her own bed. But as the months went on and he got bigger, I could see she hated taking him away from me at all. He was beginning to smile and play with his fists and be real company. 'I wonder ought I leave him with you tonight,' she'd say then, night after night. And sometimes she'd run in and dump him down in the middle of the big double bed in the room off the kitchen, but the next minute she'd snatch him up again. 'I'd be afraid you'd overlie him. You might only smother him, God between us and all harm!'

'You'd better take him,' I'd say. I used to hate to see him go myself by this time. All the same, I was afraid he'd start crying in the night, and what would I do then? If I had to go out for her in the middle of the night, it could cause a lot of talk. There was talk enough as things were, I can tell you, although there was no grounds for it. I had no more notion of her than if she wasn't a woman at all. Would you believe that? But one night when she took him up and put him down, and put him down and took him up, and went on and went on about leaving him or taking him, I had to laugh. 'It's a pity you can't stay along with him, and that would settle all,' I said. I was only joking her, but she got as red as fire, and next thing she burst out crying. But not before she'd caught up the child and wrapped her coat around him. Then, after giving me a terrible look, she ran out the door with him. Well, that was the beginning of it. I'd no idea she had any feelings for me. I thought it was only for the child. But men are fools, as women well know, and she knew before me what was right and proper for us both. And for the child too. Some women have great insight into these things. That night God opened my own eyes to the woman I had in her, and I saw it was better I took her than wasted away after the one that was gone. And wasn't I right?'

'Of course you were right,' she said quickly.

But he had slumped back against the wall, and the abject look came back into his eyes. 'And to think I shamed her as well as myself.'

I'll never get rid of him, Vera thought desperately. 'Ah, what ails you?' she cried impatiently. 'Forget it, can't you?'

'I can't,' he said simply.

'Ah, for heaven's sake. It's got nothing to do with her at all.'

Surprised, he looked up at her. 'You're not blaming yourself, surely?' he asked.

She'd have laughed at that if she hadn't seen she was making headway. Another stroke and she'd be rid of him. 'Why are you blaming any of us?' she cried. 'It's got nothing to do with any of us, with you, or me, or the woman at home waiting for you. It was the other one you should blame, that girl, your first wife, Bridie! Blame her!' The words had broken uncontrollably from her. For a moment, she thought she was hysterical and that she could not stop. 'You thought you could forget her,' she cried, 'but see what she did to you when she got the chance.'

He stood for a moment at the open door. 'God rest her soul,' he said, without looking back, and he stepped into the night.

Maeve Brennan

Born in January 1917, Maeve Brennan moved to the US with her family when she was seventeen. She began working as a copyeditor for *Harper's Bazaar* magazine, but was later offered a staff job at *The New Yorker*. There, she wrote an observational society column, *The Talk of the Town*, under the pseudonym 'The Long-Winded Lady', which was later published in book form. Brennan contributed many short stories to *The New Yorker*, many of which were collated in two short story collections, *In and Out of Never-Never Land* (1969) and *Christmas Eve* (1974). Both collections were republished as *The Springs of Affection: Stories of Dublin* and *The Rose Garden* after her death in 1993. Her only novella, *The Visitor*, was published posthumously in 2000.

The Eldest Child

Mrs Bagot had lived in the house for fifteen years, ever since her marriage. Her three children had been born there, in the upstairs front bedroom, and she was glad of that, because her first child, her son, was dead, and it comforted her to think that she was still familiar with what had been his one glimpse of earth – he had died at three days. At the time he died she said to herself that she would never get used to it, and what she meant by that was that as long as she lived she would never accept what had happened in the mechanical subdued way that the rest of them accepted it. They carried on, they talked and moved about her room as though when they tidied the baby away they had really tidied him away, and it seemed to her that more than anything else they expressed the hope that nothing more would be said about him. They behaved as though what had happened was finished, as though some ordinary event had taken place and come to an end in a natural way. There had not been an ordinary event, and it had not come to an end.

Lying in her bed, Mrs Bagot thought her husband and the rest of them seemed very strange, or else, she thought fearfully, perhaps it was she herself who was strange, delirious,

or even a bit unbalanced. If she was unbalanced she wasn't
going to let them know about it – not even Martin, who kept
looking at her with frightened eyes and telling her she must
try to rest. It might be better not to talk, yet she was very
anxious to explain how she felt. Words did no good. Either
they did not want to hear her, or they were not able to hear
her. What she was trying to tell them seemed very simple
to her. What had happened could not come to an end, that
was all. It could not come to an end. Without a memory,
how was the baby going to find his way? Mrs Bagot would
have liked to ask that question, but she wanted to express it
properly, and she thought if she could just be left alone for a
while she would be able to find the right words, so that she
could make herself clearly understood – but they wouldn't
leave her alone. They kept trying to rouse her, and yet when
she spoke for any length of time they always silenced her by
telling her it was God's will. She had accepted God's will all
her life without argument, and she was not arguing now,
but she knew that what had happened was not finished, and
she was sure it was not God's will that she be left in this
bewilderment. All she wanted was to say how she felt, but
they mentioned God's will as though they were slamming
a door between her and some territory that was forbidden
to her. But only to her; everybody else knew all about it.
She alone must lie quiet and silent under this semblance of
ignorance that they wrapped about her like a shroud. They
wanted her to be silent and not speak of this knowledge she
had now, the knowledge that made her afraid. It was the
same knowledge they all had, of course, but they did not
want it spoken of. Everything about her seemed false, and
Mrs Bagot was tired of everything. She was tired of being
told that she must do this for her own good and that she
must do that for her own good, and it annoyed her when

they said she was being brave – she was being what she had to be, she had no alternative. She felt very uncomfortable and out of place, and as though she had failed, but she did not know whether to push her failure away or comfort it, and in any case it seemed to have drifted out of reach.

She was not making sense. She could not get her thoughts sorted out. Something was drifting away – that was as far as she could go in her mind. No wonder she couldn't talk properly. What she wanted to say was really quite simple. Two things. First, there was the failure that had emptied and darkened her mind until nothing remained now but a black wash. Second, there was something that drifted and dwindled, always dwindling, until it was now no more than a small shape, very small, not to be identified except as something lost. Mrs Bagot thought she was the only one who could still identify that shape, and she was afraid to take her eyes off it, because it became constantly smaller, showing as it diminished the new horizons it was reaching, although it drifted so gently it seemed not to move at all. Mrs Bagot would never have dreamed her mind could stretch so far, or that her thoughts could follow so faithfully, or that she could watch so steadily, without tears or sleep.

The fierce demands that had been made on her body and on her attention were finished. She could have met all those demands, and more. She could have moved mountains. She had found that the more the child demanded of her, the more she had to give. Her strength came up in waves that had their source in a sea of calm and unconquerable devotion. The child's holy trust made her open her eyes, and she took stock of herself and found that everything was all right, and that she could meet what challenges arose and meet them well, and that she had nothing to apologize for

– on the contrary, she had every reason to rejoice. Her days took on an orderliness that introduced her to a sense of ease and confidence she had never been told about. The house became a kingdom, significant, private, and safe. She smiled often, a smile of innocent importance.

Perhaps she had let herself get too proud. She had seen at once that the child was unique. She had been thankful, but perhaps not thankful enough. The first minute she had held him in her arms, immediately after he was born, she had seen his friendliness. He was fine. There was nothing in the world the matter with him. She had remarked to herself that his tiny face had a very humorous expression, as though he already knew exactly what was going on. And he was determined to live. He was full of fight. She had felt him fight toward life with all her strength, and then again, with all his strength. In a little while, he would have recognized her.

What she watched now made no demands on anyone. There was no impatience there, and no impatience in her, either. She lay on her side, and her hand beat gently on the pillow in obedience to words, an old tune, that had been sounding in her head for some time, and that she now began to listen to. It was an old song, very slow, a tenor voice from long ago and far away. She listened idly.

> *Oft in the stilly night,*
> *Ere slumber's chain hath bound me,*
> *Fond memory brings the light*
> *Of other days around me.*

Over and over and over again, the same words, the same kind, simple words. Mrs Bagot thought she must have heard that song a hundred times or more.

Oft in the stilly night,
  Ere slumber's chain hath bound me,
Fond memory brings the light
  Of other days around me.
    The smiles, the tears,
    Of boyhood's years,
The words of love then spoken,
    The eyes that shone
    Now dimmed and gone,
The cheerful hearts now broken.

It was a very kind song. She had never noticed the words before, even though she knew them well. Loving words, loving eyes, loving hearts. The faraway voice she listened to was joined by others, as the first bird of dawn is joined by other birds, all telling the same story, telling it over and over again, because it is the only story they know.

There was the song, and then there was the small shape that drifted uncomplainingly from distant horizon to still more distant horizon. Mrs Bagot closed her eyes. She felt herself being beckoned to a place where she could hide, for the time being.

For the past day or so, she had turned from everyone, even from Martin. He no longer attempted to touch her. He had not even touched her hand since the evening he knelt down beside the bed and tried to put his arms around her. She struggled so fiercely against him that he had to let her go, and he stood up and stepped away from her. It really seemed she might injure herself, fighting against him, and that she would rather injure herself than lie quietly against him, even for a minute. He could not understand her. It was his loss as much as hers, but she behaved as though it had to do only with her. She pushed him away, and then when she was free of him she turned her face away from him and began crying in a way that pleaded for attention and consolation from someone, but not from him – that was plain. But before that, when she was pushing him away, he had seen her face, and the expression on it was of hatred. She might have been a wild animal, for all the control he had over her then, but if so she was a wild animal in a trap, because she was too weak to go very far. He pitied her, and the thought sped through his mind that if she could get up and run, or fly, he would let her go as far as she wished, and hope she would come back to him in her own time, when her anger and grief were spent. But he forgot that thought immediately in his panic at her distress, and he called down to the woman who had come in to help around the house, and asked her to come up at once. She had heard the noise and was on her way up anyway, and she was in the room almost as soon as he called – Mrs Knox, a small, red-faced, gray-haired woman who enjoyed the illusion that life had nothing to teach her.

'Oh, I've been afraid of this all day,' she said confidently, and she began to lift Mrs Bagot up so that she could straighten the pillows and prop her up for her tea. But Mrs Bagot struck out at the woman and began crying, 'Oh, leave me alone, leave me alone. Why can't the two of you leave me alone.' Then she wailed, 'Oh, leave me alone,' in a high strange voice, an artificial voice, and at that moment Mr Bagot became convinced that she was acting, and that the best thing to do was walk off and leave her there, whether that was what she really wanted or not. Oh, but he loved her. He stared at her, and said to himself that it would have given him the greatest joy to see her lying there with the baby in her arms, but although that was true, the reverse was not true – to see her lying there as she was did not cause him terrible grief or anything like it. He felt ashamed and lonely and impatient, and he longed to say to her, 'Delia, stop all this nonsense and let me talk to you.' He wanted to appear masterful and kind and understanding, but she drowned him out with her wails, and he made up his mind she was acting, because if she was not acting, and if the grief she felt was real, then it was excessive grief, and perhaps incurable. She was getting stronger every day, the doctor had said so, and she had better learn to control herself or she would be a nervous wreck. And it wasn't a bit like her, to have no thought for him, or for what he might be suffering. It wasn't like her at all. She was always kind. He began to fear she would never be the same. He would have liked to kneel down beside the bed and talk to her in a very quiet voice, and make her understand that he knew what she was going through, and that he was going through much the same thing himself, and to ask her not to shut him away from her. But he felt afraid of her, and in any case Mrs Knox was in the room. He was helpless. He was trying to think of something to say, not to walk out in silence, when Mrs Knox came around the end of the bed and touched his arm familiarly, as though they were conspirators.

'The poor child is upset,' she said. 'We'll leave her by herself awhile, and then I'll bring her up something to eat. Now, you go along down. I have your own tea all ready.'

Delia turned her head on the pillow and looked at him. 'Martin,' she said, 'I am not angry with you.'

He would have gone to her then, but Mrs Knox spoke at once. 'We know you're not angry, Mrs Bagot,' she said. 'Now, you rest yourself, and I'll be back in a minute with your tray.' She gave Martin a little push to start him out of the room, and since Delia was already turning her face away, he walked out and down the stairs.

There seemed to be no end to the damage – even the house looked bleak and the furniture looked poor and cheap. It was only a year since they had moved into the house, and it had all seemed lovely then. Only a year. He was beginning to fear that Delia had turned against him. He had visions of awful scenes and strains in the future, a miserable life. He wished they could go back to the beginning and start all over again, but the place where they had stood together, where they had been happy, was all trampled over and so spoiled that it seemed impossible ever to make it smooth again. And how could they even begin to make it smooth with this one memory, which they should have shared, standing like an enemy between them and making enemies out of them. He would not let himself think of the baby. He might never be able to forget the shape of the poor little defeated bundle he had carried out of the bedroom in his arms, and that he had cried over down here in the hall, but he was not going to let his mind dwell on it, not for one minute. He wanted Delia as she used to be. He wanted the girl who would never have struck out at him or spoken roughly to him. He was beginning to see there were things about her that he had never guessed at and that he did not want to know about. He thought, better let her rest, and let this fit work itself out. Maybe tomorrow she'll be herself again. He had a fancy that when he next approached Delia it would be on tiptoe, going very quietly, hardly breathing, moving into her presence without a sound that might startle her, or surprise her, or even wake her up, so that he might find her again as she had been the first time he saw her, quiet, untroubled, hardly speaking, alone, altogether alone and all his.

Mrs Bagot was telling the truth when she told Martin she was not angry with him. It irritated her that he thought all he had to do was put his arms around her and all her sorrow would go away, but she wasn't really angry with him. What it was – he held her so tightly that she was afraid she might lose sight of the baby, and the fear made her frantic. The baby must not drift out of sight, that was her only thought, and that is why she struck out at Martin and begged to be left alone. As he walked out of the room, she turned her face away so that he would not see the tears beginning to pour down her face again. Then she slept. When Martin came up to the room next time, she was asleep, and not, as he suspected, pretending to be asleep, but he was grateful for the pretence, if that is what it was, and he crept away, back downstairs to his book.

Mrs Bagot slept for a long time. When she woke up, the room was dark and the house was silent. Outside was silent too; she could hear nothing. This was the front bedroom, where she and Martin slept together, and she lay in their big bed. The room was made irregular by its windows – a bow window, and then, in the flat section of wall that faced the door, French windows. The French windows were partly open, and the long white net curtains that covered them moved gently in a breeze Mrs Bagot could not feel. She had washed all the curtains last week, and starched them, getting the room ready for the baby. In the dim light of the street lamp, she could see the dark roof line of the row of houses across the street, and beyond the houses a very soft blackness, the sky. She was much calmer than she had been, and she no longer feared that she would lose sight of the small shape that had drifted, she noticed, much farther away while she slept. He was traveling a long way, but she would watch him. She was his mother, and it was all she could do for him now. She could do it. She was weak, and the world was very shaky, but the light of other days shone steadily and showed the truth. She was no longer bewildered, and the next time Martin came to stand hopefully beside her bed she smiled at him and spoke to him in her ordinary voice.

Anne Devlin

Anne Devlin was born in Belfast. She taught English and Drama in North Antrim until she moved to Germany in 1976 and later in the same year to England. David Marcus first published her stories in the *Irish Press* in the 1980s. Her collection *The Waypaver* was published by Faber in 1986. She is best known as a dramatist, both for *Ourselves Alone* (Royal Court, 1985) and *After Easter* (Royal Shakespeare Company, 1993). She has worked extensively in TV and film. Her most recent work was the radio play *The Forgotten (2009)*. She returned to Belfast in 2007.

Winter Journey
(The Apparitions)

One afternoon in the autumn of 2003 she would walk into
a cavernous public house and sit down.

I worked here one summer in '69.

A regular was waiting, he said he remembered her.

He remembered both of them. The young Irish girls
behind the bar.

She is disbelieving of him: a regular for thirty-four years?

You were stout, he said. The other one was thin and
nervy. Read all the time.

He could hardly know what grief drove her to that place.

You went home to go to college.

I did. Would you not want to go back?

My sister in law wouldn't let me. He says.

What's it got to do with your sister in law?

She says I've no claim on the house.

Where is back?

Galway.

He asks her what she's done since that time.

I went to college, got married. Then I went to Europe.
I've been travelling.

Any children?

One. Away to university.

Empty nest.

I hadn't thought of it. Yourself?

Two, and grandchildren now.

Have you always lived here?

I have. What brings you here?

She doesn't say economic eviction because by his lights she's lived the high life:

I've just moved into a flat down the road.

They talk about many things, books mostly. He's a great reader. He mentions one particular story about an alcoholic marriage. Now why did he pick that she thinks? She gets up to go when he says: I'll walk out with you to the bus stop. They part by the red brick wall of a retirement home, one of many in the neighbourhood. He says: Call in again to the pub. I go on pension day. She says of course she will.

Strange to come back to a suburb of the Great West Road to the exact spot where she changed a tyre on the way to Germany in the winter of '76. She knows what she is doing, is rewinding the days; growing back to catch herself on. She knows that love was lost because the person who made the journey was the other one; a part of herself and she didn't wholly exist then. If she could just gather up the traces of the old route she might gather in the feelings that existed then, because she knows that she cannot go on feeling nothing at all for the person she lives with.

When Beatrice comes back from the pub she sits down in the dark flat and waits for him. He comes in expecting her to have left.

She was running and running and couldn't find the door, until she ran right into the room with him.

I've never been to Basel, Dag says, when she starts to talk about that winter in 1976.

I walked out on a relationship. I walked across the room to a table with two German women and asked them if they'd help me leave the man I was with. He followed me over and said I was having a breakdown.

One of them was called Renate; I can still see her face: Perhaps it is your breakdown she is having. Turned out they were lesbians. They lent me the money to get home.

Dag says nothing so she prompts him.

What about you? You promised to tell me about Klaus.

Suicide. We met at university. He was studying Law, but he wanted to be an actor. He turned out to be very good. He was the son of a Protestant priest.

We would say Clergyman, she corrects.

He came to Strasbourg. We shared a flat together until we were kicked out.

Why were you kicked out?

It was meant to be a temporary arrangement. Then we went to Ireland. In Dublin we did Pinter. And one night at the interval I tore into him about his performance. And he walked out; he walked right out of the theatre and disappeared. It was *The Caretaker*. I went back to Germany to run a theatre.

What happened to Dublin?

I just told you. He disappeared. And five years passed.

You went to Westphalia, was it?

Then I heard he'd moved to the area and I came under great pressure to contact him. But I never did. He wasn't reliable.

Why did you tear into him at the interval?

Because he got into bed ten pages before he should have and he had to get out again. He must have stayed in the region for as long as I was there. When I moved to Hamburg, the next thing I knew he was dead. He killed himself. Perhaps I should have called him. Didn't that happen to you?

My cousin. Jesus ... Vera. I was irritated by her. I was twenty-four and very hardnosed. A Marxist. And she was this floaty woman of twenty-nine coming late to university and then she falls in love or gets involved with the most aggressive man in the university.

She had a wedding that nobody wanted to go to. But I go. In fact I give her lunch. My partner takes to his bed with a bad back. There were about six of us. The tension was ... well you could have cut it with a knife. Three months after the wedding she turns up at my door. We lived five miles from the nearest town. And no public transport on Sunday. There had been no traffic past the house. How did you get here? I walked, she says and her face ... There she was and no one had told her.

Told her what?

That his previous girlfriend had walked around with a black eye, saying he'd hit her. She got a first and moved away. Ken went after every single female in my year without success; we laughed at him, behind his back.

He said Vera was boring. And she came to me because she said he admired me. The very same day we found her a room with the Professor of Old English, whose family were very kind. My cousin was from Ardoyne but she thought she was Anna Karenina. That's Literature for you. Later she got a job teaching in west London. About eighteen months after she moved, she rang me. She said she still loved him and wanted to go back. She found

London very fast and it frightened her. She wanted to come home. She'd spoken to him and he said he hadn't found anyone else.

That was when I told her: Oh grow up. Of course he has someone else. He's always had someone else. There's this lynx-eyed woman on the go since the day you married.

There was a strange dry squeaking on the phone, as if a door needed lubrication. Then the line went dead. And I realised I was listening to a heart breaking.

Two years later we were packing up to go to Germany: university communities are the same the world over from Japan to Sweden you find the same people. We gave a farewell party, the chaplain turned up, he'd had a phone call, Vera had killed herself.

Did your partner approve of you moving her away from her husband?

Yes. But it was the phone call I regret. I actually crushed her hope.

I've never spoken about Klaus before, Dag says.

And I told no one about the phone call from Vera. The flat Vera lived in was around here, in one of those streets near the Abbey. She's led me a long way.

Don't tell me you believe in ghosts?

She wants to tell him about the apparitions: on the road to the ferry when she first left. Vera was there like softly falling snow adding up to something and then dissolving; a snow woman.

She believed she had seen her at the far end of a hotel reception in Venice, answering to her name, picking up the key to a man's room.

It's the first real conversation they've had. Dag had loved Klaus; she had let her cousin die feeling unloved. She had to live with that. They were beginning to talk to each other.

Did you ever see those women again?

She nods: Renate and Ditta. They were music students, who paid their fees by busking for the tourists; they said I could tag along. I stayed with them for ten months. They were headed that summer for Italy. Late September, after five weeks moving through the hill towns playing music and miming tales for the villagers, we ended up in Venice. You should have seen me. I was nut brown, all flowing hair and scarves. When I looked at myself in the mirrored shop fronts I burst out laughing. I escaped myself. I had the face I wanted at last. I was beginning to add Italian to German. Dove ... which is also the name I took. We called ourselves the people of the marionette. I don't sing or play an instrument so they put a lantern in my hand, which is how I come to be leading a crowd after Ditta and her silver flute, up to the piazza where we are holding our concert. It's a combination of classical and folk. She has a peculiar coat, a rhombus of different colours. I am dressed in a bird cloak with a hard half mask. I gather up the coins. We make a lot of money in Venice. On the last night a man stepped into a photo I was taking, and I knew him. He was my ex-partner. I did something I can't explain, I said Hi. He smiles and moves on through the crowd and disappears into a hotel at the edge of the piazza.

The next morning I persuade Ditta to go with me to his hotel: I have to know if he's recognised me. We are exotic and tolerated as we trail across the pink and grey marble lobby. No one pays us any regard and I go to the desk and ask if I might call him on the house phone. I forget for a moment which language I am in and they speak to me in fluent German.

What name? a voice asks. I say his name again.

At the same time a woman at the far end of the reception desk says my name and is handed the key to his room.

Some people start journeys with a broken heart.

Dove, don't go to his room okay? Ditta says.

The receptionist has dialled the number and handed me the phone.

Then she disappears. The lobby is empty, Ditta waits at a distance.

Hi. Last night I took your photograph.

Hello Beatrice. He dispenses with my advantage.

I sit down and wait for him. Ditta has left at my urging. And she's not happy. He comes towards me and he sighs. He doesn't like anything about me. I am really without funds and I know this was the root of his disaffection with me; he begins a verbal assault about my failure to earn my living, drive a car, and function in the real world. But I'm learning a language here! This sets him off again and he complains about my desire to be a perpetual student. We walk between the pillars, him and me. We're shouting and weeping and the locals are giving us a wide berth. I can't remember anything we say but it is awful. In the portico café, in an alley in Venice he unzips his face and cries. And I do the same.

'Basta!' Ditta is suddenly walking towards me. She takes my arm and walks me out of there. I go because I'm sure I will be able to go back and finish shouting at him tomorrow. But the next day he is gone. And I go to the airline's office and try to book a flight home. An official doing the credit card checking looks at me: my face is very swollen. It's not the face I want anymore. My request is refused. Fifty pounds is all you can have. He says it very respectfully. Ditta lends me the rest.

So who went to his room?
This story isn't over. She cautions.

I am seated on the plane next to a woman who unpacks her duty free goods onto the table as if she were setting up shop. She begins to speak very quietly to me; she says she's Hungarian. I am forced to turn my attention away from the window in order to hear what she is saying so I miss my last glimpse of the lagoon. I find instead I have in my sights a taunting array of goods I can no longer afford: a scarf I have absently lingered over in duty free is lying on the table in cellophane under an opened packet of Lucky Strike, next to 200 cigarettes of the kind I like to smoke. And also my brand of French perfume. She starts talking to me about the Hungarian uprising in '56, and her own participation in it. She has launched into the middle of a political history without any small talk or preliminaries. I have been so far away all summer that I am struggling when she gets to denouncing Communist societies for the lack of freedom to travel. So I interrupt and say, you know you only have the freedom to travel if you have the money to travel.

The woman looks at me and smiles. Good argument. Now convince me of the problems of capitalism, which you so despise.

I'm bewildered. I'm pretty sure I've never spoken to this woman before so I cannot figure out when I introduced her to my thoughts on the matter. The events of the last few days have come between me and my desire to speak.

Suddenly I change my mind: You know I think '56 was a tragedy, no one wanted it to happen, neither the Soviets nor the Americans. Wasn't it sparked by a bunch of right-wing Catholics who attacked the CP headquarters and hung some party workers?

She's so angry, she gets out of her seat and moves across the aisle. When she walked through passport control in front of me a bell rang out as if a boxing match had ended.

I began to wonder how I knew all that stuff.

The hardnosed Marxist at university? he suggests.

It was something I read.

And the woman at the hotel reception in Venice?

His wife.

No she didn't believe in ghosts, but visitations from an awareness so vast it had to be expressed; a thought so insistent it materialised.

It was the pre-Lent Carnival that triggered it. She says. In 1976.

It's called Fasching. He corrects.

Right. Adults dressed up as bears, and birds, accompanied by toy-townish bands.

My partner didn't like anything about it; the truth is he didn't like me anymore. And he felt guilty but lacked the courage to tell me. She says this pointedly waiting for Dag to respond. Still he says nothing.

She knows she is going home for good this time, because she had been here before, twice. Within weeks, she goes home. Then Dag comes with her. But it isn't home for him.

He's with her until one evening, standing in a car park in the rain, when he begins to throw coins into the air with both hands. He does it twice and with such an odd expression, tracing their trajectory as they fly and then fall. It was what her infant son looked like when he discovered that soapflakes when you threw them from a box into the air, rose before they fell. The child stood in a blizzard of flakes. It's a waste, Dagmar shouted. No it's abundance, she insisted.

She gets down in the rain in the dark to collect the fallen coins she needs for the meter. He marches off towards a painted gable. Dag! she calls after him.

'He's not coming back!' The voice beside her which has spoken is that of a young man who looks like her son. He has appeared with a map. He's not wearing a coat and the temperature is dropping.

They both stare after her departing husband.

Dag! the stranger suddenly shouts.

Dagmar stops. Turns, and glimpses the configuration. He is looking into the past. He sees mother and son united against him, ten years earlier; the beginning of his decline. He sighs deeply and walks back to face the music.

He takes the map and directs the lad to a hotel nearby.

The apparitions, she marvelled, with their ability to speak out of the silence, had not abandoned her.

They travel on to the N17 to a house at the edge of the woods in the dying days of the year. She suddenly became aware of a twelve-year-old standing on a table top, glancing into the mirror above the fireplace on the Oldpark Avenue in 1963. She is being dressed in a cloak of leaves for a pantomime in St Mary's Hall.

The dressmaker, Auntie Maud, Vera's mother, is famed for her mother-of-the-bride outfits and costumes for the Opera House. Father, brother, husband, still interned from the last campaign, her aunt sews and remakes the days.

Twelve-year-old Beatrice stands on the table top, looks in the mirror and sees the bird, just as she is captured by the new music on the TV: with love from me to you. She sees that she is me, and you are in the mirror.

When she woke later her attention was caught by late afternoon light outside a lattice window high up on the wall of the room: luminous with unfallen snow. It back-lit the bare irregular branches, that cleaved to the house, while the regular grid of the diamond lattice made a map of routes that held her long enough to contemplate the irregular beauty below.

Evelyn Conlon

Evelyn Conlon is the author of four novels and three collections of short stories. Her books include *Telling, New and Selected Stories* and *Not the Same Sky*, 2013. She was editor of *Later On*, an anthology compiled in response to the Monaghan bombing and subject of a set of Italian conference papers on the Language of War. She was co-editor, with Hans Christian Oeser, of *Cutting the Night in Two*, predecessor to this collection. Her work has been widely anthologised and translated into many languages, including Tamil. The title story of her second collection, *Taking Scarlet as a Real Colour*, was performed at the Edinburgh Theatre Festival. She is currently working on a new collection, which includes a story about the Irish woman who attempted to assassinate Mussolini.

The Meaning of Missing

I think of the feeling around a person being missing as being a narrow thing. It has to be, in order to get into so many places. I told my husband this once and he laughed at me.

'Well if you can think of heartbreak as a thin piercing agony,' I began again.

He said that the turnips needed thinning, and that he was away out to the garden. He didn't like talking about heartbreak, because he had once caused it to me by going off with his old girlfriend for three months. It obviously didn't work out because he turned up on my doorstep on Thursday, June the sixth, twenty years ago. At ten past eight in the evening. He wasn't contrite, just chastened. He has been here since, but he never talks about that time. I don't mind too much, because I never admitted that I had cried crossing every bridge in Dublin, the only way to get to know a city I was told by someone, who was clearly trying to get me away from her doorstep. Go down to the river, it will be good for you. Nor did I admit to what I'd done as soon as the crying had dried up and all the bridges had been crossed. I didn't have to, and he couldn't really ask me, nor hold me accountable.

Thinning turnips, hah! You'd think we had an acre out the back, and that he was going to have to tie old hot water bottles around his knees, because the length of time on the ground was going to be so hard on them. We have one drill of turnips, a half of cabbage and a half of broad beans. Although it's not strictly an economical use of the space, I insist on the broad beans, because of the feel of the inside of them. Only two drills. They could have waited. Of course he didn't like me talking about missing, either. It's about my sister.

'She's not missing,' my husband insisted, 'you've just not heard from her.'

I often replay my conversations with him as if he is standing right beside me. I bet I'll be able to do that if he dies before me.

'For a year!'

'Yes, for a year. But you know how time goes when you're away.'

I don't actually. I've never been away for a year. Nor for three months.

When my sister said that she was going to Australia there was a moment's silence between us, during which time a little lump came out of my heart and thumped into my stomach. We were having our second glass of Heineken. In deference to the scared part of our youth, when we were afraid to be too adventurous, she always drank Heineken when out with me. She didn't want to hold the predictability of my life up to the light. I know that she had gone through ten different favourite drinks since those days, none of them Heineken.

'Australia!' I squealed.

I coughed my voice down.

'Australia?' I said, a second time, in a more harmonious tone. Strange how the same word can mean two different things when the pitch is changed. *Béarla as Chinese.* I must have hit the right note, curious but not panicked, because she smiled and said yes. Not only was she going, she had everything ready, tickets bought, visa got. She may even have started packing for all I know. It was the secret preparation that rankled most. How could she have done those things without telling me? If we were going to Waterford for a winter break I'd tell her weeks in advance.

The day she left was beautifully frosty. She stayed with us the night before, and after I had gone to bed I could hear her and my husband surfing for hours on a swell of mumbling and laughing. Apparently she was too excited to go to sleep, and he decided to get in on the act, not often having an excited woman to lead him into the small hours. The morning radio news said that if there was an earthquake in the Canaries, Ireland might only have two hours to prepare for a tsunami. Brilliant - another thing to worry about. And us just after buying a house in Skerries. At the airport, my emotions spluttered, faded, then surged again, like a fire of Polish coal going out. The effort involved in not crying stiffened my face, and yet it twitched, as if palsy had overcome every square inch from my forehead to my chin. But I was determined. I would keep my dignity, even if the effort was going to paralyse me. It would be an essential thing to have, this dignity, now that I was not going to have a sister. My husband touched my shoulder as we got back into the car, because he can do that sometimes, the right thing.

In the months that followed I mourned her in places that I had never noticed before, and in moods that I had not known existed.

First there is presence and then it has to grow into absence. There are all sorts of ways for it to do that, gently, unnoticeably, becoming a quiet, rounded cloud that compliments the sun with its dashing about, making harmless shadows. Or the other way, darkly with thunder.

'It's not as if you saw her all the time,' my husband said, unhelpfully.

'I did,' I said back.

'What are you talking about, you only met every few months.'

'But she was there.'

She wrote well, often referring to the minutiae of her journey over. But no matter how often she talked about cramped legs or the heat in Singapore, and despite the fact that I'd seen her off at the airport myself, I still imagined her queuing for a ship at Southampton, sailing the seas for a month, having dinner in prearranged sittings at the sound of a bell, because that's the way I would have done it.

And then she stopped writing, fell out of touch, off the world. My letters went unanswered, her telephone was cut off. I'm afraid, that because my pride was so riled, the trail was completely cold by the time I took her real missing seriously. And still my husband insisted that there was nothing wrong with her, just absentmindedness.

I was in bed sick the day she rang. I love the trimmings of being sick, mainly the television at the bottom of the bed, although after two days I was getting a little TV'd out. I had just seen John Stalker, a former chief of English Police, advertising garden awnings. I was puzzled as to why they gave his full title. Did the police thing have anything to do

with awnings? Was there a pun there, hidden from me? I
didn't like being confused by advertisements. If I'd had a
remote control device I could have switched the volume
down occasionally and lip-read the modern world. Then
Countdown came on. Making up the words made me feel
useful. I had seen the mathematician wearing that dress
before. It was during the conundrum that the phone rang;
it wasn't a crucial conundrum, because one of the fellows
was streets ahead of the other, even I had him beaten hands
down, and I had a temperature of 100 degrees and rising.

'Hello?'

And there was her voice, brazen as all hell got up. I
straightened myself against the headboard and thought,
'It's the temperature'. I straightened myself more and my
heart thumped very hard. It sounded like someone rapping
a door. I thought it would cut off my breathing.

'Hi,' she said.

'Hello,' I said, as best as I could manage.

'Oh my God it's been soooo long.'

The sentence sounded ridiculous and the stretched out
word was frankly juvenile.

'And I'm really sorry about that. But I'll make up for it.
I'm on my way back for a couple of months. I'll be arriving
on Saturday morning.'

Back. Not home. Well Saturday didn't suit me, and even
if it had done so up until this moment, it suddenly wasn't
going to. I was speechless, truly. But my mind was working
overtime dealing with silent words tumbling about. I could
almost hear them cranking up, scurrying around looking for
their place in the open. What would be the best way to get
revenge? She must have finally noticed because she asked,

'Are you there?'

'Oh yes,' I said.

Short as that, 'Oh yes.'

I don't think I said more than ten words before limping to a satisfactorily oblique fade out.

'See you. Then.'

I put the phone down, my hand shaking. How many people had I told? And would I have to tell them all that she was no longer missing? And had I also told them about my husband's view? And was he now right? If a person turns up have they ever been missing? How could I possibly remember what conversations I had set up or slipped into casually, over the past year? I hoped that my sister would have a horrible flight, bumpy, stormy, crowded, delayed. But that's as far as my bile could flower.

My husband went to the airport. He would, having no sense of the insult of missing. He fitted the journey in around the bits and pieces of a Saturday, not wanting me to see him set out, not wanting to leave the house under the glare of my disapproval.

By evening I had mellowed a little because I had to. It was seeing her, the shape of her, the stance of her as she leaned against the kitchen table, the expressions of her. My sister had never giggled, even in the years that are set aside for that. She had always been too wry. Getting ready for her life, no doubt, away ahead of me, I thought, always. On the third evening, by the time the ice in my chest had begun to melt, the three of us went out to our local.

'What's Wollongong like?' I asked.

'Just a normal Australian town,' my sister said, and shrugged loudly, if that is possible. And then she mercilessly changed the subject. I had thought it would have jacaranda trees in bloom all year, birds calling so busily that it would be the first thing a person would mention, sun flitting continuously on the sparkling windows of every house. A town rampant with light. I had thought it a place for rumination, with colour bouncing unforgettably off the congregation of gum trees.

'Are you sure it's just a normal town. Have you been there?'

'Yes, totally normal. Of course I've been there.'

I didn't believe her for one second.

'Why do you particularly want to know what Wollongong is like?'

'The name,' my husband said, as if he was my ventriloquist. But something in my demeanour made him hesitate, and he looked at me as if he had made some mistake.

'It's just that I met someone from there,' I said.

'When?' they both asked. Normally my sister and my husband have a murmuring familiarity between them, born presumptuously of their relationship with me. But they were suddenly quiet, each afraid to admit that they did not know when I, I of the dried-up life, would have met someone from Wollongong. Was it during her year or his three months? Damn, they would be thinking, now they each knew that the other didn't know. And me sitting there smiling away to myself. Smug, they would have been surmising. But it wasn't smug. I admit to a moment of glee but I was mostly thinking of Wollongong, and I swallowed the sliver of triumph because I am known for my capacity to forgive.

However, I didn't answer their question and went to the bar to buy my round, feeling like a racehorse, unexpectedly out in front, showing the rest of the field a clear set of hooves.

Éilís Ní Dhuibhne

Éilís Ní Dhuibhne is a novelist, critic and folklore scholar. Her short story collections include *Midwife to the Fairies*, *The Inland Ice*, *The Pale Gold of Alaska* and *The Shelter of Neighbours*. Among her novels are *Cailíní Beaga Ghleann na mBlath*, *Hurlamaboc*, *Dunamharu sa Daingean*, *The Dancers Dancing, and Fox, Swallow Scarecrow*. Her awards include the Bisto Book of the Year Award, the Readers' Association of Ireland Award, the Stewart Parker Award for Drama, the Butler award for Prose from the Irish American Cultural Institute. *The Dancers Dancing* was shortlisted for the Orange Prize for Fiction and she was awarded the Irish PEN Award for an Outstanding Contribution to Irish Literature in 2015. Her stories are widely anthologized and translated. Éilís was for many years a curator in the National Library of Ireland. She teaches Creative Writing in UCD and is a member of Aosdána.

The Coast of Wales

Opposite the flowerbed, which dazzles the eye with crimson primroses and tulips the precise pink of dentures, a woman in a yellow anorak is bent over a tap. As she fills her blue watering can, her small dog waits – he's a Yorkie or a Scottie, one of those shaggy little 'ie' dogs. He is silent, which is good because dogs aren't allowed in here. Patiently he stares at the tap.

It's attached to a slim concrete post and is almost invisible against the background of stone and milky misty sky. That's why I never noticed it before. Now this woman with the black dog illuminates it with that yellow anorak of hers, highlights it for me. There's something new to learn every time I come here. For instance, I've found out that the potted plants I place carefully on the clay dry up very quickly, even when it rains. You need to come and water them every few days. Some people know this and they've rigged up clever permanent contraptions: containers like stone window boxes, which they place on the concrete plinth, and fill with plants in season. It would be easier if you could sow something directly into the soil, but that's against the regulations.

The reason is that this is a lawn cemetery. That's another thing I've learnt: the term 'lawn cemetery', and what it means, which is that grass grows on the graves. And that men from the County Council cut this grass. They've been mowing regularly ever since spring got going, six weeks ago. These grass cutters also remove any unpermitted decorations – for example, teddy bears and plastic angels, Santa Clauses – from the graves, and throw them into the big skip by the gate. They also throw away withered flowers. You have to keep a close watch on your plants to make sure they don't decide to consign them to the skip before they're dead. All this cutting and throwing away, however, means the place is well kept. On sunny days it can look almost nice, at least after you get used to it.

I brought water in a bottle in my rucksack. And now I find out there's no need to carry water all the way from home. Water is heavier than it looks when it comes dancing out of the tap, light as stars.

This is what the graveyard looks like: an enormous housing estate, bisected by a thoroughfare. You can drive on this, and some people do, but I think that's inappropriate, like driving on a beach. Off this central artery are the cul-de-sacs, about twenty on each side. Hundreds of straight lines of graves, arranged symmetrically like boxy houses, with pocket handkerchief lawns in front of each one. True, there is a certain amount of variation in the headstones, as there is in houses on estates, but, as with them, diversity is limited by planning restrictions. The headstones must not be higher than four metres and so they all measure exactly four metres – naturally everyone goes for as much height as they can get. Apart from this, some choice is permitted, although all headstone designs and inscriptions have to be vetted by the authorities. They're obviously tolerant; there are some pretty unusual headstones around. You hesitate to use the words 'bad taste' in connection with death – another thing I've learnt. Don't be judgmental about trivial things (and everything is trivial, by comparison with what's going on in this place). But I can't warm to the shiny slabs with gold inscriptions and smug angels on top. The white marble is nicer, even when it comes with expressions of profound sentiments in lines apparently plagiarized from country and western songs, or the 'Funny Stories' page of some ancient schoolboy magazine.

His Life a Beautiful Memory, His Absence a Silent Grief.

Take care of Tom, Lord, as he Did Us, With Lots of Love and Little Fuss.

My favourites are the simple stones, plain grey, which have become more common, I'm pleased to report, over the past four or five years. (It's easy to date fashions in a graveyard.)

That's what I ordered for you. The style called 'boulder', the natural look that suits a man who wore tweed and spoke correct Irish, Welsh and Scots Gaelic. I thought it was a personal choice but I've discovered that most of the poets and writers, teachers and academics, in the graveyard are buried under similar stones. There's only one unique monument in the entire place: a wide slab of pinkish granite, thin as butterfly's wing. Only a name and a date inscribed on it in tiny Times New Roman.

The architect who designed Belfield.

Of course.

To tell the truth, I wouldn't mind one of those. A high modernist headstone that looks as if it were imported, at great expense, from Finland or some other crucible of understated good taste. But you could copy it and the next thing IKEA would be supplying the same thing in a flatpack at a fraction of the cost. They'd be all over the place.

I guess I'll stick with the country life look.

Unlike you, I know precisely how and where I will be buried (unless I am destroyed in a plane crash or murdered and chopped up into little bits and my body never found). I'll be under a homespun boulder on Row C, in the section called St Mark's, down near the wall and the old Church of Ireland. I thought when I was shown the spot that it was pretty, because it was in the shelter of the old church, with its bell tower and stone walls. The newer section of the graveyard, St Elizabeth's, didn't appeal to me one bit. It's a huge flat field that stretches despondently to the Irish Sea. The undertaker, who encouraged me to think very carefully before I made a decision, pointed out that as time went on St Elizabeth's would look 'less bleak'. The trees will grow, he said, in his mild, and mildly ironic tone. He takes death in his stride, and thinks in the longer term.

But how much time have I got?

From St Mark's there is a fine view of the Dublin Mountains, today a rich eggy yellow. The gorse. Easter egg time, almost everything in nature is yellow. Not only has it a fine view, always desirable in houses or graves, St Mark's also has the virtue of age, being in the oldest part of the graveyard, where unburnt corpses can no longer be buried – there's not enough room. For them, poor skeletons, no choice. It's St Elizabeth's; they'll have to grin and bear it, and wait for the trees to grow. But there's still space for little urns of ashes in the old section, just because not that many Dubliners choose cremation, and of those that do, many don't get a grave – their ashes are scattered in some scenic spot where they used to go on their holidays, or kept at home on the mantelpiece. Some of yours are at home too. I'm planning to scatter them on a nice headland near the place where *we* went on holiday on Anglesey, where almost everyone speaks Welsh. But I rather like having them in the house so I'll probably hold on to some. That means your ashes will be in three different places. There's no rule against it; that's the beauty of ashes. You could never dismember a body and bury bits in various places – except in vey exceptional circumstances, such as Daniel O'Connell's.

I'd have thought such ideas unhealthy, even disgusting. And terrifying. Before. Life is for the living was my motto, not that I expressed it one way or the other. But now the dead are always on my mind and I'm quite an expert on graves and graveyards. I could set up an online advice centre and may do that when I get over your death. I have quite a lot of plans for that time, for the time when I get over it, when my energy returns and I start out on a new life as a person who has lost her husband but has survived. A widow, to use that word all widows I have met – they're all over the place – can't stand. People tell me that you'd want me to start a new life, to be happy. I suppose it is a safe bet that you wouldn't want me to be actively miserable. You didn't get a chance to express any preferences one way or the other, but others step into the breach. You should get a dog. Aren't you lucky it all happened so quickly? A massage would make you feel so much better. The sort of things we'd have a good laugh at, between ourselves, over dinner. I reckon we ate about 14,000 dinners together and so had at least 14,000 good laughs. 28,000? More. It would be so great to have just one more dinner so I could tell you about all that's been happening, relay all the comments: the sublime, the absurd, the in-between.

Quite a long dinner, we'd need, to tell the whole story.

They mean well.

St Mark's is not really as nice as I first thought. The church and the ivy-covered wall block the sun in the afternoon, so our grave is often in cold shade. Today, for once, I came in the morning, and the sun is shining on you. I take my plastic water bottle out of my rucksack and pour water on the purple flower, a senettia, and the white, a chrysanthemum. It's not the kind of flower you liked, or I like, but it was the only thing in the flower shop that looked healthy enough to survive in this graveyard for any length of time. And it has lasted and looks quite good here on the grave, which needs all the flowers it can get. The boulder hasn't come yet – they're waiting for a good block of granite. As if blocks of granite come rolling down the hill when they feel like it. You'd think they'd have a regular supplier. In the meantime all you have is a little wooden marker with your name on it, and dates. It has been a great help to me, especially at the beginning when I couldn't remember where the grave was. It took me a while to remember to turn left at Mary Byrne's grave, which is next to that of Enrico Cafolla, Professor of Music – easier to remember than Mary Byrne, beloved wife, Mom and Nana. (The word 'granny' never appears on headstones.) I never go astray now.

There isn't enough water in the bottle. The flowers are alive, but thirsty. The white petals of the chrysanthemum are turning to straw. The senettia is such a strong regal purple, a deep dyed purple, that its thin blade like petals could never turn brown, but they're getting limp. I decide to walk back to the tap and get more water. It'll take about ten minutes, to go there and back, but I have plenty of time now. That is another thing. Before I had no time for anything. Now time seems to stretch endlessly in front of me, like the sea out there in front of the railway. But the sense of a wide expanse of ocean is an illusion. There is a coast that you can't see over the horizon. Wales. The land I love because it brought us such luck. After four years waiting we conceived a child there, on the first night of a holiday at Beaumaris. It's a mere sixty-six (nautical) miles away. Just because you can't see it doesn't mean it doesn't exist. And it's closer than, say, Ballinasloe.

As I go back towards the tap I notice the woman I saw earlier. The woman in the yellow anorak. She's busy at a grave. No doubt she's a widow, like me, like most of the graveyard visitors, who spent their lives taking care of husbands and have no intention of stopping now, just because they're dead. So they keep coming to the graves to pull up the weeds, to water the flowers, to plant new things. The woman in the yellow anorak is touching her headstone with both hands, and talking to it. As I pass, I hear what she's saying. 'Sandra came to dinner yesterday and we watched *Fair City*. I miss you so much, my dearest darling.'

The dog is nowhere to be seen.

The tap.

That's where the dog is, tied to the concrete post by his leash. He's a Scottie, I can see it now, I remember the difference. Black, with that long, sceptical, Scottish head.

'Hi, little dog,' I say. 'Excuse me while I fill this empty ginger ale bottle with water.'

I turn on the tap and squeeze the mouth of the bottle so it fits over the lip of the tap. This is not a good idea.

Just then, a hearse comes through the gate, followed by two black limousines; after them the straggle of ordinary cars. A few people stand at the corner, paying their respects as the hearse passes and swings quietly around the corner, making for St Elizabeth's.

I used to hate the sight of a hearse. My heart would sink if I met one on the road. But I no longer fear them now that

I've met death face to face, tried to shoo it away, and lost the battle. Now I can cast an indifferent eye on every hearse that passes by, because I've driven behind yours.

Just as the hearse turns around the corner this thing happens. The plastic bottle dislodges from the tap and a strong gush of water splashes onto the dog. Startled by the sudden cold shower, he breaks free. He can't have been tied very tightly. Off he dashes, in the direction of the woman in the yellow anorak.

And he runs right under the second big limousine, the one which probably contains the more distant relatives who are nevertheless too important to come in their own cars. I see him, all the funeral followers on the sidelines see him. The only person who does not see him is the driver of the limousine. He is such a tiny dog, the size of a well-fed rat. Dogs aren't allowed in the graveyard. The driver isn't expecting one to run out in front of him.

How ghastly. First your husband, then your dog.

This had occurred to me, in connection with dogs. And cats. Their mortality. If I get a dog, as so many people advise, it will die sometime. And by the time it dies, I will have grown to love it, even though a dog is no substitute for a husband. I'd be bereaved all over again in a different way. An easier way. But bereavement is never easy.

The hearse glides slowly along the road to Saint Elizabeth's. The first limousine turns the corner and follows it, and the second limousine turns too.

The driver still doesn't realise he has just run over a widow's dog.

But no.

No. It's OK. The dog is OK.

The car passed over him and just left him behind like a jellyfish on the beach when the tide goes out. Alive, with no more than an expression of mild surprise on his narrow face. He scampers off over the graves towards the spot where the woman he loves, who has seen none of this, is busily engaged in a conversation with someone she loves but who doesn't exist.

Animals don't know what we humans know.

All the people standing by the side of the road, including me, laugh, some more heartily than others.

His lucky day, someone says.

Yes. There's quite a bit of luck involved, when it comes to the crunch, in matters of life and death.

A short pause. We consider this observation, and savour the taste of profound relief. An exquisite taste.

I turn off the tap.

Then I kick the bottle and let the water spill over into the bed of crimson primroses, tulips the exact colour of dentures. I decide not to return to our grave. It's pointless. Unless the brash senettia, the weary chrysanthemum, get some rain and manage to soak it up, nothing I can do will keep them alive.

The mourners shake themselves, remember why they're here, and start to process sedately along the track that leads to St Elizabeth's, the railway line, and the Irish Sea. The haze has burnt off now and the water sparkles, blue as silk close to land, and a deep dark indigo, like a firm line of ink, on the horizon.

You still can't see Wales. But it is there, all right.

Lia Mills

Lia Mills writes novels, short stories, essays and an occasional blog. In a previous existence she was Teaching and Research Fellow at the Women's Education, Research & Resource Centre in UCD, with a special interest in Irish women writers. She was a founder member of the editorial groups of two experimental feminist journals: *Ms. Chief* and *f/m*. She has worked on several Public Art Commissions, including editing the anthologies *You Had To Be There!* and *Wake* (for Ballymun Regeneration Ltd). A memoir, *In Your Face*, describes her experience of mouth cancer treatment in 2006. Her third novel, *Fallen*, was published in 2014. Her website is www.liamills.com

The Crossing

In the taxi on the way to their Cairo hotel, Max and Duncan point things out to each other – women swathed in black with plastic shopping bags on their heads; swaying, long-legged camels with spiky eyelashes; donkey carts piled high with wicker baskets full of live chickens, rabbits, ducks; the carcass of a horse rotting on the riverbank. Nola says little. She feels just exactly like the open window of the car with all that rich, warm air streaming through – so many impressions rush through her that she can hold on to none of them. Egypt! She can hardly believe this is her, on the holiday of a lifetime. There's fresh trouble brewing in the region but they'd already paid for their tickets and Max said there's always trouble, they should take the chance in case it never comes again.

Duncan is their youngest, on his Easter holidays from school. His older brothers are busy with their own lives and Nola hadn't liked to leave him at a loose end for a whole week. Lately he's begun that slow turn that teenagers make, like the earth in the middle of winter arcing back to the sun. As he's got taller, feet spreading, skin thickening, voice sliding deeper into his belly, he's begun to contract away from her. She'd thought she might not have to go through this with him – he'd been an affectionate child – but no. His eyes have begun to slide away from hers in public, as if he hopes against hope that he won't have to acknowledge her as his parent. He has a way of squinting when she says things, as if the sound of her voice hurts him physically.

But it was his idea to come with them on this holiday. As soon as he heard about it, he'd perked up. 'Egypt? Can I come?' She'd been so pleased, she'd persuaded Max to agree.

The car stops at a checkpoint. Beside them, a legless man powers along the road on stumps. He pummels the ground with muscular fists to propel himself forwards, swinging and swivelling his torso along with surprising speed. As if he feels her stare, he turns to glare at her. His face is angry, determined, virile. She looks away, ashamed, although she's not sure of what.

At the hotel, they drink cocktails in the roof garden and admire the slow descent of the sun, a glowing disc sinking through an orange sky. Winged feluccas glide along the river below. On the far side, crowds of tall, blocky buildings are punctuated by graceful minarets. But the noise! Even this far up they hear car horns, whistles, music, shouts. Then the call to prayer, followed by the swell of thousands of voices calling to Allah.

Nola's men are perfectly at ease here; even Duncan knows how to order what he wants. She feels out of place: oversized, overheated, overeager. She says *please* and *thank you* too often to the people who bring them drinks and bowls of salty, bitter roasted nuts.

She's forty-five, which everyone says is young these days but there's no getting away from the fact that it's halfway to ninety, or that she's plagued by surges of blood-boiling heat, bouts of forgetfulness, sudden mood swings. Nights when hormonal storms sear through her and she has to move to the spare room for fear of disturbing Max. She's tortured by the idea that she's blown it, that somehow she failed to notice when her life was supposed to start, that she missed the vital moment when she was supposed to step up and claim it. It reminds her of an earlier holiday long ago, when the boys were small. They were late getting to the airport and even though their flight hadn't left yet, the check-in people flat-out refused to accept their suitcases and let them through. While Max argued, Nola held on tight to Duncan, a squirming toddler then, and watched their flight number climb the information screens until it was gone altogether. She'd been so young then, her life ahead of her, but she hadn't realised what that meant.

Hucksters call to them from every angle in the bazaar the next day, wheedling and persuasive. *Best prices here. No pressure.* A display of flame-coloured cotton catches her eye. The boy at the stall turns hopeful eyes on her. She knows it's a mistake to stop; she'll have to buy something now. She fingers a caftan-like top, gathering courage for the bargaining everyone says is essential. The cotton glows, soft, somewhere between gold, crimson and orange. The boy lets her bargain him down a couple of pounds from his first price. Max comes over while she's putting her change away, exhilarated. She's done it!

'What did you get?'

She opens the bag to show him. He makes a face. 'Is it for Jean?' Jean is Nola's older sister but she works in a university and still dresses like a student. 'How much did you pay for it?' When she tells him, he points to another stall where the starting prices are lower. 'Sorry,' he says.

She wanders away to a stall loaded with spices – yellow crystals of myrrh, sticks of cinnamon, whole vanilla beans. Why does she feel so crushed? That boy needs the money a lot more than she does and there's not much difference in the price – the cost of a bottle of beer, maybe. Besides, she'd paid for more than the shirt. She'd bought a vision of herself bartering in a North African bazaar; a person who would want a colour that bold; a person who might even wear it. She'd paid for the smile in the boy's eyes, the grace of his gesture when he put his palms together and bowed to her. 'You are welcome in Egypt,' he'd said, as if he meant it.

Nola reads out warnings from the guidebook in a taxi on their way to Giza and the pyramids. They should only drink water from sealed bottles; no ice except in the best hotels; if they buy drinks at street stalls or in coffee houses, they must use drinking straws; the glasses may be improperly washed. She shows them the packet of straws in her bag.

A crowd of men gathers around the car before they're even out of it, offering their services as guides, displaying trays of souvenirs. Beautiful children swarm around them, calling greetings. Max strikes a deal with a man called Ibrahim, who bats his rivals away like so many flies and leads them away up the hill.

The pyramids are empty, their treasures scattered. But the massive blocks of stone are still there, and the hieroglyphs. Nola stares and stares, trying to take it all in. Ibrahim frets when she stands too close to an open shaft, urges her back to the path. At the bottom of the hill, they meet his brother, Yusuf, outside his perfumery.

'You are my guests,' he says. 'Please to come in.'

Inside a long shaded room cooled by ceiling fans, mirror-backed cabinets display a range of enchanting glass bottles and jars. A boy whose name Nola doesn't catch offers to show her the toilet. 'Clean,' he says, 'if you wish to use.' It's embarrassing, as if they've read the guidebooks too.

They sit on a rosewood bench-seat with carved legs and patterned cushions. Yusuf talks about flowers, dabs samples of scent on the insides of her wrists. Black narcissus. Amber. Lotus flower. 'We use this on the wedding night,' he says. 'If the girl wears this, the husband will not get out of bed for a month.'

He invites them to smell a different scent. 'Red musk. I am a Muslim, I respect this. It is burned in our mosques. Also frankincense.'

'The three kings,' Duncan says.

Yusuf smiles, nods. 'Yes. From Egypt.'

After all that, Nola can't bring herself to produce the straws from her bag when the boy comes back with glasses of ruby-red hibiscus tea on a silver tray. Duncan nudges her but it's just not in her to do it. She's thirsty. The tea is blood-warm, sweet, refreshing.

Back in the hotel she takes out her purchases, several lovely bottles of different scents. 'That has to be a racket,' Max says. 'I'd say they're not even brothers. A rip-off outfit.'

Nola disagrees. 'Look at the day we've had!'

The next day they fly south along the Nile. The flight is full of local people carrying packages wrapped in brown paper and string. A few men in suits carry briefcases. As the plane banks lower, it swoops over a deep, velvety-green sea of fields under pink cliffs. Beyond the fields, the land is a dry, humped brown crust. The desert! Even Max is excited. Lower and lower they fly, until Nola makes out the tops of trees, buildings, the road. She can see right down inside houses with no roofs. There's no glass in the windows, there are no doors. A small, dark-skinned girl in a golden dress runs through a luscious, vivid field, her arms outstretched, under the shadow of the plane.

Armed guards are conspicuous outside the grounds of their hotel. Inside, women move around the pool in bikinis while polite waiters in crisp white Egyptian cotton pretend not to notice. Large pink-skinned men sweat in the sun. Beyond the pool is the river, where feluccas swoop dramatic sails. Cruise boats steam up and down, fat pale slugs on the water. A woman as old as Nola's mother would be if she were still alive squats in front of an open fire all day long shrouded in heavy veils, making stacks of flatbreads for the terrace café. '*Salam*,' Nola tries, self-conscious.

The woman's head dips. '*Alaikum Salam.*'

They visit a hotel so famous that they have to pay to get in. Max and Duncan have their drinks without ice but Nola can't resist. 'We're safe here, surely.' Her iced Coke is delicious, so cold that water beads the outside of her glass.

Their guide, a woman called Samira, collects them there, en route to the Valley of the Queens. She wears a headscarf, a long-sleeved cotton tunic, pale trousers ironed to a knife-edge along her shins.

Nola has the strongest feeling that she's been to Hatshepsut's temple before. It feels familiar: the wide, steep ascent to rows of pillars cut into a wall of rock. She must remember to tell Jean, who's taken a course in transpersonal experiences and believes in reincarnation.

She's surprised by disapproving looks directed at Samira from other tourists. She's sure she's right – it's not the Egyptian men who frown but the westerners, mostly the women.

Samira catches her noticing, raises one perfect eyebrow. 'My headscarf offends them.'

Nola feels herself blush. It seems rude to ask, 'Does it bother you?'

Samira's shrug is eloquent. 'If someone stops me from work, that bothers me.' She walks through the tourists as though they don't exist. Cool, elegant, unruffled, she talks about the queens: their consorts, their enemies, their fabulous powers.

The holiday has been such a success. Look at the way Duncan and Max are talking, pointing things out to each other. They ply Samira with questions. The looming stone sentinels give Nola the creeps but the hieroglyphs are lovely, plain and reassuring.

Samira talks about gold and jewels stolen, urns and caskets emptied. The bad luck that followed. Nola begins to feel disorientated. She stops listening, desperate to get back to their room at the hotel, to draw the curtains, take off her clothes and slip in between cool sheets in the air-conditioned dark, to drink a whole bottle of clean, cool water without stopping. She stifles a groan when their car pulls up again in the artisan's valley, among ruins that don't look much different from the clay huts that people still live in.

Inside, the walls are painted with lively scenes of people working, of everyday life. Images of men and women, families, people at work, tilling fields. At last, things she can relate to.

A guard hands her a strip of cardboard.

'What's this for?'

He smiles and waves his own strip in her direction, raising dust – she's to use it as a fan. The chambers get narrower, shallower and hotter as they go further down. The guard follows, stirring the dusty air with his piece of card. No trace of gold or jewels here, these people's offerings would have been more everyday and practical. Leather sandals, maybe. A pestle, or a bowl. Even the household items have been taken to fill the museums of the world. Nola's lungs begin to clog. She remembers where she is. In a grave. She makes an excuse, turns and stumbles back up into the light. The merciless sun beats down on her head. Sweat runs rivers down her back as she crosses the narrow sandy street, jostled by boys with big smiles, saying hello, wanting *mumyia*.

She waits for the others in a scrap of shade beside a palm. A small brown lizard darts past her foot. Plain, ordinary, busy, it would fit right into the world of the artisans, much as she would herself. Jean would have swanned around Hatshepsut's temple and imagined it was hers. On holiday together in England last year, she'd raved about the comfort, the style, the size of the rooms in the stately homes they'd visited, the clothes the women would have worn, their jewels. Nola has always known that if she lived in a house like that, she'd most likely be the under-house-parlourmaid, the one whose fate it was to be first up in the morning, to clean out the grates and lay fires for the household. No four-poster beds for her: she'd sleep on straw if she was lucky, under the kitchen table. She'd spend her mornings emptying chamber pots. She'd have little to leave behind for grave robbers. She twists the wedding ring on her finger, wonders how she'd pay the ferryman.

On the way back across the river, Samira says that the city was built on the east bank because that's where the sun rises – it's a place for the living. The tombs were built in the west, where the sun goes down, in the land of the dead. 'Only the workers lived there.'

Nola's head buzzes. She has a dazed impression that she's left herself behind, on the wrong bank.

That night, she's skewered by cramps. Her temperature shoots through the roof. When she's not sprinting for the loo she's hallucinating. The air wavers, stained with patches of colour that have survived thousands of years of sun and wind, like paint in the temples.

She lies very still in the darkened room when Max and Duncan set off on their adventures the next morning. The relief of being alone is like a cool cloth laid on her burning face. She drifts in and out of a hallucinogenic sleep, through dark tunnels into dusty tombs. Brightly coloured hieroglyphs press against her eyelids. Those birds, she thinks, their simple grace – until they come to life and swoop at her. A gold collar tightens around her neck. When she tries to tug it off, her fingers can't find it. She hears herself groan, like someone else in the room.

Her head throbs. The others are late. All of a sudden she remembers news footage of a massacre a few years back, when desperate men poured from the desert into yesterday's temple, shooting, spilling fresh blood to the sand. That's where her sense of familiarity came from. How could they have been so stupid as to come here? A sudden image of Duncan's awkward knees makes her want to cry. He is still her baby. More than anything, she wants him to blunder through the door and grunt at her.

When they do eventually come in, their voices hurt her head. She sends them off to dinner without her and passes the night in a fog, half awake. She can feel the illness ebb. For once, she doesn't envy Max his deep sleep, his reassuring, low-level snore. Her strength comes back like a tide. She likes the quiet dark, the sense of a whole continent gathered around her. Holding her up.

She wakes full of energy and slips out of the room to watch the sunrise from the veranda. Colour flushes through the garden. Birds, on holiday – like her – from a colder world, call up the new day. She feels purged, open. When she comes back inside, the others are dressed, waiting for her. There's a mound of tissue paper on the bed. 'What's this?'

Duncan smiles, shy. 'We got you something.'

'It was Duncan's idea,' says Max.

She unwraps a chunky bracelet of turquoise and beaten silver and slides it over her wrist, admires its effect on the creamy, freckled skin of her arm. They tell her about the bus tour she missed, the temple at Karnak, a stop at an upmarket souvenir shop.

'The usual tat,' Max says. 'But they had nice things too. The shopkeeper could have talked the hind legs off a Christian Brother. He'll change it if you want; it's not far away.'

'No!'

She sends them ahead of her to breakfast and takes a luxurious, refreshing shower. She dresses in good linen trousers to live up to her new bracelet, and the shirt she bought in the bazaar. It has long, loose sleeves and steep, uneven ends, not unlike the hanging corners of a tablecloth – a bit much, really – but the colour! Like a rising sun.

She takes the river path to the main building of the hotel. A kingfisher swoops and darts beside her, skimming the surface of the water. The sun is a hot hand on her back. It's going to be another searing, dry day, their last. They've more or less decided to spend it beside the pool.

On her way in to the lobby she meets Samira coming out. 'Today's group cancelled at the last minute.'

'What will you do?'

Samira spreads her elegant hands. 'See what the day will bring.'

'Join us for breakfast?'

Samira glances towards reception, where disapproval is clear in the set of the senior clerk's jaw.

'Coffee at least. As my guest. I insist.' Nola has never spoken to anyone like this before. She's quoting some film or other and why not, if it serves its purpose? She takes Samira's arm and walks her into the restaurant. Max stands up and pulls out a chair for Samira. Nola's astonished when Duncan does the same for her. 'Max and Duncan want the pool today,' she tells Samira, 'but I'd only burn.'

'What would you like to do instead?'

'Explore the town, if you're free. The real town, where people live.' It's ridiculous, how shy she feels. 'I'd like to visit a proper coffee house, somewhere you might go with friends. If you wouldn't mind. A book shop, with new Egyptian books; a cinema – anywhere with a bit of ordinary life in it.'

In the distance she can see the pink cliffs of the western bank of the river. Busloads of tourists are preparing to go over there. They'll spend their day clambering around the tombs of long-dead kings and queens, the ruins of temples, exclaiming at the scale, the grandeur, the enduring beauty of the ruins. They'll long for shelter from the sun and the unending clamour for money and attention, the pressure to buy souvenirs. She wouldn't have missed it for anything, but all that's behind her now. Today is another day.

Christine Dwyer Hickey

Christine Dwyer Hickey has published seven novels, one short story collection and a full-length play. *The Cold Eye of Heaven* (Atlantic Books UK) won the Irish Novel of the Year 2012 and was nominated for the International IMPAC Dublin Literary Award. *Tatty* (New Island and Vintage UK) was nominated for the Orange Prize and was one of the 50 Irish Novels of the Decade. *Last Train from Liguria* (Atlantic Books) was nominated for the *Prix L'Européen de Littérature*. Her short stories have been published in anthologies and magazines worldwide and have won several awards. Her short story collection, *The House on Parkgate Street* (New Island Books), was published in 2013. Her first play, *Snow Angels*, premiered at the Project Arts Centre in March 2014. Her latest novel, *The Lives of Women*, was published in April 2015 (Atlantic Books UK). She is a member of Aosdána.

The Cat and the Mouse

She steps into the room at the back of the house, softly closes the door behind her, and listens. She has sensed a dip in the light outside, the lull before rain. Since yesterday it has been this way – a pause like a large intake of breath and then, in a trigger-happy barrage against the glass roof and long windows, the rain. Her aunt in the kitchen, fidgeting with dishes; her mother in the garden mumbling into her phone. Her uncle upstairs snapping French words into a Dictaphone. She needs to hold these positions in her head; to anticipate the slightest shift in sound or intent.

Every other day she hoovers this room. At first, her mother and Aunt Babs used to move the furniture. As she got to know her way around, they moved it less and less. Now they guide her from the sidelines, in between talk about when they were London girls. Watch out for the sofa! Television coming up! Ah ah ashtray on the floor! *Ah-ah-ah.* Her mother says this, as if she's a toddler who might pick up the ashtray and start eating butts out of it, like sweeties.

The hoover beside her. She holds the cable lead in her right hand while her left hand begins its excursion, skimming over those flaws that have lately become her landmarks:

a patch of rough skin, the marks of old nail wounds, and behind the sofa, the small raised worm of air under the wallpaper that only she knows about. She still finds it an odd way to get around; odd and maybe even perverse, as if she's forcing an intimacy between herself and the house, forever feeling it up, fondling its fabrics: touching, sniffing, testing. While the house just stands there and takes it.

It would be so much easier if the cleaner did it, Madame Millet or Miyat or something. It's there in her mother's anxious voice and in Babsie's chirpy encouragement. And it's there in the cleaner's foreign words, in which she recognises, without quite knowing how, a promise to go over the room herself as soon as *l'aveugle* has finished bumbling around.

She has picked the wrong day. The minute she stepped into the room, she could tell. Stale cigar smoke like a dirty gauze on her face, meaning the cigar-smoker came back with Uncle Christophe last night after the golf club dinner. Already she knows the cigar-smoker as a man who likes to use a room, re-living his game and acting out anecdotes. There will be extra ashtrays in unexpected places, glasses on the floor, more than one type of bottle: wine or that brandy stuff made out of apples. Sometimes they keep her awake till all hours, although she would never say. Not even when her mother nags her next day, for lying on late. 'Lazy! Do you want them to think you're lazy? That you won't even *try*?'

Her mother and Babs won't have heard a sound. Their bedrooms upstairs sealed with thick glass and caged in by long shutters. That side of the house faces a road. She remembers it as a road you might see on a tourist poster, long and flawlessly straight; trees like spears on each side all the way into *la ville*.

She is the only one to sleep downstairs. In a room Christophe had specially converted after the accident. Bars all around the wall. 'Like a ballet studio,' he declared the first time he showed it to them. When he said that, she could feel her mother like a cat, bristling beside her.

Her mother says it every so often – 'Thank him.'
'I did. I do.'
'Thank him again. *Talk* to him, you know how he likes to practise his English.'

But there are only so many times she can say thank you (*merci, merci,* Mercy!) and besides she finds herself turning shy in his company, the air that lurks around him, difficult to navigate. When she came here as a child, she had no such problem. There was a cast-iron statue of a cat on the roof of the house, another statue of a mouse just above it. She had almost passed out with joy, the first time he pointed them out to her. *Le chat et le souris sur le toit.* He taught her the words in French but told her about their adventures, in his clumsy English. She would love to know if the cat and the mouse are still there but can't seem to bring herself to ask.

'What is your age now?' Uncle Christophe asks.
'Sixteen.'
'And the last time since you came?'
'I was thirteen.'
'Ahhh. Three years and so many changes.'

Christophe is a quiet man. Snotty, her mother calls him, 'snotty and permanently dissatisfied, like everyone else in this bloody place.'

It's how her mother has always referred to Normandy. This bloody place. Once when she was small, she'd overheard the two sisters talking on the terrace in the middle of the night. Through the bathroom window, the sound of frogs or maybe crickets, the clinking glass and Babsie's voice in the dark, 'Of course the people are dour. It's still here, you see. Death on the air. Blood in the soil.'

Blood in the soil! So that's what her mother had meant. For the rest of that holiday she'd hadn't been able to sleep until her mother climbed into the high double bed they had shared then. The idea of it – death in every breath you took; blood under the grass, the sand, the soil. Making everyone unhappy, the whole town, the whole of Normandy probably. Uncle Christophe most of all.

But she knows now that Christophe is not always dissatisfied. In the cigar smoker's company at least, he is happy.

At the end of the first wall, her hand comes to a stop, turns and begins moving again, this time in slow cautious arcs. Soon the sideboard will be coming up. Last week it stabbed her in the hip, the spot still tender to the touch. Everywhere danger. Their old flat in London would have been far easier to manage. Any of the old flats in fact. The last place in Wembley best of all. There, everything seemed little more than an arm's stretch away. A whole year they had stayed there; she had begun to think of it as home. Spicy smells on the stairs; giddy Indian music. Raps on the door when her mother went out in the evening, asking if she was alright. Ancient honeyed voices. This house is too big; all that space she loved as a child, she's afraid of now and the furniture has become her enemy. She remembers the rooms: a sun-kissed kitchen, bases of pots glinting like big coins from a rack. The long sitting-room. Le Salon, they called it, the same name as the hairdresser's they'd once lived above in Ipswich. There was a square table in the centre of the hall, tall white flowers in a vase that left a waft of piss on the air. In the evenings, the dining-room table heavily-laid; napkins that spread to the size of her skirt. It had been like staying in a small hotel, everywhere a touch of formality. Except for the space beyond the back garden that Christophe had left, he said, 'to become its sauvage self.'

L'herbage he called it. Her first port of call once all the cheek kissing stuff was out of the way. She would run down the back garden path, through the small blue wooden gate, long grass lashing her bare legs and flicking against her open palms. There, turning herself into a carousel, everything dipping and twirling around her – the neighbouring orchards, the distant glitter-grey sea, the vast beige beaches. Then cutting to a stop and squaring herself like a windmill, she would wait for the blur to settle. And there it was, the first holiday view of the house: the clipped back garden; the curly iron furniture; the steep-hipped roof, and of course, the cat reaching for, but never quite catching the mouse. It was what she missed most of all, during the sisters' three year silence.

She tugs on the lead. The hoover like an obedient dog, comes to her.

She feels tired suddenly, the zip gone out of her plan. But to back out now would be to throw away all those small triumphs already clocked up this morning. Last night she had decided that this was how it should be: her first solo run. No watching eyes. No guiding voices. A surprise, she could later call it. A thank you of sorts for Aunt Babs for all her kindness, like the farewell pictures she used to draw for her when she was a child. They came by ferry and train in those days. Often they hitch-hiked from Calais, telephoning Babs from the local station, pretending to have just stepped off the Paris-bound train. On the return journey there was no need to pretend. There would always be 'a little something' slipped into her mother's bag. Aunt Bab's car not yet out of earshot before her mother had the envelope whipped out and was slitting it open with her index finger.

This time, they came by airplane and taxi.

'Well, this is it then,' her mother had sighed as the taxi pulled up. 'No turning back now.'

It hadn't occurred to her until that moment, that this house would no longer be for holidays. This house was where she would learn how to be blind.

'What happened, my darling?' Aunt Babs has asked more than once and in more than one way.

'What happened that day?'

'I don't remember Aunt Babs.'

'You don't remember anything? Not even getting into the car?'

'Nothing, not a thing. I told the police already.'

'But I'm not the police sweetheart, am I? You can tell me. Did you know the driver then? Or, did he give you a lift – just tell me this, were you hitch-hiking? Alright then - did the man give your mum any money – can you remember that?'

'I told you. I told the police. All blank. Nothing.'

Later her mother questioning the questions.

'Did she ask you anything – you know, about the accident?'

'Never mentioned it. Not a word.'

'Did you tell her anything?'

'How could I tell her anything? I told you, I don't remember.'

A few days into the last holiday, the row had taken place. She had hardly known what it was all about except there had been a party the night before in Rouen and her mother hadn't come home.

'You can't do that sort of thing around here.' Babs had said, 'and certainly not while staying in this house.'

The two sisters had stood, icy and pale, the kitchen table between them.

They had called each other names; it had been difficult to know who was the accuser, who the accused:

Tramp! I'm a tramp? At least I'm not a Gold-digger? You're calling me a … You've some nerve, you bloody drunkard …

Drunkard? How dare you call me a drunkard and you nothing but a glorified…

Prostitute? He's my husband …

Husband? He bought and paid for you and you probably cost less than a housekeeper.

At least I have a home. You can't even take care of your own child.

Yes but at least I have a child, more than you'll ever get from that walking corpse.

Bitch. You're like a fucking bitch on heat you are. Any man at all. Selfish, selfish, selfish …

By then she was already upstairs pulling their clothes out of deep-mouthed drawers and rolling them into their baggage. They had walked into a late afternoon. Down the long road with its sturdy shuttered houses and the scent of apples floating on sea air. Her mother quietly crying at intervals all the way to London. Words had been spoken, she said, that could never in a million years be forgotten. But only three years gone by, and all forgotten now.

'What happened – it's a terrible thing. But at least it has brought us together again,' Aunt Babs said the day they arrived. Both sisters sobbing. Sobbing then laughing, then sobbing again.

She steps out of her slippers, begins feeling for dirt with the sole of her foot. Her feet have become almost as important as her hands. In some cases, even more important. Because it's all about tasks now, as they never tire telling her, learning them, developing them, honing them into skills. Hoovering for coordination, gardening for the senses. Tasks and skills. These two words are always there in the background, snipping at each other like blades in a scissors. The word 'blind' is no longer used and *l'aveugle* is a word she only hears from the French: the gardener, the cleaner, the old woman who works in the *boulangerie*. A peasant word, her aunt Babs said when she asked, a vulgar peasant word that should be ignored. But she has caught the word *l'aveugle* on Christophe's conversations and he is far from a peasant.

She wanted to know; to have someone say it. '*Qu'est que c'est – une aveugle?*' she asked Madam Millet.

'*Une aveugle est une aveugle.*'

She put it another way –

'*Une aveugle - c'est moi?*'

'*C'est toi ma cherie, c'est toi.*'

'En anglais on dit 'blind.'

'*Ah blegnd,*' Madam Millet said.

She pulls the lead of the hoover forward, locates the holes in the socket and coaxes the plug into place. Her foot probes its squat smooth back, then finding the control button, heels it. The hoover begins to sing. Head cocked, she listens for the subtle changes in its voice – the cackle of too much dust in its throat, the catch of a toothpick, the satiated whine that tells her it's full to the brim.

The rain will outdo these sounds, she thinks. The rain will deafen this room.

*

She wakes with the taint of apple brandy on her breath and it comes back to her then, the bottle's short neck, the dry 'toc' of its cork as she released it, above all the impressive weight of it in her hands.

She'd only wanted to move it out of the way, and then out of curiosity, had opened it. The warm breath of Christmas, the slant of the alcohol – of course, it had to be tasted. She'd gone at it like a saxophone player, bending to it, latching on with her mouth, then raising it with both hands and walloping it back. The shock of it then, like something out to kill her. She saw it as a lizard-like creature, swift and hot and spiky, a sharp swishing tail and claws made of tiny, accurate flames. She'd had to hang her tongue out of her mouth to cool it down. It wasn't a drink at all; it was liquid fire. No wonder Christophe was dour, if this was one of his pleasures.

The attack subsided, her breath returned, she'd hastily put the bottle back as she had found it, still shaken but wholly relieved to be shut of it. And then a few moments later, she'd gone back for more.

It had made her feel better, that's all. The burning sensation quickly softened and everything had become lighter: her spirits, her limbs, the tight ache that for months had been lodged in her stomach. And the worry of course: the what next? Where next? Who next?

And now here she was, lying in bed, raw throat and a whiff of nearby vomit. Her nose seeking it out - the pillow, the top-sheet, the hem of the quilt. But in these things she can only find the coy lavender scent of Madam Millet's laundry.

Fragments begin to appear, lengthening, widening, gaining substance. Her mother. The fight. Finally the whoosh of vomit.

She'd been trying to persuade the hoover to return to the cupboard. A clacking, clattering racket, and then a sudden grip on her arm and the sensation of being dragged backwards, away from the cupboard, out of the hall and with one final shove, into her room.

Spitty whispers behind closed doors.

'What do you think you are *doing?* Are you … ? You *are!* My God, you're drunk. Drunk! I don't believe this! I just can't believe this.'

Her mother stepping back. Stepping in again.

'Walking around the house, drunk at ten o'clock on a Saturday morning! Drunk and not even dressed! You can see right through that nightie. Right through it.'

'Well, no I can't actually.'

She had wanted to fight with her mother, wanted to say all those things that she'd been keeping boxed up in her head. Call her the names, she'd been silently calling her, ever since the accident. To destroy her mother with words. But she'd felt sick suddenly. A nudging sensation in her stomach like a hand groping for a way out of a tent. Behind the sick feeling, the vague satisfaction of knowing her mother couldn't shout, no matter how much she wanted to.

'Might I remind you, that we are here on sufferance? Might I remind you that only for them we would be walking the streets. Is that what you want?'

'Can I bring my hoover?'

'Is that supposed to be funny?'

Her mother grabbing her by the shoulders then: cigarette smoke still warm in her mouth; puffs of sour angry breath, the leady smell of last night's sneaky vodka. 'What do you want me to do? What do you expect me to *doooo*?'

A rag doll shake. A silent pause and then her mother gasping, 'You know something? I could fuckingwell kill you sometimes.'

'You know something? I wish you fuckingwell would!'

The two of them then, caught in a net. Carefully, silently, pulling at each other, tugging, slapping, thumping. Choking on each other's sobs.

*

After the brandy she sleeps for hours. It's all she wants now; it's her only comfort. The way it drags her down and swallows her in, depositing her in a hinterland where anything might happen.

When she finally wakes, the house is silent. She knows it's late and that everyone has long since gone to bed. Yet there's a presence beside her. For a second she almost cries out like a little girl, I'm sorry Mummy, I really am. But then an unknown hand comes and touches her arm, strokes her hair, lifts her. A spoon rests on her bottom lip, the taste of warm apple and cinnamon making her weep.

'Shhhh shhhh,' the voice says, '*Ma petite, ma pauvre aveugle*. Shhh shh.'

*

It's market day in early October when her mother leaves. There is no warning, no fuss over packing the night before, no goodbyes.

Yet she knows when she leaves for the market with Babs that when they return her mother will no longer be there.

She wears sunglasses and links her aunt's arm through the town and for a while she forgets that she can't actually see all the things Babs is describing. In the park there is the tender sounds of old men playing boules.

Aunt Babs takes her to a café and teaches her how to place the order, '*deux café, deux gaufres*. Don't forget your *s'il vous plait*.

'We'll have you speaking French in no time,' she says then, 'when your mum comes at Christmas, she won't believe it.'

'At Christmas?'

'Oh sweetheart I am ever so sorry. But your mum? Well she needs to get away for a while. It was too upsetting for her to say goodbye. But by Christmas—'

'She won't be back, Babs. I know she won't.'

For a while there is only the sound of the café and the sound of Babs smoking her cigarette.

'Maybe you're better off with us my darling,' Bab says then, 'Uncle Christophe will do everything he can to help you. And I'm here for you. You can talk to me, tell me anything, you know.'

'About the accident, you mean?'

'No. But it might do you no harm to talk about it.'

'Why can't anyone believe me? I don't remember. I really don't remember.'

*

Her dreams are more often in French now and the rented flats of the past have all but disappeared. Old classrooms have melted into the dark, as well as the toys and the friends she has sometimes had along the way. Only faces have remained. Never ageing, never changing, looking just as they did, the last time she saw them – even if she can't always remember who owns which one, or the part it may have played in her life.

What she does remember is the pure light of an English winter, the dark green of passing fields and the ditches fudged with brown ice. Bare, ink-black trees. A large tawny bird overhead. The roll and sway of the road; slate grey, stitched white up the middle. The bird again, stalled mid-air, eyeballing some small life in a field below. She was going to point it out - in fact, she had lifted her hand to do so. But in the front of the car, her mother and the man were preoccupied. Her mother's blonde hair bunned on top of the fur coat she had bought the week before in a second-hand shop. The rind of the man's neck over a navy, velvety collar. His voice refined and a little worried.

Behind the voices, a Christmas choir on a low-set radio. And that peculiar sense of peace that had suddenly come over her. Peculiar because, just a moment before her gullet had been twisted with silent rage at her mother and this posh-voiced, velvet-collared man. She'd been holding a riding cap she'd found on the floor. A hollow interior lined with red satin, the name of a girl on an embroidered tag. She had been about to ask, her voice cheeky and prepared to spoil something – who owns this? Your wife, is it? Your daughter?

Up front the words getting tighter, interrupting each other. Her mother's voice thinning to a screech; his weighted but determined.

She still can't quite find the words, nor does she want to. Only the colours interest her now, the shapes that contained them. Painting them over and over in her head in an effort to hold onto them. Sunlight squirting through trees. Harsh yellow sunlight, cat-clawing her eyes. She would have closed them but had wanted to see what the bird would do next. The sound of the indicator clicking. And the engine, stalling on the junction, jolting every couple of seconds like a nervous child waiting to jump into the turn of a skipping rope. Out on the main road a glinting river of multi-coloured steel, car after car after car.

Through the window, green fields, black trees, white ice. A tilt of auburn, mid-air.

Anne Enright

Anne Enright is the inaugural Laureate for Irish Fiction. A leading contemporary voice, her work has won many awards including the Man Booker for *The Gathering* in 2007 and the Andrew Carnegie Medal for Excellence in Fiction for *The Forgotten Waltz* in 2012. She lives and works in Dublin, her native town.

Three Stories About Love

1.

'You know what I think?' she said. 'That guy never did a day's harm. He never did a moment's harm in his life.'

She seemed so fierce, he wished he had not brought the subject up. He said, 'Right.' He shifted in his seat – a high stool on the edge of the bar – and he thought about her forearm resting on the counter top in front of him. He saw it so clearly, was so taken by the simplicity of it, he didn't even realise he was making a move on her until she took this particular part of her anatomy out of view. They were drunk. They would, possibly, sleep together. He felt immense regret. He wondered did women feel it too – this weight. Then she said, 'I'm going,' and she slid off the stool; buckling a little in the knees, when her feet touched the floor. But she recovered, and gathered her bag like her wounded dignity, and departed.

She came back in to get her phone, which was left on the counter top, and she turned to him and said, 'I just wanted to say, that guy has never done a day's harm in his life.' So he took her by the forearm – her skin was cool – and, with a toss of his head, indicated the door.

'What?'

'Come on,' he said.

The club was in a basement, and they kissed in the area outside, the drink hitting them both in the blast of cold air. But she was too drunk. Really. His heart wasn't in it. Not that he was turning it down. But he hung on to one of the railings and swung round and sat down on a step – in his good suit, actually, his interview suit – and he said, 'He's just stupid. I mean, he may be harmless but he's also just stupid.'

'You're the stupid one,' she said. 'You're the one who is stupid.'

He was a straightforward sort of guy. He wanted people to have a good time. He wanted a wife who was small and blonde. He had never really thought it through, but if he ever pictured his wife and children, she was always small and she was always fair-haired and sweet-natured and tough in her own way.

And the children, for some reason, were always little curly headed girls. They had a big trampoline and a lovely squeal. And before all that – the small wife and the little girls in their house with the nice garden – he just wanted a good time.

It was just an unlikely start. That was all. A woman's arm, on a bar-top. She had a funny face. She didn't look like a wife and she didn't talk like a good time. And the length of her. She was very long. Even her arm was long.

'Maybe,' he said. 'Maybe I am stupid.'

'You're not stupid,' she said.

'I just lost my job,' he said.

She made her way past him, her trench coat brushing his shoulder. He turned to look at her legs as they left him.

'I have a job,' she said. 'I have a great job.'

She stood at the top of the steps and took a hat out of her bag. A mad looking wooly thing.

'Come on,' she said.

His backside was cold from the step. And it was still cold when they made it into the bed in her apartment on Barrow Street. She remarked on the coldness of it. And he would have left immediately afterwards, except he had more manners than that, and in the morning she was really nice.

He didn't take her number, though. He just couldn't. When the moment came he said, 'Look at that weather,' like he couldn't wait to get out in it. But he spent a lot of time checking out her Facebook page: Una Molloy – a slice of the mad hat, one eye, one eyebrow, a picture of sunflowers in a field, 523 friends. A few days later she asked him to become number 524 and they went to the pictures and back to her place where there was wine in the fridge, she said. They did this a few times, because it was cheap, and they talked about cycling along Dublin Bay some Sunday morning, but it was all pretty awkward. He felt like a man pretending to have a girlfriend; opening and closing his wardrobe door on a row of empty suits.

One night she took him to the theatre. She said the tickets were free, though he did not really believe her and they sat in the darkness watching two guys go over and back on the stage, in some endless thing that was like purgatory: it was like watching paint dry.

'I think that might be the point,' she said. Her hair was brown and she wore flat shoes because she was so tall, and he really did think she had something lovely about her, something that was beyond him. Her long arm on the rest between their seats, bare in the darkness.

They kept drinking, on stage. A woman arrived and they all talked about a big painting that was hanging on the back wall. The woman was supposed to be married to one of the men and shagging the other one and the husband suggested champagne, so they all said, 'What ho' and it took them a while to realise that he couldn't get the cork out. The actor twisted it, and put the bottle between his knees, and they realised that he was trying not to laugh – the whole theatre realised it. He was standing in front of the awful painting, tugging at the cork, and his voice was getting smaller and lighter, as he ran out of lines.

The woman, who was smoking a herbal cigarette, looked over at him. After a moment of astonishing silence, he picked up some glasses and pretended to pour into them, with the cork still plugged in. The three of them clinked – weak with it. They pretended to drink, the tears streaming out of their eyes.

'I would just like to say,' said the husband. His voice trailed into a whimper and, after a very long moment, he tried again.

'I would just like to say.' There was a high wobble in there, like a dog yowling. The actors were in pain. The other man turned away. The woman bent slightly and held on to the back of a chair.

'Jesus that was funny,' he said, afterwards, when they reached the foyer.

'I don't know why they call it corpsing,' she said. 'But it is. It's like a dead body starting to speak or something.'

'It was really funny,' he said.

'I mean though, nobody dies.'

'No,' he said, and he looked at her, remembering the laughter killing their lines on stage, and him, in the fifth row, knowing about love suddenly, knowing it would be brilliant, reaching his hand over to touch her arm.

2.

Elaine dreamt that the baby could speak. She dreamt that the baby was, in fact talking to her, hugely and at length; endless sentences full of big words and all in a voice that was expressive and sweet. The baby was actually very interesting. Everyone in the dream wore wooly jumpers and A-line skirts with knee-high boots, and they sat in a café that looked like a painting of a café in the centre of Dublin, in the 1970s. Outside, through the canted frame of the door, you could hear the Grafton Street buskers. Inside, something terrible was about to happen, and the baby did not care.

Elaine woke to heartburn and the feeling that she was stuck to the bed, not just by the heat, but by the pull of the entire planet that lay between her and Grafton Street these days. She was in a room in Melbourne, and the baby was inside her, inside a room Melbourne. Each morning, she woke two seconds before she realised where she was, though she never forgot she was pregnant, not even when she was asleep. And this morning she could not move for the massive weight of the world beneath her and the weight of the baby above. She felt across the sheet for Joe and found him already gone.

'Joe!' she said. 'Joe!'

He came back in from the kitchen.

'You all right?' The dream had left her crying.

'What's up?'

She missed her mother. Really missed her. And it was a very big planet.

'Just,' she said. 'You're not far away until you have a baby, and then you're really, really far away.'

'I know,' he said. 'But there's lots of people here. I'm here.'

Sometimes, the moon was in the morning sky in Melbourne and Elaine could never remember if it happened that way in Dublin or if the moon only appeared at night, there, or in the afternoon. It was like she had forgotten what way the world turns. She put her hand on her belly as the baby woke and shifted, right on cue.

'Oh,' she said.

'What's it doing in there?'

'Hungry,' said Elaine.

3.

She went to see her father in the home and he was sitting up in bed, with a cup of tea on the trolley table. The air was very warm and completely clapped out, that was the first thing that hit her. There weren't three molecules of oxygen left in there, it was like inhaling sock. The second thing she noticed was the bright look in his faded old eye, because that was the way the dementia took him, strangely – it turned him into the opposite of himself.

'Hello, my darling,' he said

Maybe he didn't know who she was.

'Lara.'

He did know her. Or, at least, he knew her name. She pulled the big chair around towards the bed and sat down.

'How are you, my love?' he said.

My love. This was new. This was more again. Her father never called her 'darling', never had — not when she was small, not when she was sad, not when her mother died, not once. It just wasn't one of his words.

'I am well, Daddy. I am very well, thanks. How are you?'

'Ah,' he said. He smiled a little, and let the question go.

'Would you like your tea Daddy, will I bring that across for you?'

She was up out of the chair again, pulling the trolley across the bed. The tea looked neglected, perhaps even cold. Her father made a face when he finally got the cup to his mouth, but then he sucked the tea out, quite greedily, and it was gone. He felt for the saucer as he set the empty cup down, and she remembered that distances were a trouble to him now, he lived a little by touch, with the sight in one eye gone.

So she touched him. She took his hand and remembered the hands she knew as a child; brown from the sun with their mysterious, collapsible veins.

'That's a great bit of weather,' she said and he turned from her to the window. The sky was a summer blue, with white and ragged black clouds; the black smudged where they turned to falling rain.

'Yes,' he said.

He didn't go downhill at a regular rate. It was steps and stairs. He would be fine for a while, and then very agitated, and when he came out of the agitation he would be at a lower level, where he would stay calm for a while. There were a few weeks when he was very disturbed — roaring and shouting — and that was hard. No one liked the woman who ran the place, she was too pragmatic, she seemed to enjoy it a little. They gave him something called Atavan and that was very painful for them all because the drug was like tying him physically to the bed. But then they reduced the dose and there he was, back again. Or there was this man who called her 'darling'.

There was a tap on the door, and a little glimmer of the old Francis Mulvaney came through when the carer put a head round it to say, 'You want a hot drop, Francis?'

It was Benjamin, one of the best of them: Benjamin from Uganda, with beautiful old-fashioned English, a face bursting with goodness and good health – sometimes Lara thought she could ask him to look after her too, that she could just bring him home. But there was a twitch of distaste from her father and Lara could not help thinking, 'That's what you get, you old bigot, in your old age. That's life's little joke for you, now.'

And of course she regretted the thought immediately, though there was no escaping it: her father had been, all her life, a man of strong opinions, and many of them wrong.

When Benjamin went back to his tea trolley in the corridor, her father checked around him to see that they were, indeed, alone, then he mouthed something at her and ran a finger across his throat.

'Sorry?'

He slashed at his throat again. Then he hissed the word, a little louder.

'Priest!'

'Oh. Benjamin isn't a priest, Daddy.'

He gave her a high, sardonic look, then turned as Benjamin came in with the tea.

'Thank you so much,' he said. 'Thank you. Thank you.'

'You are most welcome,' said Benjamin.

It could be worse, she thought. Her father doing the full Cyril Cusack, sitting up like an old bishop in the bed.

'Goodbye now, Father. All best!'

After the door closed he sat for a while. Then he saw the tea in his hand and he drank it with the same pulled face and the same greed as the last cup. He set the cup down.

'So tell me,' he said. 'How is everything?'

'Hanging in there,' she said. 'Just about.'

'Good,' he said.

And Lara was suddenly bitter because things weren't great, actually, and her father would never know this. Even if she told him her troubles, he would forget them before ten minutes had passed. And it occurred to her that there was great freedom in this, she might say anything at all. She might tell him the truth: 'We are fighting all the time, Daddy.' Or, 'I haven't slept with him in two years, Daddy.' She could say, 'Oh Daddy, if only you'd died when the market was high,' because Francis Mulvaney was a great believer in the market, he had gone in there hell for leather, saying, 'Wait till I'm gone and then you'll see.' And now the market was not high, and the man in the bed was not gone. And he never knew how wrong – just by staying alive – he had proved himself to be.

'You're looking well,' he said.

'Thank you,' she said.

'A little old,' he said. 'I hadn't expected you to be this old.'

'Well,' she said.

'That's the way of it.'

'That's right,' she said.

The home was costing 750 euros a week under the fair deal, and this is what she got in return – a man who forgot to call her 'stupid' and called her 'darling' instead. Cheap at the price. A man who called her Lara because he had named her Lara. Because, in the deep freakish unknowable past, her parents sat through *Dr Zhivago* once and walked out of the cinema holding hands.

She lifted his old hand and kissed it.

'I'm forty-seven Daddy.'

'My goodness.'

'Can you believe that?'

The skin was very white.

'Are they putting cream on you Daddy? Does Benjamin do your lotions?'

He did not answer. He had lifted his other hand to touch her hair or – no – to point at something over her shoulder.

'Look,' he said.

'What?' said Lara, slightly spooked. She glanced behind her to see nothing there; a peach-coloured wall, a ribbon of paper along the dado line in apricot and jade green. I'd rather be taken out and shot, Lara thought, than be looking at that as I died. But her father's face was happy, blissed out.

'Look at your wings,' he said.

Susan Stairs

Susan Stairs received her Masters in Creative Writing from University College Dublin in 2009 and her story 'The Rescue' was shortlisted for the Davy Byrnes Irish Writing Award the same year. Her debut novel, *The Story of Before*, was published in 2013 and she has twice been awarded a Literature Bursary by The Arts Council of Ireland. She worked for many years in the art business and has written several books around the subject of Irish art and artists. Her second novel, *The Boy Between*, will be published in 2015. She lives in Dublin with her family.

As Seen From Space

Wednesday afternoon, mid-November. Fine drizzle drips from a cardboard-grey sky, sieving a pearly mesh over the sea of parked cars in the schoolyard. Jo swings in through the gateposts, side-eyeing a lanky senior sloping out the front door as she slots her Fiesta between two hulking people carriers. His hair is barbershop neat, making a tennis ball of his skull. Hands dunked in trouser pockets, he passes a pair of navy-jumpered juniors hauling a metal desk between them. Then he stops, doubles back to help. The trio shuffle along, the juniors' boyband-style fringes flapping against their eyes. Jo wonders if Glenn would stop to help like that. Or if he'd ever been given the job of relocating classroom furniture. It would be nice to know.

Newmount is not unlike Glenn's last school. A flat-roofed, rectangular concrete box set in a lake of oily tarmac with a sentry of silver birch lining the boundary wall. Jo keeps her head down as she makes her way inside. In the carpet-tiled foyer, a clear-skinned lad in a well-ironed shirt and properly knotted tie hands her a photocopied sheet. 'This is a list of teachers and their corresponding room numbers,' he says, his lips carefully negotiating a mouthful of wire-braced teeth. 'And a plan of the ground floor. I can show you round if you like.'

'No thanks,' Jo says. 'I'll manage.' The boy reminds her of Glenn. Not because he looks like him, more because he doesn't.

In the corridor, the floor covering changes to something bird's-nest-brown and shiny that squeaks under her rubber-soled boots. Rivers of condensation meander down the rain-speckled windows and the strip lighting above coats everything in a hospital-bright glaze. Framed photo collages line the walls, three, four deep: smiling sporting heroes; gold cup winners; teams of cheering medal-wearers. Other peoples' children. No point in stopping to look.

A baby-faced junior rattling a trolley offers tea and bourbon biscuits to the rows of parents waiting on beige plastic chairs. On the right, a couple exit a classroom, straight-backed, heads high. The woman – blonde, orange lipstick, skin stretched thinly over her cheekbones – thanks the teacher loud enough for everyone to hear. Jo catches the stripe-suited father's eyes – wide and searching under raised grey brows. *I'm the parent of a high-achiever*, they clearly say. Jo looks away. She doesn't want him knowing she can tell.

First on her list is Geography. Mr Boland, Room 17. She sits down, takes out her phone, the thickness of her long hair a screen against the dandruff-shouldered man to her left. She texts Glenn. *Anything you want me to say to Mr Boland?* Glenn stayed home today. It's not the first time he's faked a migraine.

No, comes the swift reply. *Did Dad turn up?*

Not yet, she replies. The bald truth of a straight *No* seems too harsh.

The man beside her separates himself from his chair when his turn comes. Jo moves along, shifting into the vacant seat where the remaining heat of his body seeps into her own. She knows Donal isn't coming. He texted last night. An 'important client visit', apparently. *Just as well it's my day off then,* she'd replied.

Mr Boland's handshake is tight and warm. 'Ah, yes. Glenn,' he says when she introduces herself. He looks down, scrutinizes the spiral-bound foolscap pad on his desk, runs his forefinger across the width of the lined page. The skin on his hands is dry, his nails ridged and flaking. A shy spring of sandy curls peeps from the neck of his pale yellow polo shirt. And his hair, coarse like fraying rope, creeps over the collar of his corduroy jacket. A poster taped to the breeze block wall behind him explains 'Weathering and Erosion' in cartoon drawings of rocks and rain and sun.

'So,' he says, leaning back in his chair, pyramiding his fingers. 'How do you feel Glenn is getting on?'

Jo swallows the sound of his voice. It slips easy down her throat into the pit of her stomach and lies there, weighty and poised, like a resting snake. She finds his eyes. Blueish green. Tiny planet earths as seen from space. And something else. Maybe it's that he looks like how she imagined. Or that there's something about him she already knows. It's been happening a lot lately – Jo seeing faces she's sure she recognises. On the street. In the supermarket. Some she forgets about as soon as they disappear. But others return in the night, oozing from the darkness when she lies down to sleep.

'I ...' she coughs. She wants to say Glenn tells her nothing and she has no idea how he's getting on. But her answer comes out as '... Fine. I think he's getting along fine.' She bites the fleshy inside of her lip and tries to make out the neat black-biroed upside-down names and grades on Mr Boland's notepad. But he comes forward and covers them, resting his elbows on the page.

'Let me show you his most recent homework,' he says, turning to the tower block of hardback copies piled on the desk. Jo studies his face – the promontory of his nose, the outcrop of his chin – and when she blinks his profile flares neon-white behind her eyelids. He slides the top hardback onto his palm, flicks through its pages. 'I haven't had a chance to talk to Glenn about it yet. Not a bad attempt. But I do have certain issues.' He turns the copy around and hands it to Jo. 'Namely the omission of the letter "O" every time he's used the word "country".'

Jo takes a look. She doesn't need to search. Mr Boland has underlined each offending word in red, leaving the skin of the page patterned with scars. She spells it out in her head – c-u-n-t-r-y – four, maybe five times, her cheeks on fire and her lips paper-dry. It could hardly be a mistake. Surely Glenn knew what he was doing? Embarrassed and flustered she says, 'I'm sorry, I—'

'No, no,' Mr Boland interrupts. 'No need for you to apologise. That's not why I showed you.' He cocks his head to one side. 'But ... Glenn is fifteen. I'm sure he knows how to spell a word like country.'

'Fourteen,' Jo corrects. 'He's not fifteen till January.'

Mr Boland breathes hard up his nose, lets the air out in a soft sigh. 'What I mean is, he's old enough to know better.'

She knows he's right. But she won't allow herself to admit it. 'It's going to take him a while to settle in,' she says. 'Just give him time.'

He looks at her for several *are-you-being-serious* moments. 'Is Glenn happy here?' he asks, eventually. 'Why did you choose to move him to Newmount?'

Her words tumble in an unordered stream. 'It wasn't a ... I mean ... our house ... we had to sell ... his father and I ... it's been hard on Glenn, he ...'

Mr Boland picks a biro from the desk, makes an axle of it, twirling it between the twin wheels of his hands. From the playing fields behind the school, rugby practice is played out. A concerto of team-boy roars and short, teacher-blown whistle blasts.

'I understand,' he says.

She hates that Mr Boland understands. That he sees the shape of their family storm. She watches as he places the biro on his notepad, carefully aligning it with the metal spiral and then lifts the blood-red mug that sits on the desk.

'If Glenn is having any problems,' he says and takes a sip. 'He should see the guidance counsellor.' His map-of-the-world gaze is a target for hers over the rim. It's like that with all men now. She wants to look in their eyes and find things she thinks she knows.

Mr Boland glances at his notepad now, scratches his cheek. 'Forty-one percent,' he says. 'Glenn's midterm exam result.' His eyebrows lift. 'He'll need to work a lot harder if he wants to pass in June. But let's see how things go. We'll reassess his progress after Christmas.' He reaches for the copybook. 'If there's anything else, you know where I am.'

Jo's hand wavers, trembles. Is that it? What does he think? That everything will have changed by then? That by some miracle Glenn will be a different boy? Her grip slackens as she stretches her arm over the desk. The copybook slips, hits the mug, knocks it over the side. Coffee splashes her jeans, her boots, before the mug hits the floor and explodes. Jagged crimson shards skitter like shrapnel in every direction.

Clumsily, she gets to her feet then stoops to start gathering the pieces.

Mr Boland rises, shoves his chair back noisily, comes out from behind the desk. 'It's fine. Honestly. I'll get someone in to sort it out.'

She stops, straightens, stands. Dizzy. Room spinning. Starry black before her eyes. He takes brisk steps to the door, holds it open, waits for her to leave. As her body passes his, the breath of some kind of history ices her skin.

Unsettled, she makes her way along the corridor, turns the wrong corner. A wave of boys buffalo in through a side door from the playing field. Muck-smeared. Steaming. The bulk of them jostling, shoving. She squeezes in against the cold wall to let them pass. Hard-muscled chests glance her shoulder. Studs clack-clack over the floor, the sound of sharpened nails hammering her brain. She screams inside. A small, thin scream that only she can hear.

'Take it easy lads,' someone says to the hoard. 'There's actual humans in here today.'

It's the grey-uniformed senior with the tennis-ball skull. Up close. Curved jaw, poppy-seeded and sure. Black eyes, lake-bottomed like a young seal's. She looks into them and thinks she sees it there. The knowing of him. How Donal used to be. Present. She should have asked for more than that. Shouldn't have made it so easy. She'd let him find the soft parts and wear them down. Until everything inside was showing. Until only the hard bits remained.

The black eyes look away and then he's gone. They've all gone. Chilly space surrounds her, solidifies the melting fact that she's here. On her own. Without.

She's in the car when she remembers she has more teachers to see. There's a point, as she nears the school gates, when she could stop, go back inside, wait in line again. But she drives on. And when she parks in the tight lasso of the cul-de-sac she realises she can't recall the journey she's just made at all. Like she blinked and now she's here, outside the house, trying to stall the burning beats of her heart.

Glenn doesn't look around when she enters the room. She watches from the doorway, the fallen statue of him stretched on the leather couch. On the TV, a girl in gold tassels and mirror-glass heels writhes to a song Jo has never heard or doesn't remember. Glenn's left foot, socked in grimy white, taps a beat against a cushion.

'Glenn,' she says, bending to switch on the lamp. *Glenn.* Donal had thought the name strong. Definite. And – importantly for him – unable to be shortened. She'd seen it as a place where echoes live. A space between mountains. What's gone, instead of what once was there.

The shadows in the room shrink in the yellow glow. She draws a breath. 'Glenn,' she says again. 'How—' And then she stops. What would she be if not for him? Where would the love go? It scares her sometimes, scares her now. She can't ask, can't bring herself to mention what Mr Boland showed her. She keeps her eyes on her son's head of fair curls, waiting for the turn that will show her his face.

'How're you feeling?' she asks.

'OK.'

'I didn't get to see them all. The teachers, I mean. I'll sort it out another day.'

He shrugs, eyes lasered to the screen. The gold-tasselled girl is now in silver gauze, her toned and muscled curves unhidden by her flimsy cloak. Jo moves into the room now, stands in front of him. She sighs. 'Turn that down.' He lifts the remote, aims, fires, drops it back on his thighs. 'Look at me, Glenn,' she says. 'I deserve that at least.'

'Yeah well maybe I don't want to.' The sentence whips hard, catches tight around her neck. The serpent of Mr Boland's voice wakens, struggles to panic up out of her throat. *How do you feel Glenn is getting on?* She swallows it down. She feels like she's choking. *Fine. He's getting along fine.*

'Mr Boland,' she says. 'He suggested maybe … maybe you could see the guidance counsellor.'

'Him? What for? What were you saying about me?'

'Nothing, I … He just thought if … Look, you don't have to. Only if you feel like it.'

'I don't.'

It's not my fault, Glenn, she wants to say. You can't keep blaming me. You understand that? None of this is my fault. She waits, studies his face for something. Anything. She wants to go to him, to kneel and fit her arms around the tender curving of his ribs. But there's too much hardness in the way. More rock than she's able to climb.

'Are you hungry?' she asks. 'I'll make dinner in a few.'

'No. I had a pizza.'

'Oh. OK.' She walks across the room. 'I'm going to lie down for a little while. Maybe we can watch something later? You see if there's anything good on.'

He speaks to the TV. 'So I'm guessing Dad didn't turn up?'

'No. Sorry. He couldn't make it.'

She's glad to close the door on his silence.

Upstairs in the bedroom, Jo looks out the window. The night is down now, spectral and empty on the other side of the glass. She pulls the curtains, makes sure their edges overlap, so that no part of what's out there can creep inside. There was nothing familiar about Mr Boland. She knows that now. It was just her eyes searching for a connection in a place where there was none. That's what she misses most. The gaze of someone who loves her back. Who knows her. Who's known her for a long time.

She lies down on the bed, looks up to the ceiling. She hates this house. Brand new and soulless. No corners she doesn't know about, no hidden secrets someone might have left behind. It will never surprise her. Donal hasn't been in it. Around eleven every Saturday, he texts Jo the word 'Here' and waits outside with the engine running, even when she replies to say Glenn's still in the shower. And at six on Sunday evening, he drives away before Glenn reaches the front door. Sometimes she catches the blocky shape of him behind the wheel and she can't believe he's not a stranger.

The landscape of their lives is not the same. The layers that built it up, even and sure, have shifted. It wasn't a natural thing, borne out of some fault line they'd always suspected was there. It was unforeseen. An avalanche she couldn't have predicted. And Glenn in the middle of it all. Buried under the fallen snow.

Out of the night, they come. Zip-wiring through the dark, ghostly and glowing like flame-lit masks. She's not sure if she's asleep, if she's seeing them in her head or if they're here, right in front of her face. The pair of planet earths appear, forest-green and ocean-blue, spinning out of the black. Close, so close. Then they whirl away. Or maybe it's she who's moving, higher and higher, retreating into space. And now she's looking down, at the shrunken world she's left behind. White bones lie on the bed. She watches as they gather themselves and float across the floor. They toe their way down the stairs, feet out in the void, snapping a jolt every time they find a step.

There's no sound in the room and the lamp is out. He's still there, planked on the couch, his outline silvered by something bright outside. She sees herself gently shaking his shoulder, his sleepy moan echoing to empty before it finds her. She's placing a hand on his chest now and, from so far away, can feel the truth of him pumping hard against her palm.

'Hey,' she says softly. 'I've something to ask you.'

He's moving, legs stretching, arms shuddering awake. Closer now and his eyes are invisible as they open. Only from above are they held by her, their deep-lake blackness staring into her own. Her hand goes to his head now and she wants to cry out, to tell herself he's someone else, he's not who she thinks he is at all. But even as she's cradling the shaven sandiness of his skull, she's breathing warm against the perfect shell of his ear.

'Tell me,' she whispers, the words spiralling soft around her tongue. 'I want to know. How is it that you spell ... country?'

Mary Costello

Mary Costello grew up in Galway and now lives in Dublin. Her collection of stories, *The China Factory*, was nominated for the 2012 Guardian First Book Award. Her first novel, *Academy Street,* won the Eason's Novel of the Year Award and was named overall Irish Book of the Year 2014. It was shortlisted for the 2014 Costa First Novel Prize, and featured on BBC Radio 4's Book at Bedtime.

My Little Pyromaniac

I had not thought of S for a long time. Then, one evening last summer just after I'd moved in here, he came walking out of the house next door. I was getting out of my car and there was just enough time for each of us to acknowledge the other, the way new neighbours do, before he got into his own car. I walked to my front door, holding myself carefully, aware of the woman and children coming behind him, then the thunk of car doors closing.

I stood in my hall, picturing the car moving along the street, the woman – his wife? – beside him, the boy and girl in the back; he, silent at the wheel, confounded by the sight of me after all these years, and the realisation that I was now living next door. And the thought that, from now on, we might, at any given moment, be only a few feet from each other, standing in our symmetrically positioned kitchens or bedrooms.

All the houses in this cul-de-sac are semi-detached, inhabited mostly by families with young children or teenagers. In the evenings the cars roll in, spilling out tired adults, children dragging coats and bags, sports gear, musical instruments. One evening, the little girl next door hopped out of S's car, dressed in a tutu. Her mother leaned into the back seat and took the child's bag and carried it into the house. She is a small, dark-haired woman, and appears to be much younger than S. The boy is about ten, the girl perhaps seven. I have watched them closely – I am not entirely convinced these are S's children.

When I was nineteen and still at university I fell in love with S. He was thirty-eight. He had a handsome, hewn face, a little like Warren Beatty's. He worked for a large investments company and lived in a beautiful Victorian redbrick with lamp-lit rooms and stained-glass panels in the front door. He was often abroad on business and sometimes a week or two would go by before I heard from him. Then we would meet and, if it suited him, I would stay over.

He would drop me off at college in his big car the next morning on his way to work or to the airport. Before I got out, I'd wait for him to say when we were to meet again. But he never did, and I carried a sickly feeling of loss and injury around with me all day. I'd let a few days pass and then I'd dial his number at night and listen to the ringing at the other end, imagining the street light shining in his front door and the lovely ivory Bakelite on the hall table echoing eerily through the house. Then, finally, a night would come when he would answer, and there would be a little pause after I said my name. He'd invite me over but I would hesitate, say that I had lectures in the morning. I had to show some restraint. I was afraid he would catch something in my voice or that even the Bakelite would betray me.

After we ended, I used to think I saw him coming towards me on the street, or entering, with other men in suits, expensive basement restaurants on St Stephen's Green at lunchtime on Fridays. Or, in more recent times, at the airport, when I'd come on those high shoe-shine chairs on the way to the departure gates and have to do a double take, thinking it was S sitting up there reading his newspaper while a young man polished his shoes. Once, about ten years ago, I was standing at a busy intersection near my apartment, trying to hail a taxi into town. It was a Thursday evening and darkness was falling, and all the passing taxis were occupied. I stood at the edge of the kerb to get the best view in all directions. Once or twice I met the eyes of car drivers as they slowed to turn left. Then a large, dark jeep, a Range Rover, approached. There was something tentative about the way it slowed and something familiar about the shape of the driver that made my heart jump. I was sure it was him. I tried not to look, but as it drew level the passenger window slid down and the man's eyes met mine. It was not S. The man looked directly into my eyes, strangely, intently, and then suddenly I knew what he wanted. He was propositioning me. I shrank back and turned and hurried along the footpath to a bus stop, with nothing left in my legs but terror. At the bus shelter I checked myself: my jeans and leather jacket, my shirt, my boots. What was it about me? Were my jeans too tight, was my hair too bright? Was I standing too close to the kerb? Is there a line, a demarcation point, beyond which a woman standing on a kerb will be mistaken for a hooker?

I keep well back from kerbs now. My attachment to such shame still troubles me. It could have been him. There was something about S – an arrogance, an authority, a furtiveness, too. He was a man used to getting his own way, a man who might send out secret signs and demands to women, and expect them to acquiesce.

On a Sunday in November, a few months in, the relationship ended. I had cycled over to his house, bearing steaks and wine in my rucksack. He was out hiking in the

Wicklow Mountains and had left a key under a stone for me. I mooched around the rooms, opened drawers, touched his folded jumpers. I stood at his kitchen window and looked out at the old tree and the wrought iron seat in the garden. I thought of him coming off the mountains, steadying himself against the car as he pulled off his boots, the damp and exhaustion of the day lodged in his bones, then the drive back to the city. I had a vision of the evening ahead, the steak and the wine, our conversation, and something in me exalted.

I tried to light a fire but it wouldn't take. I found a drum of petrol in the shed, that he kept for his lawnmower. In my youth I had seen my brother and his friends light bonfires with petrol, so I built a pyre of coal and rolled-up newspapers in the grate. I held the drum carefully but still the petrol splashed, and, when I set a match to the pyre, tongues of fire blazed up and leapt out at me, whipping at my legs, igniting the droplets of fuel on the rug, on the armrest of the sofa. I ran from the room, from the fireballs that erupted behind me, beating out a little flame on the leg of my jeans as I went.

The sound of crackling kindle still unnerves me, the mortification still scorches. For a long time I dreamt of little fires breaking out all over the place – in my shopping basket as I roamed supermarket aisles, in the nest of my piled-up hair, on my ring finger. I read somewhere that arsonists get an erotic charge and even sexual gratification from lighting fires. I can understand that – that moment of near annihilation, the juncture of sex and death, Eros and Thanatos. They like to watch fire for its beauty too, its aesthetic value. Once, I woke up on S's sofa to find him watching me. He touched my cheek lightly, delicately. I was greatly moved. There must have been other moments of kindness and tenderness too. Such moments would be worth having now, worth remembering.

I ran out of his house that day and rapped on the neighbour's door. The man – his name was Kevin – came and put out the little fires with wet towels. Then he stood and inspected the room, and finally looked at me. A huge fire engine turned the corner onto the street at that moment and sent blue light strobes around the room.

In a frenzy of fear and adrenaline, I washed down the walls and doors, wiped all the surfaces. I draped my cardigan over the armrest of the sofa. When he came in, he never noticed a thing. He kissed me in the kitchen, and went upstairs to shower. Later, I handed him a glass of wine and served up the steaks, and afterwards we carried our glasses to the front room. He sniffed the air and threw coal on the fire and it was this – the way he aimed the scuttle at the flames – that got to me, and I blurted out the whole story.

I broke down. He will kneel now, I thought, and hold me and examine my hands and ensure that I am unharmed. But he did not move. My gaze fell to his feet and I got a sudden flashback of the flames licking at my heels and the hand of death on my back. He came and sat beside me and I thought of the city and the dark night around us and I was filled with shame, and I couldn't wait to flee that house. He leaned in and stroked my hair and whispered, 'My little pyromaniac,' and then he kissed me.

In those first days after seeing him last summer, I kept an account of his comings and goings. The thought of meeting him again paralysed me. I rehearsed a few banal words to say – about what a small world it really is, and how little he had changed in twenty years. But weeks went by, and then months, and we did not meet. It is astonishing how people can live in such close quarters and yet remain remote from one another. We passed in the street, sequestered behind the windscreens of our cars. We wheeled our bins, parallel to each other, out our driveways on Sunday nights. Then, gradually, as the months passed, something shifted. The heightened state of anxiety and anticipation in which I had held myself slowly dissipated. Aided by him, I think. By some understanding in him – and consideration for those around him, perhaps even, for me – an understanding with which I would not previously have credited him.

He smokes now – I've seen the glow of his cigarette in the garden at night. Years ago he kept an inhaler on his bathroom shelf, for occasional use only, he told me. He did not seem, at the time, the kind of person who might suffer from asthma. I have known asthma sufferers – they are delicate, uncertain, sometimes stunted. One evening last autumn I watched him carry in the shopping bags and felt an appalling rush of affection for him. For his slow deliberate movements and his ordinariness. Devoid of the big house and car and the trappings of his previous lifestyle, some power has been divested of him. Whatever the cause of his comedown in the world – whatever bad luck or financial loss he suffered – he has transmuted his circumstances and is changed. In some obscure inner place, in the limbic part of himself maybe, he is changed. As if his soul has slowly awoken and shown itself in all its quietude. Or perhaps it is my soul that has shown itself in all its subtler reflections.

I work from home now. I am a freelance copyeditor and I spend my days in an upstairs room at the back of my house poring over manuscripts, sent to me electronically by publishers. I love the close engagement with a text. I love the fine anatomy of a perfectly constructed sentence.

I print out each manuscript, read slowly, insert, on almost every page, semi-colons, commas, dashes, line breaks. So many punctuation marks shunned or misplaced, nowadays, that I hold myself in readiness – tense, rigid, nervous – anticipating the transgressions. Commas, for some reason, fare the worst. Their neglect almost grieves me. The spaces where they rightfully belong beckon to me and I feel each space's ache for the tiny symbol, the cypher that gives form to a pause, a faint intake of breath, a remembrance.

These days I'm copyediting a novel – described as dystopian by the publisher – set in a post-apocalyptic Irish landscape. Not far into the novel, a gang of youths travel out of a ravaged city at night. Deep in the desolate countryside they enter a field where a flock of sheep and lambs are huddled together in the dark. The youths move quietly, stealthily. They herd the flock into a corner and slaughter the lambs, and skin them, there, in front of the mothers. Then they exit, carrying the warm bodies by the forelegs, leaving the mothers to sniff the steaming pelts and severed heads scattered on the ground. This is what hunger will do to men, the writer seems to be saying. Hunger will make savages of decent men.

From my desk I have a view onto my garden and the gardens on either side, and, of course, the sky. The weather has been subject to sudden change this summer – cloud formations in chrome and magnesium shadow the ground some days. Then, wheeling skies and downpours, even lightning. There is something elemental about living in a property of my own, moored to one particular piece of ground on this earth, that I had not experienced before, that I had not reckoned upon before moving in here.

S keeps a dog, a German shepherd that constantly paces the perimeter of the garden. She drags her limbs round and round on the worn grass, then throws herself down in a corner. I know her habits now, the pattern of her rising and pacing and resting. She stands out in the rain and the lightning – there is no kennel. Occasionally, I take a kitchen stool into my garden and stand on it and lean over the wall. The dog rises on her hind legs and wags her tail and whines. *There, there*, I say. I stroke her paws, her overgrown toenails. I feed her slices of bread and butter. I bring her water. She pricks up her ears at every sound – S's car turning into the cul-de-sac in the evenings, the doors slamming, voices in the house. She wags her tail when the little girl comes out, and the little girl wags her index finger, orders the dog to sit, stand, lie. She drags her around by the collar, presses down on the small of the dog's back, tries to straddle her. *Bold-dog, bold-dog*, she says, in a staccato voice, if the dog moves, then slaps the dog in the face. *Bold-dog, slap-slap.*

In the afternoons I drive to Sandymount and walk along the strand until I reach the rocks. I come only when the tide is far out. Proximity to a high tide or a swelling ocean induces a kind of vertigo in me, an uneasy feeling that I will be pulled in, swallowed up, brought far from any shore. But I love the cry of seagulls and the salt air. As I walk, I ponder the text I'm working on, turning over in my mind a particular clause or sentence that gnawed earlier. I meet elderly couples, dog-walkers of all ages. Day after day, I see the same faces. I feel immense tenderness for old people, for their pale melancholy eyes, their thin wrinkled skin, their diminished stature. I see them again on nearby streets as I drive away, re-entering houses, returning to routines that keep time and death and the disquiet of twilight at bay. There is an old man with whom I sometimes exchange a few words. He is tall, white-haired, patrician – I do not know his name or anything about him. One of his dogs is called

Laika. She is named after the dog sent into space on Sputnik 2 in 1957 – a stray from the Moscow streets, chosen for the project because of her placid nature, he told me. I found her photograph on the internet – she is strapped into a leather harness just before take-off, her eyes eager and shining, her ears pricked up.

The moon is huge these nights, a supermoon, the weatherman says, an optical illusion. If I mute my TV, I can hear S's through the living room walls. Ad jingles, the signature tune of the news. Last night I watched the pounding of Gaza by F16s, trolleys racing along hospital corridors, ribbons of shrapnel on the faces of children. After midnight I climbed the stairs and looked out my bedroom window at the moon. What are you doing to the tides tonight? I wondered. Pulling all of Earth's energy to you, causing an exodus of vitality? I thought of S on the other side of the wall, his head next to his wife's, his children asleep nearby. If this *is* his wife, if these are his children. I lay down and thought about the simultaneous existence of our private lives, and how we each slip into our private sleep, visited by dreams and fragments from the past, and how the same darkness, the same night, envelops us both and yet there is no name for what any of this is. There is nothing to explain how we – humans – can, one minute, lie down and reveal our most secret vulnerable selves to each other, greet the other's soul in the sex act, and then, the next minute, or the next day or week or month, part and go separately into the world as if we are strangers, as if we have not left a burn on the other.

I awoke at some point in the night, disturbed by something – an apprehension. My window was open a little and I heard a voice, low and tight and angry. *Shut up. Shut up.* I saw him, below, in the moonlight. He brought his cigarette to his mouth. The dog whined, her head held low, so timid. Stroke her, I whispered. The cigarette smoke curled from his mouth and the dog whined again. *Shut up. Shut the fuck up, I said.* He swung his open palm and struck the side of her head with great force. Before she knew what had happened, before her head had righted itself, he struck again and she yelped and slunk away into the shadows.

Long after he had gone inside, she emerged out into the moonlight and stood very still, staring at the ground. I pictured the tender insides of her head in slight disarray. Her vision blurred, the world warped, all sounds surreal. She might need to tilt her head to restore the balance of fluid in her inner ear or resettle tiny cerebral folds into skull cavities, eyes into sockets. There might be a little bleed, a swelling, a cerebral oedema. The brain might soften, and, if it does, I thought, then surely that will be a blessing, bringing, as it will, forgetfulness. She began to pace the worn grass. I watched her for a long time. I am aware of her always, there, at the edge of my being. Suppose there had been no petrol in his shed that day. Suppose I had not set fire to his house, or run away in shame. That might have been my house. Those might have been my children. This might have been my dog.

There were no sudden showers or elemental lightning today. Not a leaf stirred and only the postman and a cat prowling on the footpath disturbed the stillness of the street. I took the stool into the garden and hoicked myself up on the wall and jumped down into S's garden. The dog came, and I fell to my knees and threw my arms around her neck. Little by little she let her body recline against mine, and sighed deeply. A few minutes passed. I know now that in our hour of need, set with a seemingly impossible task, we are, like the Greek heroes, suddenly imbued with extraordinary strength. I stood and scooped her up in my arms, lifted her high. I bore her weight with ease and grace, as in a dream, and as I raised her up I felt myself raised too, she and I airborne as one, until her paws grasped the top of the wall and her weight left me and she was gone, over the top, down into my garden.

I moved with serene calm and certainty, as if it were all preordained. I crossed S's patio to the side entrance, slid back the bolt, let the door swing open. I crossed again and climbed – one, two, three – up onto the oil tank set against the wall, and jumped down into my own garden. The dog followed me inside and sat at my feet, and I laid a bowl of cereal and milk on the floor for her. I picked up my keys and went out and reversed my car up close to the front door, and opened the boot. I took the belt from my jeans and slid it under the dog's collar and led her through the hall, and willingly she came.

Shh, it's okay, I said, as I drove. She was silent, closed up in the dark behind me, but I talked anyway. All the way to Sandymount, I talked. *Nearly there, now*, I said, as we approached the street and the wooden door set into the wall that I had seen the old man enter. And still I talked. *Good girl.* I rang the bell and there came, instantly, the sound of dogs barking. When he opened the door he frowned and looked at her, then at me. Behind him, a gravel courtyard, an ivy-covered house.

'You might not remember me,' I said. 'We met on the strand a few times.'

He nodded slowly, said nothing.

'This one needs a home,' I said. I told him, briefly, of her life. Still he said nothing, just stepped back, let the door fall open, let me relinquish her into his yard.

It was Laika, the Moscow stray, I conjured on the way home. Alone in the cabin, moving through the cold and the dark, amid shoals of cosmic dust, clusters of beryllium suns. The night before the launch, one of the scientists took her home to play with his children. He wanted to do something nice for her. I did this for S, I tell myself, as I turn onto the canal. I did it to save his children from the moment when she would turn on them. But I didn't. I did it for her. I did it for me.

Now his car is pulling into the driveway. I wait. Five, six, seven ... ten minutes pass on the display of my DVD player. The children are first onto the street. Then S and the woman emerge. He says something to her and signals to the houses opposite and then crosses, diagonally, to the other side. The girl runs after him and he takes her hand and I see, instantly, the resemblance, the synchronicity, the limbic resonance. They begin at the house in the corner. He raises a hand to the doorbell.

My doorbell rings. It is the woman, with the boy beside her.

'Have you seen our dog?' she asks. Her voice is stern, urgent.

I shake my head, frown, wait for her to elaborate. 'No,' I say then.

'She's gone. The side door was open when we got home and she was gone.' Her eyes are drilling mine.

'She's probably not far away,' I say. 'She probably just wandered off.'

The woman shakes her head. 'The door was bolted – someone must have opened it ... She wouldn't know her way home.'

I keep my eyes on her. My heart is pounding. You are not worthy of a dog, I think. You people.

The boy is staring at me. He gives me a chill and I turn back to his mother.

'Did you see anything unusual today?' she asks. 'Anyone calling to our house, or anything?'

I can see S at the house opposite. Again I shake my head. 'No,' I say. 'I was out for a few hours in the morning. But I was in all afternoon. I didn't see anything.' Across the street nobody answers and S turns and begins to walk out the driveway.

She starts to move away. 'If you remember anything, will you let us know, please? The children are very upset … Someone must have seen something – someone must have let her out, or taken her.'

The boy does not immediately turn. His lingering disconcerts me and I look away, and then back again at his pale anxious face. We regard each other for a moment and I think he is going to speak. There is something he wants to say, something he wants me to decipher – it is there, a straining in his eyes – distress or sorrow or … *pleading*. He lets out a sigh and then turns and follows his mother and before I have my door fully closed he is calling across the street. *Seán*. I step into my living room and watch them stand and confer in the middle of the street. S raises his hand and rubs his forehead. He is looking in this direction, straight in the window at me, and our eyes meet. All that is within him, all he has ever seen and felt and known, all of time past, time fallen, is funnelled into this moment. Nothing is erased. The eye remembers everything.

I sit in the twilight with the TV on mute. Bombs are raining down on Gaza again. She will return tomorrow, that woman. And the boy. What was it he wanted of me? To give him back the dog? To relieve him of his sorrow? To be rescued?

I switch off the TV and sit in the dark. I think of the dog in Sandymount, pacing the yard, then standing and staring at the ground. Outside, the big moon is rising. I can feel its pull. Enormous it is, tonight.

Molly McCloskey

Molly McCloskey is the author of three works of fiction and a memoir, *Circles Around the Sun: In Search of a Lost Brother*. She was born in Philadelphia, and currently lives between Washington, DC, and Dublin.

Frogs

Sunday morning found Guy heading north on I-5 out of Portland, a thrum of life in him like he hadn't felt in a long time. It was late August, sunny, but with a whiff of autumn. He was meeting her at a place on the pier called Ardeo. He pictured champagne, something he almost never drank. He saw himself making a toast, saw her lowering her gaze, demurely. He thought of kissing her, too, and wondered would it feel creepy and disconcerting or perfectly natural and somehow a relief, the way things that wait a long time to happen, and then happen, are a relief.

They were children the last time he saw her, ten years old, their bond cemented early on when one October afternoon in the corner store, while they debated the relative merits of various flavours of a certain candy that exploded in your mouth as you ate it, a man dropped dead in front of them. As the ambulance whooped into view and the paramedics scrambled past, Guy and Kate backed furtively out the door, as though they'd been the cause of it, and ran all the way home to Guy's house.

For the rest of that school year, they were inseparable. When they weren't talking about death – sitting on the school bus those dismal rainy winter mornings, puzzling over its logistics, the multitudes they pictured jostling in some vast celestial stadium – they played. Kate was no ordinary girl. She climbed trees faster than anyone Guy knew and flew fearlessly down hills on her purple bicycle, her purple coat flapping open in the wind. In the nearby stream, she built little bridges of stone and branch, which she crossed, solemnly and gracefully, like a tightrope walker. In the pond behind her house, she monitored the metamorphoses of tadpoles into frogs, and in a little notebook drew pictures of plants and flowers. Unlike the boys their age, Kate did not, on seeing an anthill, stomp on it in the hope that ants would fly like sparks from the ground. She did not throw rocks at perching birds while imitating the sound of a machine gun, and she had not the slightest interest in setting fire to things. She was generous, adventurous and well-intentioned, and Guy was captivated by her.

The day her family moved to Seattle, they'd said goodbye in her driveway – Guy and his parents, and Kate and her parents and her four-year-old sister Nancy. It was a perfect June morning. The purple rhododendrons sat like plumped pillows at the edge of the yard. There was the slightest rustle of leaves overhead. A robin hopped across the drive. Everything seemed sharper than usual, as though the day had been tuned to a very clear frequency. He tried to think of something to say that would forestall the inevitable, but he was stricken with a sense of helplessness, and said nothing.

The next thing everyone was hugging everyone else. Even little Nancy – her fingers dusted with the orange residue of some snack, the tiniest bubble of wet emerging from her left nostril – was getting and giving hugs. Guy's father and Kate's father shook hands and patted each other's backs, as though they'd just accomplished something. Kate and Guy stepped gingerly towards each other and hugged, briefly and with the greatest awkwardness. When Kate stepped away, Guy saw the adults looking at them, all with the same tight little smiles, sad but like they might burst out laughing. His face went hot, and he looked down at the oily blacktop and did not look up again until he heard the station wagon rolling down the drive.

When Guy's family returned home, Guy went to his room and took his plastic army men out of the shoebox and staged a small war on his bedroom carpet. Here a pair tangled in hand-to-hand combat; there, behind the leg of his bed, others waited in ambush; on the mountain ranges of his bookshelf snipers perched. He did not cry.

That was more than thirty years ago. Now he had found her again. She was still in Seattle. She hadn't changed her name when she'd married, and the bulk of what Guy saw online were references to a business she'd owned with her husband – a specialty imports shop in the Capitol Hill area of the city. Everything from bracelets and blankets made by small traders in Ghana and Senegal to high-end Persian rugs and specially sourced antiques. The shop had been sold two years ago – the sale, Guy gathered, linked to a divorce. Then, a career change; she now worked for a large clinic that provided rehabilitation services for the physically disabled – prosthetic limbs, mobility aids, therapy.

He emailed her at the work address, telling only one lie – that he had happened upon her name accidentally. He told her a bit about his life, enough to make clear that he had not grown up to become a sociopath, and mentioned the name of the university where he worked, so that she could verify his implied claim to respectability. She responded the next day, used the words *surprised* and *delighted*. He thought of her breathless, ten years old, jumping off her bicycle and letting it fall on its side as she crouched to peer at something in the grass.

He knew her immediately. She was already seated at a table, facing towards the entrance, a look of calm curiosity.

She stood and hugged him gently, then stepped back to take him in. 'Guy ...' she said, shaking her head.

Her eyes were the same – a little tired, a good bit less keen and bright, but unmistakably hers. What was it about the eyes, their beautiful dogged refusal to change?

'Does it feel like yesterday,' he asked, 'or a long time ago?'

She smiled. 'Both.'

'Both,' he nodded.

They sat, scanned the menus distractedly, both ordered salmon.

He said, a little stupidly, 'You look like ... you.'

'You look like you, too,' she laughed, and leaned forward. 'So how *are* you?'

'You first,' he said.

So she told him. About that first year in Seattle, how lonely she'd been after the move, about high school and how she hadn't fit in, how she'd finally settled into herself in college, studied abroad for a year and met her husband in Rome, though they'd been in the same comp class right here at the university. She told him about the shop, how her husband had been working for a big tech company integrating computers into schools in West Africa; how she'd gone with him on a trip and that was how the whole import business had evolved.

'I'd been writing code up to then and—'

'Writing *code*?'

'Are you surprised?'

'I haven't seen you in thirty years. I have no idea what to be surprised by.'

He told her about his work. After beginning a degree in philosophy, he'd switched with some relief to the hard sciences, and done his graduate studies in botany. Now he was a plant pathologist. His current research involved isolating factors required for virus infection and generation. He said he'd become a botanist because of those days spent peering into her backyard pond, the way she'd thrilled to reeds and moss and other unremarkable things.

She smiled. 'I don't believe you.'

'It's true,' he said.

Was it? Maybe a little bit. He was flirting now. He looked at her eyes again, recalling what he'd never consciously consigned to memory. Her eyes weren't something he'd noticed much at ten, not like he'd noticed the way she ran, or her pigtails, or her yellow bathing suit with its two pieces and its tangle of strings – the things that rendered her mysterious and different. He liked who she'd become. There was a reserve, a containment, but something warm and generous too. He congratulated himself: even at ten, he thought, he had recognised substance.

At some point she said, 'And you never got married.'

'Oh, I did,' he said.

'Oh.' Her hand to her chest. 'I don't know why I had the impression ...'

Trying to sound offhand, he said, 'Maybe I give off that impression.'

*

Guy had come late to the idea of marriage. Before he met Marie, he had fallen in love twice, once in his mid-twenties and again in his early thirties. The women had been fiery, extroverted, somewhat ricocheting creatures. For a time, with both, he had felt invigorated, though with both he had reached a point of feeling exhausted by the demands of their energy.

With Marie, he had finally stopped striving for his opposite. They had met at the university where they both worked, Marie doing a post-doc in linguistics. There had been an affinity from the start, intense in its own way but quieter and less destabilising than Guy's previous affairs. It forced him to admit that deep down he had known it wasn't going to last with those other women; the relationships had been like living in a foreign country for a while, a place from which he knew he would return, enriched by many stories and a trail of acts he felt not quite answerable for.

'What if suddenly we find it isn't real?' Marie had said to him one night.

It was a strange thing to say, and Guy wondered if she had spoken her thoughts aloud by mistake. She sounded genuinely frightened.

They were lying in bed, heartbeats still quickened and limbs awry, her leg as tight as a tree root around his. He trailed a finger along her shoulder, the world coming back to him in the form of his body, which was beginning to cramp, and whispered, 'It's real.'

He nearly said it then, about marrying her, but held back.

They had been seeing each other for six months when Marie was diagnosed. She was thirty-five years old. The cancer was in the pancreas. She started chemo. For a time, she turned a vivid yellow-green from jaundice.

When the green waned, he proposed.

They wed on a ferociously windy day on the beach in Astoria, with two of Marie's friends as witnesses. They told their parents that evening, when it was done. In the hours afterwards, Guy clung to Marie – he could hardly bear to take his arm from around her waist or his eyes off of her, as though to lose even momentary track of her would precipitate her vanishing.

When she died, five months and six days from the date of her diagnosis, Guy entered a microclimate – a chill, industrial-grey grief pierced by random bursts of acute and nonsensical joy. Cycling over the bridge one spring night, all the lights sprinkled in the hills the far side of the river, and closer in, in the apartments and offices downtown, the small squares of illuminated life, framing this moment and then the next and the next after that, each unrepeatable instant, he felt rocked by astonishment. The world had never looked more beautiful, more his, as though having shown itself to him in some gesture of intimacy.

Mostly, though, what he felt was misery, oppressed by the brute weight of mourning, and the gnawing emptiness in the pit of his stomach – those words we use, like *hunger*, are not metaphors, he thought. He felt afraid of her death, as though it were something that had not yet happened, or might still be prevented.

He told Kate more than he'd intended, about Marie, her death, their wedding day. He wasn't used to talking about her. He had wanted to resist for as long as possible reducing her death to a piece of news. If he spoke about her at all, he'd wanted to do so exhaustively, and there was a point at which even the well-intentioned lost patience with the grief of others. So he had clung, until now, to a grim reticence.

211

Kate didn't say much, just listened. She was so watchful, so receptive, he felt as though a door were opening and he could step through it, bring his whole life into hers and set it down there, like some teetering, slightly comic burden.

'I hadn't meant for this to be so heavy,' he said. He tried a chuckle, which sounded forced.

'I'd rather this than small talk.' Then she shook her head. 'I don't mean – I mean I'd rather things didn't happen. But they do, and …'

'It's OK,' he said. 'I know what you mean.'

What he didn't talk about was the question he hadn't spoken of to anyone, the one that wouldn't leave him alone, the question of whether his marrying Marie had been a dishonest act. There was no doubt in his mind that he had loved her, perfectly but briefly – it was the very brevity that had enabled its perfection – but what if the doctors, instead of giving her a few months to live, had foretold years of illness? What if, instead of a swift decline, she had faced a future of gradual debilitation, loss of motor skills, limited mobility, encroaching dementia. Would he have married her? Committed himself to a lifetime of care, with not much health behind them as ballast to all that sickness? It wasn't like sticking by someone you already had a history with, it wasn't like his parents. Guy's mother looked brittler each time he saw her, thin as a twig and always with some new twist to her repertoire of pains and infirmities; his father tended her with a solicitude that seemed to border on the holy.

*

It was his mother, actually, who'd got him thinking about Kate. Three weeks before, she'd been taken to the hospital again. She'd had a mini-stroke, and in her confusion had fallen and fractured her wrist. She would be OK, for now. But Guy was aware that if the end did not come suddenly, it began like this – the acceleration of insults to the body, the sinewy snappable frailty, that look in the eyes.

As he'd sat beside her hospital bed, watching as she made her interminable way through a piece of toast, he'd begun to talk to her of his childhood, recalling things from long ago, as though to anchor her to earth, fix her to some unchangeable point safely in the past. A family camping trip to Yosemite, some nonsense song they used to sing, the day he hid a stray kitten in his bedroom, planning to raise it in secret.

She said, 'And you had that little girlfriend. Do you remember?'

He laughed. 'Was she my girlfriend?'

'The two of you were so sweet together,' his mother said. 'I imagine she's some kind of CEO now.'

Guy peered at her. 'Kate? A CEO? Really?'

'Oh, she was sharp, very focused for a child. She wasn't a dawdler, like lots of kids.'

Guy was surprised, he did not remember Kate like that. He recalled her as adventurous, expansive, life-loving. But he would never have imagined her as someone who went on to wield power, or had any wish to.

Driving home from the hospital that day, he wondered who she had become. The year after she'd moved away, everything had changed for Guy. Puberty struck, or rather stole over him, his body emitting a range of new substances: sebum, semen, sweat. He felt animal. In the mornings, he could smell himself, and he smelled feral and clammy and unfamiliar. Kate sometimes crossed his mind. He knew she must be changing, too, like he was, like the girls around him were. Had he been a bit older – fourteen, even – he might've bought a bus ticket and gone to see her. Seattle was only three hours away, he could've done it in a day. They could've lounged on bean bags in her room, listening to records and kissing all through the rainy afternoon. But by the time he did reach the age of fourteen, Kate had been relegated to the distant past, the world of childhood. Guy could hardly believe that he had ever felt that tender towards a girl, and the idea of trying to find Kate – had it even occurred to him – would have struck him as simply silly.

Now, all these years later, he felt an ache for the children they had been, for the good fortune they hadn't known was theirs, for a time when death was an abstraction linked only to strangers, and a distance of three hours akin to impossibility. He felt grateful to her. She had been, after all, his first love, and the things they'd shared – friendship, trust, affection, marvel – he knew now were rare enough in life. He thought then that he should try to find her. If nothing else he would thank her, for having been young with him, and kind. And he would tell her about his mother, too. He would tell her she was dying. He saw himself sitting in a kitchen with Kate, some indistinct interior, her hands cupping his atop a table and the two of them talking about death again, just as they had when they were children. And then not talking at all, just being sweet together, whatever that might mean at their age.

Over coffee, Kate said, 'I'll show you a picture of my son.' He thought she'd hand him her phone but she took out her wallet instead and fished through a multitude of cards until she found it. It was a head-and-shoulders shot. He looked about thirteen, hale and robust. He was wearing some kind of sports jersey, and his face was flushed, as though the game had just ended. Big grin on him and a mop of red-blond hair. A boy given to exuberance. His name was Dylan.

'He's handsome,' Guy said. The boy was neither handsome nor ugly, but it seemed the thing to say.

Kate studied the photo for a moment, as though he were someone she'd been asked to identify. 'He doesn't look like that anymore,' she said.

With an authority that sounded phony, Guy said, 'They grow up, eh?'

A beat of silence, and then: 'There was an accident.'

Guy parked behind her in the drive. As he was getting out of the car, he saw someone standing in the bay window. It was Amanda, the woman Kate had said helped look after Dylan. She lifted her hand and waved slowly to Kate, like her mind was somewhere else entirely. And then Guy saw the boy. He must've been there already, watching out the window, having heard the car. In the shadowy grey interior, the two of them had the look of ghosts.

He followed Kate inside.

The boy was mangled. He had lost the use of his legs and he seemed to have only the power of his left hand, which worked the controls on the chair. His body, which was very thin, twisted to the left as though he were making a terrible effort to turn away from them. His head drooped slightly to one side, as did one corner of his mouth, and when he looked from Guy to his mother, his eyes, because they were the only things that moved, appeared to be ricocheting wildly, like the eyes of someone bound and gagged. He was fifteen.

The accident had happened in Senegal, on a family trip, when Dylan was out with three local boys he'd met. It wasn't their fault, Kate had said, they were nice boys, good boys, responsible. Their car had been broadsided by a truck. One of them had been killed, the other two had only minor injuries; Dylan had wound up in the no man's land between death and good luck. Spinal cord injury, minor brain damage, paralysis.

With regard to her husband, Kate said, 'We didn't divorce because of it, or maybe we did. When it happened we both just became more of what we were, and we found out that he was someone completely incapable of living with Dylan, day in, day out. Or living with the loss of him. He went into this really dark shock. It was worse having him here than not.' She paused. 'I could put it another way, but what's the point?'

She had told him all this at the restaurant. So Guy had known what to expect. And yet he hadn't. He'd been prepared to enter a scene in which domestic life was a quietly heroic thing, a reminder of what really mattered. He had even thought well of himself on account of his eagerness to meet Dylan, his openness to the difficult realities of Kate's life. When she'd said in the restaurant that she should be going, she'd hesitated, which he took to mean he might accompany her, that she was inviting him to see her life. Now that he was here, what shocked him as much as the boy's condition was how locked Kate's life was to her son's, and how enormous the space left by her husband, an absence that must've pressed unbearably on Dylan. In the restaurant, the boy's fate had seemed abstract, while now it stared out at him from those eyes, an expression that seemed one of accusation and pleading, but also panic. As though the boy saw something terrible bearing down on them and could not give voice to the vision.

For a few minutes, while Kate spoke to Amanda at the door, Guy was left alone with Dylan. He wanted to connect with him, to make good on the moment, to not regard the boy with fear or aversion, as he imagined so many people did. But Dylan could speak only in guttural syllables, disconnected from each other, which Kate understood but which Guy was unable to make sense of. Instead the two of them looked at each other, Dylan's eyes occasionally rolling right or left, as though trying to tell Guy there was someone behind him, while Guy tried to convey something like apology without pity, curiosity without prurience.

When Kate came back to the living room, she said to Guy, 'Coffee? A drink?'

Guy asked for coffee, and Dylan, satisfied, it seemed, that his mother was home again, and having no wish to keep company with a stranger, executed a three-point turn, and took himself off to the kitchen. A minute later, Guy heard the crackling sizzle of a television coming on, blaring before the volume went low.

Kate brought a tray with coffee, and they sat on the sofa and talked for another while, though Guy found it impossible to relax. When he began to think he should be going, Kate said, 'Wait.'

She went upstairs and came back with a creased photo of the two of them – they were standing in front of Guy's old house wearing makeshift cowboy costumes. Guy had no recollection of the photo being taken, or of the day itself. Why had they been dressed as cowboys? He hadn't remembered either of them being enamoured of Westerns. She turned the photo over. On the back she had written the date, and the words *Guy's house*.

He took the picture from her and turned it over again.

From the other room came the *znznz-znznz* of Dylan manoeuvring his chair.

'I don't remember this at all,' he said.

217

'No? It was your idea.'

'What was?'

'The get-ups.'

'*Cowboys?*'

'It wasn't *my* idea.'

He shook his head. 'Strange,' he said.

'I think you got us to dress up a few times. And you made some kind of lasso and we lassoed things.'

'Really? Was I good with a lasso?'

'Excellent,' she said. 'Odd you don't remember.'

'I remember frogs,' he said. 'And your bicycle. And your purple coat and your yellow two-piece.'

She laughed.

'And the day you moved.'

He turned the photo over, looked at her handwriting, looked back at the picture.

'You can't have it,' she said, her voice a little teasing.

'I know,' he said.

There was noise in the other room. They both looked towards the kitchen door.

'I should get on the road,' he said.

She walked outside with him, and they stood next to his car and she said how good it had been to see him, and Guy said, 'It was so good to see you.' He glanced over her shoulder, expecting to find Dylan in the window again, but the living room was empty.

He wanted to tell her that he knew it wasn't easy, that he thought she was very strong, that Dylan was fortunate to have her. He made a ham-fisted attempt at saying these things, in answer to which she said, 'Dylan doesn't want his life.' Then she paused and added, 'And I understand that.'

She was so used to knowing this, her expression didn't change when she said it, her voice betrayed nothing.

Guy didn't know how to respond. He thought that what Kate was saying was that she wished to help her son to escape his life, to end it. But maybe she didn't mean that at all.

On the drive home, he had to keep himself from calling her. He wanted to hear her voice, but beyond that, he had no idea what he would say, or whether there was anything *to* say. He thought that to love anyone was beyond bearable. But she knew that already, and there was no point, or solace, in saying it.

It was dark by the time he reached his house. He felt drained. He dropped his keys on the table, got a beer and sat out on the porch step, his head resting against the pillar. His neighbourhood was a small world forming itself around him. The squawk and chirrup of night creatures. Footfalls, the gust of a breeze, a screen door clapping quietly a few houses down. *Even the unending ends.* Where had he read that? A poem, written by he couldn't remember who. He had said to Kate at one point, 'My mother is dying,' and she had said, 'Oh …' and put her hand over his, and it had felt so like what he'd imagined it would that it spooked him. His hand had twitched at her touch.

He might call her tomorrow, or the next day, or perhaps she would call him. Or maybe neither of them would call the other and they'd never meet again. Maybe there would be a few emails and then it would peter out to nothing, and he would wonder now and then, less often as time passed, what had become of her, and of Dylan. He thought of the boy's eyes. Of a mind that sees the unbearable looming. He thought of Kate's voice on the phone, how it might sound, who she was now. He sat up straighter, drew a deep breath, and thought of sleep, while overhead, in another passing breeze, all the leaves shivered in unison.

Bernie McGill

Bernie McGill is the author of *Sleepwalkers*, a collection of stories short-listed in 2014 for the Edge Hill Short Story Prize, and of *The Butterfly Cabinet* in 2011. Her work has been placed in the Seán Ó Faoláin, the Bridport, and the Michael McLaverty Short Story Prizes and she won the Zoetrope: All-Story Award in the US. She is the recipient of a number of Arts Council of Northern Ireland awards and was granted a research bursary in 2013 from the Society of Authors for work on a second novel. She lives in Portstewart in Northern Ireland with her family. www.berniemcgill.com

A Fuss

Rosa is at Connolly Station, in the waiting room for the Enterprise. The train is at the platform but is not yet boarding. She sits on a moulded plastic seat with her back to the glass partition that gives on to the railway lines, her rucksack tucked underneath, her head turned a little to the left towards the exit, her eyes on the railway staff who are milling around the train. Light slants in through the girdered station roof and casts arched shadows onto the tiled flooring beneath. She can still hear the drumming of the rain. There are only a few people in the waiting room, most of them in business suits, busy scrolling hand-held devices, answering messages, working on the move. There will be plenty of space on the train.

It is March, Friday, late afternoon. It means she will only miss a day and a half of work from the college library. Her manager was sympathetic, generous, when the phone call came through. It's three days' leave for a dead parent, more if she needs it but she won't need even that. She'll travel back on Monday, the day after the funeral. Her mother has learned not to depend on her; she has sisters of her own close by, one brother, a legion of nephews and nieces. By now the farmhouse kitchen will be steaming with pots of soup, water boiling in kettles for tea. They are all practiced in the theatre of mourning. Her part in it will be pivotal but small, a walk-on only. It will require a few rehearsed words, a modicum of self-control, limited exertion. She knows what is expected of her. She will be able to do it.

She has not changed out of her working clothes of neat black trousers, low-heeled shoes, a pale turtleneck sweater. It is not unsuitable attire for a wake. She has been told by her senior female colleagues that she dresses too old for her years, that she should wear make-up, style her hair; invest in a flash of colour. She overheard one of them once as she walked into the staffroom say something about a plain-clothes nun. She knows they were talking about her, but she does not wish to invite unwanted attention. Monochrome is fine. Celibacy, in her opinion, is vastly underrated.

Her uncle Colm will be waiting for her at the little red brick station wearing his dark wool coat that he keeps for such occasions. He had proposed to drive to Dublin to collect her but she had said there was no need. There would be things for him to do at home, arrangements to be made. She would get the train, catch the connection in Belfast, be in Knockarlet in the time it would have taken him to make the journey to her. He will shake her hand, offer to take her bag, say he is sorry for her trouble, which will be a strange thing to say, since it's his trouble too, but there will be no point in disputing with him the agreed hierarchy of loss. He will not kiss or embrace her. That's not the kind of family they are. He will say it's a terrible shock. You hear of these tragedies but you never expect them to visit your own door. Her father worked with beasts his whole life, he'll say, and never once made a mistake. He knew not to get between a heifer and her calf when the blood was up. They think that he must have tried to move away, caught his foot on something down there at the bottom of the low field, an exposed root maybe, or went over on his ankle in the soft ground. They think he must have hit his head off the old enamel bath the cattle used as a drinking trough. He was not a young man, that is true, but still, and he won't finish the sentence because the sentence doesn't need finishing. She's already heard it all. No one wants to dwell on the circumstances, newsworthy though they are. No one wants to think of him lying facedown, trampled into the rain-soaked earth by his own herd. It's not the kind of histrionic end they would have wanted for him in the family. They'd have preferred it if God had called him quietly, at home, in his own bed or in the armchair by the range with his feet up on the brown velvet stool. It would have been no less of a loss but they could have managed that more readily. They don't want to be an item in the local news. They're not the kind of family that likes a fuss.

Because it's her uncle's way, he will talk the whole road to the farm, but he will not say that Rosa, his sister's only child, born late to her and her husband and considered by them a blessing and a marvel always, that she should have come home to them more often, because that's not the kind of man he is; he's not the interfering kind. He will drive her up the ridged concrete road that rises from the bay, past sodden fields and dripping hedges and the bank of black-wrapped bales that will sit like mourning gifts at the side of the barn and he will say that he's never seen a March like it for rain, that there couldn't be a drop more water left in the sky. She'll wipe her feet on the thick coir mat at the kitchen door. She'll shake hands with the aunts and uncles and cousins. She'll find her mother by the open coffin in the front room with the lid propped like a great oaken kite against the pink flowered wallpaper, with her feet placed squarely on the dark red carpet, the worn part concealed, belatedly, by an unsuitable rug. Her mother will take Rosa's hands in hers and press them, and run her thumbs across the knuckles. She will not make a scene. They both know how to behave in order to get through this. They'll sit side-by-side on borrowed chairs and sip tea out of china cups that haven't seen daylight for years, not since her mother's mother was waked. They'll nibble at sandwiches that have arrived ready-made, packed into loaf bags, ferried in by neighbours; they'll nod and shake hands and thank people for coming and agree that it's a shock; they'll search long-unseen faces for some clue to recognition and sit silent and bleary-eyed by the coffin during the lulls.

And at some point, maybe tonight, certainly by the end of tomorrow, the headmaster will come to offer his condolences and she and her mother will shake his hand and say the same things to him. And when they have dispensed with the formalities, he will ask about her work in the library and she will say yes, she enjoys it, that the hours suit her, that she likes to be among books. And she knows her mother will be thinking about the day that she and Rosa sat together in that same room with the pink flowering wallpaper and the dark red carpet, when Rosa told her all the things he'd done to her in the classroom after school. When her mother had said that she must have been mistaken, that she must have dreamt it or have seen something filthy on TV, something she'd no business to see, for such a thing could not be countenanced between a child and the master who was tutoring her in his own time for the grammar school exam. And the whole time he is standing there, nodding, she will be remembering the smell of him, of cigarettes and chalk and bad teeth, and the roughness of his rag nail fingers, and his breath coming out, short, frantic, like a burrowing dog, and the way the light slanted in through the glazing bars of the high window and made a cage on the wooden schoolroom floor. And she will remember the important lesson she learned from this, from him and from her mother, that it is more agreeable to be quiet than to make a fuss by telling the truth. And on Sunday, when they've carried her father out and prayed over him, and put him back into the ground but civilly, this time, clad in oak and wearing his good suit and tie, then she will be able to go back to her quiet life in the busy city where it is possible to be alone with a bricked-up chimney of a heart without anyone remarking on it. She plans her route through the wake and funeral with military precision so that there will be no surprises, no unanticipated emotion to ambush her in the days ahead.

The automatic doors of the Enterprise waiting room glide soundlessly open and in shuffles a little white-haired lady in a purple felt beret, carrying awkwardly in both hands a red and yellow carpet bag, the base of which is almost dragging on the ground. She is wearing a white shaggy coat that reaches to her shins, what looks like a pair of soft black dancing pumps on her feet. She does not look to left or right. There are plenty of empty seats, but she walks straight past Rosa and plumps down with an exaggerated sigh onto the plastic chair to her immediate left, drops the bag at her feet. Rosa looks past her towards the exit. The train is still not boarding.

'I'm raging,' says the little woman, uninvited, as if she and Rosa are mid-conversation, as if Rosa has asked her what is wrong. 'I shouldn't have brought the carpet bag for it's far too heavy to carry.'

A woman dressed in a pale grey jacket opposite raises her eyes from her screen, glances over at them. Rosa feels scrutinised. She turns her head slightly towards the little woman, manages what she hopes is an unencouraging smile.

'The wheelie case is far easier to manage,' she says in an accent that may once have been northern. 'Only I don't like to arrive with it, for it's far too big for a weekend visit and I don't want the nephew and his wife getting a fright and saying to themselves, "Has she no notion of going home?"' She digs a surprisingly sharp elbow into Rosa's side and throws her head back for a guffaw. The woman in the suit glances over again, raises her eyebrows, a smile playing about her lips. Rosa looks again towards the exit, willing for the signal to board. 'The condiments,' the little woman whispers suddenly to Rosa, bringing her face in close, enunciating each word, 'are electronic, button-operated, for one-touch grinding. Perfect for old arthritic hands. I couldn't resist them. Half price in Baxter's.'

Rosa risks a glance at her. Small brown eyes look out from under grey eyebrows. Her face is heavily made-up in what her mother used to call pan-stick, a half-hearted blotch of orange at her mouth, as though she has tentatively kissed a lipstick, a smear of green on her eyelids. The hat is secured above each ear by a silver hairclip, each ending in a diamante star. Her earrings are a pair of purple felt flowers pierced through with a silver stud, and now that she's closer, Rosa can see two darker purple flower-shaped patches where they must have been removed from the hat. The little woman leans down; snaps open the mouth of the bag between her feet. 'And now I know why they were cheap,' she says. 'The pepper mill is stuck - won't shift for love nor money. Six triple A batteries it takes and I've changed them twice. I'll soon have my whole pension spent. The nephew'll get it sorted, though, he's what you'd call a mechanical genius, has his head under the hood of a tractor every time you turn your back. I've told him all about it. He can't wait to get a look at them.' Cushioned among cardigans and bed socks, a toiletry bag, a pink shower cap, sit two pale wooden mills, each of them about a foot in length. 'I'm daft in the head,' she says to Rosa. 'I needn't have brought the salt mill, it's working fine. Only I don't like to separate the pair.'

She snaps the bag shut, straightens up, looks Rosa right in the eye. 'Thirteen years the husband's dead this October.' Though Rosa hasn't made to speak, she waves a hand to silence her. 'Everyone has their grief. Plus, it wasn't the first death I've had to endure, though it was mercifully sudden, a heart attack, and not like the children – I'll spare you the details.' You'd think she would be used to it by now, she says, but it's not the kind of thing you ever get used to, really. 'Still,' she says, tugging her hat down lower with both hands, checking the hairgrips are in place, 'better to have loved and lost, you know the rest yourself.' She'd had an awful time of it trying to locate her Northern bus pass, she says, only where do you think she found it, in the sterling purse, of course! Some younger wiser version of her had left it there for her old senile brain to find. Not that she'll need it. The nephew will ferry her about. And now here's the train boarding at last. She reaches for the handles of the bag.

Rosa stands. 'Do you need a hand?' she says.

'No, no, dear. I can manage on my own,' and off she waddles, towards the train.

Rosa pulls her rucksack out from under her seat, walks slowly behind the little figure, keeping her distance, watches as she struggles up the step from the platform onto the train, sees that she has settled into a table seat, is shrugging her arms out of her coat. Rosa walks on to the next carriage, finds a quiet spot, sits down at the window, facing the direction of travel, puts her rucksack down on the seat beside her. She takes out a book, borrowed last minute from the library, glances at the blurb on the back cover. It's the story of a love affair, not her usual choice, but the writer is one she's read before. She had thought it would put the journey in. The train slips out of the station. She runs her hand over the glossy cover, tries to focus on the print.

When the train pulls up in Newry, Rosa still has not opened the book. Outside on the platform, in the grey light, stands a big man in green wellies, an unzipped anorak, cable-knit sweater, a peaked cap on his head. He is looking up and down the platform and then a broad smile breaks out on his face and he walks forward to meet the little white-haired lady with the heavy carpet bag. He wraps his two big arms around her and lifts her off the ground and she laughs and slaps him half-heartedly on the chest until he sets her down. He grabs the bag, crooks his elbow in a theatrical gesture and she slips her arm into his. The two of them exit the station, linked, talking and laughing, she with her little head raised up to look at him, he with his big head bent to look down at her.

Rosa closes her tired, stinging eyes. The engine idles in the station. She feels a little sickened by the smell of diesel and now there is a pain starting above her eye. She leans her head against the cool of the window, hears the soft sigh as the carriage doors close, feels the shudder through the glass as the train moves off again. Something drops on to the book in her lap. When she opens her eyes she sees that it's a bead of water, that it has fallen on to the word 'hold', that it is distorting a little the print, enlarging the word like a lens. As she dabs it away with her finger, another drop falls, and another. She puts her hand to her face and finds that her cheeks are wet. She tries to dry them with her fingers but the tears roll down, unbidden. Half-blinded, she gropes in her rucksack for a tissue but now there is a sound like someone gasping for air, great rasping sobs coming out of her mouth and shaking her whole frame. She has not made provision for this. This is not part of the plan. She doesn't know if she's crying for the little woman with the carpet bag heavy with condiments, or for her father who went out in the morning, not knowing he wouldn't come back that day, or for her mother who will never get over this, no matter how attentive her relatives are, or for herself, for the lack of love in her life, because she hasn't allowed it in. She pats her face with the tissue. After a little while, the sobs subside. She looks out the window at the factory buildings and the flyovers and the desolate, puddled lanes, at barbed-wire fences and mossy banks, at a burst of yellow whin on a hillside in the distance. The leafless trees along the track are choked with ivy. They reach up their straggly finger-bone branches and proffer dark clumps of nest like shadows on an X-ray. The power lines are strung with roosting crows. The sky is a strange green hue. From behind a barn, something rises, like a handful of soil thrown high into the air, then just at the point at which it should fall, it takes shape into a flock of starlings, turns, rises higher, dissolves into the darkening sky. She is travelling between the lights, a thing her father told her was dangerous to do. And she still has miles to go.

June Caldwell

June Caldwell is a journalist, award-winning blogger and fiction writer. She is a prizewinner of the Moth International Short Story Prize 2014 and has been shortlisted for various competitions including the RTÉ Guide/Penguin Ireland Short Story and Over The Edge New Writer of the Year. Her non-fiction work includes a biography of a Trouble's moll published by Gill & MacMillan in 2006 as well as feature articles for a host of UK and Irish newspapers and magazines. Her fiction is published in *The Stinging Fly*, *The Moth*, *Literary Orphans*, *Popshot Magazine* and RTÉ Ten as well as being a featured reader at the Italo-Irish Literature Exchange in Verona, Galway Pro-Choice and DLR Lexicon for the 2015 Barrytown Trilogy readings. She timeshares her life with *Guardian* journalist Henry McDonald and a hairy cat called Cloudy.

SOMAT

I was a controversial case. Even before Beard met Opus Dei met Speculum Man. Grey hospital cubicle punched with derma-grip, iodoform fungi, yellow tiles. Peter Papadoo giving it the: 'No more babies!' His job is not so much a sure thing anymore. He worries she will not cope. I hang above the flare; nail fur, metallic ale, unmoored. Knapsack of neurons showing me where to plop out on any given day. Mama goo goo-ing: 'We'll get by, we always do, go with it, get on with it, it's all good, don't freak the beak.' Sleep brining sleep, reflex arc, breathe, swallow, lick. Magus of my future, she is packed with a million woolly things to say to me. 'My butter fairy, nincompoop, my pickyuppy squidgy monkey. You will not stop running around. For the love of Jaysus. Oh you with the cut knees! What are we going to do about you? Rascal flower, pumpernickel. There's no stopping you! Why would I want to? So cuddly-do. Let me squeeze that sweet gooey centre of you. Come here to me now. Don't make me run! Would you look at the getup of ye.' Then it happened: I heard no more from her.

Peter Papadoo rushes in looking like a right ball of shite. Straight from work. Slathered in muck and leaves.

'This can't be fucking happening,' he says, apologising, all a-fluster. Looking for an in-the-know, big league doctor, an expert, an un-doer of crummy miracles. Awful sorry, so sorry, sinfonietta of sorry from a lot of mouths. 'A terrible thing though very rare, but I'm afraid it's now a definite'. Staff nurse crumbled in disinfectant grips him. Into a foggy cubbyhole. Flicks a chart that shows exactly how it can happen. A laminate chart. Team arrive. She won't even take Panadol for a headache. Ran two mini marathons last year. Not a bother with the other three. How can this be? 'It's rare, but not exceptional,' Dr Falvey tells him. 'We need to take her now, immediately. You wait outside. Someone will be with you as soon as we know more. We need to move now, sharp.' Plastic doors plash a sulk of dead air. This is what it's like when the planet putters out its last dingy light and a lone animal wiggles in the flourishing fade.

Beard rubs his nose with a peach linen hanky, eyes streaming. Wash away irritants, scratch, piece of grit. Paces the virgin PVC floor. Flicks pen top in out, out in, sterling silver. Hippocrates used silver to treat ulcers and wounds. He calls them over. Points to the machine. 'Bring me through it,' he says. 'Bring me through it.' 'We suspected it was related to epilepsy but …' No, not you Dr Falvey. Her. Step up. 'Is this the appropriate time?' Dr Falvey asks. There's little time. Her family is outside. It's exactly the right time. What else are they here training for? Inches forward in rumple-toe shoes; Nurse Bernie from Skerries. Pure gas at karaoke and never wanted to be a nurse but for her broad-shouldered adoptive Ma who took her on by the grace of God and claimed it as a sound idea. 'The scan shows a blood clot.' I can see that already, Beard says. And what else? What about intracranial blood flow, other vitals? 'It's not good,' Dr Falvey butts in. Let her answer, I'm asking her. 'A massive stroke on top.'

On top of what? 'On top of other internal injuries.' But are they classed as actual injuries? 'What do you mean?' It's not a trauma per se, so what is it exactly? 'Brainstem death,' Nurse Bernie says, her knees buckling. 'Excuse Bernie, doctor,' the other wispy nurse whispers. 'She's also pregnant, a few weeks in.' Well this is how you learn. Get the family in pronto. I also need to speak to Boyne ASAP. Girls, wait, girls, listen up, it's also classified as whole brain death, not just brainstem death. Make sure to know the difference. There's an important medical distinction here. Baby is still with us. Heartbeat strong. What's the husband's name? Go find Boyne. As hospital manager this is totally his ball.

Peter Papadoo shuffles in with Grandpa Brian. Brief relief that she is now in a room of her own behind reception, tucked away from the beeping ant stream. 'My sunshine, my beautiful lil' sunshine,' he says in a slurp voice, touching Mama. 'You who were always so stunning, no less dazzling now.' Peter Papadoo starts to sob. 'Don't Brian, don't.' When we took her home from the hospital she slept for a month. We thought there might be something wrong then. She barely drank a sup. Then overnight didn't she sprout up a big pink hibiscus. Tallest in her class at age six. Nicknamed the Spinning Pea because she could never sit still or do one thing at a time. She started up her own dance troupe of young 'uns, did she ever tell you that? The Beaumont Belles! Prancing around the dining room table in a heap of made-up steps and flounces. Leader of the local litter club, scrubbing up them filthy laneways at the back of the estate. Mother to I don't know how many gerbils. When she was fourteen she came back from a school trip to Paris having spent all her money on presents for us, every last blasted coin. That's the type she is. Thermometer of the Eiffel Tower on a Bakelite base.

She does not look good, not good, not good at all. Her bones splinter when her limbs are lifted. There's a piece of mould growing from her head that looks like a clouded wedding bouquet. Falvey brings in a consultant from outside. 'Numerous infections, the eyes won't close. She needs ongoing everything, there's talk of meningitis, drugs for the bowels, the stomach, a series of slow flows. She needs to be turned on the hour, it's …' Stop you there,' he says. 'I have never seen the likes. In all my years, across many countries. What have they said of the legislation exactly?' There's no machine on the planet that can keep this up. What is the confusion about? 'It's complex,' Falvey says, without being sure exactly. Sometimes that's how complex complexity is. He thinks of the vending machine Oath they all took with no sub-clause for the good poisons that might squall a swell as big as the Hill of Tara with dolmens and dirt tracks underneath. He thinks of his own daughter bouncing on a space hopper. He thinks of banshees and their pneumonic screams, how they are specifically designed to scare young boys. His mind turns to golf. There is so much tediousness and yet nothing more to do here. He takes his own blood pressure.

The media is assembling, queuing in their cars on the tar. Remember no cameras, just facts. We're not that sick. Have a good look at the Texas Futile Care Law, it's not so dissimilar to ours. No opinion pieces, leave that to the idiotic blogosphere. If there's only 20 percent chance of survival at twenty-four weeks, what hope has this mitten at eighteen? Is there anyone out there who's prepared to talk openly on this? A similar case up North maybe? Get a flaky feminist to do a lawnmower mouth on it. What are the doctors saying? Are we talking severe handicap or stillborn? How far is the State willing to go? Where is the precedent? Get an intern down to the courts, always murmurs in the corridors there. Follow the cloaks, no cacking off to Guards, keep it lean, a crisp 800 words.

Owen refuses to come to the bed. There is a wail inside his stomach that wants to plaster the walls of the world with hot pins. She is asleep too long and he can't sleep at night as a result. He never thought her to be so mean. Isaac broke so many of his toys in these two weeks, the longest running hours of his life. Even the wooden tractor bought in Galway beside the pie shop where daddy burnt his mouth on a slimy red pepper. Instead he watches the drift of skirring seagulls on Dublin's skyline, so far up the clouds look like soapy blobs that slip off the scrubbing brush in the sink after dinner. 'Why didn't Edel come with us?' Isaac asks Peter Papadoo, though he takes a little while to answer, explaining she has a snuffly nose and doesn't want to give Mama a bad cold. 'Is Mama trying to be inside Halloween?' he enquires. 'Her face looks like the pumpkin we put on the windowsill in the sitting room except for the colour.' Peter Papadoo clasps an arm around him into the tightest of hugs. The most crucial thing about being a boy of his age is to be brave at all times, to push on like a musketeer in a jumbo maze of briers. 'Can we get crisps from the machine?' Give it a minute or so more. Talk to your Mama there, tell her what you've been up to. 'What's the point?' Owen pipes up. 'It's not like she can actually hear us or maybe she doesn't even want to anymore.' No, no, no, no, no, that's not true! That can't be true and will never be true. She is just not well. It's not her fault. You do understand it's really not her fault? 'Yesterday Owen bashed the machine in the hall when the chocolate wouldn't fall out proper,' Isaac tells him. 'That's totally not true!' Owen says. 'You are making things up all the time Isaac.'

The simpering PR guy shows Peter Papadoo and Grandpa Brian how to use the Tassimo in time for the meeting. 'Pop a pod in there – Samiaza or Café Hag are pretty good – but of course it's up to you.' Grandpa Brian has his eyes hooked on the unperturbed frosted head of Boyne sitting at the long rectangular table at the very top of the room. 'I'm not in the mood for refreshments,' he says. It was all 'tragic and unfortunate … difficult, and challenging' until they put it in writing they wanted the life support switched off. Now they were being summoned to several 'briefings' per day. Talk of 'viability' and 'potential legal consequences'. Host of other fruitless buzzwords and lardy sentences stuck snug in a worn book. 'Look at the state of them,' Grandpa Brian says, pulling at Peter Papadoo's elbow. 'It's looking more and more like the Last Supper every day.'

Dr Falvey outlines what he considers to be equitable fact: mechanical support is normally only used to keep organs intact until such a time as donation is feasible. Absence of neurological activity, already determined, is legal death. In his opinion, if he may be so bold as to state it out loud right here, the Eighth Amendment shouldn't even come into it as she's already gone. Boyne cuts him off as he would a hunk of ribeye. 'It is not our job to stand on top of the law, but to serve beneath it.' Grandpa Brian reminds them that legal submissions will be heard in the morning, it will be more obvious what way to go. 'According to your own paperwork, she was very much looking forward to the birth of this child,' asserts Boyne. 'Of course she was!' Grandpa Brian replies. She had chosen names. She had decorated. She had made provisional enquiries at the same multidenominational school the others go to. The child's presence in the world was almost tactual, tangible, inasmuch as her roaming heartbeat was. 'We are heaps ahead of the United States,'

Opus Dei says. 'They don't recognise such a right until it's out and about sitting on the ground looking and smelling like a baby before it's deemed to officially be one.' Grandpa Brian and Peter Papadoo don't care if Ireland is an ejecta blanket of ignorant moon and the rest of the world is an even rougher surface still, they cannot and will not change their minds. 'It's about dignity,' Grandpa Brian informs the table. 'Our resolution is as solid and still as she is.' Boyne shuffles his papers. 'We have to be very careful here not to confuse relative with absolute value on human life, while of course trying our very best to do right by your daughter.'

Floppy liver strapped to chrome and fibre plastic in a cleaning closet on the fifth floor. Sanctify me in a sick bag. The next incy step for ethical kind. Gashed from Mama at night five days ago, Speculum Man who delivers premature babies with distinction and expert of women's parts; Beard, with the aid of Boyne's blind eye, decided it was the only way to save me from fire. They plan to grow me for twenty weeks and see how it goes. In a few weeks I'll be plump enough for a tube through the nose into the windpipe, a mix of air, oxygen and prayer. Dr Falvey will be pulled in to see me this afternoon though they have the colour of him in advance. His Facebook page shows just how much of a rancid cause carrier he is: Royal Society for the Preservation of Marine Animals, Doctors for Gaza, Great Apes Survival Partnership, No Fracking Europe, but barely able to look management in the eye or answer his wife back. He'll keep his mouth shut alright. 'O, God! O, Jesus Christ! No! How is this possible? Pure monstrous!' Beard will explain a gorgeous filthy irony – new technology from an abortion clinic in Canada – where there's no restriction on gestational limits, an exodus in reverse. And don't start going down the calculable line of Frankenstein, for pity's sake, who else will give a flying shit about me!? The country is run aground (they are saying), abortion under certain circumstances will be all circumstances before too long. This is our only chance to prove the body politic wrong. Think ahead to the golden moment, where we present our findings. The look on their faces.

A legal envoy from the courts is set to visit to clock my heartbeat for a flipchart, except I'm no longer where he thinks I should be. They will probably take a line in from another, between 120 and 180 beats per minute, steady whoosh of citizen. No visitors allowed in to see Mama now under any circumstances, because she is, let's be very clear about this, not in decent fettle. Stew meat that's been on too long, melting collagen, thawing into gelatine. Peter Papadoo can't bear to look at her face, the smile of his saucy brunette having flown the nest for sure. Her voice follows him about the house in every cupboard he opens. 'Will you just try to fold the clothes for once, not fling them!' He's down at the courts most days flagellating and flailing, trying to grab as many legal eagles and politicians as he can. 'Our hands are tied,' they tell him, with shoulder pat. 'But it shouldn't be too long now.' Grandpa Brian is burying underground, eating soil, hiding from the bloodthirsty mink as he sees it. Dr Falvey uses the phone in reception to join a tennis club. It has brand spanking new Tiger Turf that's resurfaced every year and you can play under floodlights seven nights a week. Mojitos cost only €6 for members.

She's come to get me. 'Rascal flower, butter fairy, there you are! Come here to me now. Don't make me run after you!' Unhooking tubes like you do with a baby seat in a good-sized family car. Messianic puddle on the floor is all that's left. Experiment over, hypothesis incomplete, breakthrough broken. 'You don't mind, do you, if we hang around for a small while?' Mama says. Daddy is in a right fluff and needs our support. 'Look at you! You are cuter than I thought I could ever do! Is that not a Cheshire Cat smile? Also I think it would be good for you to get to know Owen, Isaac and Edel a bit better. They're all so different … delightedly themselves. It sometimes pinches the breath right from me. Good God, they will go nutso for you though! Be prepared. Edel will likely put dresses on you. She really wanted a sister.'

Boyne's wife turns up at the hospital at the chink of dawn for a good aul bicker. His own fault for not picking an equal. He has not been home since I went missing. She thinks he's having an affair. To her it's a matter of plausible explanation. She discussed it at length with the other ladies at the gym. It's not that she's totally thick but certainly she wouldn't have even a quarter of the brainpower as him. He told a colleague when he met and married her it was all a bit of a package deal. Measure for measure, tit for tat, tooth for tooth. He'd done that 1980s' thing of spotting her across a packed dancefloor: 'That's the woman I'm going to marry!' She has zero concept of the pressure he's under now. Volumes of paperwork alone would depress an Olympic diver. Skill of skills to stop a post-mortem too. If it gets out he'll lose his bonus or even worse: there'd be a sticky public enquiry. He leaves her to the front door by A&E, kisses the sacred space between her cheek and chin and watches her disappear into a pack of parked cars. She understands now how exhausted he is. She may have made another dumb mistake thinking otherwise. The sun is back out from her skirt shadows. He pops that awkward small bone in his neck before strolling back through the double doors towards the waiting mob.

Nuala Ní Chonchúir

Nuala Ní Chonchúir was born in Dublin and lives in East Galway. She has published four short story collections, the most recent, *Mother America*, appeared from New Island in 2012. Nuala's critically acclaimed second novel, *The Closet of Savage Mementos*, appeared in 2014, also from New Island; it was shortlisted for the Kerry Irish Novel of the Year Award 2015. Under the name Nuala O'Connor, Penguin USA, Penguin Canada and Sandstone (UK) published Nuala's third novel, *Miss Emily*, about the poet Emily Dickinson and her Irish maid, in summer 2015. 'Shut Your Mouth, Hélène' is inspired by the Kate and Anna McGarrigle song, 'Jacques et Gilles'. Her website is www.nualanichonchuir. com

Shut Your Mouth, Hélène

The walking makes yellow blisters erupt on Hélène's feet. Primrose-coloured sacs of liquid, rimmed with scarlet. She bursts them at the campfire by night, after easing out of the boots that seem to shrink around her feet the further she walks. She does not complain to Maman or Papa, she knows what they will say: *Ferme ta gueule, Hélène. Hush! You are ten. Think of Ti-Pit and Ti-Jean – they are small boys. Do you hear them grouse?* It has been said more than once to her already.

All day they walk, a group of twenty, between adults and children, with one wagon for belongings, as well as a few horses and mules. The Connecticut River – and, later, the Merrimac – sparkles and spates beside them, a lure for Hélène's ruined toes and heels. She keeps her head turned to the water and imagines sitting on the bank to paddle her feet. She wishes she could swim naked as a trout through the river, the way she does in the Chaudière, with the *chutes* crashing above her like a million liquid angels tossed from on high. How she loves to bathe and dive in that river pool below the falls. She misses her home in Lac-Mégantic; she misses Grandmère and her friends and the schoolroom.

Yes, she even misses the chickens and sows who cause her so much bother with their greedy peck-and-snuffle.

'Does New Hampshire have a school, Maman?' Hélène catches up with her mother and walks beside her. She will talk to her as a way to unbalance the hunger pains that claw at her belly.

'It has schools, *petite*, but you will not see the inside of one, as you well know.'

Hélène pouts her lip. 'What will I be doing, Maman?'

'Whatever is asked of you. You'll carry water, darn clothing, knit, spin. Any chore that needs to be done.'

'I want to go to school. I miss my books.'

'*Ferme ta gueule*, Hélène! I have enough on my mind without listening to nonsense. You know you are not to speak unless you have something useful to say.'

'*Désolée*, Maman. Sorry.'

'Walk with your brothers.'

Every night at the campfire, Paddy Boyle sings sad songs. Hélène does not need to understand Gaelic to know that the songs are mournful – the tunes soar and drop in such melancholic waves, and his wife's tears flow so freely, it is clear the verses are full of sorrow. By day Mr Boyle is an angry man. He beats the mules and snaps at Hélène because she walks too close ahead of him when she is mesmerised by the river's torrents that sing to her like sirens.

'Get out from under me feet,' he bawls, making Hélène jump like a scalded rat. His huge boot comes scraping down her calf because she has dawdled too long in his path again. He yells at Maman, 'Missus, can you not rein in that child? She's away with the fairies half the day.'

Other times Hélène catches him looking at her, his tongue poked from the corner of his mouth, a furtive smile prowling his lips.

Mrs Boyle – Kitty – is a toad of a woman, wide of hip and flat of face. Her hair is cut short and Hélène doesn't dare ask Maman why. Mrs Boyle rides the wagon, perched on the back with her legs a-dangle, because she is with child. It seems to Hélène she sits there in judgment over them all.

One afternoon she comes upon Mrs Boyle kneeling by the bank of the Merrimac, praying aloud. Hélène likes the guttural, raw sound of the words: '*Go dtaga do ríocht, go ndeintear do thoil …*' It is a language that seems to be scraped up from the speaker's gut before being delivered to the tongue.

Mrs Boyle's bonnet is on the grass beside her and Hélène sees the shorn head and also whorls of scabby scalp where hair is missing. It disgusts the girl but she feels sympathy too, for what is a woman without bountiful hair? Kitty Boyle snatches up her hat and shoves it on her head when she realizes she is no longer alone.

'Oh, it's only you,' she says, looking at Hélène. She ties her bonnet strings and attempts to get up. Hélène goes to her and allows herself to be used as a prop. Mrs Boyle leans heavily on her to get her footing, her breath falling on the girl's face; Hélène is surprised to find it sweet, like Saskatoon berries.

'*Mo bhuíochas*,' Kitty Boyle says. 'I thank you.'

'Muh vweekus,' Hélène mimics, and they smile at each other.

'*Merci beaucoup!*' Mrs Boyle says, giggling a little at her pronunciation and looking to Hélène for reassurance.

'*De rien*,' she answers.

They walk back to where the others sit, alone and in groups, drinking from water cans and biting into hard tack. Hélène's papa gives the signal – a short blasting whistle through the teeth – and everyone rises, both keen and reluctant to begin walking again. The sooner they move, the sooner they might come upon a farm to buy eggs and milk. The sooner they eat well, the quicker they will gain the mills of Nashua, New Hampshire and the promised work. Then there will be money, clumps of it.

'Nearly two weeks,' says Mr Boyle, 'marching like savages.'

'Keep your pecker in your pocket, Paddy,' Jacques Aubry says, pointing at Mrs Boyle's swollen front, 'and you'll have less need for marching. Fewer mouths to feed.'

At first, Mr Boyle looks like he will thump Jacques but instead he lets a great, raucous whoop and laughs for longer than is needed. Hélène looks at Kitty Boyle, enthroned once more on the back of the wagon, but her face stays rigid, as if she has not heard anything that has passed between her husband and Jacques Aubry.

The moon slithers up over the trees, a silver coin against the navy sky; stars hang in milky drapes. Hélène could spend her whole life watching the variance of the skies and be content doing it. She means to stay awake until dawn, to follow the moon's chase of the sun, but she falls asleep. Morning fingers its way up, dragging its fleshy caul, and the night-spell is fractured. Maman heaves herself towards the campfire and pokes at the embers, sending up ash in clouds.

Hélène takes the pail to the river and dips it low for water, lying on her front so she can pull it up by the handle with both hands. A movement makes her look into the river where she is astonished to see Kitty Boyle rise out of the water before her like an apparition. Hélène drops the pail into the river and has to scramble after it; she grabs it before it sinks and stares at Mrs Boyle, who is dressed only in her underthings. The material clings to her body, clearly showing the dark parts of her breasts and the swell of her stomach where Hélène knows a babe wriggles. She stands in the water and lifts her arms as if she means to flop backwards and sail away.

'Mrs Boyle!' Hélène calls. 'Kitty!'

The woman focuses her gaze and lowers her arms; she starts to wade towards the bank. 'I'd be gone but for you came,' she says.

Hélène slips into the Merrimac and hauls Kitty out, half pulling, half shoving her. The woman seems not to want to leave the river, though it is cold. Pushing her onto the bank, Hélène squats and wraps her own shawl around Kitty's shoulders.

Mrs Boyle bows her head and says, 'I'm all right now, *a leana.*'

Hélène is not sure if she is speaking to her, or the baby that grows inside her belly.

'Where is your gown? Your shoes?'

Kitty Boyle points to a stand of bushes and Hélène fetches her clothes. She pulls them on over the woman's wet skin and undergarments, dressing her as if she is an enormous doll.

'Will you tell?'

Hélène looks at Kitty. 'I know to keep my mouth shut.'

She shivers and nods her thanks.

Hélène uses Kitty's mallet to pin down the Boyles' tent. Kitty stands with her hands tucked into the arch of her back, letting Hélène take over this small job from her. The girl is happy to help, happy to relieve her new friend of some of her tasks. Thwack goes the mallet, deep goes the pin.

Mrs Boyle teaches Hélène how to knit in the Irish way. Her cables and diamonds do not look as firm and flowing as they should, but the older woman praises Hélène's effort before making her rip it all back and start afresh. They sit on the back of the wagon together in the evenings, their needles clacking companionably. Kitty tells Hélène about her island home in the East Atlantic; Hélène tells her about Lac-Mégantic and the river and lake she loves so well.

Paddy stands by the campfire puffing on his pipe.

'Have I two wives now, hah?' he says. 'With ye both at it, I'll be wearing a new gansey in no time. No time at all.' Kitty and Hélène raise their eyes to him but do not speak; they continue with their work, the rough wool piled in their laps. Paddy points with his pipe at Hélène. 'You'll get nowhere in life without proper schooling.' He stares at the pair for a moment, spits into the campfire and walks away.

Maman calls Hélène to help her wash pots and plates. Hélène leaves down her knitting and goes to her. They carry the utensils to the river and dip them in, scraping at them with clumps of grass.

'Don't be making up to the Boyles. They're not our kind.'

'They're here with us.'

'He's an agitator. A troublemaker. Keep away from them.'

'But, Maman ...'

'Hélène!' Maman slaps two tin plates together. '*Ferme ta gueule.*'

The sun is a bright roundel in the sky but the camp sleeps on. Paddy Boyle passed around a few bottles the night before.

They held something clear and potent that made Papa gasp when he slugged, but it unfastened his tongue. All the adults drank from the bottles and they sang, laughed and talked late into the night. Hélène tried to stay awake but tiredness from walking all day and the high heat from the banked-up fire made her drowse away, the voices around her becoming liquid and slow.

Now she knows the sun's late morning heat will have warmed the waters of the Merrimac. She slips down to the bank, undresses to her skin and slides in. The river is still cool, yes, but its chill is friendly somehow, welcoming. A few strokes and she is clear of the weedy tangle of the riverbank; the current is gentle for it hasn't rained for a while. Hélène swims a bit, lets the water bubble over her mouth, flips onto her back and floats. She closes her eyes and lets the sun beat down on her face and body. She swims and drifts, eyes closed when she rides on her back. In her mind she is in the river-pool of the Chaudière, bobbing towards the spray of the falls; any moment she will feel the first spritz on her face. Opening her eyes, Hélène sees that Paddy Boyle is above her on the riverbank, watching. He flips his suspenders down over his arms and fumbles with the buttons of his trousers. His hand disappears inside his drawers and he starts to beat himself rhythmically. His head jerks backwards and his mouth goes slack but he keeps his eyes fixed on Hélène. She bobs down to tread water and looks up at him. Over the sloshing of the river she can hear him grunt.

'Come here,' he calls. Hélène shakes her head. 'Come on, now,' he croons, stretching one hand to her while the other continues to work steadily at himself.

Hélène swims downstream, looking for a sheltered spot where she can climb out and get to her clothes. Paddy Boyle follows her with his eyes and doesn't notice the approach of

Kitty or the mallet that she swings into his stomach. Paddy groans, pitches forward and falls face-first into the dirt. Kitty drops to her knees beside him, raises the mallet and brings it down onto the back of his head. The noise it makes is like the splinter of axe through wood. Kitty shoves her husband along the ground until he dangles over the riverbank. Hélène crouches in the water and looks up at her friend; Kitty stares back. She pants a little but she is as composed as a woman going about the keeping of her house. Kitty glances around, gives a sharp nod and Hélène wades forward and pulls Mr Boyle's body into the water. His face looms close to hers and she flinches and pushes him away. She and Kitty watch the Merrimac take Paddy Boyle with it, like a piece of driftwood.

Kitty offers Hélène her hand and the girl climbs from the water, sliding on the muddy bank. Mrs Boyle takes Hélène's pantalettes from the pile of clothes and helps her step into them. She pulls her gown over her head and fixes the sleeves as best she can over the girl's wet skin; she takes Hélène's hands in hers and stares into her eyes. Kitty does not speak but Hélène can hear her.

She nods to say she has understood and whispers, '*Ferme ta gueule, Hélène. Ferme ta gueule.*'

Niamh Boyce

From Athy, Co. Kildare, Niamh Boyce's debut novel, *The Herbalist* (Penguin), won The Sunday Independent Newcomer of the Year at the Irish Books Awards, and was nominated for the Dublin IMPAC Award. She won the Hennessy XO New Writer of the Year in 2011 for her poetry. She's working on a new novel and a collection of stories.

I'll Take You There

'Don't ever,' he'd say. 'Be careful,' he'd warn, 'or you'll get hurt.' And he was right, my husband, it did hurt. And so I died, in a glass house, years and years ago. Yet someone calls my name; whispers it over and over like a charm. Poor girl, do you know what you're doing? Do you know you can be heard?

Be careful.
I wasn't.

It began in the garden. He had taken you to visit his mother. I was on my knees, turning the earth, clearing the way for pansies, marigolds and geraniums with thick red petals. I smelt cigarettes. A cough came from the other side of the wall. Our new neighbour, or our new neighbour's gardener. They were wealthy enough to have a gardener, living in such a big house. I coughed myself, in protest against the smoke invading my morning. 'Hey there!' A woman squinted down at me, frizzy bob, elbows on the wall. 'Hello,' I replied. 'Do you believe in the afterlife?' she asked. I laughed, but she waited for an answer. I considered. 'Well,' I said, 'there's a house I go to sometimes in my dreams.'

Maggie invited me for tea in their conservatory. Italian tiles, Japanese prints, feral plants. 'The light on your hair ...' she said from across the room. Then, her fingers were touching my cheek. I stayed still, the glass beaded wet. She released her breath. 'I'd like to paint you. Soon. When the light is like this.' I said yes or maybe just nodded – I don't know which, I was confused by something coming awake.

Don't ever.
I did.
    The first time I posed, I was embarrassed. I made faces. Being looked at, I don't know, felt strange. Not my body or anything. I didn't think of that. No, it was my mouth that bothered me. What would she read in my expression? What would it betray? We used her spare shed. 'The studio', she called it. Window, bare walls, mattress, wooden floor. She chattered to relax me, asked silly questions. 'What's the colour of your world, when your world is good?' 'Turquoise,' I surprised myself by knowing. 'What's the colour of sex?' 'Sex? I don't know.' I didn't. 'Of love?' 'Pure duck egg. The world of love is pure duck egg.'

She made charcoal sketches, waited for the light to creep in before mixing her paint. 'Yes, yes, here it comes,' she said, scooting a brush across her palette. I felt it then, on my shoulders. Maggie said 'alleluia praise the lord' and got to work trying to capture it. I felt like the first woman feeling the warm hand of the first sun.

I didn't tell anyone, but it leaked in anyway, made me want to fill my world with colour – blues, turquoise, violet, magenta too. I wanted to be freer, like the women I saw on the beach, not caring, not wearing proper swimsuits but all sorts of mix and match, bras and sarongs. Their laughter was raucous. One of the older ones, quite fat – 'a seal,' my husband said – had no top on. Her skin was oily, and brown. He snorted; I thought she was wonderful. My own skin was so white, unseen, most of the time.

'Everyone else's house is spotless,' he said, 'other women can do it, why can't you?' Maybe I'm not a woman, I thought. But I tried, spent days on end tidying. Then I got tired of pretending I cared. We'd fight, and you'd hide. I'd find you curled behind the couch. He insisted on kindergarten. 'Do you want our daughter to spend her childhood chalking dragons on a bloody blackboard, swimming in the sea and drinking hot chocolate?' Yes, yes I did. He wanted me to be someone else, to be like him. Guarded, watching others to know how to live. I used to like to taste his lips, but we didn't even kiss then, let alone anything else. Did he kiss someone else? I didn't ask. He had hit me once, there was spit around his mouth. I had said something, taunted him. I used to taunt him.

One time we met at night. Maggie pushed the mattress under the window so the moonlight would fall on my body. The sheet stopped at my hips. I felt a draft along my side. I lay with my arm over my head, stretched as if asleep. Closed my eyes. Something rustled outside. I worried about getting caught, getting pneumonia. I trusted she'd make beauty of it, the derelict room, the curtainless window, but it was different to before. I missed my own bed at home. I missed you coming to curl in beside me. There, I was just something for the light to fall on.

She was pleased with that painting. I felt humiliated somehow, like she was saying something about me I didn't understand. 'I look old fashioned,' I said, 'from another time.' 'Timeless,' she said. I looked like a piece of meat on a butcher's block. My face was featureless, roughly shaded. 'Are you going to finish my face?' 'It's done.' I became irritated, why was I doing this? My husband would be so angry if he knew, more than angry. 'Find another model.' She topped the turps, hung a sheet over the painting. 'Fine then, go back to your life.'

I hear you cry out for your mother. I want you to know this – I'm near. And I love you still, more. There was so much I wanted to show you, but it would be enough now just to wrap you in my arms and hold you. Your hand was so small the last time you put it on mine. When I hear your voice calling, your dream becomes my dream and I run down a corridor, run towards a door, but when I get there, the crying stops, and your footsteps echo away from me.

You'll get hurt.
Yes.
    I posed one last time. In Maggie's greenhouse. There was silence, except for the sound of the brush: soothing, rhythmic. Sweat glistened in the crease of my elbow. A cloud passed over, a second of shade and coolness. An insect hit plastic sheeting over and over. My blue dress was about my waist, and the glass of the greenhouse sang blue too and he

saw me, and he saw her, and he didn't care that the light was exquisite.

I search that house you go to in your dreams, the one where you search every room for me. You're cowering behind the couch, hands over ears. Listen, I whisper, I'll give you a different place to be. Look, there's a child laughing, and that child is you. We're outside and we're free as birds. Your skin's fresh with summer, the day is pure duck egg. You say that when you grow up, you're going to fly to America and taste a real soda. And I tell you, that when I grow up, I'm going to take you there.

Anakana Schofield

Anakana Schofield writes fiction, essays and literary criticism. *Malarky*, her debut novel, won the Amazon.ca First Novel Award and the US Debut-Litzer Prize for Fiction. *Malarky* was also shortlisted for the Ethel Wilson Fiction Prize, selected as a Barnes & Noble Discover Great New Writers Pick and named on sixteen different Best Books of the Year lists. *Martin John*, her second novel, will be published in North America in September 2015 and in Ireland/UK in early 2016 (And Other Stories). She has contributed to the *London Review of Books* blog, the *Guardian, The Irish Times*, the *Globe and Mail* and more. Anakana currently lives in Vancouver, BC, with her son.

Beneath the Taps:
A Testimonial

This is my story and I'm sticking to it.

This is what I intend to say tomorrow in court. Be assured.

*

She was the middle child. She was middling in the middle. Lukewarm. The third tap between hot and cold. You could turn her a little this way and a little that, but there was always someone more forceful wedged either side of her.

*

I was a superstitious child who ever expected to sink.

*

Her arrival, briefly noted, and then forgotten, was in the middle of September. A month of in-betweens: summer bidding adios but winter not yet an adamant hello. She yowled loud because there was ever someone else yowling.

She would have to wait, because you learn to wait. They'll teach you to wait. That's how it is. Arrested in the middle. Decisively in middle age she waited no more and landed up arrested. Intentionally or unintentionally, this court will have to decide. Her solicitor, today, busy trying to influence this, labouring to create amends for her but she, belligerent, hands him a plastic red folder with a sheaf of these three pages. I didn't want them ruined by the rain, she confirms.

He doesn't read on receiving. Slots them in the middle plastic basket in the middle of the three, squatting on his desk. Bills in the top, letters in the bottom and what-the-fuckity panned into the basket between.

I didn't want them ruined by the rain will be the full extent of what she confirms in this conversational exchange with him. It's all in the document, she'll say, pointing to that middle panier. That's my story and I'm sticking to it.

*

Three children now, some forty years have since lapsed. Forty years can lapse in a paragraph, where forty minutes cannot ever lapse in a life. Head shakes the solicitor. A mother of three, past forty, with no previous convictions – how will I not get this past?

Yet

It shouldn't be so tough with drug busts and gang bangers and drunken Eastern Europeans clogging the court hearings beside her. Yet, she's a hint of the saboteur. Yet, do you hear me now? She doesn't. He's been insisting she hears. He doesn't think she has heard. Listen, he'll be insisting to her yet. Up the stairs of the court, leans towards her ear. Listen. This is the way it is. He has to be firm. Yet, she doesn't entirely nod. She half feigns a nip of a nod.

Yet, she doesn't agree this is how to get her off. No. She will not compromise. She looks everywhere but at him. She looks through him. Eyes on or above the middle of his forehead. His hairline. Eyebrows. Chin. He hasn't much of a chin. Out a window. At that potted plant on the left side of the room that needs watering. Her eyes stop-still on a pipe, the radiator pipe. Once he has finished outlining his defence of her and checking dates with her is when her eyes move. Without comment she hands him a script. This script. Eyes on the pipe, as she hands it over. It's as though she could yet move to ask a question. Yet, no, upon exit she brushes the radiator and he witnesses her hand on the pipe and up it curls in retreat. Careful, it's hot, he adds.

It's hot, she confirms.

The second and only other thing she confirms in this conversational exchange.

I didn't want them ruined by the rain.

This is my story and it's hot.

Under the Taps

I was obsessed with occupying the middle spot in the bath. I would take a bath on my side rather than my back. I wanted to be a human ruler inside the bath. The taps interrupted matters. I wasn't a long person. But no matter, the taps forced a contortion. I wasn't ever content with this contortion.

After the Taps

All my children obviously arrived in my middle. Pushed it out, a tad up before dropping it down. My middle would never quite rise again. It had a sag in it. I will say in my defence, if I am required to supply a defence, I was reclaiming my sag.

Beyond the Taps

How is it you may be wondering?

I would like to say (to the court) my grandfather was a plumber, that he fixed pipes for those women who liberated us eventually inside the post office and up on the roof of City Hall. I would like to say my father, too, was a plumber and that I had grown up around the smell of welding flames or been immersed in fixing poor-functioning water tanks. Or I could talk of the copper pipes being the reason behind all this, coupled with the dreadful water pressure in Dublin. However precise an explanation it would prove, none of it is true. My father was a bald and stable civil servant. My mother was a woman who waited for him to come home and barely complained a day in her life about anything. I did spend an inordinate amount of time in my childhood staring at taps. That was the primary evidence I might end up in the place I stand today.

I would try to place my head upside down so I could see up inside taps. I was more partial to pipe joining and hacksaws than yoyos and dolly heads. I also broke my brother's left arm with a hammer. It was an accident. He deserved it and it was a small bone that healed fast. He received a cast and people tried and failed to write messages on it. It was not as awful as it sounds. I did not pin him down and hammer his arm. We were trying to build a tent, some aspect of which became uncooperative and I missed clouting what he was holding and clouted his forearm instead. He let a wail out of himself that brought my mother, accusatory-eyed, before she yielded to my point at a bamboo stick as attempted tent pole on the ground as the intended target.

My broken-armed brother was wailing and writhing and rolling on the ground imitating football players he'd seen similarly downed on *Match of the Day*. All my mother said was how many times have I told you to leave the hammer alone? That's it she said. Help me carry him to the car. My brother more than wailed. He screamed that his bitch sister was not to put a hand near him and he would walk to the car unassisted and get her away from me. She's nothing but a witch. I was left alone in the house with the hammer while they went to the hospital. He was plied with presents and sympathy, yet it was the single most interesting thing that happened in his whole life. His handwriting never recovered mam claimed, but then she'd make any old excuse for the boys. Boys weren't cut out for this or that and boys were not cut out for helping around the house and it was only boys who should have leanings towards hammers at all.

They are both in the court today. Sat up at the back, looking smug, eyebrows ready for a raise. They have not brought up the hammer incident but it's there behind their eyelids and I am sure they will be bringing it up over lunch that will consist of a good headshake and a ham sandwich near this courthouse.

You were an awful child, my mother would sometimes say lightheartedly at parties and at my wedding, which she was right to warn me against, since I am no longer married, long since no longer married. In fact if you ever see the man I married he will likely tell you worse stories than the hammer story. He will tell you the tub truth that I was constantly in the bathroom during our marriage and it was one of several factors he attributed to our demise.

I could by turn reply that had he spent more time in the bath during our marriage the prospects would have been all the stronger for it. Genetically I have the olfactory oath and can smell a fire four streets away. I can always tell when someone has left a pan on the cooker on our street even while standing in the back garden, hanging up washing.

The above is a digression, which I do not require you to submit to the court in my defence.

The next part is not a digression: take it very seriously.

We all tolerated a less than satisfactory toilet (see olfactory providence) and a too-slim bath that it was instructed never to fill beyond the three-inch mark. We, four kids, three boys and hammer-head girl (testifying for you now) would scream unmercifully if we believed one of us was violating this staunch household bylaw. Now lads, Mam would say, there's only so much hot water in the tank and so we are all for caring and sharing or it'll be rationed by me. Rationed by her meant that one child would have to take the bath water of the last child. Note that justice was meted out via the bathwater. You were either innocent or guilty based on the amount of water you drew into the bath for the purpose of cleansing yourself.

I was the only child who was blissfully excited the day the immersion heater blew up. I still remember them men in the van. A tall man with a wide head and a strong smile who was able to squeeze into small spaces and call out things unimpeded. Frank, Frank would you pass me the ... Frank, Frank could you turn the ... The other fella Frank was unremarkable. He stood staring waiting to be shouted at. Twice I heard the main man call him a dozy bollix.

The cartography of our bathroom bothered me. There was something of a gale blowing in it and the space between the toilet and bath was wasted. There were also established rules around where the bath mat hung and the purpose for which it was intended.

Now lads, my mother would say, how many times do I have to tell you lift up the mat and hang it over the edge of the tub and it'll be dry for the next set of approaching feet. OK. OK she'd intone.

No one was listening and we weren't all lads for I was a girl. But the smartest thing about my mother was she raised us with the instructions *lads*. She knew that *lads* was the best way to be in the world. That lads would bring us to a better-functioning bathroom and in my case it has. In my most peculiar case, I should say it has also brought me into this courtroom today.

*

The Confession

There have been three bathtubs I have snuck into. I am point-blank guilty of entering these bathtubs uninvited and unbeknownst. I am guilty and should be punished although I will contest that I did no damage to any bath by lowering myself into it.

I begin this confession with the first bathtub.

Ballina

It was a party in Ballina. A house party. The place was ringing with noise. It was easy enough to slip in. A bit of a nod. People stood in the hall were friendly. Some moved to let me pass as I squeezed up the stairs. It was a wait all right to use the toilet. A woman in shoes that no foot should be punished with ahead of me, giddy with drink, *I'm dying to go, I'm absolutely bursting.* A nearby man teasing her, poking her about her middle and she yelling *stop! Would ya stop!*

I had to wait on five people before I could enter, but once inside I found the perfect setting in which to take my illegal soak.

To my memory, there was banging on the door. I ignored it. Didn't fill the bath so full and was in and out and managed my customary need to lie back and put my head under water. I left the bathroom with wet hair. There were now six people waiting. I didn't say anything except the eye wince of a mild sorry and excuse me. I exited that party as swift as I had entered it. I did not lounge about looking for a cocktail sausage. I'd had my cocktail.

Ballinrobe

I have no absolute recognition of this incident except to confirm it was an avocado-coloured bath and that I pretended to be a pizza delivery person in order to gain access to it. Obviously I was not a pizza delivery person, but the residents of Ballinrobe are most obliging and ringing the doorbell and saying I'm delivering pizzas would you mind if I use your toilet does not bring them out in rash. Carry on, they say. No problem, they say. You can and you will, they say and up I went.

This hassle-free welcome perhaps falsely indicated that all bathrooms would welcome me, with the inclusiveness of those bathroom owners in Ballinrobe. Ballinrobe might have been where my delusions about bathroom access took hold.

Ballinasloe

This is the case I am here today to face. I did not mean to give that man a fright and no matter how his statement insists his heart has never been the same since he saw me exit his bathroom – it's simply not true. Did he tell you he made me a cup of tea and that we sat together at his kitchen table? If he hadn't confessed to his daughter who made all this trouble about a perfectly innocent dip and cuppa – none of us would be here.

'She, a perfect stranger, in my bathroom. Me an old man downstairs reading the paper and watching the news.' So he's quoted in these court papers. But he does not speak like that at all. This is not the man whose bathroom I broke into. I never did any specific harm to that man, or his bathroom, beyond give him a startle. I improved his bathroom. I cleaned it after I was finished for I noticed the cleaning powder so long congealed on the top of the container and the dirt engraved into it that I don't think scouring powder was ever used on that bathroom.

Had his daughter not called to put him to bed and check on him and had she not seen me sat in at his table and looked suspiciously upon our cuppa, the man would never have said another word about it. Ask her? Ask this daughter, who sits between us now, ask what were his remarks about my visit? I recall him saying this lovely young girl has come to have a chat with me.

And there's a problem with this indictment against me. He did not have a bath at all. When I entered his bathroom and found no bath to lower myself into and saw he had only a shower, I set about cleaning the bathroom before I left. I admit when he saw me come out, he said I gave him a fright but immediately invited me to sit and that he'd just put on the kettle.

The act of trespass I am guilty of. The act of attempted anything else is a fallacy. The only act of attempt of anything was on his taps, which are inanimate, and unlikely to face the psychological damage that his daughter contests the court must reward him with.

Bring the man to this court and let us hear his story.

The Conclusion

This is the script I have asked my solicitor to present to the court. This is the script he refused to do so by telephone message an hour ago. That is why I am typing this out again. Tomorrow I will read this aloud. Tomorrow again I go to the bench to gather my sag. I have no confidence in the man representing me. He has a head the shape of an egg and we have seen historically where a man with an egg-shaped head previously disappointed us in fiction. He is not a bad or weak man. He is a man who refuses to accept this is my story.

I'm not going to say this in three languages or a loud voice so lean in, but the fella defending me in my case hasn't a clue. He's well known in the town. He repeatedly says, 'We're in good shape.' I haven't a notion what he is talking about. I admit to all my incursions beneath the taps and I supply this text as my cartography of tap baiting.

Siobhán Mannion

Siobhán Mannion was born in Ireland and grew up in Cambridge, England. Her family is from Clifden, Co. Galway. She has won awards for short fiction and radio drama, and her writing has appeared in Irish and international publications including *Eighteen Bridges*, *Stand*, *The Moth*, *New Irish Writing* and the *Silver Threads of Hope* anthology. She is the recipient of a MacDowell Colony fellowship and the Hennessy Award. She works as a radio producer in RTÉ, and is currently completing a first collection of stories.

Somewhere To Be

She takes the turn on the way back from town without thinking, the car loaded with provisions. The afternoon sun is against her as she climbs the narrow track in second gear. With one foot hard on the clutch, the other gently tipping the brake, the Fiesta silently descends the hill. She knows to pull up at an angle, away from the sharp gusts that tear across here twelve months of the year. May sunshine falls on everything, giving life to the pale yellow sand, the dark, shiny rocks at the far end of the beach, the slow-moving water of low tide which draws her gaze out to sea.

The car tips a little in the wind. Early in the mornings she comes here: to walk, to inhale the briny air, sometimes to swim. Ten long days have passed since her last visit. She unclips her seatbelt, feeling it slide back in on itself, folding her arms around her middle. Looking out through the windshield, she can pick up her own scent: on her clothes, her skin; her body hers alone to contend with. An incoming wave foams against the bare rocks. If she let herself, she could sleep.

The walk down to the water takes less than a minute. Her foot goes from under her inside the steepest dune and she falls backwards, slips some of the way down. There is no one to see her, a few weeks ahead of the summer season, this stretch of the coast almost unpopulated for another short while. She brushes the sand from her jeans, pockets the car keys, and finds her stride against the tug of the wind.

At the shore, the tide creeps inward. She moves in small steps, lulled by the wash of the water, allowing time to pass by. Soon her husband will be wondering about her, about the supplies she has collected in town: the soft cheeses ripening on the back seat, fat bottles of sparkling water and lemonade, a crate of spirits, the six-packs of beer weighing down the boot of the car. And the three boxes of balloons grabbed on a whim.

She pulls off her shoes and socks, holds them in one hand, and walks with her head back against the sky, which today is an almost uninterrupted blue, only a few stray clouds drifting high above her. Each time the wind drops, the hidden heat in the day lands. Barefoot, she stands at the beginning of the ocean, the sand giving a little under her with every withdrawal of the tide. The drone of an engine comes to her by water, one of the town's two jet skis rounding the peninsula.

A child's bucket balances on a shelf of grey rock at the end of the strand, its shellfish pattern vivid in sunlight. She makes her way to it, peers inside. Full almost to the brim with coloured shells and smooth pebbles, it slips from her when she reaches, its contents scraping down the side of the rock into a sudden heap on the wet sand. A tiny crab shell sits atop the pile, its underside cracked open, scoured of life. She picks it up by a claw and examines it, before firing it into the Atlantic. For a brief moment, it dances on the surface before disappearing out of sight.

A glance at her watch tells her there are almost four hours before the first guests will arrive; she has time. She takes off her cardigan and folds it, leaving it down where the sand is dry, a fresh breeze cooling her arms. Her watch, as usual, goes inside her left shoe, a sock pushed in behind it. Without looking around, her jeans come down. Whitecaps roll over themselves in the far off waves, the sea shimmering in the deceptive brightness of the day. A short brisk run brings her to the shoreline.

Getting into the sea, she braces herself for the familiar cold that will lock around her. Quickly, she is shoulder-deep, and then her whole body lifted. Her T-shirt is heavy, but not so heavy that it matters, and she pounds into a few strokes of front crawl, heading for the horizon, twisting herself onto her back when she needs to catch her breath; her body, fleetingly, at one with the temperature of the water.

It feels good to be in the ocean, buoyed without effort, one moment easily bringing about the next. There is no one here but her. The riding school must have trekked by earlier in the day, and with luck she will miss the regular dog-walkers. On her back, she stretches, legs together, arms flung out, her body swaying, her mind considering the evening ahead. Perhaps she will find a piece of driftwood at the water's edge, take it home and string it up with pretty lights; hang it inside the porch as a welcome.

The minutes pass. She bobs, knees at her chest, hands scooping below the surface, her torso newly cold each time she relaxes. With her toes in the air, she flexes her feet, their long thin bones fanning out. A sudden wave spills over her. She splutters, flips herself onto her stomach, and, in a sidestroke, swims slowly along the length of the beach, facing land. When she veers beyond the furthest outpost of rock, she sets her course inward again. For a time, she treads water, kicking hard, working to stay warm. Sunlight temporarily blinds her. Her T-shirt swells and empties again as she glides into a languid breaststroke, at all times keeping her head above water.

But her body tires fast, the shoreline starting to recede. Already she has had enough when her neighbour, Harry, appears on the beach, moving along the glistening sand in his halting gait, his little terrier careering ahead. She delays, waiting for them to clamber over the low rocks and on into the fields. The next wave that breaks hits her on the back of the head, sending her under. She resurfaces, sucking in shallow gulps of air, feeling her heart strike high in her chest. The sea pulls back and over her with renewed force and every part of her tenses, flung about in the swirl. She knows she must calm herself, wait it out, assume the worst has already happened. Float, she thinks, letting her limbs go slack. Be carried along by it all.

And then it is over. She propels herself to the shore, prone until her knees bang off the stones. Pushing herself to standing, her body struggles with forward motion, seaweed hooked around one ankle. She falls down on one knee, fingers shoved into the sand. A gull's caw seems near. She watches as the creature swoops in a wide arc, after something in the spiky yellow grass beyond the dunes. The undertow grabs at the ground beneath her, and, with effort, she crawls away from it, up onto dry land.

Her wet clothes drag at her as she moves into the lee of the rocks, out of the sting of the headwind. Leaning over, she lets her arms dangle, her hair fall forward. Water drains quickly into the sand. Her legs shake. She takes in a long deep breath, holding it for as long as she can manage, before carefully releasing it.

'Hello, Grace.'

'Harry. I didn't see you there.' Her shivers throw a tremor into her voice. She picks up her jeans, clutches them in front of her. He appears not to notice anything strange, that she is not in her wetsuit, but a drenched T-shirt and underwear.

''Tis well for you. Here on a Friday.'

She says nothing to this, scraping a hand through her hair, freeing her face.

'We haven't seen you here this past while,' he continues.

'No.'

'Were ye away somewhere?'

'No. No. Just busy with things.'

Harry nods. 'Big party tonight for himself, I hear.'

'That's right.'

The dog barks at the horses coming over the hill, all the riders leaning back in their saddles. She squints up at them, glad to have a reason to look away. Each horse breaks into a trot as soon as it reaches flat sand, the riders quickly finding rhythm, rising easily in their stirrups.

'You're bleeding,' says Harry.

'What?'

He points at the ground. Blood wells from a gash along the top part of her foot, bright red against her pale skin, dissolving into pink rivulets where the dripping water meets it. Together, they watch its progress, while she waits for the pain.

'Probably not as bad as it looks,' he says, using his leg to manoeuvre the skittish dog away from her.

'Right,' she says, hugging herself, teeth chattering.

'Well, we'll be off. See you now.'

'See you, Harry,' she says. It is her habit to smile, but today it won't come. He shuffles away. 'Drop by later if you like,' she calls out. 'You'd be more than welcome.' He waves one hand high in the air without turning around, and she understands that the next time she will see him will be right here where they stand.

The last in the convoy of horses is already climbing back up onto the grass, jerking its young rider while trying to gain a foothold in a shallow dune. She pulls her sodden T-shirt over her head, lets the air at her wet skin and underwear. The buttons of her cardigan momentarily defeat her. She unfastens her bra, slides it down one sleeve, her breasts heavier, unsupported. Only then does she notice that one of her shoes, the one with the watch inside, is missing. Its mate lies undisturbed where she left it, telltale paw prints scuffed across the sand.

'Harry!' she yells, dragging on her jeans, running on her toes into the sharp grass, avoiding rabbit holes and rabbit droppings. But already they are out of earshot, her voice swallowed by the wind. She curses out loud, reads the sky. She knows she cannot delay, her shadow long beside her. Back on the beach, she works her cut foot into the lone shoe, leaving the laces loosely tied. The single sock covers her left foot and, with uneven steps, she retraces her journey to the car, squeezing her wet things as she goes, marking a dark trail in the sand.

Time stops in the instant quiet when she yanks the car door closed. Pulling her jacket onto her lap, she finds comfort, heat, pleasure in it. A box of crackers sits within reach inside a bag behind the passenger seat. She tears at the cardboard, rips open the plastic wrapping, eats two in one go, and then two more. At the turn of the ignition, air blasts from the heater, gradually becoming warm. Her broken skin burns inside her open shoe.

Three missed calls flash up on her mobile. *Back soon my love x x*, she taps out in reply. Immediately, he tries to call her. She flinches, studying herself in the mirror inside the sun visor: the dented shadows under her eyes; her cold, reddened cheeks; the ends of her hair beginning to stiffen into saltwater curls. After the beep of a message, again the quiet.

The clutch presses against the ball of her socked foot, the car seeming too close to the ground, its machinery heavy around her. She grips the steering wheel with both hands, feeling lopsided. At a bump in the track, her cargo bounces in the boot. A sheep wanders across the lane, a streak of luminous orange sprayed on its side. She jams on the brake and takes up her mobile again.

'Hello?' she says, at the sound of breathing.

'Hello,' says the child.

'Hi, darling. This is Grace.' She asks the girl for her mother, hears the handset being dropped, the disjointed murmurs of television and family in the background.

'Hey, Grace.'

'Hi there. One of your sheep is out on the road.'

'Not *again*. I'll sort it out now. How's the birthday boy?'

'He's grand. I'm just on my way home.'

'Well, shout if you need anything. We're around.'

'Thanks. See you later. Looking forward to it.'

She ends the call, sighs, registers the time and closes her eyes to quell a slight panic. When she opens them, the sheep has pressed itself up against the car, on the driver's side. From here, she could reach out and put her hand on its tangled wool, feel its breath on her palm. It fixes her with its glinting eyes, angling its head in a way that unnerves her. She revs the engine, willing it to move on, her heart jumping inside her.

It has taken more than a week for her body to empty itself, for all traces of new life to fall away. She has scared him, she knows this, with her long silences, her animal howls. Quiet now their days together, quieter than they have been for a while. The two of them have lain on the couch, the pieces ebbing out in slow tides between her legs. Time reduced, once again, to no more than this day, this night.

Out on the main road, her body shifts behind the wheel, re-centring itself, the car seat damp beneath her. Sunshine slides over the way ahead, its glare reflected in the windows of a cluster of holiday homes. She accelerates with her sore foot, letting her head lean back against the rest, pressing the pedal in little bursts, gaining on home with nothing coming at her.

Through the hard land she travels, where little grows without being beaten back by the wind, where the gorse and fuchsia thrive, fed by the rain. Home now, almost, the hour later than anticipated, she remembers the driftwood, wonders would there have been any there, had she gone looking. Tonight, they will have drinking and talking, laughing and singing. Later, the last of them, dancing themselves into a spin, hauling each other up and tumbling down again.

Until, finally, the glowing tips of two cigarettes against the blue-black sky. Night air soothing her scraped foot, between the strap of her high-heeled sandal and the silver varnish of her nails. Seeking each other's skin for nothing more than shelter, huddled in the cool grass, under constant stars. A slow kiss on her shoulder. A stray balloon attempting to take flight. And above them, the dawn breaking, pink and ragged and new.

Eimear McBride

Eimear McBride studied acting at Drama Centre London. At twenty-seven she wrote her debut novel, *A Girl is a Half-formed Thing*, and spent the next decade attempting to have it published. Eventually picked up in 2013, it went on to receive the inaugural Goldsmiths Prize, the Baileys Prize for Women's Fiction, Kerry Group Irish Novel of the Year, the Desmond Elliot Prize and the Geoffrey Faber Memorial Prize, among other short-listings. She occasionally writes and reviews for the *Guardian*, the *TLS* and the *New Statesman* and is currently finishing her second novel.

Through the Wall

It moves in my ear from through the wall, this time not like I've heard. Brickwork notwithstanding and water-pipe clang. Is that him? No. TV. No. The dog.

Smoothing Easter egg wrappings out with my son on an almost Pentecost day, next door's dog still alarming with the plaintive yelps that mail flitter usually abates. I ran my nail on purple foil till its wrinkles turned to glide and passed him the done sheets to be closed inside books for later cutting out as planets. Twinkle twinkle little star, his small cheer a sting in my eye. But the God, the God, dog going on till. Would you ever shut up! I shouted. And the instant I did, realised next door was in, probably sat right there in their kitchen with him. Ah balls! So much rowing all these months and they never once said a thing. And before that too, the year before, the baby, screeching the night. Doesn't bother us, they'd say when I'd apologise. Never mind, they mightn't have …

Heard it shortly after. The baby toddling to stare in the street. Police cars! he roared Are coming here. I've annoyed once too often, I thought. When I grabbed him though, to drag him back, it was an ambulance instead, cracking the gravel, light decking the kerb as they bounced a stretcher out. I knew in the split I was off the hook but someone else was on. Minutes later her grey ponytail caught the breeze and her forehead, below it, wan. Did her husband know? I wondered. Should I go out? I'd no number to call. We were only ever smiles in the street or the occasional extended hello. Is that a bump? she'd asked when I was five months gone. Congratulating when I said Yes. Saying how much she'd always loved children, despite not wanting them themselves, which spared me the weirdness of strangers affronted by my general lack of coo. Bit of a surprise, I said But a good one … of course. You'll be fine, she said. I said I hope so. Or the day her old car passed its MOT, her yippeeing along the street. But really only the inconsequent ends of being good-fence neighbourly.

I saw him follow them out then, shirtsleeves in the rain, obliviousness working like raincoat enough, so I de-gawked from the windowpane.

In the evening I didn't answer the phone. The needle to fight not there. When the texts about visitation went beyond irate, I pressed hard Power Off for a change.

That night I didn't hear her cough through for the first time since moving in and numbered all the nights I had, guessing whether her husband found it annoying. And their dog quiet too. That was odd, not barking at every last thing. My half-empty bed creak, in the first pool of dawn, our shared wall's loudest sound of living.

One time we got up at the crack of it, to make some car trip somewhere. I saw her at their window, waving, as he set off to collect his first fare. Although the street was godforsaken, glum beneath council-rationed lights and freezing to the point of kettles on windscreens, there was an all-in to her smile. For the next bickerous two hours it wormed me, the outliving petty I presumed it meant and thought I'd been her the year before, not limping down the road of no retreat.

The next morning hopped to with the early refrain of I want to have a wee. A minute too late and I was out by the bin binding tabs round a sogging nappy. I saw the neighbour pull in. The look of him, each fissure swoll to its edge, his eyes a flagrant beaten. I … I … How is … ? She died, he said Two hours ago but when I found her … I knew she wouldn't come round. I'm sorry, I said and scrabbled to add I'm so sorry. But he was already gone. Which flicked me on through to finality. Don't go to bed on a row, they say. Our grubbed bicycle chain of mortality slips off so quick to become oily stains. So with plastic and piss still under my nails I went in to my child inside, screaming now for Ready Brek and signifying the extent of my have.

In the days after fro-ings, I cowered, not wanting to catch him out by the bin, then have to think of something to say or be disapproved for wasting what he'd had dragged away. In the end I brought a card, one of a lake because I didn't know what she was – definitely the look of an atheist though, the cheeriness I suppose. I didn't go to the funeral or after either. I thought that was for family and friends and I was a shouter at dogs on her deathbed but he thanked me for it all the same.

I have listened with alchemical calm ever since and stopped answering my phone. In the yard I hush my toddler to listen to the neighbour's spade going one two in the garden that together they often dug. Without her he's keeping on with it. Is that the shock? Or love? Or is it he just likes gardens and her absence is giving him time? It helps me consider my meanness, since my husband left I often have. She seemed, in life, never wound that tight. I never heard a cross word pass between. She walked without fraught and even her vandalised flowerpots didn't knock a fig while I, recently ready for fury, cursed whoever had. Ah, probably drunk students just fucking about, she had said and content with that. I've never had as much give in me. I think that should make me ashamed. I cover it as best I can but I suppose it drove him away – the meander down from ever and ever to I can't help being this way. And if I grew tulips or geraniums now what might they symbolise? The tightness in my chest when the test said yes? My husband's distress when I said Oh no? My inability to fall for motherhood as quickly as pregnancy proposed? I move my finger along the wallpaper to the little wound I find. Here the cot box scraped, going up the stairs, and we began to fight. I didn't want everything getting destroyed and he kept shouting Life is different now. I couldn't give in or understand the wherefores he offered, or whys. You'll change, he said not understanding why I mightn't dream that to be or how odd his insistence that I become else didn't move him to be less stationary. Who wants to segue into wearing fleeces and using words like 'snug'? But really I mean: what struggle had made, I was unprepared to shrug off. When my son was born I could take my eyes off him and wanted my husband to take him off me. I did all I should but I didn't love him either, until he was six months at least. In the pictures from then I am awful because that was the truth. Not clinically, postnatally, more like aghast at the smithereens I'd been blown to. I'd have foxgloves. I've heard they foretell a death. Making new life certainly decimated the one I had cherished and the grow that grew after on my scorched earth was still too unwilling for him. So if daffodils? His disappointment in me. Fuchsia, the imperfection he could not concede. Jasmine, the desire exhaustion recedes and what for making home bricks and slate? Back then I tangled until my son first knew my face. He could tell before me that we shared flesh. That first smile taught me we belonged together – whatever of it I could make. And the door closed. I closed it on my husband's dream of the white work-surface life he wanted as real. Manifested as dead lines on lifting the receiver and a pocket filled with hotel receipts. See? See? I can too, he said Choose to not choose the family we've made. If you won't play Mum I won't play Dad. Creak and creak and SLAM. Which means I'd plant Rosemary too, for remembrance and the claimed comfort in his aloneness she gave. Blooms to signify how, despite myself, I became someone else anyway.

I come to sit often now, head against the shared wall, eavesdropping on the sound of the neighbour's loss. Willing it to help my soul click over itself into a knowable groove. And as I make dinner and wash the clothes and read my son stories and wipe off the snot I still wonder, of these duties, which I should find joyous then try to think of my neighbour alone.

Today we met, out by the bins. At first shame said Oh just ignore him. I did, sidled sideways to chuck the recycling in then thought to shame Who are you? How are you doing? I asked. He raised his head. Good days and bad – as I might have expected. She was such a lovely woman, I said She was always so kind to me. He smiled and said She was the best. In my life she was every single thing I wanted. Not many people get that … you know yourself. And I pricked in defence but knew. Sorry, he saw, said, I didn't mean ... just ... I see you with your son and I wouldn't change a thing but ... I just miss her every day. No I understand, I said and did. Not with elucidating lights or torrents of meaning. Just a glimpse of the simple dissatisfaction of being despite the effort of getting there to here. As the squall came up for Ready Brek it seemed the walls of my world somehow settled themselves. My son was the in and my husband the out and the workable fine those had become.

Tonight I hear it – first time since – old howl of their dog. His now. And know his grief isn't my own. So when it rings out I answer my phone – woman-up to responsibility. There's a bellow on custody and arriving tomorrow. If you like, I say How's about noon for you? We should probably try make it routine and, god knows, I'd love Saturdays off. So take him out, why don't you, with Rosemary? I don't even care how this sunders him because I remember he was the conservator of such things as who was who and what went where. I ring-off, then go upstairs to fill my bed, knowing though my son will slip in in the night. I'll make room when he comes but sprawl before it and think, one day too, that will change.

Belinda McKeon

Belinda McKeon is the author of two novels, *Solace,* which won the 2011 Faber Prize and was named Irish Book of the Year, and *Tender*, published in 2015. She lives in New York and teaches at Rutgers University.

Long Distance

You want to live in a place where nobody notices a runner. Where nobody pays you the slightest bit of heed. You want to live in a place where you are just one more thing on the horizon of things unbothered with; just part of the rainfall, part of the wind-gust, part of the pile upon pile of day upon day. You want a place where nobody will come up to you later and say, ah, I saw you out running there, out on the road. Ah, you like the running, do you? You do be at it out in the States, I'd say, a good bit, do you? Fierce good exercise, by all accounts. Fierce good, isn't it meant to be, for the heart?

Alison's heart is at her like a temper now. She is out of practice at the running, is the truth of it, and anyway she is used to the treadmill, or to the elliptical, with its cradled soup of motion, not to the up-and-down juddering of anything real. Pounding, her footfall. Ragged, her breath comes and goes again. And knee-niggle, and headphone-tangle, and off the scrag and onto the tarmacadam, and downhill now, and with downhill comes the swoop she came out here seeking in the first place, although she did not know that she was seeking anything at all (in her head now, her husband David snorts disbelievingly): that moment when fields and drains and cloud-dragged skies and shit-stained cattle seem, in the late June light and how it lies on them, beautiful, so beautiful, and sentiment blooms in Alison's bloodstream, and foolish notions pluck at the catgut strings of her nerves –

But now she is onto the main road, and must stop to let the traffic past at its ordinary, homicidal momentum, and again it is just knee-niggle, and headphone-tangle, and some fucker bouncing the heel of his hand off his car horn because he has nothing remotely better to do.

(Not that Alison is, to his attentions, indifferent. Not that the sound of him, the fact of this guy, whoever he is, having noted her, approved of her, is going to slide away as though it is nothing at all. An eye is an eye. A nod is a nod. Passing muster is a hell of a lot easier here, on the stretch of road down the way from her mother's – yes, her mother's – house, but it is nonetheless passing muster.)

The headphones are more tangle than music now. The track is one she is tired of listening to, anyway. She is tired of them all; she needs to put a new playlist together. Hadn't she intended to do this for the flight? Which was another misguided idea, in a whole family of them: because would she have wanted to listen to running songs, strapped into seat 14F somewhere over Greenland, somewhere over the unthinkable reach and plunge of the sea?

Anyway. Her mother will be wondering where she is.

*

The second to last time she was here, which is to say home, which is to say *home* home – emphasis is where the heart is – Alison stopped running at this point on the lane. This point on the lane – she knows from long experience, she knows from the twitch and jostle of her very cells – is the point beyond which things become audible from her parents' vegetable garden. Things such as running. Things such as walking. After this point, every move that disturbs so much as a pebble on the lane can be heard; every step squeals on you, betrays you. These things are not audible from the polytunnel, maybe – though who knows what a ready ear can discern? – but from the garden itself, they can be heard as clear as a cry. And it was in the garden itself that you would, until very recently, find the person who preferred not to grow things in the polytunnel, who preferred to grow things in ground that had no way of hiding from the cloud-dragged skies – and who, if you came running down the lane for any reason other than an animal that needed to be caught or pulled, or a neighbour who needed to be gone to, had his way of turning, and looking at you, and changing things.

Changing what you thought you were up to. Changing what you thought, fool and all that you were, that you had somehow managed to become.

(Though he could also, Alison finds herself allowing now, still running, have been merely looking. Merely noticing. Merely turning to see who it was, and was it her, and would she be turning to him, and saying hello –)

(It has been one of the hardest parts of these past months, this business. This business of her mind, the way it has insisted upon serving up the harmless, reasonable versions of all the moments Alison has carried with her, for decades, as non-negotiable sores. Alison negotiates for a living; Alison deals in things that are valuable partly because she says that they are. So Alison does not like this; this shifting. She does not like the way it pulls away from her and turns around to show itself as something other than what she believed it was. It is possible, she knows, that she has come back here to send this shifting on its way.)

*

Officially, she has come back here for a birthday dinner. A birthday dinner for a now impossible age, but that should not mean they cannot celebrate it – this, at least, has been the gist of Alison's emails to her siblings; that should not mean they cannot gather together in its name.

'In its *name*?' David said to her, when she used him as a sounding-board for the initial suggestion. 'That's an interesting way of putting it.'

'Shut up,' Alison said, and turned back to her laptop. *In its honor*, she typed instead, and sent it before she had a chance to think again about it, and only spotted afterwards that she had used the American spelling for *honour,* and that this was something else over which Emma and Louisa would sneer in the emails they would probably already be writing to one another about her noble proposal, but honor-slash-honour was the least of it, and she didn't care if they all thought she was an interfering Yank lickarse: she did not think their mother should be alone in Clonbraghey on that day.

Great idea, Emma responded. *Good thinking*, Louisa said. *Grand*, said Martin, and *I don't mind*, said Pat, and *Whatever you want to do yourself*, said Michael, which was precisely what their father would have said, except not in an email; except muttered, with a baffled-looking toss of the head, and fuck, she misses him so much for things for which she never expected to end up missing him – and yet the garden, the garden, and all the moments on the garden's wavelength, all the stares, all the silences, all the days and nights of a house of children, and a woman, living, hardly blinking, in the grip of his seething, in the heat of his muted, injured roar –

Don't worry, we'll organise everything, Emma and Louisa said. *All you have to do is turn up.*

'Bitches,' Alison spat at her computer screen.

'Why do you say that?' David said.

'Take me down to Passive-Aggressive City,' Alison said.

'But maybe they mean it. Maybe they *are* grateful to you for suggesting you all get together.'

'Is that the kind of thing they're teaching at the William Alanson White Institute these days? Jesus Christ.'

'The language you use around this really is interesting,' David said, his head to one side. 'It's Messianic, a lot of it, I mean; have you noticed that? It's –'

'Oh, get to fuck, would you,' Alison said.

David is American, needless to say. He has a private practice on the Upper West Side, where most of the shrinks are, roosting in the co-ops like crows in an old plantation, and he is post-post-post-Freudian – which, he likes to joke, is like being Off-Off-Off-Broadway, except with even smaller office space and even larger persecution complexes – and he does a sideline in hypnosis therapy, which is nothing but verbal snake oil, as far as Alison is concerned. Well, what had she expected, David wanted to know, after the first time he counted Alison down and clicked his fingers at her, as she lay on his beige brocade daybed, trying to guilt herself into concentrating on the feel of her breath expanding and contracting her diaphragm? How were you meant to get anywhere near your own unconscious, concentrating on something as anatomical as that? But what had she been expecting, David had wanted to know? Had she been expecting to wake up and find that everything was different? That she, the person, the woman, the wife and daughter and sister and gallerist and lazy runner Alison, was somebody else instead?

Well, yes, sort of, Alison had said, and David had smiled his untranslatable smile.

*

Her mother grows all sorts of things in the polytunnel. Early potatoes, and cherry tomatoes, and strawberries, and even kale. That kale, the star of New York society, should turn out to have been, all along, an ordinary, muck-covered staple in Irish vegetable gardens is something over which Alison loves to exclaim - which is, she realises, another reason why her siblings regard her as having well and truly left the building, but really, kale – who knew? And in the polytunnel her mother also grows beetroot, and cucumbers, and stalks of Brussels sprouts that looked to Alison, at Christmas, like huge clusters of tumours, but that was just the way Alison's unconscious was acting the prick at Christmas; everything looked either like a tumour or a father.

The polytunnel had been her father's, actually; the six of them had gotten together, for his seventieth, and bought him the swankiest model they could find online – the swankiness intended to serve as a kind of panacea against any perceivable shabbiness in the fact of six grown adults, six successful professionals, having to pool their money to buy their father a birthday gift, because shouldn't there be six lavish gifts, really? Shouldn't there be a polytunnel *and* a ride-on lawnmower, *and* a wax jacket from Barbour, *and* a new border collie to replace the one that had met its maker under the front wheels of Bernie Flanagan's jeep, *and* – was that six things yet? Why were seventy-year-old fathers so bloody difficult to buy for?

What their father actually would have liked for his birthday was an endless line of credit on Donedeal.ie, the website to which he devoted every minute not spent in the vegetable garden; it gave him a deep, world-rectifying pleasure, Alison could see, to trawl through the posts offering used balers and strimmers and – yes – polytunnels for sale; cars and kitchen cabinets and job-lots of coat-hooks; hideous gold jewellery and half-empty tins of emulsion and boxes of schoolbooks covered in S Club 7 stickers. Alison knows it feels world-rectifying, the pleasure, because Alison feels it herself when she dives into the sites she herself keeps on her bookmarks bar. There is always, sunk into those pages, the feeling that an ordered, layered, perfectly furnished life is within reach; that the clicks will bring into being a settling of experience, a fitting of everything needed and everything already, awkwardly in possession into their rightful slots. Days will go the way you want them to, because all demands for those days will be at hand; nothing will elude you and nothing will evade you and nothing will taunt you with the image of itself as precisely the thing that you should, at any given moment, have had. You will be ready. You will be armed.

(Swanky price tag notwithstanding, the polytunnel still looks like a cross between a caravan and a condom, sitting there between the cabbage patch and the rhubarb hill.)

(And you can buy hospital beds on Donedeal.ie, it turns out; again, who knew? Not *actual* hospital beds, needless to say – that is, not a spot in an actual hospital bed in an actual, potentially helpful hospital ward – but heavy iron things, with rails and knobs and levers, to assemble in your own front room.)

(The front room is back to normal now. It is, once more, the room in which nobody spends any time, and in which all the furniture, carefully coordinated, sits and looks around at itself, waiting to be used.)

Her mother, when Alison comes, still running, into the yard now, is at the sink in the back kitchen – probably peeling potatoes, even though she has been forbidden to lift a finger in the preparation of tonight's dinner – or rinsing clothes too delicate to put through the machine. She stirs at the sound of Alison. She lifts her face from the potatoes, or from the delicates, and she looks out to where Alison stands panting and stretching, and she smiles.

*

And her mother is not working at potatoes, and her mother is not being a hard-working washerwoman – how dreary, how utterly shallow of Alison to have thought so – but at roses. Roses, laid out long, seeming mobbed by their own teeming greenery – how can there be so many leaves? – on the dulled, scrubbed steel of the draining board. Her mother, wearing yellow gloves, is snipping the lower stems away with her secateurs, letting the ends drop into the sink or onto the floor, wherever it is that the angle sees to it that they fall – and what about that? Is that, Alison wonders, something that her mother would have done before? Something to think about? That little carelessness, that little ease and openness in the neglect of things –

'Finished?' her mother says.

'Finished?' Alison says, not understanding.

Her mother arches an eyebrow. Perfectly shaped, Alison notices; recently plucked, or threaded, or whatever it is that rural Irish women, nowadays, get done. And is *that* something you would have the presence of mind to think of? Is *that* something you would bother with, not three months on?

'Finished your run,' her mother says pointedly.

'Oh,' Alison says, taking off her terry headband, feeling a little surge of pride at its sweat-soaked whiff; she balls it up in her hand. 'Yeah.'

Her mother twists again with the secateurs. 'See anyone you knew?'

Alison shrugs. 'I hope not?'

Her mother glances at her. 'Why hope not?'

Alison shrugs again; she becomes a teenager the second she steps inside these walls. It is retinol for the emotions; it is a shot of hyaluronic acid right into the hormonal glands. 'You know,' she says, but her mother has already stopped considering Alison's stance on who you might see or by whom you might be seen; her mother is gathering up her huge crop of roses.

'Now,' she says, thrusting the scarlet bluster of them under Alison's nose. 'How's that?'

'Great red,' Alison says, which strikes her, immediately, as the wrong kind of thing to say – or as the wrong way, rather, to say the right thing; *great red* is something you would say about a bottle of wine. Or, more likely for Alison – because Alison does not really care how great, or red, a bottle of wine is, as long as it is a bottle of wine – about a painting, a painting in front of which you might be standing with a client, trying to talk them into shelling out whatever record-breaking sum the gallery had come up with as a price this time. It might be a Borga, maybe, or one of the big older Rollinses, one of the *Catastrophe* pieces that took up almost a whole wall. You'd say, *such a great red*, and the client, in their Wednesday afternoon Prada, would nod, and you'd already be thinking about what to do with the commission, and the client would nod again, and the handlers would take the painting back to the storeroom to be processed and packed. Donedeal-dot-insanity. Donedeal-dot-emperor's-clothes.

'Anyway,' her mother says, into the roses. 'They'll make a lovely centrepiece.'

'Oh? You're putting them on the dinner table?'

'*You're* putting them on the dinner table,' her mother says, easing the roses back down the sink as carefully as Alison has seen her deposit a sleeping grandchild into a bed. 'I want you to make one of your displays for me. You remember you used to make me those lovely displays?'

Alison remembers. She remembers, with a vividness that astounds her, the way that the spongy firmness of floral foam always set her fingernails on edge. She has to rub at them now with the pads of her thumbs to get rid of the feeling; how can it just be hanging around, waiting for her, in this way? She shakes her hands out rapidly to be rid of it; her mother, noticing the blur of motion, looks at her with a frown.

'What's wrong with your hands?'

'Nothing.'

'I hope you're not getting my bloody arthritis.'

'I don't think so.'

'Shaking them out like that won't be a bit of help for them, if you are. Omega 3, that's your only man.'

'No, no, I'm OK.'

'You'll need four or five of these for the centrepiece. I'll put the other ones in a vase. It'll be a nice way to welcome the girls. Whenever they finally decide to grace us with their presence.'

'I'm sure they'll be here soon,' Alison says apologetically, although it is still two hours from the time when Emma and Louisa are due to arrive. 'They said —'

'Oh, I know what they said,' her mother says, all her attention seeming, now, to be on one of the stems.

'It'll be nice to have everyone together again,' Alison says, and stares at the line, its echo, in an instant welter, aghast. 'Everyone, I mean —'

'Look at that for precision,' her mother says, cutting Alison off. She has turned, and now she lifts the rose up so that Alison can consider it; it is the filigree of scent, something both ancient and vital, that catches Alison by surprise.

'It's lovely,' she says, which is evidently not the reaction her mother is seeking; she points to one of the leaves curling in on itself beneath the petals, and at once Alison sees. Several circles, exact as though made with a tiny hole-puncher, are cut into every leaf. They are all over the stems; they are all over, she sees, looking down, the parts fallen into the sink and onto the floor; they look like a virus still thriving and still spreading; a virus of blankness and space.

'Leafcutter bees,' her mother says, with what sounds like reverence. 'They use the pieces to make their nests.'

'Jesus,' Alison breathes, touching around one of the circles with a fingertip. She and her mother are standing very close to one another now. She can smell her mother's skin.

And she is sure – feeling slightly less proud of the sweating, now – that her mother can smell hers.

'Ah, they're no harm,' her mother says. 'Sure you'd only notice them if you looked up at them too close.'

'Yeah,' Alison says.

'Amazing, isn't it, the kind of thing that goes on,' her mother says, and she lays the rose back down beside the others. 'I'll get these ready for the hall.'

*

'She's allowed to be too OK, if she wants to be,' is what David says that night when she phones him, after the dinner dishes have been put away again, after her siblings, smiling and waving, have driven back to Killoe and Carrick-on-Shannon and Newbridge and Enfield and Phibsboro with their commentaries racing out ahead of them, sharper than the glare of their headlights, on the road. 'She's allowed to be any kind of OK she wants to be.'

'Yeah.'

'You are too.'

'Yeah,' Alison says, stretching her legs out on the front-room sofa; the action knocks a green velvet cushion to the floor. 'It's just, you know.'

'I know,' David says – which, it seems to Alison, is incredibly lazy, professionally speaking; because aren't you supposed to push someone, when you do what David does? Aren't you meant to draw them out, when they neglect to finish their sentences, when they lean on the clichéd, empty expressions that stand in for saying the things that need to be said?

'You know,' she says again, and again David says, in his soft and easy murmur, that he knows.

In the hall, she hears her mother lock the front door. As well as the lock built into the knob, there are two deadbolts - one at the top of the frame and one at the bottom - and there is an alarm system, complex and paranoid, that the others had installed for her parents after it became clear that the burglaries in the area were not going to stop. Gangs of thugs, happy to tie up people who could have been their grandparents, and beat them, and leave them for dead. Every night it comes again as something possible. At least, Alison finds herself thinking, he never had to go through that.

(This is a thing she has found herself doing lately. A kind of retrospective-bargain-making. A kind of consolation-collecting. *You're allowed to deal with it however you want to deal with it,* David has said.)

'I have to go,' she says, and she hangs up before David can say any more.

'I have to go,' she says again, to the empty air.

Lucy Caldwell

Lucy Caldwell was born in Belfast in 1981. She is the author of three novels and several stage plays and radio dramas. Awards include the Rooney Prize for Irish Literature, the Dylan Thomas Prize, the George Devine Award for Most Promising Playwright, the BBC Stewart Parker Award, a Fiction Uncovered Award and a Major Individual Artist Award from the Arts Council of Northern Ireland. Her most recent novel, *All the Beggars Riding*, was chosen for Belfast's One City One Book campaign in 2013 and shortlisted for the Kerry Group Irish Novel of the Year. She was shortlisted for the 2012 BBC International Short Story Award for her short story 'Escape Routes' and won the Commonwealth Writers' Award (Canada & Europe) in 2014 with 'Killing Time'. Her debut collection of short stories, of which 'Multitudes' is the title story, will be published by Faber in 2016.

Multitudes

Visitations

The consultant comes into the room with eight or nine others. We are so new to this, barely twenty-four hours new, we don't yet know what this augurs. With the consultant is the registrar, and two SHOs, the senior nurse and the other nurses and even the student nurse who knelt beside me at 3 a.m. last night and told me how her newborn son was premature and had to spend the first six weeks of his life in hospital. Our son is a full-term baby of nine days old and we're still hoping this is nothing serious, a little bug, a false alarm, and after the momentary comfort I felt ashamed. I catch her eye now and smile and she smiles back but is the first to look away although it's only later, much later, that I remember this because right now and without any preamble the consultant has started talking and the first words she's said are: it's not good news.

Platitudes

Words don't fail us: the problem is the opposite, there are too many words. Too many words with too many syllables.

There are also words we wish there weren't, two of them in particular. Fifty percent.

Numbers games

Fifty percent. Fifty–fifty. Heads or tails. Yes or no. We look at each other and say it with horror: fifty–fifty. But as the hours accumulate (two, three, twelve, twenty-four, thirty-six) and his temperature still won't come under control, we start to say it with a desperate sort of hope. Fifty–fifty. We'll take that. There's also *half of all survivors*. We'll take that, too. We'll take anything. We read and re-read the leaflet the consultant left us with, which isn't even really a leaflet, just five smudged and increasingly dog-eared photocopied pages stapled together in the left-hand corner. We read it hoping there's a paragraph or sentence or statistic we missed. There never is.

He is so young we don't even know yet what colour his eyes are going to be

The kingdom of the well and the kingdom of the sick

In the darkest hours of the night, which aren't actually dark at all but punctured by the red and green glow of machines and the flashing yellow numbers and the strip-lighting from the corridor and the bright lights of the nurse's station outside, my panicking mind, plundering its reservoirs, throws up all sorts of flotsam and jetsam, disconnected images and half-phrases half-remembered, a desperate attempt to make sense of things. The kingdom of the well and the kingdom of the sick is a phrase from – it comes to me – a Susan Sontag essay that I read as a student; somehow I've retained that much, although I haven't read the essay in question for years. The words go round and around in my mind, like the refrain from a catchy pop song lodged. The kingdom of the well and the kingdom of the sick. It's true: we have crossed a border. When people phone us from the distant lands of their own lives, their voices are tinny, distorted; there is a time lapse on the line that's not just the hospital's patchy reception. Over the last couple of days those closest to us have learned our new vocabularies and try them out with clumsy tongues. How are his temps, his obs, his bloods. Ceftriaxone, Nystatin. Recannulate. IV push. We are acquiring new vocabularies at a rapid pace, strings of acronyms and shorthands – GBS, PCR, LP. Some of these are almost familiar from teenage years spent watching *ER*. Get me an EKG and a Chem-7. 90 over 60 and falling. Clear. When the doctors use a word we don't understand we nod and then, when they're gone, we Google it. New immigrants to this land, we don't want to admit our weaknesses, our failings. We will master this language and in doing so we will wrest back control. Systolic, diastolic, puls/ox, stat. Or maybe it's not that at all. Maybe the hope is that, if we learn this new language, if we abide by the rules of this foreign land, keep our heads down and be thankful and eager and subservient, then one day we will be allowed to go home, or else we will blend in until we can slip back unnoticed over the border.

Mother's milk

He is too weak to feed and so I feed him a drop at a time, hour after hour, drop after drop after drop on the tip of my little finger. Then I express milk into a syringe and squeeze half a millilitre at a time into the corner of his flaccid mouth. Some of it he manages to swallow; most just dribbles away. I miss, even through the new mother's pain of cracked and bleeding nipples, his hot, sugary little mouth, the urgency of his latch, the pinching tug of his feeding. My breasts are swollen and hot with useless milk, the skin taut and shiny with angry red patches. I hook myself up to a hospital-grade pump and press the button to drain the milk out of me, my nipples swelling to raspberries. The little yellow-lidded bottles line up; all the milk he should be, isn't getting. I've always thought 'nursing' a coy term for feeding a baby, a euphemism to avoid saying 'breasts'. But now I understand it. I am looking after my son in the only way I can, nursing him better one drop of milk at a time, hoping that everything the baby books say about the miraculous properties of breast milk is true. When they say I will have to stop feeding him while they analyse my breast milk to make sure I'm not infecting him through it, I want, momentarily – and before I am ashamed of the thought and its despicable self-indulgence – to die.

Where have all the flowers gone?

It seems to have become the song I sing to him, rocking him in my arms to sleep. Sometimes I have to sing it several times before he succumbs, and so we go round and around and around, the young men becoming soldiers becoming graveyards becoming flowers over and over, generation after generation of them. Just a few miles from our window, people are pushing ceramic poppies on wire stalks into the ground around the Tower of London, commemorating the hundred-year dead. That world feels as far from us here and now as those old dead young men do. Sometimes I go on singing long after he's finally slipped into sleep, limp and heavy in my arms, the monitor wires and IV drips arranged carefully across the tight white sheets of his cot and fed into the glut of incessant beeping machines. I sing over the noise of the machines and I sing myself into a sort of daze. Sometimes I try to sing alternative endings for the soldiers (Where have all the soldiers gone? They've all stopped fighting every one) but nothing I invent will break for long the cycle of graveyards and flowers, flowers and graveyards. Sometimes I try to sing other songs. But I find I can't remember the words to 'Blowin' in the Wind' or 'My Grandfather's Clock', or even my own childhood favourite, 'Down By The Lock Hospital', and 'Puff the Magic Dragon' works for a while but then is too lurchingly sad: dragons live forever, it goes, but not so little boys. My mouth is suddenly dry and my throat is cracked and I go back to the flowers, no less sad, really, but blessedly meaningless, now, the hundredth time round.

Days

The days pass. We lose count of them. Someone asks if we would like to speak to the hospital chaplain. We say no and so he (she?) never comes but something about the offer – the combination of doctors and priests, perhaps – makes me think of the Larkin poem. I Google it and it is shorter than I remember. We no longer live in days. We live in an endless present tense that's both day and night and somehow neither, demarcated by obs every four hours, different drug cycles every four, six, eight and twenty-four, the combinations meeting and receding in an elegant quadrille. We save his nappies to be collected by the nurses and weighed. We roll them up into fat little bundles and line them up on paper towels, the time neatly written on the top right-hand corner, and we note their frequency and contents in a log chart. We keep feeding charts too: which side, how long, with what degree of vigour. These days are a particular time outside of time, like the air in the negative-pressure room, suspended, cut-off, an endless turning in on itself. Darkly, as much as we long for time to begin again, we hope that it won't, because its beginning again could mean the other of two things.

Personality

Here are the things we know about him. He hates his cot. He wriggles and writhes and thrashes and cries and stiffens his little back flat as a board until we pick him up and I lay him on my stomach, mewling and hiccupping, until he falls asleep. His cot, its bars painted blue and bright green, is called 'Inspiration' and it is where people do painful things to him, though they all tell us he is too young to make the association. I don't believe them. He knows. I know he knows. Other things we know about him. His smell and the particular warm heft of him, the feeling of his rapid hot little breaths against our chests or into our necks, and his shuddering exhales, and the way his arms fling up above his shoulders in abandon when he sleeps and his drawn-up, froggy little legs. These are things every parent knows: but they are also specific to him, to us, as if we are the first in the world ever to know them. Other things. He has, somehow, at just a week and a half and against all the odds, begun to smile. We know the doctors will say this is impossible, say it is wind, or involuntary movement of the muscles, and so we document it furiously, tapping series of pictures into our phones, taking videos, before we look at each other and put down our phones and just smile back at him, eyes thick with tears. Yes, we say, that's right. Yes. Other things. We loved him as soon as he was born, bashed-up and purple and battle-scarred, and we loved him fiercely and surprisingly, and what we said to him and to each other was, It's *you*, because it was *him*, and it had been all along, and it made such sense, that heady overwhelming flush of recognition. Other things. We knew he was unwell. We knew. Even without a rash or a temperature or any of the leaflet's other signs, we knew he wasn't himself and we pushed for a second opinion and this, and the brief hours it won us, might be what spares him.

Peripheral Venous Cannulation

When we were admitted it took three doctors six attempts to cannulate him, and eventually they had to bring up special equipment from Neonatal, a lightbox to shine through his veins, which were too thin to be seen by the naked eye. The cannula lasted a day before the vein gave up and the whole procedure needed to be done again. It's been redone three times now: his veins collapsing one after another under the intensity and duration of the IV drugs. He's had the right hand, the left, the right again, the left foot. This time there is talk of them putting the cannula into his scalp and we recoil and say, Please, no, please. We look at his scalp and we see the juicy veins just under the surface and we say, Please, only as a last resort. The nurse says, If they have to do it that way they'll give him a little cap to wear, it will be OK, you won't see anything. We kiss his hands and feet and forehead and cry, both of us, and then we leave the room before the doctors begin but we hear his cries the length of the corridor, and until we've put two double doors between us. My own left hand is still aubergine from a failed attempt to cannulate me during his birth. I run the fingertips of my right hand over the bruise and then press down as hard as I can.

The reasons (we tell him) to stay in this world

During my – our – protracted labour, I tell him, I used (too much and incorrectly) gas and air and went temporarily crazy, although I thought I was perfectly lucid at the time. I started stamping and swaying from side to side and chanting in a deep, loud, atonal voice, and in between contractions explained to my husband, politely, patiently, and in my normal voice, that I was in the middle of a shamanic rite, calling the spirit of our unborn child from where it was roaming on the plains, telling him – we didn't know the gender, but I already knew it was a him – that the time had come to be born. I tell our son this now, how I called his spirit into this world and I tell him that I will fight for it against the forces that want to suck it back. My husband lists all of the containers – our word for them, an obscure joke whose origins we can't now remember – that we have bought to put him in and keep him safe. His car seat. His bednest cot. His Sleepyhead pillow. His Moby wrap. His Babybjörn bouncer. His baby bath with its moulded sponge insert. His highchair with a newborn attachment. There are half a dozen of them, a dozen. My husband reaches the end of the list and begins again, a litany. We tell him it's a beautiful world. The cheap pocket radio is talking of Gaza and Ebola and Operation Yewtree and global warming and we look at each other and tell him, as parents must have murmured to newborns for decades, centuries, that it's his job now to make the world better. At some point we stop giving reasons and just tell him, Stay.

Fiction

For the first time in my life, fiction has failed me. I can't imagine myself out of myself, or even imagine doing so.

One evening, when I am so exhausted I can't imagine how I'll last through another night, my husband offers to read to me. He picks up a magazine and opens it at random and reads a review of a new restaurant in Brooklyn. It is the first time in our lives that he has ever read to me. Between sentences, perhaps even between words, I dip in and out of sleep. Our son is lying in the crook of my husband's left arm, naked but for a nappy, limbs limp, mouth open. My husband reads, self-conscious. I have never loved him as much as I love him then. He turns a page and reads his way through a poem, stumbling slightly. The poem is a son's memories of his father, a lifeguard, and the one time he saved people from drowning. It moves from concrete memories to abstract musings, from the people saved and lost that day to the sky above and the ceaselessly moving waves. Read it again, I say when he finishes, and after that, And again?

Multitudes

Before we are born, we decide in advance the lives we are going to live, the events in them, the people, the choices. We decide according to the lessons we want to learn and all of us have lived here many times over, learning new and different lessons, meeting over and over the same people in endlessly new configurations. I dream this in the light hot daze of one snatched nap, in the sweat of the faux-leather chair-bed and the stiff, faded cellular blankets, and for a few minutes when I wake, it all makes sense and the ancient wisdom in my baby's grave and luminous eyes is obvious and I think, You're here to teach me too and for a moment I even have a fleeting grasp of the lesson.

Homeward

And then, almost as quickly as it started, it is over; we are being told his clinical signs are good, they've been stable for forty-eight hours now and so we can go home; they need the room and we live near and can bring him in three times a day to receive the rest of the course of his IV drugs. So we are suddenly packing a week's worth of accumulated things – a cheap supermarket duvet and my breastfeeding pillow, energy bars and packets of dried fruit, crumpled clothes and toothbrushes and the pocket-sized radio, unread magazines and tubes of nipple cream, piling everything haphazard into the plastic laundry sacks the nurses have given us because we don't have any other bags. Then we're leaving the room and walking the length of the ward and through the double doors and along the corridors and into the lift and down and through more corridors, through the main reception and into the concrete and litter of a Whitechapel afternoon, the knots of smokers and the traffic fumes, the flapping tarpaulins of the fish and vegetable stalls across the road and the racks of flimsy fluttering chiffon outside the sari shops. My husband has gone home every night to sleep, and has been to and from the supermarket on errands, and he strides on ahead carrying the baby in his car seat but my legs are wobbly; I've been out of the hospital – out of our son's room, in fact – only twice in seven days, when it all got too much and I walked through the corridors and took the lift down to the entrance hall to stand in the sunlight with the smokers and cry. It feels too soon to be going home. It seems as if they've only just told us how seriously ill he is. Fifty–fifty. We are the first fifty, or the second, the right fifty. It's chance, luck, Alexander Fleming in 1928, nothing we've done, and this makes us fearful. The ferocity I felt through the nights in hospital, the conviction that I could and would fight for his soul, has melted away in the daylight, and now it's just the three of us, left to watch and wait and muddle through. Wait for me, I say, suddenly terrified, and I heave the laundry sack over my shoulder. We have to stay together. We have to: that's all there is.

Storytelling

He's too young to remember any of it, they say. He won't remember a thing. We think of his eyes in pain, black with incomprehension and fear and bewilderment, and we are not so sure, and we agree more out of politeness even than hope. He is talking to himself as I write this. Gurgles, coos, the occasional indignant squawk. Heh-gooo, haw. Uh-heh, glaaaaa. Eoow. Batting with his right hand, now finally out of its cumbersome bandage, a green bird with rattling beads in its tummy, suspended from a loop on the playmat he lies on. He is utterly absorbed. Ah-gooo, haw. Heh-eoow. Are you telling a story? I ask him, as I kneel down beside him. He looks up at me, beams his gummy little grin, and even as I smile back at him and rub his fat little stomach my own stomach lurches. It will always be like this, I think. But perhaps it always is. Sometimes he smiles as he is sleeping, and sometimes he sucks down imaginary milk. Sometimes his tiny face creases and his chin quivers and he cries out his distress cry. Then we rush to pick him up, but even by the time our hands are around the soft heavy warmth of his swaddled body he is gone again, the memory, if that is what it was, already, at least momentarily, forgotten.

Lisa McInerney

Lisa McInerney was born in 1981 and just about grew up to be a writer of contemporary fiction. Her debut novel, *The Glorious Heresies*, was published in 2015. In 2013 her story 'Saturday, Boring' was published in Faber's *Town & Country* anthology, edited by Kevin Barry. 'Arse End of Ireland', her take on life in a Galway council estate, won Best Humour at the Irish Blog Awards in 2009, which was a surprise as she wasn't aware she was being particularly funny at the time. Lisa lives in Galway with a husband, a daughter, and a dog called Angua.

Berghain

Fall in off the main road, lurch down the cement block passage and along the side of the unlit car park: the way to bulk-bought shots and manifold bass drops and orange-legged young wans. Club Whatever The Fuck they were calling it these days, held every Saturday and Bank Holiday Sunday in the function room of Kenny's Hotel. And the guardian – a turn up for the books – Andrea Devlin, sitting in sickly yellow light in the ticket booth, hair scraped and smoothed back, like a black shadow on the crown of an egg.

Not an awful lot Alan could do about it now, standing in the queue and half-mouldy. Fuck, though.

'What?' grunted Ja, teetering on some unseeable brink between the tarmac and the plaster wall.

'I fucking hate that wan.'

She might have married one of the Kennys; he couldn't see Andrea Devlin deigning to sit in a ticket booth on a Bank Holiday Sunday night. Not the way that wagon had been back in school, with her sneer and her ramrod poise.

'What'd she do on you?' Ja asked.

'She's a weapon is all.'

The weapon lopped off the topmost end of the queue. Ja moved forward with his hand on the wall to his right. A dangerous tactic, broadcasting a rickety gait. There was a bouncer stationed at each end of the queue. Fat bastards both. The one by the booth window was bald as Buddha, but he had the ignorant over-shoulder stare so deftly practised by pricks of his vocation. No room for error with him flanking the bitch. Ja made the beginnings of a belch and clamped his mouth shut. His cheeks puffed.

'Stand up straight, Ja, for fuck's sake.'

Underfoot the tarmac glittered, wet, spotlighted and dashed here and there with cigarette butts and lost coins. The thirst was spreading. There had been pints back in McGee's. One short: whiskey – he couldn't remember what brand. From that door to this was a ten-minute walk; not long enough, logic suggested, to slough off a man's buzz. That was the town for you. It clipped your wings and tightened the muscles on your brow and under your throat and shoulders as soon as you were back in it; you festered here, you cultivated headaches, your temper pinched.

No need for soundproofed doors when the Kennys owned half the parish. From the dancefloor inside came a persuasive beat and the methodical come-ons of a girl band high on hairspray and auto-pitch.

Alan wanted to be indoors, if only for the open dispensary in the far corner: bitters and syrups, pitchers and shots, doled out amply and swiftly by straight-faced girls in top-knots. And the curve of young wans' shoulders as they filed up to be served vodkas and dashes, the bulging of their cleavage, the winsome torment of hemlines bobbing up over dimpled thighs illuminated in swooping rainbow lights. The possibility of the ride: eight quid before midnight, a tenner after.

But here was the guardian of the double doors and the salacious spectacles within: Andrea Devlin.

Alan approached the booth at a slight angle so that he could stand between his old enemy and his old friend – Jarlath Brady, fine hurler, new father and line operative – and said, 'Two.'

Andrea Devlin narrowed her eyes and the left corner of her mouth twitched and slowly stretched.

'Not tonight, lads.'

'What? Why not tonight?'

She recognised him and she had no problem with his knowing it. 'You've both had a skinful already, haven't you? Go home and sleep it off, maybe?'

'Bullshit,' he said, and then, 'Bullshit, Andrea.'

Nor did that faze her. 'Sorry,' she said, and clownishly inverted her smile.

This is why he hated coming home. This petty superiority from kings and queens of Muck Mountain. Tallied points from years and years back. Shapes cast on old rivalries, rankings, reputations.

At school she was so up her own hole she had to be rolled to class. She presided over a knot of wink and nudging nail-filers. She sat in his row for Maths and French. She delighted in getting people's names wrong. *Colin Allen?* she guessed, persistently. *Alan Collins*, he corrected, too patiently, willing to give her the benefit of the doubt because he doubted his own significance; they were in a year group of a hundred and twelve; she couldn't be expected to remember everyone. One day he got flustered enough with her obscured cruelty to trip over his own tongue: *Colin Collins*, he said, and she dropped the act and laughed with great and shrill malevolence. He was Colin Collins until he was further abbreviated: *Cuh-Collins, C-C-Coll-Collins*.

He was gawky in those days – tawny-haired, all elbows, in possession of a forehead on which could be sold advertising space – but he was bold enough to hate her for prompting his self-sabotage.

Now the Buddha bouncer pitched towards him. An open palm was held an inch from his shoulder, cordially, insistently.

Through his teeth, Alan Collins asked Andrea Devlin, 'D'you think you're minding Berghain or something?'

She wouldn't give him the pleasure of a furrowed brow or a neck tipped to the side. Like she knew what Berghain was. Which she fucking didn't – how would she?

Beside him, Ja accepted the verdict with the weary sigh of a man rearranging his priorities; he had shifted from thirst to hunger; he was thinking he'd mangle a burger.

Alan walked with him to the end of the queue – a journey of four strides and an itch, a capacity for trouble, a righteous pique.

He'd done Berlin's Berghain – Europe's most beautiful den of iniquity – on three separate occasions and on each he'd watched the rejects take the walk of shame from the top of the queue to the very, pitying end. Some of them re-joined the hopefuls: swapped hats, or pinned their failure to articles of clothing and tried to shed the proxies. Some of them left, vowing to sober up, dress sharp and fly right, and attempt the process anew in an hour.

Each time Alan had been admitted first go.

Now he retook his station behind three girls and a fella in pale jeans splashed front and back; the lad was animated and loud, and for a long moment the second bouncer paid no heed to Alan's slotting back in place.

'Come on,' Ja said, and now the bouncer parted his gloved hands and approached.

'I'm not leaving,' Alan said.

'Come on, to fuck.'

'I'm not leaving. I'm not drunk, I'm dressed right, I'm able to pay, I'm going in.'

Ja felt the bouncer drawing near and jammed his hands into his jeans pockets.

'Suit yourself,' he mumbled.

The bouncer took his place at Alan's side and forced cool cajolery.

'Move along now, please.' This was directed at an entity somewhere to the northwest of Alan's neck. 'Come on, you heard the lady.' Knocked down a notch. The bouncer sternly fabricated a frown, aimed this time square in the middle of Alan's shoulder.

'I don't accept the lady's authority.'

The bouncer hovered.

The pleasures beyond the double doors would doubtless have little to recommend them to anyone not tied to this place by blood or tradition. Little to recommend them even on that stipulation. As it was, there was an incestuousness to the rigmarole, penned in and conducted by Andrea Devlin and her suited goons. Familiar faces welded to familiar faces, a predictability to the dancers' couplings, even to the paths beaten through the shuddering crowds: here be drunken pairings; here be women, trooping like ants to the toilets; here be young men made still by their own awkwardness, moving only now and then to bring a tumbler to a thin mouth outlined by a two-day beard.

Walls and all between them, he could see it. Shit had changed that little.

A group of girls on the dancefloor, humourless about their rhythmical capacities, insistent about space owed to them. Turned out in sequined flats extracted from their handbags on entry. The balding, bloated DJ in his LED-festooned booth, one hand on his hip and the other on the Stop/Start, watching them shake their arses. Their dogged precision rankles, so he grimaces. He counts tracks passing on a set pre-mixed by a third party. One of the dancing girls objects to an incoming song. She throws her arms in the air and mouths hostile protest at him. These girls in the sequined flats like to think of themselves as avant garde. They arrive early and stake out territory near the DJ so that they can broadcast to him his successes and his mistakes. The more they drink, the more insistent they get. He fucking hates them.

On the other side of the dancefloor, a girl has just been singled out by a particularly dopey git on account of her short skirt and the velocity at which she moves through the crowd. He cops an emphatic handful of arse. She turns. Her assailant isn't expecting that. He pretends not to see her. He grips his pint glass and stares off over the rim like some stalwart outdoorsman gauging clouds on his horizon. The offending hand is quietly retracted; he snakes it back around his buddies' tucked-shirted bodies and slips it into his pocket. The groped girl gets right in his face. He pretends not to know what she's talking about, but his cheeks are puce and his forehead shines.

The seats down the back, to the side of the bar, exhibit couples. There's a girl – there is always a girl – who has had enough to drink to make her regrettably audacious. Her pals don't notice. Comrades aren't there to police antics, even when they can skilfully predict the next day's hangover-driven horror bout: *Oh my God, why did I do that? I don't even fancy him.* She allows her partner's palm to travel from her thighs to her backside; if they're lucky enough to be in a corner he may even hitch up her hem and push his fingers into her as she slides her hand down the front of his jocks. There's an edge of skittishness and it's enough to stop either getting off, but someone will notice, someone will take a picture, somehow it'll end up on the internet; it's a script that's easily read.

In the women's toilets there are three young wans. They squish into one of the cubicles but the door won't shut for them. There's a heart-to-heart. One of them's said something. The other two wish to set her straight and calm her down; she's in the mood for neither love nor logic. Mascara's caked under her lower lash line and smudged at the corners of her eyes. There's glitter on her cheeks, on her jaw, on her collar. One of her friends begins to rub her back. This girl's jaw is going ninety: her mood is augmented. Hardly good yokes in town, not in this day and age. Coke, maybe. Adulterated sediments, cut in a port city by an indebted teenager hardly disciplined enough to follow precise measurements. And now here, hoovered up by some knobbly-kneed young wan who's full sure of her counterculturalist credentials and at the same time shit-scared that her mam will find out.

Alan Collins reached the head of the queue once more. Flanked now by both bouncers, he set his jaw and said to Andrea Devlin, 'One.'

Beatifically sour, she replied, 'We reserve the right to refuse admission.'

'On what grounds?'

'On the grounds,' said the Buddha bouncer, 'that you're two sheets to the fucking wind, buck.'

A smattering of stragglers, none below the limit of those two sheets, emerged from the murk and filed behind him, insofar as the listing fools could file. Andrea Devlin grew bold in the immunity awarded by her sheet of acrylic safety glass. She crooked a hand and beckoned the nearest dawdler.

The fella, whose blue and red checked shirt had creased out over the left hand side of his jeans, jogged Alan's arm as he overtook him.

'You've been asked twice now to leave,' said the Buddha bouncer.

'Do you not think you're making a bit of a fool of yourself?' chided his counterpart.

'I'm not drunk,' said Alan. 'Why can't I go in, when I'm not drunk?'

The Buddha bouncer laid a firm hand on Alan's shoulder. Alan shrugged him off. He arced the scrappy queue and stood behind the revellers. All were promptly admitted.

'This is ridiculous,' Alan said.

There was scope here for reason. He could scrape a smile from the jowls formed by his tucked chin; he could; hadn't he been feigning benevolence long enough? Was that not what he was paid so well for up in the capital? 'Communications Director', the kind of title ambiguous enough to wreck the heads of his hometown's plebeians but impress the erudite. *Oh, that sounds important,* he imagined his mother's friends cooing. It was important. It fucking was. He had made something of himself.

Through his teeth he said, 'I'm home for my father's birthday. Some of my family are here already; I'd like to join them. I'm not drunk. I'm absolutely fine.'

'Well, so you say,' Andrea Devlin smiled, 'but you say it slurring, Colin.'

'Oh, fuck you!' He slapped both hands against the glass and she jumped; there'd be pleasure in that, once the temper ebbed. 'Fuck you, I have a right to be here! I belong here as much as you do!'

The last few words he delivered under stress, as the bouncer closest to him grabbed at the back of his shirt and swung him into the wall. His palms came up and he flexed against the blocks and saved his nose and chin. He rolled around with his hands up as if in surrender. The Buddha bouncer raised a finger. 'Don't you move.'

'I'm calling the guards.' A muffled promise from the booth.

'Do!' said Alan. 'Do *infuckingdeed*. I know my rights.'

And right he was too, for getting out of this torpid shithole. Right for leaving school adequately battle-hardened and with nary a visible scar. Right, in a perverse kind of way, to take the memories with him and allow the negativity to fuel him; right, fuck it, dead right.

Wrong to return. He felt that regret every single bloody time. There was something discomfortingly comfortable about driving back over the county line, like settling into an old couch, the springs of which might at any moment quite literally tear you a new arsehole. It was a raw dichotomy: the feeling of belonging, but belonging on the fringe. The diminishment of it, almost physical, almost hunching his shoulders and stooping him over his own gut. Home, where the family are. Home, in the taste of boiled carrots and the smell of diesel and the sensation of mud splashing and curtains twitching and chattering, endless chattering, on things the bastards both knew and had to guess at.

All he wanted was a fucking drink.

'You know what's wrong with her, don't you?' Alan asked the bouncers. It was his turn to point. He stabbed at the ticket office. 'She just hates to see anyone she used to look down on climb away up over her. She thinks I've no right to have prospered. She'll exert now the only authority she has left … And what a hollow authority it is. Keeper of maggots. Shepherdess of wasters and blaggards. Not such a far cry from blowing Davy Hughes and Thomas Fanning one after another out behind the community centre at the Valentine's disco, ha?'

There was no reaction but a delayed flurry of lapels and limbs as one young Garda and two bouncers endeavoured to extract Alan before the early birds ducked out of the nightclub doors and turned their beaks towards one of two main street chippers. Ankles in fists and elbows locked. Alan went rigid and then flopped. The weight of rejection spread over his chest. Then came the buoyancy of blissful resignation.

'I'm better than all of this shit,' he shouted.

He could no longer see Andrea Devlin. Blessed be the boys in her absence – hateful, beautiful bitch.

'I'm better than this,' he crooned, as they carried him from the grounds and left him scuffed and prone on the broken path outside. 'I've been in Berghain.'

Roisín O'Donnell

Roisín O'Donnell was born in Sheffield, with family roots in Derry. At eighteen she moved to Dublin and studied English Literature at Trinity College. On graduating with first-class honours, she travelled and taught abroad before returning to teach and write in Dublin. Her work has appeared in journals such as *Popshot*, *Structo* and *Colony*. Her stories have been anthologised in *Fugue*, *Unthology* and *Young Irelanders*, a collection edited by Dave Lordan. She has been shortlisted for several international competitions, such as the Cúirt New Writing Prize and the Wasafiri New Writing Prize. Her work has been nominated for the Pushcart Prize and the Forward Prize, and she has received honorary mentions in the Bath Short Story Award and the Fish Flash Fiction Prize. In 2015 she received an Arts Council bursary. Her debut collection of short stories will be published by New Island in 2016.

Infinite Landscapes

'*Abeyomi had always known I wasn't destined to stay in this world,*' the young Simidele wrote on the back of a cereal box in looping purple ink. Even as a child, Simi was in the habit of noting down her experiences, never suspecting that thirty years later I would use her box of scraps to piece together the legend of my origins. Simi's writings, along with Abeyomi's memories and the cuttings I have pasted in my scrapbook over the years, have allowed me to reconstruct a narrative of sorts. And when friends ask why I waste so much time trying to put together Simi's story, my usual response is to shrug and tell them, 'If you don't know your roots, then you can't understand where you're coming from.'

Abeyomi was my grandmother. She was a proud Yoruba woman with a high forehead and an obsession with the music of the Chieftains. Memories of her evoke the caramelised fragrance of frying plantains, the ripple of Irish reels from the kitchen and the tropical flowers of her *gele* head wraps. She arrived in Dublin in her early twenties and started work as a nurse at St James's. There she met my granddad, Cathal O'Doherty, a plumber from Dún Laoghaire, who landed in at A&E one morning with his left leg scalded from a boiler incident. 'He'd the cheek of the divil,' my grandmother told me, 'there he was, in a right state, blisters all over, but that didn't stop him from asking me out to a dance.' My grandparents married soon after, settled on Tivoli Avenue and started planning a family.

Years of heartache followed. Time after time, they visited the Early Pregnancy Unit at the Rotunda. Time after time, the monitor showed nothing but darkness floating around inside Abeyomi's womb. The watery oblong of a pregnancy sack with nothing inside it. There were always the same words of consolation, '*Not to worry love, you'll have another one soon … You'll be back in here before Christmas.*' The same room in the Rotunda, reserved for moments of shock, disappointment, grief. The same cups of milky tea. And then the long drive home to Dún Laoghaire. Silence gathering between them like the stillness before snowfall.

This cyclical pattern was eventually shattered when my grandmother came home one winter evening, slammed the door behind her and shouted, 'Cathal! We have a heartbeat!' Her hands trembled as she told him about the scan she'd had. The pregnancy she'd kept secret. Elated, the couple splashed out and ordered Domino's pizza for dinner. But later, once they'd settled on the sofa for the evening, Abeyomi pressed pause on the remote and put her hand on Cathal's knee. 'Love,' she said, 'this won't be a normal baby.'

Onscreen, a blonde girl was paused open-mouthed in her soaring rendition of 'Wind Beneath My Wings'. Cathal took his wife's hand and gave it a squeeze, 'What do you mean, "not normal", love? I've always said I'd love any child that we …'

'No,' her black eyes watered into inky pools. 'This child will be *abiku*.'

'It'll be what?' Cathal asked.

'Cursed,' she hiccupped, 'a child of the spirits.'

Cathal kissed her forehead. 'Ach love, that's just quaint old superstitions, so it is.'

Just then, the TV un-paused itself, and the blonde girl soared into her chorus, '*Did you ever know that you're my here-oh-oh-oh …*'

Tutting as if the singer had offended her personally, Abeyomi re-paused the telly and threw the remote down so hard that the battery fell out and rolled under the sofa. She folded her arms across her chest, 'Cathal. There is *nothing* quaint about a spirit child.'

Abeyomi was forty-three at that time. She had lived in Ireland for more than half her life, but still held onto her Yoruban beliefs. Whether her baby had been conceived by the Liffey or in Lagos did not make any difference to my spirited grandmother. Among Yoruba, it was considered serious bad luck for a child to take up residence in the belly of a woman who had lost so many other children before. So, that night, Abeyomi called her mother Sama Nanosi on Skype. The wise-woman of Kwara crouched over a cola, her dreadlocks brushing against the webcam as she listened to her daughter's story.

'Mark my words,' Sama Nanosi nodded. 'This child will be *abiku*. A spirit child predestined to forever come and go.'

Abeyomi came off Skype with a list of tricks and remedies. From that night on, she began leaving a pair of open scissors by her bedside, to scare the spirits away. 'Don't be daft love,' Cathal said as he watched his wife wincing over a cup of egg shell soup. 'Sure the doctor said everything's grand. There's no need for all this fuss.' Abeyomi ignored him. My grandmother loved her unborn child enough to drink that egg-shell soup, even though it was like drinking her own fingernails. Sighing, my grandfather left her to it.

He busied himself by decorating the spare bedroom with rainbow wallpaper, while in Abeyomi's belly, the child grew stronger.

And on the day newborn Simidele O'Doherty first opened her shocking green eyes in the Rotunda Hospital, my grandmother's suspicions were sadly confirmed. Little Simi burst into life shuddering and wailing from the scars of past lives barely lived, and suffering withdrawal symptoms from the spirit kingdom she had left behind. As Abeyomi had dreaded, through her umbilical cord Simi had absorbed the spirits of all the other lost babies gone before. Simi would never settle in the skin of one personality, but would always be changing between one soul and another. She was fated to be seduced and misguided by the spirits, to read minds and skip between dimensions and to be eternally distrusted in a world which fears the unfamiliar.

Concerned for the fate of their newest family member, the Yoruban side of Simi's family tried all they could think of to shift the *abiku* out of her. Abeyomi and Cathal's terraced house on Tivoli Avenue received a constant flow of calls and emails from aunts and cousins in Kwara and Oyo, bearing advice and remedies. 'Keep away from iroko, baobab and silk cotton trees,' a cousin in Kwara advised, becoming offended when Abeyomi pointed out that these trees do not exist in Ireland. Sama Nanosi suggested they should avoid all trees altogether, for these were the seating places of spirits. 'Stay out of bright sunlight,' an aunt from Oyo told them, 'and no crying over the child. Each tear you cry, she will convert for diamonds in the spirit kingdom.'

Kneeling by Simi's bedside, Abeyomi turned to her Gods. 'Leave her be,' she implored Olofi, the conduit between heaven and Earth. 'Let her stay,' she begged the supreme god

Eledumare, 'Give her the spark of life, Ayé. Allow my daughter to stay.' And each afternoon, she wheeled Simi's pram around Dún Laoghaire in relentless circles while she tried to discover where the child had hidden her spirit key. An object whose discovery would convince their daughter to stay.

But all the incantations to Eledumare, the late-night vigils and the open scissors left by the child's bedside were to no avail. Each morning, Simi's green eyes would carry glints of the electric dreams she'd woken from, and it was clear as day to anyone present that Simidele O'Doherty was as much an *abiku* child as ever.

Growing up, I often heard stories of how Simi's youngest years were spent tousling among the spirits, who delighted in playing mind games with the humans. Simi's earliest drawings show the spirits as semi-transparent light shapes lingering around her. A recurring image shows a spirit in the shape of a cat. Its bluish tail curled round Simi's leg, its red eyes flashing. Other pictures show spirits of Abeyomi's dead babies as soft pink cloud shapes scampering after Simi across the floorboards. 'Sometimes we'd see a shadow dashing across the bathroom wall,' my Granny told me, 'or we'd hear a buzz, like the frantic flutter of a trapped night moth. Other times, I'd step into a patch of warm light and I'd know there was something there. Not quite living. Not quite dead. *Something.*'

Some of my grandparents' tales of spirit mischief have been retold so often that they have worked their way into my memory. I now imagine I was there to witness the events myself. My favourite story is of how Abeyomi lulled the downy-haired Simi to sleep in her cot one day, only to find her dozing in the unlit oven a few minutes later. Face grimy from oven grease. Smelling of last night's chicken burgers.

The back of her head marked by the oven shelf. Then there's the story of how Cathal locked the front door one night only to find it wide open the next morning. He still describes the eerie stillness. The soft sea brume seeping around the door frame. Nothing had been stolen, but a strange sadness had crept into the house like a sea fret.

'Honest to God, I was almost beginning to believe your Granny's stories,' my grandfather told me. He was reminded of whispers he'd heard as a wain of changelings and fairy forts. And he began to view Simidele as a volatile and potentially dangerous gift.

To an outsider, Simi's antics might have seemed like normal toddler tantrums. Playing chase with the dead babies, Simi would often toddle along with her arms crossed behind her back to prevent anyone from holding her hand. Set on a headlong track like this, without her chubby arms to balance her, she would often fall. She'd sit and wail, then she'd pick herself up and start running again. No one but her parents would have suspected there were ghosts and lost children chasing after her.

'Simi's imagination is just wonderful,' a second class teacher at Scoil Mhúire beamed at the O'Dohertys, as she slid the child's copy book across the desk between them. In front of Cathal and Abeyomi, a diary entry in Simi's loopy handwriting was illustrated with pictures of pink and turquoise spirits dancing the limbo in the sand.

'*On Saterday we went to the beech and I said Daddy can the spirits com in the car and daddy said no they fuking can't and then the spirits got angree and playd in daddys enjin and then daddys enjin wouldn't start daddy said forfuksake and then he fix it and then the spirit babees playd wid me outsid and then we sleept.*'

'Simi's an imaginative child,' Cathal laughed nervously.
'Incredible,' the primrose-bloused teacher gushed.

Throughout her childhood, Abeyomi and Cathal
worried that Simi's strange behaviour would make her a
target for school bullies. 'I spent my life fearing she'd be
picked on,' my grandmother told me. But she need not have
been so concerned. People's assumption that strangers are
interested in their lives meant no one ever noticed Simi was
psychic. Alternative lifestyle trends ensured that when Simi
spent two days up a sycamore in Phoenix Park or turned up
at Scoil Mhúire with her hair bright blue, people presumed
she was simply being hip. No one would have guessed that
the spirits had tied her to the sycamore with thistle strings as
forfeit for a bet. Or that the lost spirit babies had puked in
her hair until it turned blue.

At worst, my grandmother told me with a sigh,
Simi's peculiar abilities led people to make incorrect
assumptions about her. Strangers often assumed Simi
was a generous and considerate person which, apart from
the odd moment of hormone-induced benevolence, she
was not. When Simi enquired after a stranger's dying
grandmother, or warned a classmate about an impending
personal catastrophe, people presumed the alluring green-
eyed girl was being kind. But in such cases Simi was just
showing off.

Reading between the lines of Abeyomi's stories, I
imagine Simi's personality was one of someone whose
parents had spent the first twelve years of her life enticing her to stay. Whenever Simi caught a cold or fell over
in the yard, Abeyomi feared the worst. The cold would
develop into pneumonia. The scraped knees would turn
septic. The bumped head would clot into a concussion.
And yet, Simi continued to stay. On the back of a free

Dublin postcard, she wrote, '*It's like swinging in a hammock between worlds. Surrounded by the spirits of deceased relatives and future generations. Soothed by the tug of both past and future.*'

In her mid-teens, Simi began to create collages by sticking bits of broken tea bags and nettle leaves onto paper plates and smearing these with colourful inks. Her Leaving Cert art exhibition was unlike anything the school had ever seen. By the age of eighteen, Simi's creative brazenness secured her a place at Dún Laoghaire College of Art and Design. On Simi's epic baroque canvases, spirits crawled and coiled around bystanders' heads. In her most impressive piece, burnt toast, used condoms and nail clippings depicted a naked woman strapped to a plantain tree whilst playing an Irish harp.

'*Simidele O'Doherty's intercultural narratives reflect a vibrant new era of Irish Modern Art,*' one of the *Irish Times* articles in my scrapbook claims. '*What O'Doherty achieves in her work is to open a dialectic between the local and the international, by interposing traditional Neolithic symbolism with Yoruban oral traditions.*'

Within months of graduation, Simi's striking 'spirit collages' were highly sought-after. But Simi's paintings puzzled and divided the critics. In an infamous TV interview for *Modern Art Now*, the art critic Ben Dawson asked her, 'Do you find the complex duality of your Nigerian and Irish identities to be the cause of a necessary aesthetic clash in your work?'

'No,' Simi replied, 'but I find your question to be bleedin' annoying.'

Such interviews soon garnered Simi a reputation as one of Ireland's most obnoxious artists. Sales of her paintings soared, enabling her to earn a modest living and to rent a small studio overlooking Dún Laoghaire harbour.

Simi's diary describes how, on a damp December evening when she was twenty-five, she walked into the Sea Bar on the quayside at Dún Laoghaire. She knew instantly the barmaid was two-and-a-half days pregnant. That the fat couple sitting by the window would shag in seven different positions that night. That the old man at the bar would break his wrist next Tuesday, and that the friend he was talking to had cancerous cells mutating in the backs of his eyelids. But when she turned her attention to a man sitting alone at a table in the corner of the pub, she found his aura was a black hole which offered neither a glimpse of past or future.

Frustrated, Simi glared at the man until he was socially obliged to walk over to her and ask in a polite BBC accent, 'Sorry, do I know you from somewhere?'

'No,' Simi replied. But she allowed the man to buy her a pint and stare at her, while she tried unapologetically to force entry into his past and burgle his future.

'Could I perhaps have your number?' the Englishman asked.

'Guess it,' Simi replied.

From the start of their relationship, the Englishman must have had doubts about Simi's temperament. I suppose it took a middle-aged chartered accountant not to notice the glint in Simi's eyes. And the way she slipped out of bed at night to tiptoe naked in search of the spirits, who whistled to her from behind the double-glazing of the man's semi-detached home. Abeyomi and Cathal encouraged this relationship, openly relieved their daughter's spirit was finally being tamed by the attention of this grey-suited businessman from Sussex.

Simi married the Englishman on an August day which smelt of rain, and for a short time things seemed normal. In one diary entry, Simi describes only how the spirits retreated in a huff to the slopes of the Sugar Loaf Mountain, and the spirit babies, starved of attention, started wasting away. Around this time she stopped painting sadistic spirit orgies and started painting insipid still lifes which didn't sell. Her diary entries thin out at this point and become grocery lists. *'Peas, fairy liquid, toilet roll, marshmallows ... To do: hoover kitchen, phone dentist, unblock shower in ensuite.'*

Futile as it is to reimagine the past, I've often amused myself by wondering how things might have turned out if Simi's life had remained poised in that fragile equilibrium. This story might have unfolded differently had it not been for one late summer evening two and a half years later, when Simi was walking along the Harbour Road at Dún Laoghaire and saw a tall black man leaning against a wall waiting for her.

In one of her diary entries, Simi describes how *'daylight was fading and the wet grey road snaked into the distance. A sharp sea breeze gathered itself up into a crescendo as I crossed over the road and into the man's smile.'*

'Good evening…' the stranger said. He took her hand and Simi knew right then she had been found. Located. Pin-pointed with GPS. Her lost trajectory plotted across a dark and empty sky. The man was an *abiku* too and Simi recognised him as such because he smelt of congealed spirit baby puke and he was able to study her very intently without ever looking at her face. He said he was from a small republic with no name, and that his name meant 'hope' in a language no one could understand. 'I've been waiting for you for a thousand years,' he told Simi.

'I know that,' she replied.

Unfettered by the chains of human caution or obligation, Simi fell headlong into this new love. And for a brief chink in time they were an island. A two-person planet. Meeting always at the harbour wall, or in the park's lush seascape. These infinite landscapes which the *abiku* man craved. He told Simi stories of a landlocked republic, mischievous goats, lackadaisical goat-boys, praise poetry and a people praying for rain. 'In my country, spirit children are worshipped,' he told her. 'That's why I'm going back there. I never felt so shamed and belittled as I have felt here.'

'I'll come with you so,' Simi told him, but he shook his head.

'Let's face it. There's nothing for you in my country, Simidele. For your sake I would stay. But I can't live like this.'

'For feck sake, take me with you!'

'Simi. You wouldn't be happy in my country … and Ireland doesn't hold much for me.'

'You stupid eejit!' Simi screamed. 'You know we'll both be bleedin' tortured!'

The *abiku* man laughed and stroked her cheek and Simi knew right then that their joint fates were sealed. They were destined to hunger after each other throughout all eternity, as after an enticing mirage which melts into the glare of a summer road.

'But why the hell did he have to leave?' I once asked Abeyomi.

My wise grandmother stroked my hair. 'I don't know, pet. I guess sometimes in love the wrong decisions are made for all the right reasons.'

'The abiku man told me time would heal,' Simi wrote in her diary, *'but the spirits didn't want time to heal.'* The spirit babies began smashing alarm clocks, watches, digital radio

clocks, grandfather clocks and egg-timers onto the cracked tarmac of the Harbour Road. The air was stung with the confused whir of seconds shattering. On their last evening together, Simi and the *abiku* man sat on the harbour wall and watched a P&O ferry rest on the skyline. The ship seemed immobile, and yet it had soon disappeared beyond the lighthouse, out of sight.

At this point Simi's dairy entries become sporadic. The pages clogged with indecipherable scribbling which could be either words or pictures, it's impossible to tell. It seems Simi wallowed in her pain in the weeks that followed. Unable to tolerate his wife's mood swings, her naked wanderings and the way that she now screamed out another man's name in the middle of the night, her English husband moved out and filed for a divorce. Abeyomi reckons when the Englishman left, a couple of the spirit babies tagged along with him and pestered him for years to come.

'Simi soon became lonely in that house, surrounded by depressed spirits and unsold still lifes,' my grandmother told me, 'so she moved back home with us.'

'Ach sure, she'll get over it,' my grandfather Cathal suggested when the first wave of Simi's sadness flooded their house on Tivoli Avenue and killed off all the petunias. Abeyomi shook her head, wondering after forty years of marriage if this Irish man would ever learn. Surely everyone knows what happens when a spirit child sets their eye on something?

And initially Abeyomi presumed it was grief swelling inside Simi, making her belly bulge like a full moon. By the time Simi admitted that she was pregnant, she was already four and a half months. 'The child of a spirit child?' my grandmother almost choked when Simi told her the news.

Simi shrugged. 'Let's pray it's not bleedin' *abiku*, right?'

To my grandparents' surprise, in her third trimester, Simi returned to her studio and began to paint again. In the *Encyclopaedia of Modern Art* on my bookshelf, this period has become known as 'Simidele O'Doherty's Late Renaissance'. This is the phase art historians have been most fascinated by. In one of the cut-outs I keep in my scrapbook, the renowned art critic Síle Reinhart wrote, *'it is no exaggeration to say the canvases produced by O'Doherty during this ninety-day period altered the course of Irish art history.'*

On these stressed panels, spirits float along intricate Celtic spirals. I keep prints of my favourite pictures in my scrapbook. Sometimes I run my fingers along the colourful patterns, imagining how Simi splattered each canvas with paint, until the pigments worked under her fingernails. In the only two surviving photos from this time, Simi resembles one of her own creations, with her wild hair, green eyes and paint-sparked skin.

Her diary describes how she painted each day until she was exhausted and then threw herself down on the ground of her studio to sleep. *'There are no spirits with me these nights,'* Simi wrote on her studio wall in spidery black paint, *'I left them all by the harbour wall with horizons draining from their eyes.'* And one night, Simi did something she'd never done before but had always known she was capable of. She read her own future and saw the desolation of life without her soulmate. She saw a single bed. Microwave dinners for one. Numbness, like being trapped in one of the low-lying clouds over Dublin. She saw that she would spend the rest of her life searching for a shard of emotion she'd never feel again.

My grandmother often talks about how, when Simi's waters broke, the lights went out over half of Dublin Bay.

Emergency generators kicked into motion, and the residents of the city were overwhelmed by a wave of nostalgia.

'Surely to God, she doesn't seem to want to live,' Doctor Casey in the Rotunda puzzled, as she analysed the rain-dance of Simi's slow green pulse. Sometimes the spirits would sneak inside Simi's heart monitor, causing it to tango with hope before the doctor's eyes. Other times the spirit babies would fart on the life-support machine, causing alarm bells to blare and stressing out the entire hospital.

As Abeyomi sat by her daughter's bedside, Simi's eyes were focussed on a landscape far away. 'I already knew she was gone,' my grandmother told me with tears in her mahogany eyes, 'and it was only then I realised the stupidity of placing human limits on an *abiku* child.' Until that moment, Abeyomi had failed to understand the truth about Simi. Her consciousness – her *ori orun* – could never be tied to human form. Simi did not fear death because her spirit was sure to continue, so what reason was there to feel frightened?

My mum was the great Irish artist Simidele O'Doherty. Family legend has it that just as Simi left this life, I entered it and opened my earth-brown eyes with the wail of one whose spirit was entirely my own. They called me Ife from the Yoruban word for love and wrapped me in one of Simi's old blankets.

The rest of the story has been the subject of countless songs, books and bio-pics. No doubt you are familiar with the story of how the grief-stricken grandparents eventually brought themselves to clear out Simi's studio. Thinking to use the money towards my schooling, they started to auction off the paintings. Abeyomi and Cathal were shocked when their daughter's epic final works garnered seven-figure sums.

'We had no idea that her paintings would cause such a stir,' my grandmother told me.

I often wish my grandparents had kept the famous canvases, but over time I've come to settle for posters and the prints in my scrapbook. Many of Simi's masterpieces now grace the walls of embassies, government buildings and the drawing rooms of heads of state across the world. Her most famous painting, 'Infinite Landscapes', has pride of place in the National Gallery of Ireland, and I call in to see it on my way to work sometimes. Her legacy put me through college and secured my future. The *abiku* man never returned.

Meanwhile, as a baby I showed no signs of being a spirit child. I would doze in the cot where Abeyomi had left me, and would allow Cathal to cradle me for hours. My toddler years were marred by nothing more than spilt milk, crayoned-on wallpaper and the odd tantrum. But in the nights that followed, my grandparents always left my bedroom ajar and a small pair of blunt-bladed scissors propped by my bedside with their legs wide open, just in case.

Ife O'Doherty, Dublin, 2015

E. M. Reapy

E. M. Reapy is from Mayo, has an MA in Creative Writing from Queen's University, Belfast and was a founding editor of wordlegs.com. Her work has been published internationally and she has read at festivals and events in Ireland, the UK, the US, Argentina, Australia and New Zealand. In 2013 she represented Ireland and was listed for the PEN International: New Voices Award. She received an Arts Council Literature Bursary to complete her debut novel, *Red Dirt*, which will be published in 2017.

Gustavo

'Chile?'

'Yes. Chile.'

'And he's your friend?'

'Yes.'

Who has friends from Chile? Who even knows anyone from Chile?

She's seven months pregnant and is having a rough time with iron injections, swollen feet and bouts of morning sickness still. Her tiny frame is cartoonish with the bump.

We are eating pizza and watching *CSI*. She drops it casually but I can see her slyly eyeing me, waiting for my response before she takes the next bite. He's staying with us. For two nights. This Chilean.

'He's travelling Europe. He wanted to drop by while he was this side of the world.'

'Where did you meet him?' I ask. I probably shouldn't ask. I just know. She won't lie to me. Especially now she's pregnant. She's excruciatingly honest, setting an early example for the bun.

'I met him in Rio. When we went to Carnaval. Years ago, Tom. Gustavo is a great guy. You'll really like him.'

'Was he your boyfriend or something?'

She goes silent. 'Not quite a boyfriend, no. But I stayed with his family and he showed me all around Santiago and they were so kind to me. Especially considering I didn't and still don't have any Spanish. But what we did—' she pauses. 'Not quite a boyfriend. No. Hey, feel.'

She takes my hand to the bump. The baby is kicking. It melts me without trying. I can't be angry with her. I kiss her head and get up to turn the hot water on for her bath.

The Chilean arrives.

I let him in.

He's got a big bag on his back and is wearing a colourful scarf around his neck, PLO style. His hair is jet black with silver threads flickered through his beard. His eyes are bright and brown; his skin is dark; his purple sweater clashes against him and against the scarf with a level of cool that I'd never be able to pull off. He's a handsome bollocks.

'Tom?' He kisses me. I squirm.

Lydia waddles quickly out to the door, squealing. 'Gustavo.'

He squeals back, 'Lydia, *linda*. Wow, look at you.' He kisses her and makes a bump on his own stomach. 'Is beautiful.'

She is beaming at him. She says nothing, just smiles up at him. I am looking up at him too. He's a good three inches taller.

'Is alright if I leave bag down?'

'*Sí, sí*,' Lydia says and she is fucking smitten. 'Gustavo. Gustavo.'

That's all she says. I tap him on the shoulder and say I'll show him to his room.

He's so full of good energy that I want to kick him when he bends to scoop his bag back up.

'Your house is very beautiful,' he says, his teeth dazzling me.

'It's alright,' I say.

Lydia is still grinning. Something has lodged itself in my stomach and it is in flames. Gustavo asks if he can have a quick siesta.

'You can have anything you want,' Lydia says.

He's been asleep for over three hours. Me and Lydia are in the sitting room, not talking. I don't know what will come out of my mouth if I speak. So I say nothing. I linger and listen for any weight on the floorboard to show he's up. Lydia is cutting her fingernails with no strategy. The clippers click erratically and she adds the sheared nail to a pile on her bump. Sometimes she just goes for them with her teeth.

There's a creak from upstairs. Lydia stands, throws the nails into the fireplace. I find myself wiping down my clothes, primping my hair. We both listen. He's walking around. I can picture him. Strutting. Probably has a six pack and a massive erection.

'He'll be hungry,' Lydia says, looking at me with pleading eyes, like she's the hungry one.

'So?' I say.

'Well, I can't move around the kitchen, Tom. Would you—'

I interrupt her by getting off my seat and stomping towards the door.

'Thanks, pet,' she says and applies a smear of Vaseline across her lips.

We have a box kitchen. I've been meaning to knock a wall and extend it but I haven't had the time. Now, as I fry some sausages and eggs for Gust-suave-o, the walls seem to be coming in on me.

I don't think Lydia would cheat on me. I don't think she's that type of girl and she hasn't been óverly horny since going into these later stages of pregnancy. She gives me the odd rub or we have the odd fumble but we're both getting a bit scared now with the arrival getting closer.

She lumbers up the stairs as I poke at the pan.

But what if she did cheat on me?

Four prong marks scar the pinky-grey skin of the sausages as I pierce them with the fork.

What if she's gone up there to—?

He'd smile at her, his mouth so alluring and she'd take his hand and put it on her ass, turn around for him. Bend over for him. The bun getting prodded in the head.

That's my baby inside her.

The fry squelches in the oil below me and smoke rises as the meat burns. I turn on the loud oven fan and dash to open the window but it's too late and the fire alarm screeches.

Two sets of footsteps on the stairs.

Lydia enters. 'Jesus, Tom,' she says and picks up a teacloth to wave off the smoke.

'I wasn't paying attention,' I mumble.

Gustavo stands in the doorway as I inspect the food. It's burnt one side and raw the other.

He beams at me. 'Is alright,' he says and rubs his belly. He urges me with his smiles.

'Ye'd probably eat anything where you're from,' I say and plate him up.

'Tom,' Lydia says, hands on hips and sour-faced.

I'd go for pints but I can't. I can't leave him there in the front room sitting on the couch like a puppy, smiling and excited. I can't leave him with her.

Lydia's shattered around 9 p.m. and says goodnight.

Gustavo kisses her right cheek before she leaves. '*Buenas noches mi amiga,*' he says. My teeth grind.

I rise to escort her upstairs, almost frog march her into our bedroom. She kicks off her shoes. We're using the new cot for our laundry. I fling her socks into it.

'What am I going to do with that fella?' I ask.

'Can ye go out or something? He's very nice. He'd be in good form doing anything at all.'

'I'm not bringing him to the pub. What if I know people there?'

'What?' Lydia says. She blows out a breath and scratches her hair. 'Sometimes, Tom, I don't understand you.'

If my pub mates are there, what would I say? This is Lydia's Chilean lover from back when she was wild, when she'd feck off to South America on her own without money or language and have a bloody great time, meeting the likes of him. Those good old days when she'd drink and smoke and party for three or four nights in a row and still be laughing as she puked. When she was gamey and had that come hither glint in her eyes.

Jesus, those days when I met her first.

She was working two jobs, in a bakery and tutoring an autistic kid. I saw her on the quays. She was rooting in her handbag for something as she walked. I thought she'd seen me and would avoid me but she didn't. She banged into my shoulder, falling backwards onto the ground with the impact. I should have moved out of her way. I felt terrible as I picked her up.

'I'm sorry,' I said, afraid.

She looked at me with huge blue eyes and took a gulp. 'I was looking for these.' She laughed, pulled out a big ball of tissue and opened it. Two pink donuts lay on top of each other, half mangled and squashed. 'Take one.'

'OK,' I said and that was it. I became we. Lydia and me.

'Well, what'll ye do so?' she asks as she strips off her dress. She rubs some lotion onto her face and neck and squeezes the bottle into her palm for a big blob of white, sweet-smelling moisturiser to massage over the bump. She looks utterly beautiful as she concentrates.

I sigh. 'We can go for a walk or something.'

We walk along the canal. Gustavo doesn't attempt to talk but every so often he turns to look at me and smiles when I acknowledge him. I want to smash his face. He's so fucking annoying.

He stops suddenly, nudges his head forward. I give him a shrug. He does it again. I check what his gaze is towards. A bunch of guards squaring out a 'DO NOT CROSS' section with tape on the path ahead.

It's not a terrible neighbourhood we're in but it's not the best one either and seeing them gives me a cold feeling at the base of my spine. I think of Lydia, struggling to get comfortable in bed. I think of the bun, all foetal position and toasty inside her. The depth of my love for them both scares me sometimes. The fierceness of it.

'Is bad?' Gustavo asks.

'I don't know, Gustavo,' I say. 'Will we check it out?'

He nods.

We walk to where the guards are and see flashing lights and florescent hi-vis jackets. Everyone's breath fogs in the night air. A body has been fished out of the water, it seems. It's been covered with a sheet. I know looking at it; so does

346

Gustavo. His eyes widen and he folds to his knees, blessing himself.

I bend down to him. 'Hey, hup, get up. Don't be down here.'

'Is a child,' he says, tears streaking his cheek.

'It's OK,' I say and put my arm around him. I try to get him off the damp ground, get us away from this sight.

He's sobbing deep and his body is buckling in the middle. We move to the nearest street.

'Gustavo,' I say. 'Here, it's awful but we can't – we have to be strong.'

'I,' he says and pauses, points at himself, 'I – two childs.'

'You have two children?' I try keep my voice even but know it's gone up a bit.

'*Sí*,' he says and pulls his wallet out of his pocket. He shows me a picture of two gorgeous curly haired kids with sallow skin. 'Esme *y* Rodrigo. They are in Madrid. I go soon. I got visa. At last. My wife,' he says and flips a different section of the wallet to show me a black-eyed woman with thick eyebrows and high cheekbones. He smiles though his chin is trembling. 'I miss. I sad. I no see for very, very long. I wait. But soon. In Madrid. With my family.'

'Come here, Gustavo,' I say and pull him to my chest. I grip him. He cries into my shoulder.

He gathers himself upright when he's finished. Sniffs. 'I sorry,' he says.

I hush him. 'No. No need for that. Come on.'

They stare as he enters, pipe down, give me conspiratorial looks.

I order two pints and move the stool out for Gustavo. We sit in silence and wait for them to settle, wait for the head to be added.

The bartender hasn't the tact of his customers. 'Who's that?' he asks, laying the pints on beermats.

'This,' I say, 'is my friend, Gustavo. He's from Chile.' I put my arm round him again.

'Chile?'

Gustavo takes a sup; it leaves a creamy trail on his moustache. He swallows and gasps, wipes his lip with the back of his hand.

'Is good,' he says.

He lifts his glass to me and nods. I give him a smile.

Eimear Ryan

Eimear Ryan was born in 1986 in Co. Tipperary. Her stories have appeared in *New Irish Writing, The Stinging Fly, The Irish Times, The Dublin Review*, and the Faber anthology *Town & Country*. Her awards include a Hennessy First Fiction Award and an Arts Council bursary. She lives in Cork.

Lane In Stay

She felt that she should do something to mark her husband's passing – a personal project, some self-improvement – so she learned to drive. It was harder than she imagined. Her husband had made it look easy. He drove while consulting the map or groping under his seat for the Al Green CD he loved, one hand stroking the wheel, open-palmed. She drove with her hands clamped firmly at ten and two.

She got lessons from a boy forty years her junior from the local town. He always stared straight ahead, avoiding her eye, even when she pressed a fifty euro note into his hand at the end of every lesson. She knew it wasn't personal; it was just her husband's death, lingering like an awkward joke at a party. Nobody knew what to say to her.

The interior of the car looked different from the driver's side. The seat was moulded to the contours of her husband's body. There were remnants of him everywhere: the door pocket stuffed with music and chocolate bar wrappers that she couldn't bear to vacuum away.

She practised every day; she had time, in her widowhood. Driving even infected her sleep: she dreamt of hill-starts, of endless three-point turns, of cars driving towards her in the wrong lane. She awoke with handbrake precision. When the time came she sailed through her test, and drove home feeling reckless and free.

In the last few weeks of her husband's short illness, he told her not to be lonely. *Go out,* he said. *Meet new people. Have a life.* That's what he would've done had she been the first to die. But then it was different for him. He was on parish committees and hurling backroom teams; he could hop onto a high stool at Kennedy's and talk to whoever was beside him. The pure ease of him.

She loved him, but by no means had he been a perfect husband. There'd always been indiscretions – even a love child, about ten years into their marriage. The other woman had been local; though she didn't know who it was, she fretted that it was someone she knew, someone she liked. When she went into town, she sometimes scrutinised the faces of twentysomethings, looking for the shadow of her husband.

She tried to honour his deathbed request. She developed a routine: every Saturday evening, she readied herself, got into the car and left. It took her two hours to reach the coast, driving in any direction. She would make for a city or a big market town. She'd wear every piece of jewellery she owned, a long dress, a shawl. She would go into a hotel bar, order a Jameson on the rocks, and wait. It was never long before a man approached, looking for company, asking if she was OK for a drink. She usually let them buy her one.

She knew she was a point of fascination. She drank steadily but was careful to never appear drunk. Men who were young enough to be her sons approached her, asking what was she doing out on her own, at her age. Their eyes skimmed over the curves of her body, the clinging swirls of fabric, her neat cap of downy grey hair. Some of them told her she reminded them of their mothers.

The men would drink themselves to the point where they had the courage to reach out and touch her face. Her skin was creased, but still soft. Sometimes she pulled back in a kind, maternal way, and they would splutter and apologise and blame the drink. Other times, she went home with them.

She thought she saw her husband, sometimes. A man coming towards her on the street, smoking a cigarette, would turn out to be a woman eating an apple. She stared at strangers who shared a trait with him: a beard, a dark coat. She began to harbour a belief in ghosts.

She willed him to reincarnate. She was alert for the way a crow might turn its head, or a cat yawn with its whole body, the way he used to. She looked into young mothers' buggies and expected to see his knowing eyes smirking back at her. She was the one who hadn't wanted children, and now she cursed herself for it, for failing to hold on to even a piece of him.

Tonight's candidate watched her from across the room for two hours before summoning the courage to approach. He was in an armchair, hunched over a low coffee table, pretending to do the crossword. She bided her time.

He was a bulky man, but so was her husband. They bore it differently, though. Her husband's heft was like a bulwark against the world; he seemed insulated inside it. This man wore his weight apologetically, like a ratty old coat. She felt a pang of pity; she allowed him in.

Later, at his apartment, all shyness melted away. When he bent her over the couch, the blood rushed to her head. She had the phantom sensation of hair tumbling, tugging at her scalp; the long hair of her youth. It was different from sex with her husband – there was no way she could pretend it was him. But she still enjoyed it.

Grief was like a creature from folklore, sitting on her chest while she slept. Her excursions began to leak into midweek. She tried to pick a quiet time when there wouldn't be much traffic, when her only company would be the wildlife: the slink of small animals on the narrow country roads, or a flock of dark birds in the evening sky, like fragments blown from a fire.

She would enter the city in the murky dusk, the street lights just beginning to spark up, reminding her of the glow of her husband's cigarettes as he smoked out the kitchen window before bed. It hadn't even been the cigarettes that killed him, in the end – it had been some other, stealthy mutation. It could have happened to anyone.

Her lovers would ask her to stay till morning, offering to cook her breakfast, expressing concern about the long drive. *I don't mind,* she'd reply. *I like long drives. I can listen to music.* Actually she did mind, travelling in the dark from Cork, from Galway, from Kilkenny, from Limerick. She minded being trapped in the dark capsule of her car, hurtling into blackness. She couldn't see her hands on the wheel; the night seemed to invade the car. Her eyes were tricked by tail lights and she'd hallucinate hitchhikers, heavy machinery, trees blown into the road.

After every journey she'd arrive home, climb into their old shared bed, and whisper into the pillow what she'd done, and who she'd done it with. *I'm meeting new people*, she'd say. *I'm living my life.*

*

Six months into widowhood, she made the mistake of becoming attached. He was a tall, stringy Corkman, a businessman who told her he had no time for relationships. He said he found it hard to talk to women – except for her.

He talked about everything: how he really wanted to be a doctor but didn't get the points; his mother's early death; his disabled younger brother whom he worried about constantly. In return, she told him about the hotel bars, the men. How she'd been a virgin when she married. How she'd become convinced that her teeth were about to fall out; they tingled as if preparing to wrench themselves from their roots. She tongued them when she drove, daring them to make a crone out of her.

When they went back to his place, he only ever wanted to lie down, hold each other and talk. Sex was something he paid for, she gathered. She was irritated by the way he compartmentalised his life, but then, wasn't she doing the same thing? Still, she liked him for his staccato accent, and because he reminded her of her husband – his directness, his sardonic humour.

Though she rarely saw the same man twice, this one became a habit. She would drive down midweek, or whenever he could meet. She would feel her pulse quicken as she drove through the tunnel at the outskirts of his city, with its puzzlingly inverted instructions painted on the tarmac, commanding her to LANE IN STAY.

When they were apart, she would text him from under the covers, curled up, the smartphone glow flooding her tired eyes, and thought of reading by flashlight as a child, her mother scolding her: *You'll ruin your eyesight.*

He asked her to stay the night once, and for him, she broke the rules. He made her breakfast with charming nerves, checking that she had enough juice and coffee, forgetting where the spatula lived. It was a pleasure to watch him move about the kitchen, quiet and smiling, like a tall sturdy geisha. Her husband used to make her breakfast too, but with a flourish, as if conjuring French toast from the midmorning ether. This man, by contrast, made humble scrambled eggs, pouring in entirely too much salt. But she ate them with gusto, savouring the shrivelling saltiness on her tongue and lips like a kiss.

Something changed between them that morning, and they found themselves undressing again and going back to bed. The sex was warm and straightforward, like him. Afterwards, he cried in her arms and told her he'd never felt such intimacy in his life. She rocked him, dismay seeping through her. She'd thought he understood that this wasn't about him. But he was coming undone in her arms, and she knew there was no way of explaining. She left as normal, giving him a kiss at the door, and drove home. In the tunnel, she weaved around the other cars, ignoring the directive to LANE IN STAY. As she was passing over the Blackwater, she pitched her phone into the river. She didn't trust herself not to text him again.

She fell back into her old routine – Saturday nights only, different towns and cities, different men. She drove home from Kilkenny one night, slightly drunk, knowing she was tempting fate, that she'd be put off the road if she was caught. She wouldn't know what to do with herself then, sitting at home, trying to distract herself with bad television, or the death notices on the radio, or by staring into the fire until her vision blurred. The things widows were supposed to do.

There was someone thumbing on the outskirts of the city, on the road that pointed home. He stood in the faint wash of a streetlight. She slowed down and squinted to make sure he was really there; most of the hitchhikers she saw turned out to be trees, or wheelie bins. But this one was real. When she saw who it was, she almost laughed – it was the boy who'd taught her to drive, whose name eluded her. He looked tired, unsteady on his feet. She stopped the car, skimmed her mind for his name. It was a new-fangled name – Darcy or Bradley or Cassidy – more a surname than anything.

Davin, she called, easing down her window. He looked shocked that someone had stopped for him, even more shocked that it was her. He ducked his head and peered in the window, and her heart quickened, keeping pace with the tick of the indicator.

She'd only ever really seen Davin in profile before, sitting sullenly beside her during driving lessons, deliberately not looking at her. But his eyes, the cast of his brow – they were achingly familiar.

I'll take you home, she said. He got into the car.

He made small talk, though in her jolted state she'd have been fine with his usual silence. He'd been at a college friend's birthday party, he explained. But there'd been a fight. Something stupid and drunken – he could see that now – but he'd stormed off, and it would just be hassle to go back. He'd been planning to walk home if necessary – all the way back to their sinkhole town in the midlands. It would have taken all night. She smiled at this. *Aren't you lucky I came along?*

She looked at him; no longer the boy from the driving lessons, but a revelation. His arms looked coiled with strength. His jawline, dark with stubble, revealed no acne. He couldn't see her watching him in the dark.

You're a good driver, he said, *but you've been drinking*. He must have smelled it on her.

When they were nearing home, he turned to her and looked at her in a way he never had through all those lessons. He said he was sorry for his gruffness before; that he hadn't known what to say to her. *I don't know if you know this,* he said, *but your husband – he was really good to me.*

The turn for their town was coming up. The night sky spattered onto her windscreen; she flashed the wipers.

He was friends with my mother, he went on, *and I suppose he was always kind of like an uncle to me.*

They stopped at a set of lights. There was no other traffic this time of night. He seemed unaccustomed to talking about emotional matters and he stalled, puttering out of words like a broken engine. She put her hand on his knee, the way she used to with her husband when he drove.

Do you want me to take you home? she asked.

He didn't object when she pulled up to her house, not his, and unlocked the front door. He followed her mutely. Inside he was nervous, asking for a cup of coffee – *if it's not too much trouble; it might sober me up.*

When she came back from the kitchen, steaming cup in hand, he had taken off his jacket. He was crouching beside her husband's CD storage tower, running his fingers over their spines. Her eyes lingered on the hollow between his shoulders, a space that would fit the flat of her hand exactly. He stood, holding up a CD. *Sly and the Family Stone,* he said. *I love this record.*

She took it from him in exchange for the coffee. His shy smile as their fingers touched nearly undid her. *Davin,* she thought – the one she'd brought home. She wondered if her husband had named him. She shrugged off her own coat, inserted the CD in the stereo, and pressed play.